ORDINARY SECRETS

A ZORDI WORLD NOVEL

SECRETS
TRILOGY
—1—

ORDINARY SECRETS

MELISSA LAM

12Bunnies
Publishing

ASIN B0DPZJGGSR
ISBN 978-1-964502-00-7 (ebook)
ISBN 978-1-964502-01-4 (paperback)

Developmental editing by: R. D. Langr
Editing, cover design, and proofreading by: Enchanted Ink Publishing
Author photo by: AB-Photography.us
Logo art by: A. Krause Studio

www.authormelissalam.com

For Joe.
You are the type of husband women deserve.

CONTENTS

CAPTURED IMMUNE

PLAYLIST

Chapter 1: "Show Me the Meaning of Being Lonely" Backstreet Boys
Chapter 2: "Warning Signs" Alex G
Chapter 11: "Love's Just A Feeling (feat. Rooty)" Lindsey Stirling
Chapter 13: "In My Head" NIGHTBREAKERS
Chapter 19: "Shivers" Ed Sheeran
Chapter 22: "Touch (Acoustic)" Little Mix
Chapter 24: "Treacherous (Taylor's Version)" Taylor Swift
Chapter 25: "Not a Bad Thing" Justin Timberlake
Chapter 29: "Medicine" James Arthur
Chapter 32: "Suffocate" J. Holiday
Chapter 34: "Because You Live" Jesse McCartney
Chapter 38: "Mercy" Shawn Mendes
Chapter 39: "Arcade" Duncan Laurence
Chapter 40: "Oh So Sorry" PVLN

CONTENT WARNING

Welcome to Forbidden Love Bistro! Today's four-course meal is brimming with intense emotions and flavors that linger.

Appetizer:
Profanity Poppers
A bold blend of spicy words and f-bombs.

Soup:
Slow-Burn Bisque
A simmered fusion of death, violence, and domestic violence, topped with a sprinkle of attempted rape.

Main Course:
Steamy Love Linguine
Packed with passion and spice (for taste buds at least 18 years or older).

Dessert:
Cliff-Hanger Chocolate Cake
A decadent finish that will leave you craving another slice!

1

―――

TREY

It's easy for me to screw things up. I've done it countless times. From little things like saying the wrong thing at the wrong moment, to big things like not saving my parents from getting blown up. Today is a day I'm determined to get right.

I can do this. I can do this, I chant in my head over and over, as if the more I lie to myself, the more I'll believe it.

I continue internally chanting as I pull my car up behind a white Honda Civic parked on the side of a busy highway. The car's hazard lights flash as I idle my car about two truck lengths behind it and pop my door open.

Sand and gravel crunch beneath my shoes as I head toward the Civic. Rumbling car engines whiz past me, blowing my dark hair around. I drag a shaky palm through the longer strands at the top, trying to make it all stay in place, but my attempts are useless. The second a semitruck flies by, my hair is ruined again. *I guess the messy look will have to do.*

Off in the distance, the burning California sun blurs the air. It's warm on my skin. It would feel much warmer if my body's natural equilibrium wasn't working to cool me down. I'm grateful for this bodily function that all Zordinary humans

1

have, because the last thing I want is to look like a sweating pig the first time I meet this special woman.

As an effort to keep my hands from jittering, I shove them into my jeans pockets and keep crunching the gravel.

Just don't mess up, I tell myself. Easier said than done.

Things have to go well today, because if they don't, that's it.

The end.

My life will be meaningless.

Liz usually smacks my arm whenever I'm being "dramatic," but it's true. My success today will be the beginning of making my parents' deaths count for something. If I can continue and *finish* the work they left behind, I'll be able to say that I did something they can be proud of. I'll be able to say that I brought something of value to this world. Whereas right now, I'm just the pitiful son of two Zordinary researchers who hasn't done anything nearly as impactful as his parents did before they died in a "house fire."

For years, I've lived with that story.

Today, I have a chance to change the ending—and it all starts with getting this special woman to tell me everything about her. To do that, I need to gain her trust. To do that, I need to get close to her. But first, she needs to know that I exist.

Over the last month, I've written out tons of plans outlining how I can stumble into her at a grocery store or strike up a conversation with her at a coffee shop. Unfortunately, all of those ideas went straight into the trash.

Now, I'm not gonna say this meeting her on the side of a busy highway idea is any better, but this is the most promising, so I'm hoping this works. This *has* to work.

Then again, a thousand things could go wrong. I could trip and fall and make a fool of myself. She could shoo me off. She could—*Oh no.* A mess of tight black curls peeks out from the front passenger seat.

She could have a friend with her. *Dammit!* Of all the things I planned for, not once did I think she'd have company. She's never had a friend with her on the way home from work before. Why does she now?

Abort! Abort! Abort! my brain shouts. My feet don't listen. They keep moving. I've already reached the trunk of her car, and the women have probably already seen me. I can't stop now, or I'll look like a crazy person.

That is how I feel though—crazy.

What makes me think I can pull this off? Or that this will work at all? When I got assigned this mission, I was told my objective is to get close to this woman so I can find out what makes her immune to Zordi powers. Considering she's an Ordinary and doesn't know that people with powers exist, she doesn't even know she's immune.

So, I'm supposed to ask her lots of questions to learn as much about her as possible. Sounds simple enough, but what if she doesn't have the answers I'm looking for? And if she does, what if she isn't willing to share them?

Only one way to find out.

I step up to the passenger-side window with my hands still hiding in my pockets. In the seconds it takes for the glass to roll down, I pathetically forget all the lines I rehearsed this morning.

Maybe my uncle is right. Maybe I'm not cut out for this field-agent thing. Although, this *is* my first mission. I could go easier on myself.

Nah. This'll be my first and *last* mission if I fail. *I have to do this right.*

Bending at the hip, I offer my friendliest of smiles. "Hey. Need some help?"

My attention locks onto the beauty behind the wheel. When her gaze meets mine, my heart drops. Her round coffee-colored eyes are more captivating in person than they are in the pictures I've been studying. I knew she was gorgeous, but *damn!*

"Flat tire," she says, telling me information I already know.

"Want me to take a look at it?" I ask.

Her friend arches an eyebrow. "Do you know how to bring tires back from the dead?"

"How 'bout I assess the damage, then we can go from there?"

The friend gestures a pink-nail-polished hand out the window. "Be our guest."

Both women climb out of the car and meet me at the back right tire. I've seen these two together before. Since they hang out pretty often, I'm assuming they're good friends. I don't know the Black woman's name or anything about her. She looks around the same age as the brunette—twenty-two-ish, only four years younger than me.

I kneel and pretend to inspect the blown rubber. What I'm actually doing is trying to process the strange sensation of *knowing* there are two women behind me yet sensing only one.

Excitement radiates off the Black woman in waves, colliding into my head. I wish I knew what was lighting her up so much. That's the downfall of my gift—it only tells me *how* a person feels, never why.

"What happened?" I ask, even though I know damn well what happened. Still kneeling, I twist around to face the ladies. The sun almost blinds me, so I cup my hands above my forehead and squint. Within seconds, my Zordi eyes adjust and the women become crystal clear in my vision.

"We don't know." The one I can't take my focus away from moves all of her long waves to rest over one shoulder. "We heard a loud pop, then the car swerved a little."

I don't have to pretend to sound concerned. "Did you hit anything?"

"Thankfully, no. I pulled over right away, and we were about to call for a service when you showed up."

Thank fuck. The device I planted into her tire last night was supposed to leak the air out *slowly* and *safely*, not pop it. Some gadget that was. The point of my mission is to get information. I can't do that if this woman gets hurt. From now on, I'll make sure all my mission plans put her safety first.

With a hand against her car, I stand and lightly kick the blown tire. "Bad news, ladies. Doesn't look like you'll make it anywhere with this." I know the answer but ask anyway. "You got a spare?"

They shake their heads.

"I could take you to get a new tire. I'll even help you put it on."

"That's very nice of you, but"—the brunette hooks a thumb toward her curly-haired friend—"her brother's a mechanic. We'll be okay."

My hopes deflate like a thumbtacked balloon as I rub a hand over my stubble. What are the odds that she'd have a friend in the car with a brother who's a mechanic?

"He hasn't responded to my calls or texts yet," the friend says. "Maybe we should accept the help from . . ." She circles a hand in the air.

I thrust my palm out. "Trey Grant."

With a sharp gasp, the friend's mouth pops open. Her excitement from earlier that merely waved through my head now smacks me in the face. "See? I knew it! I freaking knew it! I told you it was him! You're in that pop rock band that plays at the Soul House, right?"

I try not to show how thrilled I am that she's recognized me. Not because I like the attention, but because this could work in my favor. I flash her a giant grin. "Yep, that's me. And your name?"

"Javina Abrams." Finally, she shakes my hand, which has been outstretched and waiting. "I went to one of your shows a few months ago. I bought your band's album that night, and I've been watching all your music videos on YouTube ever since." More elation comes from her. It's so strong, it's drowning out the emotions of all the people driving by.

"Thank you. That means a lot to me." And I mean it. I get compliments on my band often, but when it comes from someone who seems as genuine as Javina, the words carry more weight. I offer my palm to the woman I came to meet. "And your name?"

"Ari," she says, lightly returning my handshake.

This isn't the first time I've touched her. The first time was two weeks ago when I "accidentally" bumped into her at a restaurant. I made sure our bare arms brushed as much as possible while keeping it brief. I don't normally need to touch someone to sense their emotions, but since I can't sense this woman at all, I thought maybe the physical contact would help. It didn't then, and it's not now either. *How is she doing that?*

As if my hand is scorching hers, she tugs her arm back, then her gaze falls to the grass. *Whoops.* I definitely didn't mean to hold on to her for longer than socially acceptable.

Finally, her name registers in my brain. *Ari? That's not right.* "What's that short for?"

"Arella, but everyone just calls me Ari."

"Arella is a beautiful name. It suits you."

She smiles bashfully, and I can't tell if it's because she liked the compliment or because she hated it and is simply being nice. I've never had to guess how people feel before—ever.

"Anyway, could I help you get a new tire?"

"I don't want to inconvenience you." Arella fidgets with the bottom of her yellow T-shirt. The logo on the front reads *Sunrise Daycare.* Javina's wearing a matching shirt. Seeing them in their work attire makes it easier to not get caught already knowing that they work together.

"It's not an inconvenience at all," I say with a bright smile. *It's the very reason I'm here.*

"Well, I wouldn't want to inconvenience your friends." Arella gestures toward my car.

Fuck. I was hoping she wouldn't notice my friends. Like how I didn't plan for Javina to be here, I didn't plan for my friends to tag along either. I meant to come *alone* during this part of my assignment. The only reason I didn't was because Liz guilt-tripped me into having dinner with her and Kevin.

During band rehearsal earlier, I refused dinner three times, until Liz whispered, "We need to cheer him up. You know his mom just got diagnosed with breast cancer. He's worried about losing her."

I would've been a dick to say no. How could I? I'd lost my mother too. If taking Kevin out for sushi would help take his mind off his mom for a while, I'd comply. As long as my friends didn't interfere with my plan today.

Just as Arella mentions my friends, my car doors swing open, then Liz and Kevin step out. *Dammit.* My friends' energies float toward me, all light and curious. They have the right to be curious. After I agreed to dinner, I volunteered to drive without telling them we'd be taking a detour.

"What's the holdup?" Kevin shouts on his way over. His jet-black hair is so gelled up, the wind from the passing cars isn't affecting it at all.

Next to him comes Liz with a peppy bounce in her step. "Everything okay?"

"Just a flat," I say as a semitruck zips by us.

Liz stops at my side. Her nearness causes the Zordi sense in my chest to tingle. It reminds me that Liz and I are the kind of humans who are born with powers and the people around us are not.

Like I did earlier, Liz squats to examine the busted tire. "There's no fixing this. The hole's too big."

"You ladies need a ride to a tire shop?" Kevin asks. "We could take ya, right, Trey?"

"Yeah," Liz adds through a yawn, covering her mouth with a satin-gloved hand. "There's probably one not too far from here."

Why did I think for even a second that my friends would be an interference? Of course they'd want to help. They're good people like that. Now that I think about it, having a woman with me could increase my chances of getting Arella to accept my help. Women are more likely to trust other women than a man they've never met. If I had been smart, I would have planned for Liz to be here from the beginning.

"See?" I beam with a renewed sense of hope. "You're not an inconvenience at all."

Arella turns to her friend. "Why don't you call your brother again?"

Javina rolls her eyes. "I could, but I ain't seein' the point of that when we've got three perfectly capable helpers standing right here."

I hold back a grin. Javina just made it to the top of my *befriend now* list.

Arella thinks, then nods. "Okay. Let's grab our things."

On the inside, I jump up and down like a giddy child in a toy store. On the outside, I play it cool. "We'll be in my car."

Liz claims the front seat like she always does as Kevin plops into the back behind me. I don't take my eyes off Arella while she and Javina saunter over with their purses in hand.

Arella slips in first, settling on the middle seat next to Kevin. I'm gifted with a perfect view of her in my rearview mirror. Our eyes lock for half a second before she turns to click her seat belt in. I'm still staring at her as she sets her little purse on her lap and Javina climbs in.

Once everyone is buckled, I force my eyes back onto the busy highway. When I get an opening, I join the flow of traffic.

Liz wastes no time twisting around to wave a gloved hand at our new additions. "Hi, I'm Liz."

"I know!" Javina's exhilaration rushes through my head again. "You're one of the two girls in the band, right? The soprano and dancer?"

"Yep!" Liz's lips curve upward. Her spirit does the same. Out of everyone in the band, Liz enjoys meeting our fans the most.

Javina leans forward to lock eyes with Kevin. "And you're the bass guitarist, right?"

He nods with a closed-mouth smile. "Mm-hmm."

"Don't you play the guitar too?"

"Yeah. I'm not as good as Trey though."

"Lies!" Liz reaches back to slap Kevin's boney knee. "Kevin's just being humble. He's amazing on guitar. He's also our tenor and does most of the creative video editing for our YouTube channel."

"Impressive! I'm Javina." She points a finger at her chest, then places a light palm over Arella's thigh. "This is my bestie, Ari."

That nickname is still confusing me, because I've been referring to her in my head as Arella. I never knew she went by anything else. There are just some things a manila folder can't tell me—hence why I'm here.

"Are you two from the Los Angeles area?" Liz asks.

"I'm originally from Chicago," Javina says.

Liz's jaw drops with a little gasp. "I'm from Chicago too! What about you, Ari?"

"I've lived almost everywhere in Cali," Arella says, all soft and sweet.

"How long have you been in LA?"

"About four years."

I've never been more grateful for Liz. Not only am I learning things about Arella that aren't in her limited file, but I'm also not doing the work. Liz doesn't know about my mission. If she did, she'd be doing a hell of a job assisting me. Apparently, I need the help, because I can barely think with this beautiful mystery in my back seat. All the free space in my brain is consumed with trying to sense her.

"So what cover song is gonna be your next single?" Javina asks.

Liz puts on her thinking face. "It's an acoustic rendition of a Backstreet Boys hit, right, Kev? Are we allowed to tell them which one?"

Kevin shrugs a shoulder. "Why not? It releases tonight for Throwback Thursday. It's 'Show Me the Meaning of Being Lonely.' "

Javina gasps. "I love that one!"

After she gushes about the Backstreet Boys for a minute, she spits out a long string of questions. When is the next original music video coming out? What's the craziest fan encounter you've ever had? Do you normally get recognized everywhere you go?

Liz and Kevin do a great job answering everything while I contribute nothing. Actually, I stop listening after a while. My mind is buzzing with all the puzzling thoughts I have about the quiet woman behind me.

Is Liz's mind power working on Arella? I want to ask, but I can't do that in a car full of Ordinaries. That would break the number-one Zordi law: Never reveal anything from the Zordinary world to an Ordinary. Maybe after sushi tonight, Liz and I can—

"T?" A gloved finger taps my shoulder.

I jolt, and the car goes quiet. "Hmm?"

Liz dips her eyebrows at me. "I asked if you know where we're going."

"Oh." I clear my throat. "Yep. There's a tire place just off the next exit." *The one I Googled last week when I came up with this plan.*

"Anyway," Javina says, stealing the attention back, and I'm

happy for it. "How far have you guys gotten on your next original album?"

Perking up, Liz shares some general details about our band's second original album, which we've been working on since we released the first one. Liz's details aren't anything our band manager doesn't want us to reveal.

The whole time, Arella stares out the windshield with a blank look on her face. One would think that after observing her for the last four weeks, I'd be sick of looking at her, but I'm not. It's not only because she's stunning, either. I'm desperate to know how she's deflecting my gift and if she knows she's doing it at all.

If I shut my eyelids, I wouldn't even know she was in this car. I sense that Liz is happy. Javina is still exhilarated out of her mind. While Kevin's got a content look on his face, he's a little anxious on the inside. As for Arella . . . nothing.

When we arrive at the tire shop, Liz and Kevin opt to stay in the comfort of my car's air conditioning. I gladly leave the engine running for them, then volunteer to escort Arella and Javina inside.

"Well, aren't you a gentleman?" Javina says when I hold the door open for them.

I return her smile with my own.

Besides a gray-haired man reading a magazine in the waiting room, the lobby is empty. The scent of fresh rubber fills the air. At the same time a burst of joy rushes through my head, a round of laughter comes from the other side of the glass wall where three cars are raised on lifts. A group of eight-ish people in red polo shirts surround the vehicles with various power tools.

From behind me, something vibrates. Javina digs through her purse before pulling a phone out.

"Ooh! I gotta take this!" She rushes back outside with her phone pressed to an ear as her excitement spikes again. I'm getting the impression that she's easily excitable.

For the first time ever, I have Arella to myself. This is my chance to say something—to find out something valuable about her. Sooo, what do I say, and how do I say it? It figures that it'd be *now* when my brain decides to shut down. No words—at least none that form intelligent sentences—come to mind.

Like a sheltered teenage boy in the presence of an attractive female, I fidget with the zipper of my black leather jacket. I pull it halfway up my chest.

Then down.

Up again.

Stop it!

I shove my hands into my jeans pockets.

Then I take them out.

In once more.

What should I say?

Hey, Arella, you come here often? Dumb question. She's only here because of me.

Sooo, you work at a daycare. You like kids? Another stupid question. Why would she work at a daycare if she despised children?

How 'bout that heat, huh?

A glass door slides open, releasing me from my inner torture.

"Hi there!" says the cute blonde woman with a black smear of oil running down the front of her polo. "How can I help?"

Arella steps up to the counter while I stand off to the side, pretending to be interested in a chart on the wall that asks, "When do you need new tires?"

It's strange. Even without Arella's emotions hovering in my head, I still feel extremely aware of her presence, her every move. Usually, I know exactly how far someone is from me by how strong their emotions come through my head. With

Arella, I sense nothing, yet there she is, existing merely ten steps over.

As discreetly as possible, I lock my gaze onto her back and focus my gift on her. The only thing that comes is the emotions of the blonde behind the counter. It's as if Arella isn't there at all.

For the last month, I've kept my distance. Now that I'm here, I don't know what to do with myself. I need to touch her again. The brush of our arms and our little handshake isn't enough to confirm if physical contact can or can't break down her immunity walls. I was told that if I can find a way to break through her invisible shield, it might help us figure out how she's immune. Do I have the first clue how to do that? Nope. Not one bit.

As Arella finalizes the payment, I make a mental note to pay her back for this. There's no reason she has to spend her hard-earned money on something I caused. I'll be sure to get her something she needs but can't afford for herself. Something at least triple the price. It's the least I can do.

Within no time, we've got a new tire in my trunk and our seat belts secured again. Liz and Javina dominate most of the conversation on our way back. They talk like they're old friends who haven't seen each other in months. I don't mind. It gives me a chance to regain myself. I don't normally get nervous around women. Apparently when it matters, I lose all sense of control.

Back at Arella's car, I grab some tools and get straight to work. Before today, I have changed a tire all of two times, with the sole purpose of practicing for this moment. I didn't wanna look stupid.

"Can I help?" Arella drops to her knees at my side.

I startle, falling backward onto my tailbone. My ass lands on the jack. A few curse words—all beginning with *F*—fly through my head. I'm not used to people sneaking up on me without me sensing them first.

"Sorry. I didn't mean to scare you." She lets out an adorable laugh, making goose bumps run up the back of my neck.

"It's all right." I chuckle lightly as I pull the jack out from under me and hand it to her. "Could you turn this little knob to lower it enough so we can fit it under your car?"

"Sure." Arella sets the jack down, then gathers all her hair toward the top of her head. I'm mesmerized by the way she swiftly ties it up within seconds. Once she's done, her eyes meet mine and she flashes me a tender smile.

Shit. I've been gaping at her with my mouth slightly open. *Way to play it cool.* Tearing my attention off her, I go back to loosening the lug nuts.

As Arella lowers the jack, I feel the need to make conversation with her, except I can't think of anything to say. *Do I even know how to talk to women anymore?*

Behind us, in the grassy ditch, Liz, Kevin, and Javina seem to have no problem making conversation. With all the noisy cars passing us, I can't make out every word they're saying, but from the little I can catch, it sounds like they're still talking about music. *Would Arella like it if I talk to her about music?*

"Done." As she leans over to set the jack near my feet, I catch a whiff of her light floral scent—lavender and springtime.

Does her scent have anything to do with her immunity? Probably not, although I've been told not to rule anything out. It could be *anything* that shields her from Zordi powers.

When I finish loosening all the lug nuts, I push the jack under her car and twist the knob. After a few turns, the car lifts off the ground.

I continue twisting it up. "Do you know where to get rid of this blown tire?"

"Where?"

I banked on her not knowing. "I can take care of it for you."

"No way. You're already helping plenty."

"It'll be my pleasure. One less thing for you to worry about."

She opens her mouth, seemingly about to object, then stops. "Thank you, Trey. Seriously. You're doing so much for me, and I don't even know you."

"Let's get to know each other, then." *Wow!* Those words weren't practiced, yet they sounded right. *Gold star for me!*

The air stands still as I wait for Arella's response. Seconds pass as I keep working the jack up. Her reply never comes.

Good going, dumbass. What kind of pickup line was that? I sounded way too forward. Might as well have used the "Hey, did it hurt when you fell from heaven, 'cause you look like an angel" line.

"Sorry," I say because I don't know what else to say.

"For what?"

"Trying to flirt with you. I'll assume your silence means it's unwelcome." I've had her semi-alone for all of two minutes, and I've already fucked up. *Figures.*

"Oh. It's okay. I mean, um . . . ." She's struggling to find her words, and I wish I knew why.

Am I making her nervous? That's not my intent at all. If anything, I *need* her to be comfortable with me.

"Honestly," she says gently, "I'm not used to men trying to flirt with me. I didn't realize that's what you were doing."

I freeze to gape at her. "What? You're gorgeous. Do you really expect me to believe that guys don't hit on you *all* the time?"

At first, she blushes, then her head droops. "They don't."

"Well, good." I return to working on her car. "That gives me more of a chance with you."

She shakes her head, rolling her eyes. "Don't waste your time on me."

"You wouldn't be a waste of time." I almost scowl at her

for thinking that of herself. "Are you single?" I already know the answer. Unless she's got a boyfriend she hasn't seen for a month, this woman is very available.

"I . . . am . . . single," Arella says slowly as if giving herself time to think. "That doesn't mean I'm looking though."

I don't like that answer, so I take that information, crumple it up, and toss it into the recycling bin in the back of my head.

Once the car is lifted off the ground enough, I twist off the first lug nut and hold it out to her. "You mind hangin' on to these so we don't lose 'em?"

She flips her palm open, and I drop the first one in, making sure to brush my fingers against hers. The physical contact does nothing. She's still blank.

We work together until the old rubber's off. When I'm home later, I'll dispose of the tiny device that's probably still stuck in that rubber somewhere.

After the new tire is on, I lower Arella's car to the ground, then slide the jack out. With a grunt, I push myself up and slap my dirty palms on my thighs. "You're all good now."

"Thank you. Here, let me pay you." She digs out her wallet from the purse hanging by a strap across her body.

I slash a hand through the air. "Don't worry 'bout it."

Not listening, she holds out three twenties. "Seriously, take it. Calling a professional would have easily been four times this."

"It's okay, really." I push her cash away, then give her hand a gentle squeeze. "I'm just happy to help."

She flinches, and the color washes from her face. A woman has never reacted to my touch that way before. Instantly, I let her go and step back. Within seconds, the tension in her shoulders releases and she lets out a breath.

Glancing up at me with those big brown eyes, she forces a tiny smile. I know that smile. It's the same one I use whenever

I'm trying to hide my pain. *What pain is she trying to hide? And does it have anything to do with her immunity?*

Arella stuffs her cash back into her purse, then hugs herself, looking anywhere but at me. "Thanks again."

Perking up, I pretend that my next idea is a spur-of-the-moment one. "Hey, so, my band is performing a show tomorrow. Would you wanna come out to support us?"

"I can't," she says way too quickly. "I work tomorrow."

"Our set starts at eight. You work that late?" If she says yes, she's lying.

"I don't. Where is it?"

"It's a cool music bar downtown called the Soul House. Great food, great service, and I hear the entertainment's not too bad either." I wink and immediately regret it. *Why did I do that? I'm so lame.*

"Um . . ." she says, biting her lip. Not the reaction I expected. "How much are tickets?"

"For you? Nothin'. I'll put your name on a special VIP list so you can walk right in. It's last minute, so you'd probably have to sit at the bar, but it's still a good spot."

"Oh. Um . . ."

Javina materializes at Arella's side, gripping her arm. "Ari, this kind man just helped us out, then offered to put you on a VIP list to see his show tomorrow. Do you understand that their tickets are hard to get last minute? They're usually sold out for weeks in advance. *Weeks*, Ari. Weeks. If you don't go, I will."

And that's the reaction I was hoping for.

Arella straightens her back. "I'll come if Javina can come too."

If that's what it would take to get this woman back into my space, done. "Great. I'll put you both on the list for tomorrow. Javina Abrams and Arella . . . Sorry, I never got your last name." I already know it, but it's important to hear it from her.

"Rance."

"Perfect. I'll see you tomorrow, then."

While this didn't go exactly the way I had imagined it, I still accomplished what I needed to, and that's what matters.

Phase one—complete.

Now on to phase two.

2

ARELLA

The gratitude I have for Javina will never end.

Tonight is our monthly movie night. Since we also happened to be scheduled for the same shift, we carpooled, and I'm glad for it. If it wasn't for her recognizing those people, I wouldn't have accepted their help. I know better than to get into a car with three strangers. What if they were serial killers? Since we're still alive, I'm going to assume they aren't.

I can't believe I agreed to go to their band's show tomorrow. Bars aren't my thing, but it's Javina's thing, especially the music ones. So I'm happy to go if it'll make Javina happy.

She's practically dancing in my passenger seat. "All right, babes, you're never gonna guess who called while you were getting a new tire."

I merge my car into the leftmost lane. "Your brother?"

"Nah. Still haven't heard from him. I'll give you a hint. We should stop somewhere for a celebration cake."

I knit my eyebrows together, then my jaw drops. "You and Rachel got approved for the apartment?"

Her face falls. "I wish. We should find that out next week."

Javina and her girlfriend have been apartment hunting for almost three months. Every place they've toured is either a dump or the rent is too high. Last week, when I found out that my upstairs neighbor was moving, I texted Javina and told her to apply for it.

"Okay, I'm just gonna tell you." She grins with all her teeth. "I got the promotion!"

"What!" I squeal. "I knew you'd get it!"

"Thanks. I wasn't confident. I was up against Carrie, who has been at the daycare for, like, three years longer than me."

"Yeah, but you work harder than Carrie does."

"If there's anyone who works the hardest, it's you. You always do all the extra shit nobody else wants to. I still think you should have applied."

Our director hinted to me that if I applied, I was guaranteed the position. I didn't apply because I knew Javina really wanted the job. I also knew that if our director didn't promote me, she'd pick Javina.

She'll be better at it, anyway. My strengths reside in handling the kids. Javina is better at all that leadership, organization, and technology stuff—all the skills she'll need to be the best assistant director Sunrise Daycare has ever had.

In the grocery store, Javina stares at the cake options for way too long. Nothing fits her expectations for the "perfect celebration cake," so we get popcorn instead.

The sun sits along the horizon in hues of pinks and purples as we arrive at my apartment in Culver City. Out of habit, I step out of my car and scan the lot to see if *his* car is around.

When my tire blew, I thought the source of my problems was *him* again. *He* has been messing with my life for years. It wouldn't have been the first time he'd sabotaged my vehicle either. Thankfully, my flat today was just an accident.

When I finish doing a quick eye sweep of the area and don't see his car, I let out a breath.

"Don't sweat it, babes." Javina throws up a closed fist. "If he was here, we both woulda taken him. He'd be leavin' with a bloody nose and a limp."

I offer Javina the biggest smile I can manage. *I love this woman.*

The first thing we do when we enter my apartment is kick our shoes off, then drop our grocery bags onto my kitchen counter. Javina takes the liberty of rummaging through my fridge for a can of root beer. I'm not a fan of root beer. I only stock my fridge with it for her.

"Did you tell Rachel about the promotion yet?" I slide my finger under the flap of the popcorn box. It tears open easily.

"Yeah. I texted her as soon as I got off that call." Javina takes a long chug from her can. "We're celebrating on Sunday."

"Why Sunday?" Today is Thursday. It's rare for Javina to go more than a day without seeing Rachel.

"She's on a business trip and won't be flying back until late Saturday night."

I unwrap the plastic off the popcorn. "How are you guys going to celebrate?"

"Probs go out for dinner and get drunk on wine."

I chuckle. "Nothing like living your best life."

Minutes later, we've got a bowl of yummy, extra-buttery goodness in hand as we head to my living room.

"Pick out somethin' good for us," Javina says as she shuffles down the hall. "I'll be right back."

My butt makes a light *thud* as I flop onto my worn garage-sale couch. The TV brightens to life with the hit of a button. I scroll through our entertainment options, logging some choices into a mental list. Most are true-crime related. Javina and I like to judge the way murderers get caught and discuss how we could have done it better.

"Yo!" Javina calls from the bathroom. "When are you planning to fix this gaping hole in your wall?"

I still have nightmares about that fist flying at my face. When I ducked, his fist ran straight into the drywall with a *crack!* He bled quite a bit. While I bandaged him up, I secretly wished he had broken something. That was the moment I knew I had to get out.

A week later, I was busy packing a bag when he arrived home early from work. Getting caught trying to leave only made a bad situation worse. For weeks, he barely let me out of his sight. He stole my car keys and hid them. Every day, he'd drop me off at work and pick me back up. The daycare became my safe haven, and I'd dread whenever my shift ended.

When I wasn't working, he'd lock me up in our apartment and try to brainwash me into believing that I was nothing without him. Sometimes, it worked. Other times, I wished for him to get hit by a bus.

During those dark days, whenever Javina asked if we could hang out, I'd lie and tell her I already had plans. Eventually, she caught on. The day she pulled me aside during our lunch break and vocalized her suspicions, I burst into tears. It didn't take me long to confess how I'd got the marks on my face that I'd been hiding under layers of foundation and concealer.

That night, Javina showed up with her buff dad, her athletic brother, and her two heavily tattooed uncles. All of them had broad shoulders and stood to at least six three. While one guarded me, the others threw all of my ex's things out the door—literally. Socks were scattered across the grass, and his can of shaving cream exploded all over the sidewalk.

For the next few weeks, Javina's family took turns camping outside my place to ensure he stayed away. Javina still talks about how much she loved seeing the fear in my ex's eyes when four large Black men showed up and wouldn't take *no* for an answer.

"I'll do it eventually," I say, hoping I'm speaking loudly

enough for Javina to hear. "I haven't found the motivation yet."

"Want my help? I can't imagine staring at a hole in the wall every day while I do my business."

I've thought about patching it up, but then I'd need to patch up the three holes in the bedroom. In the middle of our fights, he used to point at those holes and say, "*That* is what happens when you disobey me and try to fight back. Just do what I say, when I say it." That normally scared me into submission because he was right. Fighting back only ever made him more violent. It was always easier to just give him what he wanted. Now, I hide those holes behind artwork and framed photos. If I only had one hole to fix, it'd probably be done already. Four is a daunting project.

I would cover the hole in the bathroom with a picture if it wasn't in such an awkward place—right below the towel bar, slightly to the left. My bath towel usually hides it, and nobody except Javina ever comes over anyway, so why bother?

Besides, whenever I see that hole now, I'm reminded of the naïve, trusting person I used to be. I'm reminded that I don't need a man or his money to make it. Over the past eight months, I've picked up a weekend nanny job to cover his part of the rent. I've learned the difference between real love and the love to control. I've even learned that I can make jokes and laugh out loud without his permission. Seeing this hole now reminds me that I'm stronger today than I was before, and it encourages me to continue to be strong.

The toilet flushes, and the sink runs, then Javina reappears in the living room. "Sorry, babes. Didn't mean to bring him up again."

"It's fine." I force a smile—something I've learned to do well. Yeah, I'm getting better, but time hasn't completely healed me yet. There are still things that shut me down. Like whenever I see or hear his name. Whenever I catch a whiff of alcohol. Whenever a man gets too close.

I've been relearning that not every man who touches me wants to bruise me. My brain knows it, but it's harder to convince my body to know it. I still tense up whenever I'm touched by a man, which is progress from eight months ago, when I'd practically break down in tears.

In the beginning, my ex's touches were loving and didn't leave bruises. The first time he slapped me, we were in a heated argument over something I can't even remember. He promised it would never happen again. And it didn't . . . not for another four months. Eventually, his slaps turned into punches, his promises turned into begging, and the months between those fights became weeks or days.

He spent a lot of nights conditioning me into believing his behavior was my fault and that I deserved it. Apparently, I didn't listen, I was too defiant, and I questioned him too often. After a while, I just obeyed. Whenever he talked, I listened. Whenever he told me not to wear something, I didn't. Whenever he came home late, I stopped asking where he had been. I know now that his actions were not my fault and that I never deserved it.

Javina plops beside me and digs her hand into our popcorn bowl. "One last question, then we can be done talking about him."

"Okay?" I keep scrolling through the movies, even though my brain isn't registering any of the titles. I'm too focused on what Javina has to say next.

"When's the last time you saw that low-life bitch face?"

"A month, I think."

Thirty-seven days, to be exact. And yes, I keep count because thirty-seven is a record—a *huge* record.

Unfortunately, that means he's bound to reappear soon.

3

____

TREY

In the back lot of the Soul House, I pull my car up next to Kevin's.

"Thanks again for taking me out for sushi, guys," Kevin says as he pops his door open. "I really appreciate it."

"You're welcome, Kev," Liz says, waving one of her gloved hands. "See ya tomorrow."

I wave too. "See ya, bro."

The second Kevin is in his car and has driven away, Liz turns in her seat to face me. I already know what she's gonna say. "Oh my god, T. Please tell me you got a reading off that Ari girl."

"Nope. Did you?" I know this answer too. Why else would she be asking?

"I couldn't smell her at all!" Liz clasps a hand against her temple.

The way she describes her mind power, the first of three powers all Zordis are born with, is weird. I guess, simply put, "smelling people's souls" is exactly what her mind power does.

Whenever Liz gets within an arm's reach of a person, her mind senses the quality of their soul and interprets it into a scent. If a person's soul is good, they could smell like freshly baked muffins or blooming flowers in a field. If a person's soul is bad, they could smell like sewage or a two-week-old corpse.

"I feel better now that I know it wasn't just me. Pense que me estaba volviendo loca." *I thought I was going crazy.*

"You're not going crazy," I say, underutilizing my conversational Spanish skills. I don't practice the language enough with her. The only time I speak Spanish to Liz is when I want to say something I don't want the rest of the band knowing.

I press the button to turn my engine off since it seems like Liz and I might be here for a while. "If you could smell her soul, what do you think it would smell like?"

"She seemed like a good person, so probably something like an apple cinnamon pie straight out of the oven, or maybe some flowers."

Liz is probably right about the flowers. Maybe Arella's soul would smell like lavender. I guess we'll never know.

Liz says that my soul smells like roasted marshmallows on a campfire and the wick of a burning candle. What's interesting about her mind power is that it gives her the ability to guess a Zordi's elemental power, our second gift. Within seconds of meeting me, she knew my element was Fire.

"Do you think it's possible she doesn't have a scent?" I ask.

"Do you think it's possible she doesn't have any emotions?" Liz makes a good point. "Everyone's got a soul, T. Unless they're dead, and Ari looked very much alive to me. I thought about it during dinner and thought maybe her soul is neutral. Now that I know you couldn't sense her either, I don't think that's the case." With a jolt, Liz gasps. "What if she's a robot?"

Not missing a beat, I fake the same big gasp. "What if she's part of an alien invasion team that's scoping out our planet to strategize the best time to attack? You can't smell alien souls, can you?"

With an eye roll, she smacks my arm.

I rub the spot she hit, pretending like it stung. "In all seriousness, do you think if you took your gloves off and shook hands with her, you'd catch a memory?"

"I dunno, but I'm not willing to test that."

A body power is the third and final gift every Zordi is born with. Liz's allows her to see people's memories. She calls this gift more of a curse because she can only see a person's most painful memory—the one that haunts them and tears them apart inside.

Thankfully, her gloves act like a barrier, but they don't keep the terrible memories she's already caught from replaying in her head at night. Because of that, Liz can't stay asleep for long. She always lurches awake, screaming from the scenes playing out on the back of her eyelids like a private horror movie.

If given the opportunity to trade my body power of telekinesis with Liz's of memory catching, I'd do it. I wouldn't even think twice about it. Liz deserves to be saved from the agony of living through everyone else's suffering night after night, and I'd gladly volunteer.

Unfortunately, trading powers isn't a thing, so I do my best to help Liz feel comfortable in other ways—everything from letting her cry on my shoulder to shutting people down whenever they get a little too curious about her gloves.

When I first met Liz four years ago, she claimed she wore gloves because she's a germaphobe. I knew it was a lie, but I didn't care enough to interrogate her. It didn't change that she needed a dance partner to enter a competition with. I was taking dance lessons at the studio Liz still works at when my instructor recommended me to her.

For the next few months after that, I met with Liz at the studio to help her choreograph a winning routine. One day, she hadn't put her gloves on yet, and I accidentally grazed my hand against hers. She froze, and her terror shot through my body like an arrow through the heart.

It all happened so fast. One second, her eyes were screwed shut with a pained look on her face. The next, she let out a sharp gasp and erupted into tears.

Because many mind and body powers are viewed as intrusive or dangerous, it's part of Zordi culture to keep that information private. Elemental powers are widely discussed, though, since everyone has one of four: Fire, Water, Earth or Air. That's why I didn't know that Liz was a Memory Catcher. It's also why I didn't understand her suddenly crying for no reason.

My uncomfortable response was "You okay?"

"Trey . . . you—you were there."

"I was where?"

Without hesitation, she explained what her hands could do. "You told me your parents died. You didn't tell me that it was because of something traumatic or that you witnessed the whole thing happen."

I blew up at her. "You crossed a fucking line! Using your body power on me like that? Really? Find yourself a new dance partner for your stupid competition. I quit!"

I hurled all my things back into my backpack and stormed out of that studio without any intention of ever returning.

Liz ran after me, unwilling to let me leave. I was unwilling to hear her out.

"I'm so sorry, Trey. I didn't mean to. Your memory came to me when our hands touched. I can't control it. Trust me, if I could choose, I'd rather be an Ordinary."

I was already halfway to my car when I froze right there in the parking lot. I understand what it's like to not have control of your powers. Often, I've wished to be an Ordinary too. It's common for Zordis to long for better powers. What's uncommon is for us to long to be completely powerless. The moment Liz said those words through tears, it hit me that maybe, just maybe, I wasn't alone.

Fuming a little less, I allowed her to talk me into staying.

That night, instead of dancing, we had a lengthy heart-to-heart conversation—a form of torture for me.

"I'm sorry I got angry," I said, apologizing for the tenth time. I felt like an asshole for yelling at her the way I had. "It's just that . . ."

"You don't have to explain," Liz said when I couldn't find the words. "I'm glad I saw your memory—for your sake."

"How's that for *my* sake?"

"It'll be good for you to have someone to confide in. Someone who understands you. Now I know why you're so closed off."

That last comment didn't make me feel any better. I am fully aware that I shut down the second anyone asks me a personal question, but to hear Liz verbalize it? I felt called out. I had half a mind to walk out again.

"I'll make it even with you," she said. "I can tell you about something that kills me deeply too."

So, she did, even after I told her it wasn't necessary. She told me all about the most disturbing memories she'd caught over the years and how they still affect her. She even shared some of her own dark memories—of things she's experienced herself.

I listened in awe of her every word, mostly in awe of her. I'd had no idea how much agony hid behind those bright smiles and cheery hugs. Liz had fooled me into thinking her happiness came easy.

Looking back on it now, I realize that Liz told me all those dark things because she needed someone to confide in too. Before me, she never had anyone she could share that pain with. No one had ever wanted to share it, especially not her family. There she was, carrying the weight of all those distressing memories on her own two shoulders, and I was more than happy to help her carry that burden. I still am.

If everyone knew all the shit Liz has been through, they'd have as much respect for her as I do. Liz has the kindest, most caring and understanding soul I've ever known. For that, I will protect her at all costs.

"Why do you think our gifts didn't work on Ari?" Liz asks, drawing my attention back to her.

"I'm not sure," I say. *But I'm gonna find out.*

4

———

TREY

THE SECOND LIZ GETS INTO HER CAR AND DRIVES AWAY, I reach back to feel around the fabric of my back seats. It doesn't take me long to find what I'm looking for. When I do, I carefully fold the strands between a napkin from my center console; then I drag my phone out to call Victor.

"What?" my uncle answers, all clipped as if I'm interrupting a meeting with the fucking president.

"I got the sample."

"Good. Come to Shadow Ridge. Now."

I pull my phone from my ear to glance at the screen. "Now? It's really late."

"And?"

I should just do whatever he wants. It's easier that way. "All right. I'm coming."

Zordis only need to sleep half as often as Ordis. Lucky for me, I slept last night—not that Victor knows that. What if tonight was my night to rest?

"Can you send a Teleporter?" I ask.

"I only have one Porter right now. He's busy, so you're on your own. Don't dawdle." *Click.*

Huffing, I shove my phone back into my pocket. With a Teleporter, I could be at the Ridge within seconds. Now, I have a three-hour road trip ahead of me and another three hours back.

Whatever, I guess.

I start my engine, then head toward my house. Once there, I switch my car out for my motorcycle. Riding it will make this last-minute errand feel less daunting.

Going with Liz would make it feel less daunting too, but she doesn't know that I'm a Zordinary Innovations Research and Development Agency agent. It's better that I keep that information from her, too. She wouldn't approve of me working for a group of Zordis who operate outside the zovernment on their own terms. Besides, it's against ZIRDA policy to tell people in our personal lives that we're ZIRDA agents.

While ZIRDA does good things, the secret organization has a reputation for being a group of vigilantes. Like how we're working to discover what makes some rare Ordinaries immune to our powers. After that, we'll figure out how to replicate their immunity, then ZIRDA will be able to overpower and take down the people who killed my parents. As for me, I'll sleep better knowing that the people who destroyed my family never get the chance to hurt another little boy ever again.

Three hours later, I'm near my hometown, about halfway up the dark mountain. On the side of the road, I cut the engine and dismount my bike. A refreshing breeze grazes my cheeks as I yank off my helmet.

Since there's a shortage of parking lots in the middle of nowhere, I flick my wrist, and my Harley lifts off the ground. It floats in front of me as I tuck my helmet under my arm and hike off the road, through some tall grass.

I trek through the woods until I can't see the road

anymore. In the air, my bike follows my hand movements, maneuvering around every tree in its path. As I lower my hand, it eases to the ground behind two thick tree trunks, where it'll stay with my helmet until I return.

On foot, I march deeper through the forest in search of the perfect hover-log. The denser the woods get, the more I lose the moonlight, so I open my hand and imagine fire. A glowing ball of red and orange appears in my palm. Its warmth on my skin offers me a tiny sense of comfort between the dread and loathing of coming back to this place. I use the volleyball-size fireball to illuminate the ground until I spot a piece of wood about the size of a skateboard.

With a turn of my wrist, the log glides through the air toward my ankles. I knock on it a couple times to make sure it's sturdy enough to hold my weight. It is, so I step onto it and kill my flames. As I lift my hand, I'm carried into the air above the trees.

I fly so fast that the wind whips across my face like I'm in a speeding car with my head out the window. Below me, the treetops are a dark trap waiting to swallow me whole if I fall. Of all the times I've flown above this forest, I've never fallen.

I used to hover-log over this area every day just to get to school, and I despised every minute of it. Doing this again reminds me that I didn't grow up in a normal house like normal kids with a normal family.

I tilt my head back to gaze at the stars. Maybe my parents are up there somewhere, watching me. Does knowing that I'm working on the research they started make them proud of me? Or do I need to *complete* their research for that to happen? Either way, I'm going to finish this for them—no matter what it takes.

By the time the familiar peak of a mountain appears, my throat is dry. The still and silent mountain seems to say, "What are you doing back here?"

Trust me. I'm not happy about this, either.

Even though I lived at the Ridge from the age of seven to eighteen, I never called it my home. All of my memories here are of bloody noses and nights spent locked alone in my bedroom. I can't count how many times I planned to run away, or how many times I was told to leave and never come back. In a way, staying was rebelling. Also, I had nowhere else to go.

The closer I get to my destination, the closer I hover near the treetops. I'm not ready to land yet though. Up here, I don't have to watch for booby traps. If I had to hike this, like many do, I'd have to study where the traps are. I don't come around often enough to do that. The only other time I've been back here since I moved out was last month when Victor called to assign me this mission. Otherwise, I wouldn't have come back at all.

I used to watch the weekly footage of wayward hikers tripping the traps. Some traps release snakes. Others release swarms of hornets or fire ants. Anything that keeps people from getting too close to this ZIRDA base.

In addition to the animal deterrents, small speakers are hidden in the trees that play bird sounds all day and crickets chirping all night. The extra noise masks the sounds of the waterfall that veils the entrance to Shadow Ridge.

Since I'm up in the air, the sounds of the waterfall reach my ears before it comes into view. The base's entrance hides beneath strategically grown trees that blend in with the rest of the forest. Through a slight break in the treetops, I dip my hover-log down and stop just above the grass. Then I step off and drop my hand, making my hover-log return to its former useless state on the ground.

A towering waterfall stretches before me, cascading into a small lake. I used to spend hours swimming in that water, mostly because there isn't much else for children to do around a secret hideout. Cable couldn't have been installed out here even if I'd wanted it. As for the Internet, Victor made it a rule that children aren't allowed to use the Ridge's satellite. Since I was the one and only child who lived here, it was obvious who he made that rule for.

Trickles of cold liquid splash onto me as I enter the cavern behind the waterfall. My footsteps echo in the darkness. I open my hand and imagine fire until warm flames appear. I throw my fireball into the air and keep it floating a few feet ahead of me as I trudge deeper into the hollow.

Tiny cameras embedded into the rock wall follow my movements. I know where most of them are hidden. As I look for them, I spot more cameras that weren't there before. They seem to have doubled.

Waving, I wink into one of the thumbtack-size lenses I've never seen before. The security guards hate it when I do that. They think their camera-concealing skills are top-notch. For the untrained eye, they probably are.

After a couple minutes, my fireball illuminates the Ridge's entrance—a wide door that looks like any other part of the cave. With my hands flat, I feel around the rocks for the little hole. Once I find it, I stick my index finger in and press it against a fingerprint scanner.

Beep! Beep! Beep! With a mechanical screech, a ten-foot section of the rock wall retreats inward, then slides to the left.

Two men in security guard uniforms greet me with unwavering frowns. The zense in my chest spikes, confirming what I already know. Their aggravated energy seeps into my head, bringing my already shitty mood down more.

" 'Sup, Carlos," I say to the older one. He's been working here for as long as I can remember.

"Don't think I missed that wink," he growls.

The younger, more muscular guard hooks his thumb toward me. "Who's he?"

"Big V's annoying nephew. He used to live here and liked to play practical jokes on me."

I played jokes on Carlos because he was an easy target. This other guy though . . . He must be new, because I've never seen him before. He's got a scar down his left eyebrow and looks like he lifts trains for fun. As a kid, I wouldn't have played jokes on him. I wouldn't have even considered it.

"You know the drill," Carlos says. "Arms up."

After being frisked, I take the elevator down from the sixth floor to the fourth. When the elevator opens again, I find two more guards waiting for me with stony expressions. The bulkier one gestures for me to follow him.

Based on their fancy suits in place of security uniforms, I'm gonna assume these men are Victor's personal guards. Each of them has a wired device in his ear. If they were standing next to the president, they wouldn't look out of place. The only difference is that they aren't carrying any weapons. As trained ZIRDA agents, *they are* the weapons.

The bulkier guard stomps ahead of me while the skinny one trails behind. Our footsteps echo loudly against the walls of the wide hallways. As we turn the corners, I catch glimpses of more uniformed guards. When I lived here, it was never this packed with security. *What changed?*

We arrive at a locked door, where the bulkier guard holds his ID card up to a black device on the wall. A tiny light flashes green with a soft *beep*, and then the door unlocks. On the other side is another long hallway with more doors. At the end stand two guards posted outside a set of double doors. One of them scans their ID card and gestures for me to step into Victor's office—alone.

Chilly air nips at my skin as the door shuts. My body's equilibrium immediately works to warm me. Victor's office feels cold because it's huge for no goddamn reason. There's barely anything in it. A giant desk sits smack-dab in the middle, and behind that are a bunch of filing cabinets. Otherwise, there's so much open floor space that he could fit at least four king-size beds in here.

Victor, in a brown tailored suit, scowls at me from his colossal office chair behind the U-shaped desk. His emotions slap me in the face, somewhere between frustrated and angry. It's nothing new. I wish I could say his hostility is because of the stress from being the head of a ZIRDA base. I'm sure he's got lots on his plate, but Victor's hostility is only ever directed at me. Whenever he talks to other people, he's always firm but never demeaning.

"What took you so long?" Victor turns his finger in a circle above his mug. His wind power spins the metal spoon around.

I want to say that if he had sent a Porter like I asked, I would have been here hours ago. Since that'll only piss him off, I say, "Traffic."

My uncle flashes me a foul look. We both know there's no traffic at three in the morning.

"What's with all the extra guards?" I ask, desperate to change the subject. I take a seat in the small wooden chair on the other side of Victor's desk.

Every little movement sounds like nails on a chalkboard. The chair creaking beneath me. Each clink of Victor's spoon against the side of his mug. The cold air blowing in from the vents.

Silence always irks me. It makes me feel lonelier than I already am, so I usually play music around my house to cover it up. Ever since Aunt Jodi left him, Victor's opinion of music is that it's "for the weak." To him, my career choice is simply a "pathetic grab for attention."

"We've discovered moles," Victor says, scratching his forehead.

"Moles?"

"Yes, as in double agents. Royals."

My heart shrivels up at the mention of Royals. "How many have you found?"

"Two, and we took care of them appropriately."

I know exactly what that means and feel no remorse. The

Royals deserve that fate for all the innocent lives they've stolen —especially my parents'. Instead of fighting for the development and growth of Zordis like ZIRDA does, the Royals would rather cause chaos and destroy any sense of peace in the world.

ZIRDA has been around since before the Grand Separation in 1326. Before that, Zordinary humans lived in harmony with Ordinary humans. Besides being born with powers and different bodies, we're all the same. Everyone just wants to be happy.

Unfortunately, some Ordinaries didn't see it that way. They felt threatened by anyone with gifts, so they manufactured a poison that affected only Zordis and distributed it through alcohol. Two million of us dropped dead within a year.

After that, it was clear that Zordis weren't safe anymore. Our choices were to either eliminate all the Ordis who wanted us dead, or go into hiding. So the zovernment recruited eighty-nine of the world's most powerful Scrubbers to alter the memories of all Ordis at once, erasing our existence from their minds. Sadly, not all Zordis agreed with this decision, and they came together to establish the Royals.

They're the Zordis who believe that we were robbed of our freedom. They believe that because we are born with powers, we are entitled to power over Ordinaries, a mindset I can never understand. Some Royals go as far as believing that Ordinaries don't have a place in this world at all. Those are the people who scare me the most.

The Royals want to control all governments and be treated like kings, hence why they named themselves *Royals*. They will stop at nothing to get what they think they deserve. They have gotten and will get rid of anyone who stands in their way. Unfortunately, while in the middle of working their Immunes project, my parents learned what happens when you stand in the way of the Royals.

Now, ZIRDA doesn't work only on the development of Zordis but has also established an anti-Royals department. The department that I'm now a part of. The department that I've wanted to be a part of since I was seven and was told the truth about who caused the explosion that killed my parents.

Victor stops spinning his finger over his mug, and the spoon goes still. "Where's the sample?"

From the inner pocket of my leather jacket, I pull out the folded napkin holding the three strands of Arella's long hair. The woman has so much of it, I'm surprised I didn't find more lying around on my back seat.

Victor accepts the napkin from me, setting it on his desk. "I'll have our lab techs run their tests on this right away."

"What are you looking for in her DNA?" I ask.

"Defects. Anything abnormal for an Ordi. We'll also see if there are any matches to the other two Immunes we have DNA from."

"How are those missions going?"

When Victor gave me this assignment, he told me that there are two other agents doing the same thing I am. Even though I've experienced being around an Immune myself, it's still hard to imagine that there are other Ordinaries out there like Arella. How many more? I have no idea, because according to my extensive research on the z-net over the last month, being immune to Zordi powers isn't possible.

Victor shoots me a venomous look. "You know the rules. Missions are not to be spoken about between agents."

I know that. I was just trying to make conversation, but whatever.

"Are you making any progress with the girl?"

He's not gonna like my answer, but it's the only one I have. "This might take more time than we thought."

Originally, Victor and I estimated that this mission would take about two months. Three, max. I spent the entire first month observing Arella from afar. Now I'm almost through week five, and all I've got is some hair in a napkin.

I continue, "She seems reserved. Not quick to trust people."

"Work around it!" Victor snaps. The long horizontal scar on his neck shifts as he swallows with anger. The scar reminds me that a Royal almost took his life too—on the same night my parents died.

"You need to think more like a woman," Victor says. "If you were in her shoes, what would make you trust someone enough to spill every little detail about yourself?"

I think about that for a moment. The only person I've ever trusted enough to tell almost everything to is Liz, and that's only because she's seen the worst of my memories. Otherwise, I would always keep my lips sealed around her. Even now, I still don't tell her everything.

Apparently, I've taken too long to think, because Victor scowls at me. "It's simple. To get, you need to give. If you tell her personal things about yourself, she'll return the favor."

"Tell her personal things? Like what?"

Victor bends back in his chair. "I don't fuckin' know. This is *your* mission, so *you've* gotta figure it out."

With a nod, I say, "Fine, but I still need more time."

"The longer you take, the longer you're postponing the process of figuring out how to reproduce her immunity. We need this to have an advantage over the Royals. Can you imagine how much easier it would be for us to overpower them if their gifts can't affect us? The sooner we can destroy all their bases and capture their leaders, the sooner we can stop them from killing more innocent people. So stop wasting time, and go get the information we need."

Ever since a Royal tried to kill him, Victor has dedicated his life to eradicating the Royals. Over the years, he's gotten more and more bitter about how they're still a thriving organization of violent criminals. He'll probably stop at nothing to take them down.

What Victor doesn't realize is that I feel the same. I want the answer to Arella's immunity just as much as he does. I want to take down the people who killed his brother—my father—just as much as he does.

That's why when I arrive back home, the first thing I do is grab my laptop and log in to the z-net. A few thoughts occurred to me during my three-hour ride home, and I'm itching to do some research.

In the search bar, I type, *Is it possible for an Ordinary to be part Zordinary?*

My theory is that maybe, by some fluke in the biological laws of reproduction, Arella could be half or even part Zordi. If so, maybe immunity is her gift.

After reading many articles written by reputable professors and medical zoctors, I conclude that the answer is no—being part Zordi is impossible. The Ordinary egg isn't strong enough to hold a Zordi sperm. The aggressive Zordi sperm always destroys the Ordinary egg upon impact. On the other hand, Ordinary sperm isn't strong enough to penetrate the cell walls of a Zordi egg. Most of the time, a Zordi woman's body kills off the Ordinary sperm before it can reach the egg, anyway.

So I ask the search bar another question: *Is it possible to block the zense?*

Since it's not possible for a person to be part Zordi, maybe Arella is full Zordi. Maybe her immunity can block that tingle we get in our chests whenever we get near one another.

After some reading, I conclude that it's also impossible to block the zense. Even Zordis with dormant powers will still activate the tingle in other Zordis.

Back at the search bar, I type, *What can make a person immune to Zordi powers?*

I get the same information I got all the other times I

researched this question weeks ago, which is nothing. The bottom line is that since people don't know that Immunes exist, there's no information about them.

But if Immunes have existed since before my parents were killed, how is there not a single article about them? ZIRDA can't be the only people who know about Immunes. The zovernment has to know they exist too, right? So why isn't there any information anywhere?

5

TREY

I SENSE IT BEFORE IT COMES. FROM BEHIND, LIZ'S BUBBLY energy fires through my head like little pellets. Her heels clack rapidly across the backstage floor until her front slams against my back. The zense in my chest tingles as I fall forward off my barstool and catch myself right before the guitar in my lap hits the carpet.

Not even for a second does Liz release her arms from my torso. "Hey there, T-Bear!"

"Seriously, Liz? You act like you didn't just see me all day yesterday." *And every other day.* Dramatically, I pry myself out of her grasp, pretending she's a slimy slug.

With a huff, I plant my ass back onto the barstool. Once Kevin's guitar is repositioned over my thighs, I go back to changing the strings for him. He's been saying that he needs new strings, but he hasn't had the time to do it with all the stuff going on with his mom, so I figured I could help.

I twist the knob for the E string a few times. "You still trying to get that T-Bear thing to stick?"

Liz has been calling me that for the last few weeks. "I'm not trying. It's already stuck."

I throw my head back and groan.

"Ya know," she sings in her soprano voice, "I only call you that because ya hate it."

"I don't hate it," I grumble. "I just don't prefer it."

"Whatever." She narrows her eyes playfully. "You secretly like it."

"Do not." I do, not that I'll admit it out loud.

Liz is the only person I allow to call me silly names. She wears yellow every day of her life while she struts around the Earth spreading joy to everyone in sight. Even the people who don't deserve it—like me. For that, she can call me any stupid name in the book.

With a swoop, Liz flings her purse onto the sectional couch shoved against the wall, then heads to the mini bar for a bottle of water.

Our backstage area is one big room with our instruments lining the perimeter. In the middle sits a large open space where we like to rehearse. Down the hall in the back are some bathrooms. Across from those is our recording studio, where I've occasionally brought women in for a good time. I haven't done that for a while, because the last time I did, the redhead I invited in used teeth. My dick was sore for a week. Never again.

Liz claims a spot on the couch and pulls her yellow satin gloves off by the fingertips. The gloves flop onto the coffee table. I've come to appreciate the short moments when Liz's hands are bare. It doesn't happen often—only when it's just us.

It takes me another minute to finish tuning Kevin's guitar. With a flick of my wrist, the instrument hovers through the air, back to its stand. Then I join Liz on the sectional, resting an arm across the back.

She tucks one of her cherry-brown curls behind an ear. "Sooo, I read some of the comments on last week's music video."

"I thought we decided you weren't gonna read online comments anymore?"

"I didn't wear gloves for that video shoot," she says a little defensively. "I wanted to see what the fans' theories were."

"And?"

She chuckles. "The best theory was that I've been replaced by an alien clone and aliens are allergic to gloves."

I let out a loud *ha!* "Yep. That makes way more sense than the fact that you did your scenes alone, so you didn't need hand protection."

"I know, right?"

Over our four years as a band, our fans have drummed up hundreds of wild theories as to why Liz always wears gloves. While most people accept her excuse of being a germaphobe, many others like to spread theories about her having robotic hands or that she's hiding Hispanic gang tattoos.

It used to bother Liz. Now she owns it as her thing. Our sassy band manager, Monique, says that having a "thing" is great for branding. It gives people something to recognize Liz by. It's endearing when our hardcore fans come to our shows wearing satin gloves of their own. Monique has suggested that we slap our band logo onto some gloves and sell them as merchandise, but Liz refuses to monetize her curse, fearing that if she does, it'll get worse. I don't blame her. I'd feel the same.

"I sense three people coming." I point at Liz's gloves. They fly off the coffee table and land in her lap.

"Thanks, T." She doesn't hesitate to slip into them as Kevin swings the back door open. Sunlight radiates into the room while he holds the door wide for Marcus and Emmy to enter.

"Grant!" Marcus shouts. Our fans have labeled our drummer as the tough guy of our band because he's a tall, broad-shouldered Black man with a "Come at me, bruh!" resting face. On the inside, though, he's a softy, especially when it comes to his girlfriend. "Lemme ask you somethin'. If, before you walk into a gas station, you ask your girl if she wants a snack and she says *no*, can she get mad at you for not buyin' her a snack?"

I cock my eyebrows up. "No?"

Marcus turns to Emmy, who's barely a step behind him. "See, babe?"

Emmy, our band's pianist and alto, scowls at him. "Liz! If your man comes out of a gas station with three snacks for himself and none for you, then refuses to share *one* potato chip, do you have a right to get pissed?"

Liz laughs, pushing herself off the couch. "I mean, I'd be a little ticked."

With a flash of red curls, Emmy turns to slap her boyfriend's arm. "See?"

"It's never just *one* chip!" Marcus says. "One always turns into the whole goddamn bag."

Kevin makes a few *tsk tsk tsk* sounds as he wiggles a finger back and forth. "Word of advice, man: Always get your girl a snack."

"Whose side are you on, Chan?" Marcus gapes at Kevin. "She told me she didn't want nothin'!"

"Nah, bro." Kevin shakes his head. "They *always* want somethin'. And if they don't, now you got an extra snack."

Marcus glances at me with a *back me up* look.

The most I can offer him is a shrug. "Kevin knows what's up."

Knowing he's lost this one, Marcus mutters something under his breath as he takes his spot behind the drum set.

We're able to rehearse a few songs before the opening band arrives. Around that time, our crew members trickle into the room.

By seven, our openers are on stage while my band is backstage with Monique, talking through our upcoming filming schedule. I'm barely paying attention, for two reasons.

First: I don't have anything going on in my life, so whatever dates work for them work for me. Second: I keep checking the time every two minutes. Arella should be here soon, and the clock on my phone seems to get slower with each glance.

Forty long minutes later, our security manager peeks his head backstage and motions for me. Earlier, I asked him to come find me whenever Arella got here.

Emmy is in mid-sentence when I shoot off the couch.

"Be right back," I say.

"What?" Marcus says as I rush away. "We're goin' up in like fifteen minutes."

I ignore him as I exit through a door and come out at the side of the stage. I scan the crowded restaurant for her face but don't find it.

"Where is she?" I ask.

Our security manager points with one of his thick tattooed fingers. "At the far end of bar."

Even through the dim lighting and all the people surrounding her, my eyes pin onto her immediately. She's got her back facing me, with all her wavy chestnut locks pulled into a long braid hanging over one shoulder.

The openers are in the middle of performing their closing song as I make my way toward Arella. Occupied tables of all sizes cover the floor from the stage to the back wall. From a side table, a pair of young women shout my name over the music. I flash them a smile and a quick wave. Instant giddiness flies through my head. Then comes their disappointment when I don't stop to chat with them. *Sorry, ladies, but I've got more important things on my plate.*

Tonight, for phase two, I have two objectives. First is to ask Arella out on a date. I need to keep seeing her until I find out what makes her immune. Since it could be *anything* that causes it, I need to learn as much about her past, her family history, her genetics, and whatever else as possible.

My second objective is to get her to tell me all the basic

information I already know about her. I would hate to slip up and mention something I know that she hasn't told me yet.

Arella, looking as stunning as yesterday, has her phone pressed to her ear as I approach her from behind.

"What do you mean, you're not coming?" A pause. "You're kidding . . . No. I can't be here without you, Javie." Silence, then she groans. "All right, fine. No, it's okay. Yes, really. Mm-hmm. I'll see you tomorrow." With a deep sigh, she sets her phone onto the bar counter.

Now's my chance.

"Hey." I slide onto the empty barstool next to her.

Arella jumps back a little, clasping a hand against her chest. "Ah! You scared me."

"Now we're even."

She crumples her eyebrows together before making an *oh!* face. "That's right. I scared you yesterday while you were fixing my tire. Thanks again for that."

"No problem. Where's your friend?"

Arella rolls her eyes, but her irritation doesn't shoot through my mind like it should. "Javina's girlfriend flew back from a work trip early as a surprise. Apparently, that means Javina needs to go to the airport and ditch me here by myself."

"You're not by yourself. You've got me."

"But won't you be up there?" She points at the stage, just as the opening band's final song ends.

The floor vibrates with an eruption of cheers as the lead singer waves at the crowd. The lights go wild with bright neon colors flashing back and forth. The singer says his last thank-yous, then vanishes behind the black curtain with the rest of his band. Slowly, the stage lights dim out as the cheering fades and transforms into a loud hum of conversation.

I have little time left, so I throw a hand up to get one of the four bartenders' attention. The guy with an eyebrow piercing spots me right away and offers me a curt nod as he finishes the drink he's making.

After he sets two drinks in front of a young Asian couple, he approaches me. The name tag pinned to his upper chest reads MITCH. I've never seen him before, so he must be new.

"What can I get for you?" Frustration simmers in Mitch's gut. I wonder what from.

"I've got my card on file under Trey Grant." I gesture to Arella. "Anything she wants is on me tonight."

Mitch squints his eyes. "Huh? What d'you mean you've got your card on file?"

"Just tell Sophie I'm covering her bill."

The guy scoffs. "And you are?"

I don't expect the new guy to know who I am. Still, he doesn't have to come at me with that snippy attitude. Twisting on my seat, I hop off and head toward the nearest table.

"Excuse me," I say to the group of men shoving onion rings into their mouths. I grab the little acrylic sign off their table. "I'm just gonna borrow this for a sec."

I hand the sign to the bartender, then point at my face. "That's me. Tell Sophie this guy is getting this girl's bill, 'kay?"

"Cool." Mitch tosses the sign back to me, and I catch it easily. He's lucky I've got good reflexes, or I would have dropped it from his shit throw. From under the bar counter, he pulls out a laminated menu and shoves it at Arella. "Be back in a jiff."

I should speak to Sophie about Mr. Rude and Unfriendly later. He's not someone I'd want bartending at my joint. No doubt, Sophie doesn't want him either.

After I return the sign to its original table, I reclaim my place next to Arella, who's reading the menu. "What're you in the mood for?"

"Thank you, but you don't have to pay for me."

"No worries. Sophie gives the entire band and crew a huge discount. She says we help bring in most of her income."

I check the time on my phone. Monique is probably freaking out right now about me not getting mic'd up. I'm gonna hear it from her later about how I purposely do things just to piss her off, even though that's never my goal. If Arella wasn't such a vital puzzle piece to finishing my parents' research, I'd be back there already.

While Arella focuses on the menu, I focus on her as if staring longer will make my mind power kick in. So far, nothing. *Damn, she's beautiful though.* Undoubtedly the prettiest Ordinary I've ever laid eyes on. Strands of wavy locks fall out of her braid, framing her rosy cheeks. Long black lashes surround her hypnotizing brown eyes, and her nose has that delicate small and rounded shape about it. All her features fit with her sweet and gentle demeanor.

Arella sets the menu down and turns to me with a shy smile. "Am I that interesting to watch?"

I smile back sheepishly. "A little."

Mitch returns with that same snippy tone. "You decide on somethin' yet, sweet cakes?"

Sweet cakes? I can't stop myself from shooting him a dirty look. Mitch pretends like he doesn't see it, but I sense it when he does, the moment his nerves spike. Subtly, I give him my best *I'm this close to hitting you* face.

"I'll have some water and the chicken nachos, please," Arella says, never acknowledging Mitch's stupid pet name. Maybe she doesn't care that he called her *sweet cakes*, but I do.

"Cool." Mitch snatches the menu from her, then leaves.

Now that he's gone, it's time for me to make good on my mission. "So, Arella, do you work anywhere besides Sunrise Daycare?"

Her shoulders stiffen. "How do you know where I work?"

"You and Javina were wearing the same T-shirt yesterday. I just assumed . . ."

"Oh, right." She relaxes. "I'm also a nanny over the weekends. How about you? What do you do?"

"You know what I do. I'm a musician." I nod my head toward the stage I'm supposed to be behind right now.

"Do you do anything else?"

"Just this."

Her fingers play with the end of her long braid. I can't tell if she's doing it out of habit or because she's nervous. Here I am, playing that guessing game again.

"If you don't have another job, what do you do in your free time?" she asks.

This is supposed to be me learning about her, not the other way around. I answer anyway. "Doing what I do keeps me busy enough. We film videos at least once a week and rehearse a lot. Then there's all our writing and recording sessions. I also do a lot of the background work like song arrangements and producing. When I have free time, I like to ride my Harley around the suburbs, read, work out, you know."

"Sounds like you've got it good."

I purse my lips together into a thin line. "Sure."

Something I've learned about life is that the way things look on the outside isn't always what they are on the inside. I would trade away the Internet fame and everything I have if it meant I could live the life I would have if my parents had never been murdered.

"What do you do in your free time?" I ask.

"Um, are they looking for you?" Arella points toward the stage. I turn at the hip to find two crew members up there, cupping hands to their eyebrows and surveying the crowd.

Dammit. I've never been this late. Monique is gonna kill me.

"You're staying for the whole set, right?" I force my ass to slide off my seat.

"How long does it go 'til?"

"Ten."

"Oh, that's kind of late." She tugs at the bottom of her shirt. "I'll stick around for as long as I can."

"It'd mean a lot to me if you stayed. I'd like to know what

you think of our music." I *need* her to stay. If she leaves, I'll have to plan another run-in with her. At that point, it might look suspicious.

I see the battle she's having with herself in her head, even though I can't sense it. I've gotta get her to stay, so, with the sweetest puppy-dog eyes I can muster, I add, "Please?"

After a moment, she lets out a breath and smiles sweetly. "All right. I'll stay for your whole set."

Thank fuck. "Great. I'll come find ya when I'm done."

Backstage, the openers are getting their instruments packed up as I beeline past them to my electric guitar. Liz and Emmy each have a microphone in their hand, flashing me a *what the hell* look. Kevin, with his bass guitar strapped over a shoulder, taps the invisible watch on his wrist. Marcus spins his drumsticks around his fingers, shaking his head at me. The crew members are all in position, ready to roll. The only person not in sight is Monique, and I count it as a W.

I'm about to swing my guitar strap over my head when a large hand shoves me so hard, I'm launched forward a step. It's Marcus, and his mood swarms around me like angry bees. "Bro, you missed our entire pre-show routine. I was 'bout to send out a search party."

I throw both hands up in surrender. "I'm here now. No need for the helicopters."

"I had ten dollars on you hiding in the bathroom, whackin' one off." Marcus huffs as he makes his way back to join the rest of our band near the stage door.

Our gray-haired sound manager replaces him. "I bet twenty dollars." He hands me my earpiece.

I shove it into my ear, then hook the mic pack to the back of my jeans.

Our sound manager marches away as his voice bellows through my earpiece. "Found Grant. He's ready."

Monique growls my name through the device. I know it's her from the same exasperated tone she always says my name in. "Trey Grant, I swear to Lord Jesus, you be givin' me more aneurysms than all six of my children put together."

I ignore her. She says that about me at least once a week.

Our sound manager responds with a chuckle. "Monique, you say that about him every week, yet ya still like the kid."

"I'd like him more if he didn't purposely try to make my job harder."

I chuckle to myself, then press a button on my mic pack. "Monique, we all know you enjoy yelling at me as much as I enjoy making you yell at me."

She growls again. "Get to your position, Grant."

I rarely get nervous before a show., but tonight, my mind feels chaotic. My body's here, about to perform, but my mind's still with Arella, trying to figure her out.

Focus! I order myself as my bandmates and I step out onto the stage, still hidden behind the giant black curtain. On the other side, the audience is screaming at the top of their lungs. I allow their intense energy to rush through me and take control. Hopefully, it'll drown out the tension in my stomach.

The crowd gets louder when the lights flash and our intro music drops over the speakers. A heavy drum beat with a guitar riff plays, then comes Liz's recorded voice.

"Like a sunrise on the darkest day or a shining star within the black sky, you'll always see us because we are . . . Flames in the Night!"

The crowd chants along with the countdown. "Five. Four. Three. Two. ONE!"

As my bandmates march out from behind the curtain, the rumble of screams pulsates through my veins. I'm always the last to come out. When I do, I lift my guitar into the air, and the crowd gets wilder. Their rush of exhilaration slams into my head so hard, I almost lose my balance.

With my Empath powers having the range of a quarter mile, I can sense hundreds to thousands of people at once. Usually, I'm able to minimize my range to only those within a few steps of me. It makes the emotions of everyone else in the distance feel like a low hum—still present, just not as loud.

On stage, I like to expand my range to everyone in the audience. Being able to sense every single person as I perform is one of the few perks of this empathy gift—a gift I never would have chosen. Not that anybody gets to choose.

Marcus ticks off four beats on his drumsticks before going into his drum solo. After eight measures, I enter with my guitar. After that, the rest of the band joins in, and we play our usual opening song, "Fired Up!"

The more I sing and play, the more I lose myself in the moment. Music has always been my escape. It helps me forget about my bullshit childhood and seeing my parents die in front of me.

6

—————

TREY

EIGHTEEN YEARS AGO

I'M ABOUT TO FINISH BUILDING THE FIRST WALL OF MY LEGO castle when Mama comes into my bedroom and sits on the floor with me.

"Hey, honey." She grabs my teddy bear and puts it in my lap, then drags her fingers through my hair. I usually love it when she does that. Tonight, I know she's only doing it to distract me from how she feels. I can't ignore it. Her heartache is making my heart ache.

"What's wrong, Mama?" I rub the wetness off her cheek with my fingers. *Did I do something wrong?*

"Nothing's wrong."

"Then why are you crying?"

She wipes her tears off on her sleeve, then pats her lap. "Come here, baby."

I listen to my mama and crawl onto her legs.

"Let's sing our song together," she says.

Last year, Mama wrote a song for me. She said that whenever I'm sad, I should sing the song and it'll remind me

55

that everything will be okay. I love the song, and we've been singing it together every day.

I pull Andy, the bear I named after Daddy, closer to my chest as Mama and I sing.

> *When you're lost without me,*
> *you'll always have Andy.*
> *When you feel you don't belong,*
> *hug this bear and sing this song.*
> *Look to the sky when you feel down.*
> *Know that things will turn around.*
> *Work twice as hard to the finish line.*
> *Now it's your time to shine.*

Mama kisses my forehead. "I love you so much, honey."

"I love you too, Mama."

Daddy's footsteps thump down the hall, stopping outside my bedroom door. "It's time to go."

Mama doesn't move. She keeps running her hands through my hair.

"Suzie . . ." Daddy says as his tense feelings rush through my mind.

I think of earlier that day when my parents made my favorite pancakes with strawberries and whipped cream. I turned my entire plate into a tower of white fluff. Mama and Daddy couldn't even tell there were pancakes underneath. I think about how happy I felt while eating it. Any cheerful thought will work as long as I think about it hard enough, then push it into Mama's head.

She smiles, squeezing my hand. "Thank you, but you know I don't like it when you do that."

"I just want you to be happy," I say as she pushes off the carpet.

I slide out of her lap and look up at her. She wipes more

tears off her face, and it makes me want to push more happiness into her.

Daddy always says there isn't a point to having powers if we don't use them. Mama always says it's okay to use my powers as long as I don't hurt anyone. *Does making people happy hurt them?*

"Listen to me, son." Daddy kneels at my side and points at the clock hanging on my wall. "You see that shorter arrow pointing at the nine?"

I already know how to tell time. The clock says it's nine thirty-six.

"When that short arrow reaches the twelve, if Mama and I aren't back yet, run to one of the neighbors' houses, okay? And take Andy with you."

"What time will you be back if you're not home by midnight?"

Daddy swallows, looks up at Mama, then back at me. "If you get hungry, there are some leftovers in the fridge." He stands and pats my shoulder. "Be a good boy now."

Something bad is happening. I know it. I can *feel* it. Maybe if I cry and tell them I don't want them to go to work, they'll stay.

No. They'll still go. They always do. Besides, I'm seven now. Seven-year-olds don't cry.

"Goodbye, honey." Mama leans down to kiss my forehead.

"Wait. You said to never say goodbye. Goodbye means forever."

"I'm sorry, baby. I meant bye for now."

Outside the living room window, my parents run through the rain, get into their car, and drive away into the darkness. I drag my feet back to my room and slump over my bed, waiting for the short arrow to tick away from the nine.

Usually whenever my parents get called in to work, Aunt Debbie comes over to watch me. Earlier, Mama told me that Aunt Debbie couldn't come. Mama asked if I could stay home by myself. I told her that I'm old enough. Besides, I've stayed home by myself before. Most of the time, it's only for a few minutes while my parents run to the store.

Vroom! Every time I hear a car, I rush back to the living room window. The cars never stop, and there have been at least six cars now.

When the short arrow points at the ten, water pours onto the house. It's so loud, it sounds like all the kids at my school are stomping on the roof. To try to block out the noise, I point at the TV. It turns on with a bright screen that hurts my eyes for a second. Once my eyes are clear again, I sit in my spot on the couch. I always get the middle cushion because I like to be right between Mama and Daddy.

I wiggle my fingers at the TV, pressing buttons until *The Lion King* plays. With another wave of my hand, a blanket floats off the floor and drapes over my legs.

My eyes get sleepy as Simba and Scar battle on top of Pride Rock. I shove Andy behind my head to use as a pillow. His fur is soft and—

BOOM!

The front door bursts open.

I yelp and fall to the floor, getting tangled in the blanket.

"What was that?" a deep voice asks.

I peek my head out from under the fleece. Two tall people are standing in my living room. *Who are they?*

With heavy footsteps, two more people rush into my house.

The biggest guy points at me. "It's their kid! Get him!"

I toss the blanket over my shoulder. A fireball the size of a baseball appears in my hand. My fireballs aren't as big as Daddy's, and I've never cared—until now. I throw my fireball at the biggest guy and don't even wait to see if I hit or missed. The second I let it go, I run.

The carpet rumbles beneath me like I'm standing on train tracks with a moving train coming right at me. I fall and hit my face on the corner of a table. I cry as I rub the pain in my cheek.

"Come here, you little shit," a big man says from behind me.

I twist around, then scream as I crawl backward away from him. Behind him, a fireball shoots through the open door. It sets one of the bad guys on fire. My skin burns, even though it's not *my* body on fire.

Two more people run through the door. It's too dark to see who they are, especially when they're moving so fast. One of them throws a fireball at the bad guys. If they're fighting the people who are trying to hurt me, that means they're good, right?

I don't stick around to find out. On my hands and knees, I crawl away. I'm about to turn in to the kitchen when a fireball lands right in front of me. I scream with my arms over my face. The flames burst upward, blocking my way.

Hide! I need to hide! I crawl until I've shoved myself into a corner behind an end table. Hopefully, no one can see me here. More fireballs fly around the room. I can't tell who they're coming from or who they're aimed at.

A woman screams as something sharp jabs into my side. I pull my shirt up to check my skin. Nothing's there. My face burns like someone's thrown a fireball at my head. My body's going numb, and I think I'm going to puke. I haven't learned how to stop my body from feeling other people's physical pain yet. Daddy says I should be able to once I'm older, but I want to be able to do it now.

More flames consume my house, destroying everything. All the people are screaming and shouting at each other as my body continues to ache. A chair cracks into pieces against the wall by the TV. I dare one look up, only to find a vase flying at me. It shatters right above my head. I throw my arms up as the glass falls over me, and liquid drenches my shirt.

"Honey?" Someone shakes my shoulder.

"Mama?" I open my eyes.

A long cut runs along her bottom lip to her chin. Blood drips from it. She's got another cut on her forehead, with even more blood running from that. Suddenly, my head and lip hurt too.

"Run outside!" Mama shouts over the crash of someone being thrown against the floor.

She yelps as she's jerked away from me by her hair.

"Mama!" I shriek, reaching for her.

The big man who yanked her climbs on top of her and punches her in the face. I feel it in my cheek.

Then again.

And again.

And again.

The man shocks her with a lightning ball. She cries out as my body shakes.

"No!" I throw my unsteady hand up and launch a fireball at the guy.

He only flinches as it hits his arm, falls to the floor, and rolls away. The tall guy behind him flicks his wrist in circles. A tornado appears in front of me, sucking me into it. The air leaves my lungs as I spin until my back slams against the wall. I fall to my knees and gasp for a breath.

I'm still dizzy as someone lifts me into their arms. I'm about to blast them with a fireball until I see his face. It's Daddy—with a gash in his cheek. It's so deep, it looks like part of his face is falling off. Red streaks pour from his wound, all the way down to his chest.

"Outside! Now!" Daddy points at the coffee table. It flies up and crashes through the big living room window, landing in the front yard. Glass falls everywhere.

My back hits the couch. I scream and grip the cushions as Daddy waves his hand, and I'm flown out the window on the couch.

It crashes next to the coffee table, bounces once, then tips over, dumping me onto the muddy ground. Water pelts my eyes. I can't see. I can't—

BOOM!

My house explodes into a giant mushroom of fire. It throws me backward. Heat pricks my skin as I fall to the ground. Pain bursts into the side of my head. A high-pitched ringing sound pierces my ears. I can't hear anything else.

I wipe the water from my face. It feels weird. I glance at my hands. They're red. Why is the water red?

I have to get up. I have to help my mama and daddy.

I try to push off the grass, but my arms don't work. I collapse into the mud, and then darkness takes over.

7

ARELLA

I'M TOTALLY GOING TO KILL JAVINA. WHILE I'M AT IT, I'M going to kill Rachel too. If it weren't for them, I wouldn't be sitting at a bar by myself.

Once Javina told me that she wasn't coming—last minute, I might add—I figured I could stay for a few songs, then leave. Screw Trey and his show-stopping smile and those puppy dog eyes.

"It'd mean a lot to me if you stayed." How is a woman supposed to say no to that?

I munch on a cheesy chip off my plate of nachos as Trey effortlessly performs a guitar solo on stage, his second of the evening. There's no denying that he's talented. His fingers slide up and down the guitar as if it's a part of him. I can't imagine how many long hours it took him to learn how to play that fast and make it sound good.

While everyone in the band has singing parts, Trey seems to have the most. It doesn't seem like anyone's disappointed about it, either. When he's not singing or playing the guitar, he's behind the drum set, banging some drumsticks all over it. When he's not doing that, he's behind the piano, delivering a perfect tune. If the crowd isn't impressed by how many instruments he can play, it's probably because they're too busy gawking at his arm muscles straining the sleeves of his leather jacket.

Midway through the show, the rest of the band disappears behind the curtain and Trey performs by himself from the piano. He sings with his eyes closed and his lips practically making out with the microphone. I wouldn't be surprised if all the women here wished they were that microphone right now.

After he finishes the song, he thanks everyone, and the lights go dark. A second later, the spotlight returns as Liz, Kevin, and the other female band member take the stage. The women perform a perfectly harmonized song with Kevin on the guitar. I'm just as mesmerized by their voices as I was by Trey's.

From behind a ketchup bottle, I find one of those table signs displaying the band's picture. All five of them look like models, with their flawless faces and matching outfits. Trey's in the middle, wearing the same thing he wore yesterday and is wearing today: a black leather jacket over a plain black V-neck that hugs his torso. In the picture, he's got the same styled hair and stubbly beard. The only difference is that he looks slightly younger in the picture, but not by much.

"That picture is over a year old," someone says from behind me. "We're getting them updated soon."

I twist on my barstool to find the dazzling man I was just admiring. When our eyes lock, my heart kicks up a notch. My body reacted like this around him yesterday, too. It's not like me to get this excited around men. Usually, I'm trying to escape as fast as my legs will carry me. Right now, that urge is absent. If anything, I'm a little drawn to him, and I can't figure out why. It's not like Trey's the only attractive man in this city. A cute guy made conversation with me at a gas station this morning, and not once did he make my stomach flutter the way Trey is.

I pretend like his presence doesn't affect me as I tilt my

head toward the stage. "Aren't you supposed to be over there?"

"Nah. It's solo time. Everyone gets to show off their individual talents for a while and give the others a break."

I do my best not to stare at his can't-help-but-gawk-at-them features. "It's fun to watch your band perform. I didn't know you played so many things. Which instrument did you learn first?"

"Guitar. I first picked one up when I was—" Trey catches that my attention has slipped to the two ladies with eager smiles standing behind him. He flips around.

The one with teal blue tips in her blonde hair perks up. "Hi, Trey. Can we get a picture with you?"

"Oh, sure." He drapes an arm around the blonde's shoulder and flashes his pearly whites. Her friend snaps a few photos, and then they alternate.

"We've both been huge fans ever since your first YouTube video went viral," Blue Tips says. She goes on and on about how much she loves his music and, more so, how much she loves *him*. Her friend adds to the conversation by asking him question after question. They sound as fangirly as Javina did yesterday, except I'm bothered by them and not by Javina.

They steal Trey away from me for so long, it's Kevin who's got the stage to himself now.

"Thanks again, ladies," Trey says halfway through Kevin's solo. "I appreciate the support."

It's obvious that he's trying to close the conversation, but the ladies don't take the hint. They keep fawning over him and praising *him*, not his music. I can't tell if he likes it or not.

Patiently, I wait until Trey presses a finger against his earpiece. The fangirls are still blabbing as he listens to whatever is being said on the other end.

With a groan, he takes a step backward toward the stage. "Sorry, ladies. I gotta go before my manager chews my head off. It was great to meet you both."

Finally, the ladies say their goodbyes, then depart into the sea of people around us.

Trey turns back to me. "I'm really sorry 'bout that. I gotta go back up. We've got a meet and greet right after this. Would you mind coming to that for a bit? I won't make you stay long. I promise."

I don't know what possesses me to do it. Maybe it's because I know the answer he wants to hear, or because I'm a people pleaser. Maybe it's because throughout the show, I've been in awe of him and I want to keep being awed. But I say, "I'd love to."

The bright smile that spreads across his cheeks makes my heart swoon and confirms my decision. After he thanks me, he sprints off behind a door marked BACKSTAGE. AUTHORIZED PERSONNEL ONLY.

The moment he's gone, those two fangirls materialize on either side of me.

Blue Tips speaks first. "Do you know Trey Grant? Like, personally?"

"Uh . . ." I don't *know* him. Not really.

The other girl doesn't wait for me to respond before she asks, "What's he like in real life? Is he like what they say online?"

"Um, what do they say online?"

"You know, that he's charming, mysterious, and really good in bed."

"Oh. I—I suppose I don't know him like *that*."

"Does that mean you're not on his list?"

I scrunch my face together. "His VIP list?"

"No. His *list*. You know . . ." Blue Tips nudges my arm with her elbow and waggles her eyebrows up and down. "Of people he's fucked. I've heard he's into doing it with his fans."

"And sometimes with multiple at the same time," the other girl adds.

Are these ladies trying to have a threesome with him?

Wait . . . Is that why Trey invited Javina and me here tonight? Was he trying to entice us into his bed? If so, he chose the wrong woman. I'm not interested in being anyone's plaything.

"No," I say firmly. "I'm not on his list."

"In that case," Blue Tips says, grinning, "can you get us into the meet and greet tonight? Tickets were sold out, and we really wanna go."

"Uh . . ." I don't know how to respond. Thankfully, I don't have to, because a thick guy with a long scruffy beard comes up behind the girls and speaks for me.

"Ladies, leave her alone. If you wanna bang the guy, find your own way. You're making her uncomfortable."

That's putting it lightly.

Blue Tips shoots Scruffy Guy a dirty look. "Mind your own business."

The man uses his large body to stand in front of me protectively. "Walk."

The girls glance at each other, then silently agree to leave. They mutter foul words under their breath as they slither away.

"Thanks for that," I say once they're gone.

"No worries." The towering man sticks out a hand with a smile. "I'm Dex."

"Ari." I shake his thick palm. That's two days in a row now that I've shaken hands with a man and didn't feel violated by it. I'm making wonderful progress.

Dex slides onto the empty barstool next to me and takes a swig of his beer. "Pretty name. Where ya from?"

"Around here," I say vaguely. While I'm grateful he told those girls off, it wasn't an open invitation to befriend me. He seems to think it was though.

As Kevin leaves the stage and is replaced by Trey and Liz, Dex asks about my age and what I do for a living. I give him undetailed answers like "A woman never shares her age" and "I work with kids." Then I move the subject back to him. I've learned that most men like talking about themselves more than they like listening to women talk, and Dex is no exception.

My nachos are gone by the time I've heard all about Dex's plan to get rich as a travel agent. I fake laugh and nod whenever appropriate. Listening to him go on and on about himself reminds me of why I don't enjoy first dates. I have yet to go out with a man who genuinely wants to know more about me than he wants to brag about himself, though I've only been on three first dates, so I don't have the best pool of results.

"And I got this one after I moved to San Fran." Dex points at his huge upper forearm where a detailed dragon is inked into his skin. He's been yammering on about his tattoos and love for dragons for about fifteen minutes now. Judging by the way he talks about dragons, their diets, and what their scales feel like, I'd say he thinks they're real.

Mitch, the rude bartender, interrupts Dex's tattoo-flaunting session. "Another beer?"

Dex hands Mitch his empty bottle. "Yeah, and how about a cocktail for this pretty lady?"

I shake my head. "No, thanks."

"You sure?"

I'm positive. "Thank you, though."

"It's my treat."

"No, really. I don't drink." That's not something I usually tell people right away, but I don't want to seem impolite.

"How 'bout a lemonade, then?"

I shrug a shoulder, giving in. "Sure."

Mitch departs, then comes back with a glass of icy lemonade and another beer for Dex. I take a sip of my drink. It's sweet and tangy, exactly the way I like it.

Once the bartender takes off to help the next customer, Dex goes back to mansplaining dragons to me. I thought turning my entire body away from him would indicate that I have no interest in dragons, but nope. He's too self-absorbed to pick up on any of my social cues.

Thankfully, the entertainment is a good distraction. Trey's now playing an acoustic guitar and singing a duet with Kevin. For a second, Trey locks eyes with me, and my heart skips a beat. I must have imagined it though. There's no way he can see me from all the way up there with all those bright stage li—

Someone taps my arm. "Ari?"

I flinch, jerking my arm back.

Dex puts a hand up, palm forward. "Sorry. Think I lost you there. You didn't answer my question."

I take a well-needed sip of my lemonade, holding back a groan. "What was your question?"

"I asked if you've ever been to Europe."

"No."

"Well, as I was saying . . ." and he goes on yapping.

The more he talks, the less I pretend to listen. I nod occasionally while keeping my eyes on the amazing entertainment.

After a few more songs, my lemonade is gone and Dex is *still* talking. About what? I have no idea. My grandparents taught me to always be nice to people, but I'm losing my patience with this guy. Also, my head feels hazy. I'm hot, I'm sweaty, and the room is swaying.

"You all right?" Dex asks. At least, I think it's him. I've shut my eyes to block out the flashing lights that are suddenly way too bright.

"I'm getting a headache." Placing my elbows on the bar, I dump my head into my hands. The music's way too loud. Every bass drop feels like it's rattling my brain.

"You wanna go home?"

"I'm fine."

"You're turning red." Dex catches me with his enormous hand as the room tilts to the side. "And now you're falling . . ."

I understand that he's only trying to stop me from crashing to the floor, but him grabbing me like that makes me want to recoil into myself. I'm close to shoving him away. I don't because I don't want to be like that anymore. It's exhausting to be scared all the time and to wonder if the hand on my body will leave another bruise. I want to be a normal person—someone who can be touched by a man without dying on the inside.

"I'm gonna get some fresh air." I toss the long strap of my purse over my shoulder, then get to my feet.

Dex puts his beer down. "I'll come make sure you don't fall over."

"No, thanks. I'll be fine." The room wavers as I navigate through the crowd from my seat to the door.

Fog settles into my brain as I stumble into the warm night air. The massive line of people waiting to get inside earlier has disappeared. It's quieter out here than in there, which helps me feel a tiny bit better—right until a car drives by with lights as bright as the sun.

"Be careful." Someone steadies me with an arm on my waist.

I flinch as my eyes meet with Dex's. I thought I'd told him I'd be fine, but apparently I'm not if I can't even walk straight.

Dex keeps me upright as I shuffle behind the restaurant to sit on a patch of grass under a looming palm tree. I pretzel my legs together and throw my head into my hands.

What's going on? Why does my head hurt so much? Was it something I ate? *Wait* . . . Did someone drug me? My head springs up.

"You okay?" Dex squats in front of me with concern etched into his face.

I peer over Dex's broad shoulders to scan the area for my ex's car. I wouldn't put it past him to slip some money to the bartender to drop something into my lemonade, and then when I come outside, he attacks me.

My vision is blurry, but from what I can tell, his car isn't here. *Maybe he parked it in a parking garage?*

"Looking for someone?" Dex asks, glancing back.

Was it . . . ? No. It couldn't have been Dex. I kept my hands and eyes on my drink the whole time, and not once did he reach for my lemonade.

Rummaging through my purse, I pull out my phone. The brightness of the screen makes me screw my eyes shut again. "I'm going to call my friend to pick me up."

"I could take you home?" he offers gently.

Yeah, right. "No, thanks," I say kindly yet firmly.

"I don't mind."

I mind. "I appreciate the thought, but I—"

The world tips upside down. All I can see is the back of Dex's jeans. His hard shoulder digs into my stomach, and my purse flops against him as he steadily carries me across the parking lot.

"Hey!" I shout. The word barely comes out. "Put me down."

I struggle to raise my arms. My attempt at punching the guy looks like my hand twitched. My leg doesn't lift when I tell it to. Neither does my head.

No! I scream at the top of my lungs, but it doesn't reach my ears.

A car beeps, then a door opens. I can't pry my eyelids apart. Warm leather presses against my cheek. My mind races to all those kidnapped, raped, and murdered women I watch true crime shows about. *Am I about to become one of them?*

I try to scream again. Nothing comes out. I try to move but fail. My legs are moving, but that's because Dex is pushing them into the car. I tell my legs to kick him. They don't.

The door slams shut as a deep voice bellows, "Step. Away. From. The. girl."

"Don't worry, man. She's my girlfriend. She's just had too much to drink."

"Get away from her," the other man growls.

"Fuck off."

I wrench my eyes open just enough to see Dex's giant frame bend forward as he grunts. His head snaps back as the other guy punches him again. With a growl, Dex swings his fist at the smaller man, who ducks and strikes Dex in his jaw.

Vomit is coming. It's slowly creeping up my throat.

Someone lets out an ear-piercing scream, then wails. I think it's Dex. At least, I *hope* it's him.

The door flies open. Someone's warm palm cups my cheek. "Are you okay?"

I try to force my eyelids open, but they don't budge.

8

———

ARELLA

T HE BLINDING SUNRISE SHINES THROUGH MY TINTED WINDOWS. I drag my blanket over my face. *Why does my blanket smell like a man? And since when are my windows tinted?*

I jolt upright. The blanket I don't recognize slides down my front.

Whose bed is this? It's king-size, I think. I can't tell for sure; I've never been on one. The sheets are gray and silky, not purple and cotton like the ones at home.

I'm alone. *Is that a good thing?*

The denim shorts I wore last night are still on. As is my shirt. *Good sign.*

The other side of the bed looks slightly made. *Another good sign.*

On the nightstand are three bottles of cologne, a lamp, and a book with a dragon on the cover. Visions of a scruffy-bearded guy sipping beer zip across my mind like flashing lights. He went on and on about his dragon tattoo.

What happened last night? I try to remember, but my memory fails me. Everything beyond dragon talk is a blur. Am I at that guy's house? *Oh, god. I hope not.*

This bedroom is twice the size of mine. Maybe triple. The

72

white walls are bare. *How am I supposed to figure out whose house I'm in if they don't have any personal pictures hanging up?*

After scooting off the gigantic mattress, I peer into the walk-in closet. Dark jeans and plain T-shirts are hung in neat rows. Whoever's closet this is doesn't wear any color.

The master bathroom is complete with a jacuzzi and a shower as big as my entire bathroom. This house belongs to someone with money, that's for sure.

I press my ear against the bedroom door. Silence. No movement, either. After taking the lampshade off the lamp, I unplug the lamp and grip it tightly. Anyone I feel threatened by is about to become a victim of my lamp bat.

As softly as I can, I open the door and tread down the hall with sloth-like footsteps. Maybe I'm in *his* house. Then again, he could never afford something this nice. Not without Daddy's money. Nor does he read.

I keep tiptoeing over the soft carpet. Sunlight gleams from the other end of the hall. A familiar scent floats up my nose. I'd know that smell anywhere. *Bacon.*

When I round the corner to where the sizzling is coming from, I raise my lamp bat, ready to strike.

The tall man in front of the stove jumps. "Shit!" His spatula somersaults onto the hardwood floor with a clank.

I freeze with my weapon up. It's not the man I was expecting.

Trey scoops up the spatula, then wipes the floor with a towel. "Dammit. You've really gotta stop scaring me."

Trey Grant? That's who lives here?

"What's with the lamp?" he asks. I'd like to think he feels intimidated, but the knitted brows and hint of a smirk on his lips tell me he's more amused than anything.

I keep my lamp bat held high and muster up the sternest voice I can. "What happened?"

Nonchalantly, Trey slides two slices of bread into a toaster. "How do you like your eggs?"

My eggs? What? He's asking me that as if I casually stay overnight at his house all the time. Maybe he's used to women waking up here, but I'm not used to waking up anywhere except in my own bed.

"What happened?" I ask more firmly this time.

"I'll tell you once you put my lamp down."

If Trey wanted to hurt me, he would have already, right? Sighing, I set his lamp onto the island.

"Is scrambled okay?" Trey asks, all light and gentle.

"Um, sure."

From the refrigerator, he pulls out a carton of eggs. "What do you remember?"

"I remember being at the Soul House. I was watching your band play and . . ." Then I was thrown over the shoulder of a giant man like a sack of potatoes.

"Did you know that dirty-mouthed motherfucker?" Trey's tone has lost all his earlier gentleness. It's ironic that he's calling Dex dirty-mouthed when he's no better.

"No."

"He drugged you."

My jaw drops. "How? I nursed my lemonade the entire night."

"I know. I was watching you. More specifically, him. You kept talking to him, so I thought maybe you knew each other. I never saw him put anything into your drink, so I called Sophie. She owns the bar. I told her what happened. On a hunch, I asked her to check out the new bartender. She found drugs on him. Lots of 'em. The cops were called. Got a text from Sophie this morning. Apparently, Mitch and Dexter were in on it together, and this wasn't their first time."

A shudder runs down my spine. If I'm not the first, what happened to the others? I don't think I want to know.

"What now?" I ask.

Trey turns back to the stove and flips over the sizzling bacon. "They're both arrested and are probably gonna go away for a while. Sophie is gonna do a better job at performing background checks before she hires. I get that she's short-staffed, but she can't just take in anyone off the street."

"Was that you who beat up Dex?"

"Once I saw him take you outside, I jumped off the stage to make sure you were safe. At first, I couldn't find you. I was really worried, Arella."

The idea that Trey was worried about me stirs a little flutter in my belly. Just another one of the many uncontrollable reactions my body has to him. Like the way my heart jumps through my shirt every time he says my name.

"Thanks for coming after me. I'm very grateful."

"Me too, Arella. You have no idea."

There he goes saying my name again, making my insides leap. No one ever calls me Arella, not even my grandparents. I've been going by Ari since kindergarten, when none of the other kids could remember how to say ah-rel-lah, so my teacher suggested that we shorten it. I liked it so much that now, barely anyone even knows that Arella is my real name. Most people think Ari is short for Ariana, and I don't care enough to correct them.

The toaster pops up with some perfectly browned bread.

"Butter?" Trey asks as he grabs a ceramic dish from the cabinet.

My stomach rumbles. "Yes, please. And thank you, Trey, for everything."

"No problem." He smiles sweetly, then gestures toward the row of barstools on the other side of the massive island. "Take a seat."

I claim the rightmost stool, leaving the other three empty. Trey's back faces me as he cracks a few eggs into a buttered pan. No complaints about the view. His rippling muscles are practically bursting out of his white T-shirt. His dark-chocolate hair is tousled in that just-out-of-bed sort of way.

Last night, he had a dreamy, superstar aura about him. Now, in gray sweatpants, tossing eggs around in a pan, he looks . . . normal. Or as normal as men with model-like faces can look.

From the fridge, he grabs two cartons of juice and holds them up. "Apple or orange?"

"Apple, please."

He pours me a glass, then one for himself. I accept it and take a sip, shivering a little.

"You cold?" he asks.

"Kind of." Although I do get chilly easily, it feels like Trey's got his air conditioning extremely high. I suppose he can afford it. I mean, look at this place.

He shuts the stove off, moves the pan off the heat, then pads down the hall. Within seconds, the air conditioning stops humming.

"You didn't have to turn the air off just for me," I say when he comes back. In his arms is a throw blanket, which he drapes around my shoulders. My body betrays me again as my heart dances around from his nearness. I'm beginning to think it's impossible for a woman not to react like this around him.

"I wouldn't want you to turn into a popsicle," Trey says, and his tender smile makes me smile back.

"You're probably the only person in California who just turned off their air conditioning in the middle of summer."

He chuckles and nods. "Probably. I can turn it back on later."

Concentration is painted over his face as he arranges our food onto square white plates. He sets one in front of me, then one in front of the chair directly on my left. Then he sits there. Oddly, I'm okay with it. A year ago, I would have freaked out. He's so close that I can smell him. His scent reminds me of the bedsheets I woke up in this morning.

Wait a second . . . "Hey, if I slept in your bed last night, where did *you* sleep?"

"The couch."

Behind us sits a long couch in the massive living room. It faces the huge tinted windows looking out into a cul-de-sac. *Why are all his windows tinted?*

Maybe Trey's a drug dealer. He doesn't want people to be able to look in and see him making his deals. It would explain how he's got such a nice place. He can't afford all this on a musician's salary, can he?

Something about his living room feels off. All he's got are end tables with lamps on them. No messes of any kind. No clutter. No pictures on the walls. His place looks like a page out of a home décor magazine.

"How many bedrooms do you have?" I ask, then take my first bite of bacon. *Mmm.* It's perfect. Soft yet crunchy.

"Four. One master and one music room. Upstairs is my workout room, and the other room sits empty."

"This seems like a lot of space for one guy."

"It is. If I could, I'd probably just rent a one-bedroom apartment near a gym. I only bought this house because when we started the band, we needed a place to play, and I figured this was more economical than renting an apartment *and* rehearsal space. Then a year later, we got in at the Soul House, and now, I'm stuck with this."

I glance behind me into his living room again. It hits me why it looks odd. "Where's your TV?"

"Don't have one."

I consume the rest of my delicious bacon strip in one breath. Apparently, I have no self-control. *Is there such a thing as self-control when it comes to bacon?* "Are you not a TV person?"

"I didn't have a TV growing up." His face falls for a second before he flashes me a fake smile. "Anyway, your car is in my driveway. Our security manager drove it here for you last night."

"Really?" I hop off my seat to look out the window. Sure enough, there's my white Civic next to Trey's black Lexus— another item that seems outside of his musician salary. He can't be getting paid *that* much, can he? He has to be doing something else.

I return to my chair and readjust the blanket over my shoulders. "Thanks, Trey. Seriously."

"Like I said, no problem." He continues eating his eggs as if helping me with a flat tire, saving me from getting kidnapped, then making me breakfast—all within three days —is nothing.

"Is there anything I can do for you in return?"

"Nah." He waves a hand through the air. "It's all good."

I feel like I owe him, although I don't know what I can get for a guy who seems to have everything yet nothing at the same time. If I could, I'd get him some pictures of his family to hang on the walls. It would add some life to this place.

"Do you have any siblings?" I ask, then take a bite of my toast.

"Nope. You?"

"Me neither. I'd probably have siblings if my parents didn't pass away so young."

Trey stops eating to stare at me.

I know the question he wants to ask, so I answer it. "Car accident."

"Oh."

Whenever I tell people that my parents are gone, they usually say they're "sorry" out of politeness. Trey doesn't do that, but the sympathetic look on his face feels more genuine than any sorry I've ever received.

I have a bite of my scrambled eggs. "It's okay. I don't remember them. I grew up with my grandparents."

"Are they still around?"

"Yeah. I'll probably go visit them soon. How about you? Do you see your family a lot?"

Trey clears his throat and gazes aimlessly at his half-eaten plate. "Not really."

Judging from the desolate look in his eyes, he doesn't like

talking about his family. Maybe they don't get along. That would explain why he doesn't have any pictures of them.

I should change the subject. "This breakfast is amazing. Are you normally a good cook?"

"Eh. I wouldn't classify myself as good. I'm decent. I only started cooking this year."

"What made you start?"

"Liz. She was sick of me ordering pizza whenever she came over."

I laugh, admiring his blunt honesty. "Does she come over a lot?"

He nods, scoff-chuckling under his breath. "Enough to drive me crazy."

"Do you not like when she comes over?"

"Eh. Depends on what I'm doing."

Playfully, I narrow my eyes. "In other words, if you're in the middle of something with another woman, you don't want her barging in."

Trey laughs, and the sound of it lights a spark in my chest. "Thankfully, that's never happened, and I hope it never does."

"Would Liz freak out and get all jealous?"

"Nah. She's not like that. *We* are not like that."

Ever since I saw Trey and Liz sing their duets last night, I've been a little jealous of her. The way they looked at each other, danced together, and held hands seemed to be on a level of comfort above friendship. I thought maybe there was something between them. *Maybe not?* Or maybe that's what Trey wants me to think.

"Are you like that with anyone?" I ask, and I'm not sure why. His relationship status shouldn't matter to me. Still, I'm curious.

"Nah, I'm not seein' anyone."

I let out a *pfft*. "I find that hard to believe."

"I could say the same about you, Arella. You really expect

me to think that a woman as stunning as you is actually single and not looking? Come on."

"It's true. I *am* single, and I'm *not* looking." Suddenly, I'm no longer convinced by that last part. The way Trey just called me "stunning" has my lips curved into an immovable grin.

I picture the two of us together, holding hands, kissing, spending our nights cuddled up watching movies . . . The vivid images come to my head too easily.

"Why aren't you looking?" he asks.

Because I'm too busy still trying to get rid of the last boyfriend. "I'm happy being single." Not completely a lie. I'm very happy. Although I am comparing my current level of happiness to my level of sadness when I was with an abusive man.

"Everyone says that until the right person comes along," Trey says with a smirk. "Maybe yours came along on the side of a highway."

I knit my eyebrows together. "I've barely spoken two words to Kevin. I highly doubt he's right for me."

Dramatically, Trey slumps his shoulders. We both know I knew what he meant. "I wasn't talking about Kevin," he says.

"So, what? You were talking about yourself?" I try not to show how much that piques my interest, because again, I'm not looking . . . right?

"Is it out of the realm of possibilities for that to be true?"

"You barely know me."

"You're right. How 'bout we get to know each other over dinner?"

Dinner? With this guy? A man who looks like he just walked off the cover of a magazine?

"Uh, you're not really my type," I lie because I can't have dinner with him. Getting involved with me is a whole can of worms he doesn't want to open. Until my ex is officially out of my life, I can't start something new. Especially not after what happened with the last guy I had dinner with. I can't put anyone else in danger like that.

"Not your type?" Trey jerks his head back like he's offended. He probably is. I'm sure he's used to being everyone's type. Women probably throw themselves at him left and right. I witnessed it firsthand when those fangirls were practically begging me to help them get into his pants.

"Yeah." I avoid his eyes by playing with the bits of egg still on my plate. "I'm not really into guys like you."

"Guys like me?" He sets his fork down and twists on his stool to fully face me. His tone goes from sounding offended to slightly hurt. "And what exactly is the type of guy you think I am, that I'm not good enough for you?"

"Oh no! I didn't mean it like that. I just . . . Oh, never mind." I slash a hand through the air, trying to end this conversation before I dig myself into a deeper hole.

"No, no," he chuckles, not because anything is funny. He's chuckling to hide how much my rejection is damaging his ego. "Please, do explain. Don't leave me hangin'."

"Come on, Trey," I say, smiling as an attempt to keep things lighthearted. I don't mean to hurt him. This is for his own good. "You've got a long line of women who'd love to have your attention. Don't waste your time on me."

He leans over to look out the living room window. With a hand cupped to his forehead, he squints as if trying to see better. "Hmm . . . Where is this *long line* of women you speak of?"

I giggle at his overdramatic silliness. "I didn't mean literally. Just that there's plenty of women out there who'd want to date you."

"Who says I want to date any of them?"

"Don't you?"

"Only if *you're* in that line."

I can't see it, but I know my cheeks are turning red.

How can I tell Trey that this is for his sake without explaining the situation with my ex? Would anything I say stop him from having an interest in me? I don't even know why he's interested at all. We just met, and he knows nothing about me, yet I've caught him staring at me more times than not.

I can't think straight. There's no denying that I'm attracted to this man. Who wouldn't be? Stunning blue-gray eyes. A handsome smile. *And those arms* . . . The fangirls last night were right about his charming personality. It must be working, because I'm actually considering accepting this dinner thing.

"Arella . . ."

My name sounds so sweet coming from his lips. I want to keep hearing him say it.

"Could you give me a chance?"

I ponder it for a moment, even though I already know which way I'm leaning. "How about this? We can go out for dinner, but not as a date. Could we go as a couple of new friends grabbing a bite to eat?"

He flashes me the biggest grin. "I'll take what I can get."

9

———

TREY

Phase two: complete. Not without a mishap though. I don't feel bad for breaking that crooked-teethed goat-fucker's ankle last night. Sex predators don't deserve sympathy. Honestly, he's lucky I didn't break more. I wanted to, especially after Arella passed out.

For a moment there, I thought she died. I checked her pulse at least seventeen times before I was satisfied. I almost took her to the hospital, until I figured that Healing Water would work better than any medicines the Ordinary doctors would give her.

While she slept, I sponged Healing Water into her mouth. It didn't hit me until three sponges in that the Healing Water might not work on her since it derives from Zordi powers. Once the color returned to her face, I knew it was working. I don't know how it worked, but I'm glad it did.

Am I allowed to use Zordi products on Ordinaries? *Nope.*

Could I get into deep trouble if anyone ever finds out that I did? *Abso-fucking-lutely.*

Do I care? *Hell no.*

All I care about is making sure that Arella is okay.

I stare at the taillights of her car leaving my street as I call my uncle to give him the update he asked for.

"Find out anything yet, kid?" Victor says when he answers. No *hello*. No *hey, how ya doin'?* I don't know why I'm surprised.

"Nothing out of the norm so far," I say as I pace my living room with the phone pressed to my ear.

"What have you learned about her childhood?"

"Not much. I've barely been able to talk to her." *Fuck.* Why did I just say that?

As the CEO of ZIRDA California, Victor assigned me this mission. As my uncle, he threatened to beat me up if I fail. I don't mean in the philosophical sense, either. He will actually bloody me up. I should be more careful of what I say and only tell him things that will make him think I'm accomplishing something.

Victor's tone turns icy. "Isn't that the fucking point of your mission? To talk to her?"

"I was planning to last night, but some bastard at the bar drugged her and—"

"Well, make sure it doesn't happen again! If you don't have any progress to share, why the fuck are you calling?"

Um, because you asked for an update? I can't say that. Instead, I say, "I do have progress to share. She finally agreed to go out on a date with me." Technically, she agreed to dinner as *friends*, but Victor doesn't need to know that.

"Wait a fuckin' minute. You haven't even been on a date yet?"

Shit. "Like I told you, she's reserved and—"

"Don't call again until you have something good to say!" *Click.*

Really? Sometimes I wonder why I give a damn about getting Victor's approval. He's an asshole to me more days than not. Most of all, he's not my dad. I can't even say Victor's *like* a dad to me. Sure, he took me in after my parents died, but it's not like he actually took care of me. At a young age, I was forced to learn how to fend for myself.

Sadly, Victor wasn't always like this. He used to be that fun uncle who came over with new toys—just because. We used to play basketball in the driveway for hours. He'd take me out for ice cream after dinner, and we'd go for walks around the park. Many of my weekends were spent at his house, where we'd stay up all night eating spray cheese straight from the can.

Then one day, out of the blue, Aunt Jodi left him. I guess coming home to a half-empty house and a note about her finally finding her soul mate is awful. But I don't understand how Victor's personality took a complete one-eighty after that. All of a sudden, he was always angry and hated my guts.

It was normally Aunt Jodi who hated me, not Uncle Victor. She used to push me out of her way and call me a "piece of shit" under her breath. She'd take my favorite toys and shove them down the garbage disposal in front of me. Once, she kicked me down a full flight of stairs and claimed it was an accident. Since she never acted that way in front of my parents or Victor, no one believed me when I told them.

After she ran off with another man, it was like Victor felt the need to replace her—as if there always had to be someone who bullied me. I used to overhear my parents talk about Victor's overnight attitude change. They were just as confused as I was.

I would give anything to not only have my parents back but also have my loving uncle back. That's partly why I want to succeed in this mission so much. This is the first time he's ever trusted me with anything important. If I can do something he'll be proud of, perhaps our relationship can be better. No, I don't expect us to have sleepovers with spray cheese again, but it'd be nice to finally have a conversation with him without all the animosity.

I spend the rest of my morning planning out my "dinner as friends" with Arella.

After lunch, I head to the Soul House for band rehearsal. By the time I'm done with that, performing our two-hour show, and doing our lengthy meet and greet, I'm exhausted.

Back in my dark garage, I park my Harley next to my car, then kill the engine. Still on the bike, I drag out my phone to do the one thing I've been thinking about doing all day: text Arella.

Before she left this morning, she entered her number into my contacts. I wanted to text her earlier but didn't because I didn't want to seem desperate.

The screen glows in my face as I search for her contact and send her a text.

> Hey gorgeous! Thanks for putting your name into my phone as Arella. It made it easy for me to find you. 😊

Now comes the waiting game.

I stare at the screen for a full minute to see if the little dots will start jumping around. Nothing happens. She's probably not by her phone. Or worse, she read my text and ignored it. Or maybe she's already sleeping? *Dammit, I'm being pathetic.* I've never sat around waiting for a text from a girl before.

The moment I hop off my bike, I freeze. Someone's emotions hover toward me—coming from *inside* my house. *What the fuck?*

I tiptoe through the door, being as quiet as possible. No lights are on. I don't hear anything either.

Whoever's here probably didn't hear my garage door open, because the emotions I'm sensing from them are content, not scared, and, oddly, a little horny.

I tread down the hall to where my gift leads me. It's not until I'm near the bedroom that my chest tingles, and suddenly, I know exactly who's here.

I stomp through the door. "Get out."

Jess doesn't even bother looking up at me. "Is that any way to greet a person?"

She's lying on my bed with her ankles crossed over each other. The lamp's on, and she has one of my naughty magazines flipped open over her thighs. Her low-cut pink tank top gives me a full view down her shirt, leaving nothing to the imagination. Based on the wrappers on the floor, I'm gonna say she's been in my pantry.

"How did you get in my house?"

Keeping her attention on the photo of the topless woman, she gestures toward a key on my nightstand. "I know where you leave it outside."

"Good. That means you know where to put it back." I lift my finger, and the key flies into the air. When I drop my finger, the key falls into Jess's lap. I wave at the door, and it swings wide open, coming to a halt just before it hits the wall.

Finally, Jess looks my way and tosses the magazine and key over her shoulder. They land on the carpet with light thuds. "You haven't seen me in months, and you're kicking me out already?"

Jess is never an easy person to get rid of. Maybe if I'm nice to her, she'll leave faster. I soften my tone. "What's up, Jess?"

She pouts. "My boyfriend dumped me."

"The Teleporter?"

"Yeah."

Jess and I used to have an on-and-off relationship. I haven't seen her since she started getting serious with her boyfriend—ex-boyfriend now.

"I went to see him today." Her sadness drenches me like heavy rain from a gray cloud right above my head. "I thought maybe we could work things out. He doesn't want anything to do with me anymore."

I sigh, plopping next to her on the edge of my bed. I have no idea what to say to make her feel better. Thinking of a happy time and pushing those feelings into her might work.

She continues talking before I can think of anything happy. "I thought maybe if I showed him that I want him back, he'd want me too. But all he said was—" Jess's skin bubbles as her shoulder-length blonde hair transforms into curly black dreads. Her skin fades from a California tan to a deep bronze until there's a brawny Black man wearing a pink tank top next to me.

Jess drops her voice into a deep, husky tone. "You're too fucked-up for me. Go get your shit together."

Her skin bubbles again and her hair grows, turning blonde until the real version of Jess is back.

"Sorry," I say because I suck at pep talks. Also, her ex is right. She does need to get her shit together, and that's coming from me, a man who never has his shit together.

She stares at me with a dark expression in her eyes. I know that look. Before she can say anything, I'm back on my feet with my hands in my pockets. "Not tonight, Jess."

"What? Why not?"

Because I have important shit to do. Besides, even if I wasn't in the middle of something, I still wouldn't want to have sex with her. This woman only ever shows up when she needs a rebound fuck. Yes, I've always allowed her to use me, but I've been getting sick of our relationship existing on only *her* terms. She's never here when *I* need her.

Five months ago, when I was going through a rough patch, she wouldn't even answer my texts. Now that I think about it, I'm still fuckin' pissed.

I hook my thumb toward the door. "So, you gonna leave, or what?"

"Seriously?" She gives me a look like I've just smeared mud all over her shirt. "Can't you *feel* my pain? I thought *you,* of all people, would understand."

Of course I can feel her pain, and it's exactly why I don't want her here.

"I want to get fucked like an animal, Trey. And you're the only man who's ever rough enough with me to do it right."

"Jess, you can't just break into my house and demand that I fuck you. Especially when you haven't spoken to me in over five months. Plus, you went through my shit." I point a stern finger at the empty chips bags on the floor.

"I'm sorry, okay? I couldn't talk to you back then because of my boyfriend. He didn't like me talking to any of my exes. As for tonight, I didn't want to be alone. It's not my fault you weren't home when I arrived. I didn't think you'd care as long as I made it up to you . . ."

With her best *screw me now* face, she hooks her fingers through my belt loops and yanks me in. As soon as she flips her emotions to make me feel what she wants me to feel, I'm a goner. Within seconds, my energy feeds off hers, and it's not long before she's won the fight. Her erotic emotions take over my mind, and the next thing I know, she's beneath me—topless.

As I kiss her neck, I wonder if I would still want this if I weren't feeling what she's feeling. It's hard to know. While I rip my shirt over my head, I decide it doesn't matter. As long as she wants this, that's all that matters.

It doesn't take me long to finish. It's been at least a month. I lie on my back, panting as I pull the rubber off and toss it into the air. When I point a finger at it, it flies across my bedroom, landing into a little trash bin in the corner.

Jess scoots toward me and props her head on my shoulder. Then she rests a hand over my chest as she lets out a little exhale. My body stiffens. She knows how much I hate cuddling, yet she does it to me anyway. I know how much she hates when I shove her away, so I make sure to do it extra rough this time.

On my way to the bathroom, in the corner of my eye, I see her roll her eyes like she's disappointed. Call me an ass, but it's not like I've never warned her. As if it'll make things better, I offer her a little shrug. "You know I don't like cud—"

"Yeah, yeah," she says. "I know."

After we're both cleaned off and dressed, Jess asks for a loan. Without hesitation, I grab my wallet and offer her two thousand dollars, knowing I'll never get it back. We've gotten to the point in our relationship that when she asks to "borrow" money, we both know it's a gift. I've never asked for the money back, and she's never offered. I wouldn't accept it anyway.

Jess struggles a lot financially. Her father walked away before she was born, and her mother died of a z-drug overdose before her second birthday. The way she grew up consisted of hopping around from foster home to foster home where nobody wanted her and even fewer people cared.

I'd probably be in the same financial situation if my parents weren't the researchers who discovered how to turn Healers' tears into usable products that keep their healing abilities. Royalties for Healing Water, Healing Goo, and Healing Spray are like a never-ending gold mine. Lucky for me, I'm the main person reaping the benefits.

Jess waves to me from the Uber as it drives away. I'm not even back in my house before I've got my phone out.

Yes! I've got a text from the woman I've been waiting to hear from.

> I figured if I added myself into your phone as Ari, you'd get confused.

I smile. A *real* smile. Not one of those fake ones I use out in public.

> I am a man. We are easily confused creatures.

My phone buzzes within seconds. I'd like to think she was on the other end, waiting for me to text back.

I'm very familiar with your kind. 😉

You excited for dinner tomorrow?

Yes. Dinner. With a new FRIEND.

OK, friend. Let's carpool. I'll come pick you up. 😊

I can meet you at the restaurant. Thanks tho.

You don't even know where we're going.

I would if you told me.

It's a surprise! What's your address?

I've been to her apartment before—plenty of times. I'm always parked on the street, hunched in my car, studying her routine. I've never been *inside* her apartment though, and that's where I need to get. Seeing her living space might help me know her better. There's only so much a background check and Google searches can tell me, which is nothing of value. Her background check was pretty blank, and all I got from Google were pictures of people who weren't her. She doesn't have any social media for me to scroll through, either. It's like she's purposely making this harder for me.

My phone buzzes.

Okay, we can carpool.

Her next text includes her address.
Then my phone vibrates again.

You know, one of these days, you'll learn that you can't always get your way. 😜

I snort. Funny that she thinks I always get my way. I

figured out as a child that life will hand me rotten lemons and there's nothing I can do about it.

Some might say that living with Victor wasn't *that* bad. A kid can survive demeaning comments and some violent outbursts here and there. A few smacks to the face usually shut me up. Nothing I couldn't handle. To make myself feel better, I always compared every hurtful thing Victor said or did to seeing my parents get blown up. After that, taking a few hits was nothing.

10

―

ARELLA

At exactly six o'clock, someone lightly thumps their knuckles against my apartment door.

I jump in front of the mirror to inspect myself one last time. The extra minutes I spent on my makeup paid off. I look like I'm glowing. My lacy plum-colored dress falls just above my knees, and my hair features more defined waves, thanks to my curling wand.

I know, I know, tonight's not a date. That doesn't mean I can't look cute though. I was never allowed to wear anything like this around my ex. He would yell at me for dressing like a "slut." To him, showing legs is "asking for it." Now that I'm done living by his rules, I'm going to wear whatever I please.

The second I open the door, Trey whistles through his teeth. "Damn. If I knew I was gonna have competition, I would have tried harder."

I almost laugh. There is no competition, and if there was, he'd win. Trey looks more gorgeous than the last time I saw him. I'm not even sure how that's possible. Hair fluffed up, perfectly trimmed stubble, and an irresistible smile to top it all off.

He's in his usual black V-neck that hugs his broad

93

shoulders and a pair of jeans that hangs a little low on his narrow hips. If he raised his arms up, I'd probably get a glimpse of those defined abs Google images showed me earlier.

"Ready?" he asks with the sunlight hitting him in just the right way for me to see how smooth his skin is. I'm jealous. I want skin like that. I'll bet he's never had a blemish.

I nod eagerly, yet not as eagerly as I feel. "Ready."

As he leads me to his car, my eyes scan the parking lot. I think we're in the clear. If my ex was here, we would have known by now. He would have picked a fight with Trey the moment Trey knocked on my door.

How embarrassing would that have been? Now that I think about it, maybe this dinner thing isn't a good idea. What if, when Trey drops me off later—

"I've been looking forward to this all day," Trey says, cutting into my thoughts.

I fake a smile, pretending that I wasn't thinking up ways to end the evening right now. "Me too. Where are we going?"

"It's a surprise, remember?" Trey opens the passenger door for me—like a gentleman. "Hop in."

I don't move, even though I appreciate his kind gesture. "This isn't a date, remember?"

He rolls his eyes and chuckles. "Just get in."

Once we're on the road, Trey turns the radio down. "How was your nannying job today?"

"Wonderful." I tell him about the four kids I spend every weekend with and how we finger-painted dinosaurs on canvases. "How about you? What did you do today?"

"Sunday is the band's day off. I literally just sat around until it was time to pick you up." His tone is gloomy, like he wishes he had other things he could have been doing. I imagine him in his big living room, all by himself, aimlessly staring at a clock. Surely, he was more productive than that.

Trey flicks his blinker on and speeds to pass a slow car.

"So, you told Liz that you've lived everywhere in Cali. Where'd you live before you moved to LA?"

I can't believe he remembers that. I didn't think he was paying attention to anything that was said in the car the day we met. He seemed so out of it. "I moved here from Brawley. It's a small town about three hours south of here."

"Where'd you grow up?"

"My grandparents and I have moved around every year since I was little, so I kind of grew up everywhere."

Trey merges between two trucks, then into the left lane. "I see. What are your grandparents' names?"

"Phil and Roxy."

"Last name?"

I'm not sure why their last name matters. I tell him anyway. "Ward. How about you? Where did you grow up?"

"Three Rivers. It's near Fresno."

"Did you go to college there?"

He keeps his gaze aimed out the windshield. "Nah. I never went to college. You?"

"I studied early childhood education at UCLA. Originally, I wanted to be a kindergarten teacher. Then I realized my passion is baking. I want to have my own bakery someday. I already have a name picked out."

"Which is?"

"A Slice A Day." Just saying it out loud gets me excited, even though the reality of that dream is so far away.

"What do you like to bake?"

I can't believe he's actually asking questions about me right now. More so, I can't believe he's not trying to tell me stuff about himself that he thinks will impress me. I thought that was a first-date standard for men. "I do it all. Mostly cakes and cupcakes, because I love to decorate."

"I'd love to see some of your work."

I perk up. "I've got a blog you could check out."

"That's cool. Could you send me the link? I can take a look later."

"Sure." I'll text him my link, but I have no confidence that he'll ever enter my website. Trey doesn't strike me as a man with an interest in cake decorating.

"When did you start baking?"

I spiral into my story of getting my first Easy-Bake Oven and always helping Grammy in the kitchen. Trey listens with nods, asking the occasional follow-up question. I can't remember the last time I spoke this long without a man interrupting me. Usually, I don't even talk this much. With Trey, I can't stop. Although I could go on and on about baking.

"Enough about me," I say a while later. "Tell me about your hobbies."

"I don't have any."

I eye him. "You play music."

"Yeah, but it's also my career, so does it still count as a hobby?"

"What about your nonprofit organization? Is that a hobby for you?"

Trey turns his head to stare at me. "How do you know I have one?"

"Oh, I—um, I might have . . . Googled you."

Chuckling, he shakes his head at me. "Don't believe half the shit you read."

"You don't have a nonprofit?"

"I do, but the rest is trash."

I twist at the hip to face him. "Like what?"

"Tell me what you read, and I'll tell you if it's true."

"You can play over twenty-five instruments?" I've already seen him play three. Twenty-five blows my mind. I can't even play one.

He pauses with a thinking face on. "True, probably. I haven't really counted."

"You produce all of your band's work?"

"Half true. I do most of it, but it's not all me."

"I read something about how you broke someone's car window while filming one of your music videos."

"Hey." He lifts his pointer finger, laughing. "It was an accident, and they weren't supposed to be parked there."

I tap my chin. "Seems like my research has been accurate so far. What about the Liz rumors?"

Trey groans as his hands slide down the steering wheel. "Which ones?"

"The ones about how you two date on and off, and you're always leaving her for other women."

He laughs, and it eases the pang of jealousy in my belly. "Liz told me about that one. Those people twisted my interview into something it wasn't. They asked me about my relationship with her, since our fans are always pinning us together. I told them that Liz means a great deal to me but I'd never make her my girlfriend. They reworded it, saying that I was sleeping with her but refused to commit." He sighs deeply. "Media these days."

Why does it thrill me so much to hear that he doesn't have a thing with Liz? I mean, he's already said it before, but hearing it again feels more validating. *This is not a date*, I remind myself. *This is not a date.*

"Anything else you read about me?" he asks.

I read that his parents were killed in a house fire. It made me feel bad for asking if he saw his family often. I can't believe he didn't mention that his parents were gone when I told him about mine. Anyone else would have. Not many people lose both parents to tragic accidents as young kids. Why didn't he want to tell me that we have that in common? Maybe it's still hard for him to talk about it. Either way, I'll try not to mention that I already know, since he obviously didn't want to tell me, but maybe he needs a little push.

"I read a little about your foundation and how it supports

school-aged kids with deceased parents. Tell me more about that."

Trey goes back to gripping the steering wheel at the top. "Not much to tell. We just offer free mentors, tutors, and funding for therapy and after-school activities. Whatever keeps the kids busy."

"That's wonderful of you." I gave him the perfect opening to tell me about his parents, and he didn't take it.

"Eh. Don't give me too much credit. It wasn't my idea. It was my friend Sharon's. I agreed to finance it with the expectation that I wouldn't have to get too involved. The extent of my duties is transferring a chunk of my bank account over each month and signing a few papers here and there."

"Oh, I'm sure you do more than that."

"I really don't. I used to mentor one of the kids. I stopped once . . ." His face falls.

"Once what?"

He rakes a hand through his dark locks, keeping his eyes glued to the road. "Uh, about five months ago, my mentee kid —he, um, he . . . passed away."

The car goes silent as Trey swallows his pain, and it makes my heart ache for him. "That must have been really hard."

"Yeah, well, I never wanted to be a mentor. I got guilt-tripped into it. Once Elliott was gone, I decided getting close to the kids wasn't for me, so I quit." He clears his throat. "Anyway, do you like pasta?"

I take the hint. "I *love* pasta."

"Good. We're going to my favorite pasta place in Long Beach."

"Long Beach?" I didn't realize how long we'd been driving for and in what direction. I assumed Trey was taking me somewhere in LA.

He must see the discomfort on my face. "Is that okay?"

"Isn't it too late to change plans now?"

"I can turn around and we can go somewhere else, if that's what you want."

Do I want that? If we're going to Long Beach, the likelihood of us running into my ex is low. One would think that with living in a big city like Los Angeles, he'd be harder to run into, right?

Wrong.

Living on the other side of the city doesn't stop him from showing up behind me at the grocery store. Or getting gas at the same time and station I'm at. Or "coincidentally" going to the dentist at the same time too. Yes, I can't even get my teeth cleaned without him following me there.

"Actually, Trey, I think Long Beach sounds wonderful!"

11

TREY

THE RESTAURANT HOST LEADS US TOWARD AN OUTDOOR corner table under some twinkling string lights. The other tables are occupied by people sipping from wineglasses. From a small stage at the front of the patio area, a violinist in a flowy dress plays an enchanting upbeat melody. Couples dance together in the grass, their energies full of warmth and lust.

"Your waitress will be here shortly," the host says as she sets two menus onto our table, then leaves.

Almost everyone here is horny. I sense it from most of the men and plenty of the women. I need to be careful about not letting their emotions control me. If Victor was here, he'd tell me to embrace it. He seems to think that having sex with Arella as soon as possible will get her to trust me faster, which will get her to tell me her secrets. I don't know Arella very well yet, but I know her well enough to know that Victor's method is more likely to scare her away.

"Wow," Arella says with her jaw slack. I pull out her chair, and she accepts it without making another comment about how tonight *isn't* a date. "This place looks way too romantic for a *friendly* dinner."

And there it is. After draping my leather jacket over the back of my chair, I sit on the other side of our cozy table. Whether she considers this a date or not, I've already told Victor it is.

"You've been here before?" she asks.

"Yep. This was one of the first places our band played at. We did acoustic covers of lovey-dovey songs all night."

"Hi." Our waitress sets two glasses of water onto our table. Her exasperated energy shoots at me while her cheerful tone comes out through a smile. "Would you like to try our house wine?"

I turn to the exquisite woman sitting across from me. Before I can ask her if she prefers red or white, she smiles and says, "Water's fine. Thank you."

I guess getting her tipsy to talk is out of the equation. "Me too, thanks."

"Awesome. I'll give you a moment."

Once the waitress leaves, I take the silverware out of my cloth napkin and drape the napkin over my thighs. Liz taught me to do this the first time I ever ate at a fancy place. I hope it makes Arella think that I'm a proper guy and that I know shit.

I pick up my menu and pretend to read it. "Are you sure you don't want any wine? I'm treating."

Arella responds sweetly yet firmly. "I'm sure. And no, you're not treating. I don't want this to be a date, remember?"

Of course I remember. She's reminded me so many times now, I'm beginning to think she's trying to convince herself, not me. "Friends are allowed to treat each other."

Ignoring me, Arella flips over her menu to read the other side. I already know what I'm getting, so while she chooses what she wants, I keep my menu in my hands and concentrate on trying to sense her. With all my might, I narrow my eyes on her and fire every ounce of my mind power her way. My energy tightens in on her body, straining to latch onto something, *anything.* The only thing I get is the sexual tension of the man behind her.

After a full minute, all I've accomplished is a headache.

"Do I have something on my face?" Arella asks when she sets her menu down.

"No. You're just beautiful and easy to stare at."

"So . . . you admit you were staring?"

I chuckle, nodding. "You'd do the same if you were in my shoes."

We make small talk for a bit before our waitress comes back. Whatever upset her before is passing, because her mood is calmer now. Arella and I place our orders, then the waitress takes our menus away.

Leaning forward, I rest my arms on the table. "So, tell me more about your grandparents."

Arella unfolds her cloth napkin, then sets it onto her lap the way I did. "What would you like to know?"

"You mentioned that you guys moved around every year. Where do they live now?"

"They're still in Brawley. After I graduated high school and came to LA, they decided to stay."

"Are they retired?"

She takes a sip of her water. "Yeah. Gramps was a mechanic. Grammy stayed home with me."

How odd. What kind of mechanic gets a new job in a different town every year? It's not a career that requires traveling. That makes me think he was running from something. Question is: What and why? Then, once Arella moves out, all of a sudden, he's done running? Something's not adding up.

"If they liked moving around so much," I say, "why aren't they anymore?"

Arella shrugs like there isn't anything more to this. "It's not the moving they loved. It's the living in different places. The adventures. The new experiences. Since I was in school, they didn't get to explore the world like they wanted to. Moving around the state was a good second option until I graduated.

Now that I'm not around, they travel all the time. They're currently in Alaska until tomorrow. In two weeks, they're off to Brazil."

I guess that's a possible explanation. Still, I think there's more to it. Either that or I want there to be more, so I'm looking for it.

Arella continues, "They get antsy when they stay in the same place for too long."

I can relate to that. The minute I graduated, my uncle told me to get out and "find my place in the world." I packed up the little I had, bought a car, and went wherever life took me. I'd stay in one city for as long as it suited me, then I'd pack up and do it again.

The longest I've lived anywhere since I left home is LA, and that's only because of my band. I'd like to think I've found my place here, but if that's the case, why do I always feel like I don't belong?

The violinist finishes her piece, and the crowd erupts with applause. In the grass, a few couples swaying together mosey back to their seats. After some thank-yous, the violinist turns a page in her book, then returns the instrument to her shoulder.

"What about you?" Arella asks as another tune fills the air. "Do you like to travel?"

I'm not a fan of how she keeps spinning our conversations back to me. Talking about myself depresses me. Plus, that's not the point of this dinner. "I do. I've been to lots of different places. How 'bout you?"

"I haven't gone anywhere outside of California."

That's odd. How has a girl whose family loves to travel not been anywhere except this one state?

"What's been your favorite place to visit so far?" Arella asks.

"Besides here, I lived in Spain and France the longest, so maybe those two."

"Did you pick up the languages there?"

"Only conversationally."

Her face lights up. "Have you ever been to Paris?"

"Of course."

"Ah!" She throws her head back, swooning. "I've always wanted to go there. I've heard they have the best bakeries."

Although I can't sense it, I can *see* her strong desire for Paris. *Seeing* her feelings but not *feeling* them is like I'm watching TV, where people are expressing emotions I can't sense.

"Trey?"

My head jerks up. "Huh?"

"You got quiet all of a sudden."

"Sorry. I was thinking."

"About?"

I clear my throat, trying to think of a lie. Nothing comes to me, so I go with the truth. "You. Just wondering what you're feeling."

As impassive as ever, she says, "I feel fine."

Well, I've accomplished nothing. All I've got is more questions. How do I ask her if her grandpa was running from something, without sounding like a psycho?

"House salad with the dressing on the side," our waitress says, placing it in front of Arella. "Caesar for the gentleman."

While we indulge in our salads, I ask Arella about what her favorite movies and books are, because it'll help make my questions about her family and childhood less suspicious. Victor wants me to rule out that her immunity is caused by something that happened to her as a kid. Besides the annual move and being raised by her grandparents, she seems to have had a normal upbringing.

One of Victor's many theories to explain Arella's immunity is that she was experimented on in a lab as a baby. By the way she talks about how much her grandparents love her, I doubt they would have allowed that to happen.

Another one of Victor's theories is that Arella possesses

some kind of gene defect. To me, she looks, sounds, and acts like any other twenty-two-year-old Ordi woman.

The most ridiculous theory Victor had is that Arella came from another planet. It's only the first date, but I'm pretty sure I can rule that one out. Arella seems as human as anyone else.

"Wow," she says, wiping her lips off on her napkin. Two empty pasta plates sit between us. So far, I've learned a lot about her, yet nothing at all. "That was the best Alfredo I've ever had."

"I'm happy you think so." I clean off my hands and nod toward the grass. "Now that we're done eating, do you wanna dance?"

Dancing is the main reason I chose this place. While we slow-dance, I'll have permission to touch her for an extended period of time. This will be a great opportunity for me to continue my physical research because, sadly, the verbal kind is getting me nowhere.

Unfortunately, Arella shakes her head. "I can't dance."

"It's easy." I stand and hold my palm out to her. "I'll teach you."

"Um, you go. I'll watch."

I make a crumpled face at her. "I'll look like an idiot slow-dancing by myself. Is that what you want?"

Grinning, she nods eagerly.

She thinks I won't do it. Clearly, she doesn't know anything about me.

Challenge accepted. "All right. I'll dance solo."

Arella's eyes go wide as I saunter away. She whisper-yells, "Trey! I was kidding!"

I wasn't. I stop at the top of the patio steps and say over the heads of couples eating, "You gonna come dance with me?"

Her head shakes again.

Without another word, I hop down the steps and join the sea of couples swaying to the melodic notes. With gusto, I put my hand on the waist of an invisible woman and pull her close. My other hand holds her invisible palm up, then I twirl her around the grass.

The more dramatic my turns are, the more Arella loses it. She laughs so hard, she's slapping her knee. I don't care that other people are staring at me like I'm stupid and ridiculous. I know I am, and that's the point.

"Okay, Trey," Arella says through giggles over the railing. "You can stop now."

"Nah. Miss Invisible and I are enjoying ourselves." I continue for another minute before the song ends. To finish my performance strong, I spin my lovely dance partner twice, then dip her for a solid beat. Only once the crowd claps for the violinist do I make my way back to the table.

"Oh. My. God." Arella's still giggling. "I can't believe you did that. Aren't you embarrassed?"

I plop back into my chair, unashamed. "It made you laugh. The embarrassment is worth it."

Arella's cheeks fade into the most adorable shade of pink as she giggles some more. Whatever I'm doing, it's working. She's becoming more comfortable with me. Soon, she'll be comfortable enough to tell me the information I need.

12

ARELLA

"The Big Ka-booms?" My stomach aches from all the laughing.

Ever since Trey stopped frolicking around the grass like he's a cartoon character, he's been telling me funny stories about the early days of his band.

"Yep, that was our first unofficial band name. Kevin and Marcus came up with it. They were arguing over whose dick was bigger. Marcus said, and I quote, 'Bro, I'm Black. When I take mine out, it falls and goes ka-boom.' "

I could sit here all night listening to this man tell me stories. "How did you end up becoming Flames in the Night?"

"The brains of the band, of course. Liz and Emmy were our final additions. They wanted a name that represented our band's diversity. Kevin is half Chinese, and Liz is half Hispanic. Marcus is Black, and Emmy's family is from the UK. Liz said that our diversity makes us stand out. What stands out better than fire in darkness?"

"You boys are so lucky you have Liz and Emmy around."

"No kidding. Without them, we're a—" Trey's head snaps to the right. A frown replaces his smile as he glares off into the trees.

I glance that way but don't see anything to be frowning about. "Everything okay?"

His head whips back to me. "Uh, yeah." Forcing a half smile, he says, "What were you saying?"

"I wasn't. You were."

"Oh, right. I was saying that without the girls, we're a mess." His head snaps to the right again. This time, his face twists like there's something sour in the air. Under his breath, he grumbles something. It's so quiet, the only words I catch are "ignore it."

Ignore what?

For a moment, we sit in silence. Trey glares at his water glass with a crumpled look on his face like he's contemplating life—hard. He must come to some sort of decision, because with a creak of the wicker, he's out of his chair with his wallet out.

After tossing three hundred-dollar bills onto the table, he says, "Stay here. I'll be right back."

And just like that, he's gone. He doesn't even grab his jacket before sprinting away as if the restaurant is on fire.

Where is he going? Curiosity takes me over as I grab my purse and his jacket and run after him. It probably looks like we're pulling a dine-and-dash, but I'm confident those three bills will cover double what we ordered and a hefty tip.

When I catch up to Trey on the sidewalk, he's glowering at the groups of people strolling the busy street.

"Are you okay?"

He jumps and flips around. "I thought I said to stay at the table."

"Yeah, but—"

He doesn't let me finish. Roughly, he snatches his jacket from me and shoves his arms into it. "Stay here. Please. I'll be right back."

Without waiting for me to respond, he runs off again, zigzagging around pedestrians with the speed of a wild animal chasing its prey. I run behind him, a little less aggressively, spitting out apologies to the people with crooked faces left behind in his path.

I almost lose him when he turns a corner down a backstreet. At the end of the alley is shouting and laughing. Three teenage boys stand over a smaller teenage boy on the ground, kicking him. Before I can process anything else, a loud voice yells, "Stop!"

The three teenagers jerk their heads up. The bulkiest one steps forward with his hands up in surrender. "Chill. We're just playin' a game."

Trey gestures toward the boy on the ground. "It doesn't look like *he's* having fun."

"No worries, dude," the tallest teenager says. "We're all friends."

Trey turns to the boy, who's still covering his face with his arms. "You okay, buddy?"

The boy sits up, making a movement with his hands, and mouths something.

"He's fine," the bulky teenager says. "It's just a game."

Trey scowls, then moves his hands around too. The kid on the ground widens his eyes as he picks himself up. He rubs his ribs a little, then moves his hands again. It takes me a moment to realize that he's using sign language.

When Trey communicates back the same way, the three bullies drop their jaws. I do too. I had no idea Trey knew sign language.

After he signs back and forth with the boy for a moment, he turns to the bullies with a grimace. "Get outta here."

"Look, dude, you don't understa—"

"Go!"

It doesn't take more than a second for the teenagers to realize that they don't have a choice. Their shoes stomp against the pavement as they dash off. Trey's gaze follows them until his eyes land on me. His expression turns stony. I wish I would have stayed at the restaurant, if only to have avoided that look.

The Deaf boy plucks the lid off a garbage can and chucks it. It clanks to the ground with an echo. After some digging, he wrestles out a backpack from the trash, pats it off, then throws a strap over his shoulder.

Turning to Trey, he signs something. I don't know anything more than the ASL alphabet and baby signs from working at the daycare. All I catch is the boy saying thank you. The rest is lost on me.

As I approach Trey's side, he gestures at me and signs my name in letters. He does it so fast, I barely catch that it was my name.

"Arella, this is . . ." Trey pauses and signs as he says, "Sorry, what's your name?"

The boy moves his fingers so fast, I can't understand.

"Lucas," Trey says.

I wave. "Hi, Lucas."

The boy waves back and signs to me.

"Nice to meet you," Trey interprets. "You have a beautiful name."

"Thank you," I say and sign.

Trey turns to the boy as he signs, "Don't allow those boys to haze you anymore. It's not worth it, okay? Do you need a ride home?"

With a shake of his head and another thank-you, Lucas limps out of the alley.

Once he's gone, Trey shoves his hands into his pockets. "You ready to go, babe?"

My insides dance at the sound of him calling me *babe*. I used to cringe whenever my ex called me that. He only used pet names when he wanted something. Or when we were around other men. Or when he was apologizing for the night before. Hearing Trey call me *babe* doesn't elicit that fight-or-flight reaction from my core. I actually like the sound of it.

As we speed back to LA, Trey talks my ear off about everything except what just happened. This entire evening, he's been asking me buttloads of questions about me and barely talked about himself unless I asked a question first. Now that he's suddenly openly sharing, it makes me think he's filling the silence just to ensure I don't have a chance to ask him about Lucas.

I'm barely paying attention to his words. My mind is reeling about how he knew a teenage boy was getting beat up in an alley—from the restaurant.

"How do you know sign language?" I ask, interjecting into whatever story he's telling me about a time he used to live in Georgia. Or maybe it was Oregon.

Trey clears his throat. "Uh, Elliott, the kid I used to mentor . . . He was Deaf. I took private lessons so I could communicate with him."

"How did you know Lucas was in trouble?"

His fingers curl tighter around the steering wheel as he swallows. "I thought I asked you to stay at the restaurant."

"Sorry, I didn't listen."

He scoffs loudly. "I see that. I asked you to stay because I didn't want you to get hurt."

"I didn't."

"That's not the point." He breathes out, all exasperated. "Can we just forget that ever happened?"

Moments like these with my ex always turned into fights, until eventually, my choices were to keep quiet or get smacked. I really don't want to fight with Trey. I don't think he'd hit me, but I miss the lighthearted conversations we've been having all night.

Playfully, I lower my voice to a whisper. "You can just admit that you're Superman. I can keep a secret."

My tactic works, because Trey perks up, laughing. "I'm not Superman."

"So, you're Spider-Man, then? You've got Spidey senses that tell you when someone's in trouble?"

He chuckles lightly. "Not even close."

For the rest of the car ride, I don't mention Lucas again, even though I want to, because knowing things like that isn't normal.

As Trey pulls into the parking lot of my apartment, I subtly glance around for *his* car. When I don't see it, I let out a breath of relief. Day forty and counting. *Maybe he's done stalking me . . .*

"Did you have a good time?" Trey asks after he parks his vehicle.

I offer him a genuine smile. "I did."

That was the best dinner I've had in a long time. Plus, I haven't laughed that much since, well . . . before my ex. I hate that I allowed him to take away my happiness for so long.

"Thanks again, Trey. Tonight was fun." It was so fun that a part of me doesn't want to leave. I'm enjoying his presence, and the way he looks at me like I'm the only person in the room who matters. Unfortunately, this was a one-time thing, and as much as I don't want to go, I have to.

I'm about to grip the door handle when a firm palm on my shoulder pulls me back.

"Hold on a sec. I didn't get a chance to ask you out again."

All the air leaves my lungs as I screw my eyes shut. The world around me stills. The hand gripping my shoulder is the one that used to bruise my face. It's the one that used to control me in ways that still haunt me.

He yells at me. "You can't wear dresses like this, you whore!"

I try to get away, but his fingers claw into me like talons wrapped around a mouse.

"Don't you dare walk away when I'm talking to you! We're not done!"

"Arella?" Trey's gentle voice pulls me back. His hand is gone. It's in his lap now, away from me, not hurting me. "You okay?"

Nodding, I force a smile.

Judging by the way Trey crinkles his forehead together, he's not buying it. "You sure?"

"I'm fine." My voice shrinks so much, even I don't believe it.

Slowly, he leans into me, and I catch a whiff of his scent. He's wearing a sweet cologne that smells nothing like Nathan. Usually, my ex smells of gin and cigarettes.

In almost a whisper, Trey asks, "Do you wanna talk about it?"

I glue my lips together and shake my head. I can't talk about it. Not with him. I'll start crying. Talking about it is like reliving it, and I've already lived it for enough years to never want to do it again.

I feel him staring at me. He's probably debating whether or not to push this subject further. Like how he didn't want to explain Lucas, I don't want to explain this.

Finally, Trey leans back and smiles warmly. "I'd love to see you again."

My voice comes out soft. "I don't know if that's a good idea."

His face drops. I wait for him to lash out at me and yell at me for not giving him his way. I wait for him to call me a bitch because I'm being "disobedient."

Instead, he tenderly asks, "Can you explain why?"

Because I'm starting to like you. I can't admit that.

Because my ex-boyfriend is a psycho and will scare you off like he did the last guy—with a knife. Telling Trey that will prompt more questions.

Because Nathan is still under the impression that he can control my life. That will make me sound pathetic. I hate acknowledging that my three-year mistake still has power over me. Not as much as he used to—just enough to keep me fearful.

I've been doing everything I can to cut ties with him. Telling him off has only made things worse. Never leaving my apartment isn't feasible, and never coming home is the same. I've tried looking for a new place to live. Unfortunately, all the other apartments I've toured are smaller for twice the rent. He'd find me anyway. Filing a restraining order did nothing more than get his deputy chief father involved. After that, it's like the entire police force was on his side.

Am I ever going to get my life back? I hate that I can't spend one night out with a guy without my past huffing down my neck. Tonight was the first time in a while that I've felt some peace. I felt *safe*. Being in Long Beach made me feel like Nathan couldn't find me. Being with Trey made me forget about him altogether. I can't allow my ex to keep doing this to me.

Eventually, things need to change. I just wish I knew how to make it happen.

13

TREY

It's been two days since I had dinner with Arella. We've been texting back and forth so much that my phone is almost always in my hands, but I have yet to see her again. She has yet to mention it, either. Two days is long enough to wait before giving it another shot.

> Hey beautiful! My band and crew are coming over tonight for a little get together at my place. You wanna come? Javina and her girlfriend are welcome too.

> Hey pretty boy! It's Javina. Ari and I will be there. What time? 😬

I grin at the text. I purposely waited until I knew Arella was at work with Javina before texting her. I figured that if Javina knew she was invited, she'd convince Arella to come.

> How about seven?

I text her my address.

> Thanks, hot stuff. We'll see ya then! 😈

> Sorry, you'll have to excuse Javina and do the same tonight too. She has no boundaries. I'll see you tonight.

> Can't wait!

Fuck yeah. Now all I've gotta do is convince people to come over.

When I arrive at the Soul House for rehearsal in the afternoon, the backstage area is empty. After my bandmates show up, I mention the idea of having a little get-together. Marcus and Emmy are the first to jump in.

"I'll bring some snacks!" Emmy says.

"I'll get the drinks," Marcus adds.

"I'll provide the pizza," I say, glancing at Kevin, who looks hesitant. "And we can set up a poker table."

He flashes me a *you know me so well* grin. "Pizza? Poker? I'm down!"

By the time we're done working and everyone's in my backyard, my "little get-together" has turned into a huge party. I figured that since it was last minute, only a few people would show up.

And I thought wrong.

Not only is most of the crew here, Kevin's two older brothers are too. Like Kevin, they heard *poker* and couldn't resist.

Upbeat music blasts over my speakers. Cardboard boxes of pepperoni pizzas decorate a long fold-up table. A few crew members have brought their dogs and are chatting by the fire pit. Everyone else is scattered around playing card games, mixing drinks, or telling stories on my patio.

Arella and Javina are the last to show up. Javina struts through the wooden gate first. Behind her comes Arella in a flowy white sundress that shows just enough cleavage to get my dick to harden. My gaze skates down her slender legs. My hands twitch from wanting to run my palms up and down her skin. I know I'm supposed to only get information from her, and I shouldn't be as attracted to her as I am, but damn, she's fucking gorgeous.

I wave from the pizza table, hoping my boner isn't noticeable. "Hey, ladies! Thanks for comin'." In my head, I thank Javina profusely for being here. I doubt Arella would have come on her own.

"Thanks for the invite!" Javina says.

"Wow. There's a lot of people here." Arella has all her hair tied into a braid falling over one shoulder. Wisps of wavy curls frame her face as she eyes the crowd.

"Apparently our team didn't have much else going on tonight," I say.

"T!" Liz calls from a distance. "Come! Monique wants us to take a quick band pic for the socials."

I groan out loud. These "quick band pics" are never quick. Monique usually makes us pose for a few minutes so she has enough content to work with. While I'm glad she takes care of our band's social media, I'd rather not have to take pictures all the time. But I've learned it's easier to comply than to resist, so I take a step backward, away from the only reason I have all these damn people at my house.

"Help yourself!" I gesture toward the food. "I'll be right back."

For longer than necessary, I smile, I pose, and I put my hands where I'm told. The second Monique says, "Awesome job, everyone!" I beeline back to Arella, who's quietly nibbling on some pizza crust.

Unsurprisingly, Javina has inserted herself into a game of poker. Arella looks like Javina's plus-one as she stands behind her friend's chair, watching the card game.

"You look beautiful," I say once I'm back at her side. Under the sun and in this dress, she looks like she's a glowing angel sent from the heavens.

Arella glances up at me with a sweet smile. "Thanks. You don't look too bad yourself."

I receive compliments all the time, but they never feel the way it does when Arella says it. When other girls tell me I'm hot, it's because they want me to fuck 'em, and it feels like a transaction. When Arella says that I "don't look too bad," I believe her.

I tilt my head to the side. "You wanna go for a walk?"

She gives me a look like I've just stumped her with a riddle. "Um, shouldn't you stick around? It's *your* party."

"Nah. Nobody'll miss me."

"Um, I don't know if I should leave Javina here alone."

Without taking her eyes off the poker table, Javina speaks over her shoulder. "Go for a walk with the man, Ari! I'll still be here when you get back. Except I'll have double the money in my pocket."

The boys around the card table erupt into laughter.

"Yeah, right." Kevin chuckles. "Start weeping!" He throws his cards down, face up. It's a full house. Three queens, two jacks. Kevin's brothers groan, chucking their cards at the table. Laughing, Kevin snatches the chips from the middle.

I'm not a poker person. My ability to read emotions tells me exactly when someone's bluffing. It's not fun when I'm basically cheating.

Arella pops the last bit of pizza crust into her mouth, then throws away her paper plate. "Okay, I'm ready."

We're just through the wooden gate when Liz shouts at me. "T!"

I twist on my heel with an exasperated "Whaaat?"

"Where ya goin'?"

"For a walk."

She flashes me the same look Arella did when I suggested that we ditch my own party. "Okay . . . ? Don't be long."

"I won't, Mom."

Liz responds with an eyeroll, then goes back to her conversation with Emmy.

When Arella and I make it to the sidewalk, I shove my hands into my pockets. I have the urge to offer her my arm to hook hers through, but I'm pretty certain she won't accept it.

I've got a hunch as to why Arella's so jumpy whenever I touch her. I think she's been abused. I used to be jumpy, too, whenever Victor raised a hand around me. Once I got as tall as him, he stopped hitting me like that, and I stopped being jumpy.

Considering Arella is all of five-two, with skinny arms that resemble tree branches, whoever abused her is probably *still* bigger than her. I doubt it was her grandparents, since she seems to adore them and vice versa. If I had to put money on it, I'd say it was an ex-boyfriend.

"I'm glad Javina forced you to come out tonight," I say as I shift to walk on Arella's side closer to the street.

"She didn't force me. When I saw your message at work, I mentioned it to her. I'm not really a party person, so she thought I was going to say no, which is why she stole my phone and texted you."

I raise my eyebrows with a smile. "So . . . you wanted to come?"

"Mm-hmm."

Hearing that makes me feel like I'm doing something right. "Javina seems like a good friend."

"She's my bestest friend." After a few steps, Arella asks, "Who's your best friend?"

My answer comes easily. "Liz."

"Does she always keep tabs on you?"

"Sometimes. She thinks I'll get into trouble if she doesn't."

"Is she right?"

I purse my lips together, tilting my head from side to side. "Kinda."

"What kind of trouble do you usually get into?"

"Fights, mostly. When I was in school, I'd get sent home early for fighting in class. My teachers suggested that I join after-school programs as a way to help me control my anger, or some bullshit like that."

"Did you?"

"Yep. Theater, art, football, soccer, basketball. None of them worked."

After-school programs work for most kids, like the ones my foundation supports. Being able to do something fun outside of their depressing homes helps them forget about their dead parents. I only wish it had worked for me.

"It sounds like your bad-boy phase started young," Arella says.

This isn't the first time someone's called me a bad boy. I wouldn't say I'm a bad person. It's not like I purposely tried to pick fights with the other boys at school. It's that when they didn't stop bullying me for wearing the same three outfits, I couldn't stop my fists from pounding into their faces.

Three outfits were all I had. Victor didn't care enough to provide anything more. The only reason he paid for me to join all those after-school activities was because it kept me away from him.

"You seem to be more tamed now," Arella says. It warms me a little because "tamed" seems to be something she wants. I'll be tamed or whatever else if it means she'll tell me if she's ever been experimented on in a lab. "I mean, you might try to *look* like a bad boy sometimes, but I think that's just a defense mechanism."

"Defense mechanism?"

She narrows her eyes at me, smug. "Don't act like you don't know."

"I don't."

"If Liz keeps tabs on you, that means the fighting didn't

stop once you got older, right? I'm guessing bars or clubs? Maybe both?"

"Right . . ." I don't like where this is going.

"I'm also going to assume you have a history of drugs, drinking, and sleeping around. Maybe you still do. Either way, I think you like to *look* like a bad-boy because you think it keeps people away. You probably think that's easier than actually letting people in, because the fewer people you get close to, the fewer people you have to lose."

I freeze to gape at her. I've never thought about the reason why I keep people at a distance. In school, people were either afraid of me or pitied me, and I didn't want to be friends with either. Even now, I see my bandmates all the time, and besides Liz, they don't know that much about me. What Arella said has some truth to it. Letting fewer people in does mean I have fewer people to lose.

Her dress twirls around her thighs as she turns to face me. "I'm sorry if I'm wrong. I'm just saying this because of the way you talked about losing Elliott and how it made you never want to mentor another kid."

I clear my throat and resume our walk. "So, um, anyway . . . Tell me about your plans for the weekend."

She offers me an understanding smile as she returns to a steady pace at my side. "I'm going to visit my grandparents."

Last night, I did some digging into Phillip and Roxanne Ward. Roxy's background check came back mostly empty, which checks out because she was a stay-at-home grandma.

As for Phil, his background information is fishy as hell. A few auto shops came up as past employers, but I didn't see a new employer every year like Arella claims happened. Either he was getting paid under the table or someone has tampered with his records. In addition, neither of her grandparents' information revealed past addresses. It's like someone went through and deleted as much as they could. Question is: Who and why?

"Are you staying there for the whole weekend?" I ask as we wait on a curb for a car to pass before crossing the street.

"I'll leave Friday after work and come back Sunday evening."

I guess I won't be able to see her this weekend . . . "What do you guys usually do?"

"Sometimes we go out to eat. For sure we'll play board games, and I'll bake something with Grammy."

"Did you play a lot of board games growing up?"

"Mm-hmm. You?"

"Not really." By that, I mean none at all. The idea of Victor breaking out Candy Land with me is unimaginable.

"If you didn't watch TV and you didn't play board games, how did you spend your childhood?"

If I tell her how I spent my childhood, she won't believe me. Hell, *I* wouldn't believe me.

She'll think I'm joking if I tell her I grew up under a mountain in a secret compound. She'll think I'm insane if I tell her that a few weeks after I moved in, I discovered that burning down trees with the fire that comes out of my hands made me feel better.

At the age of eight, I spent most of my after-school hours trying to make money to buy myself new clothes and shoes.

At nine, I was put into training with the new ZIRDA agents to learn how to fight properly. Victor allowed me to learn in hopes that it would help me control my gifts better. Either that or he got off on seeing me get beat up. Whichever it was, it didn't change that whenever I got too upset, my powers would get out of hand. My room used to light up in flames almost once a week, and things would fly all over the place.

How I spent my time as a kid isn't something I want to share with Arella.

"I went for a lot of walks," I say, thinking about all the

times I hiked the forest for a good tree to burn. It's the truth, just not the specific truth. "And I worked out a lot."

"Were you a chubby kid?"

"No, but I enjoyed exercising." *If getting beat up by people twice my age counts as exercising . . .*

Victor didn't tell the adults I trained with to go easy on me. They were told to fight hard, and they did. The worst part is that along with my own pain, I could feel theirs too. It made me twice as weak.

It wasn't until I hit puberty and finally learned how to block other people's physical emotions from mirroring onto me that I began winning fights. Otherwise, I was basically used as a punching bag.

Arella and I loop around the sidewalk to head back toward my house. Before we arrive there, I need to ask her out again. I just don't know how.

"I checked out your blog last night," I say.

Her eyes widen. "You did?"

"Yeah. You make cakes look like works of art displayed in a museum."

"Wow. I didn't think you'd actually look at it."

With any other girl, I wouldn't have. But this is Arella, and I need to learn everything about her. I hoped that going through her website would give me some insight on who she is. All I got out of it was a craving for baked goods.

"Do you make money on your site?" I ask.

"Some. Not enough to live off of. It's based on ad clicks and how high the traffic is."

"That's how my band makes money on YouTube, too. Ad partners and brand deals. The more clicks and views, the bigger the paycheck."

Arella steps over a large crack in the sidewalk. "You must make a ton of money on YouTube if you're able to split it between the band, hire a crew, and still have enough to afford a four-bedroom house in Brentwood on your own."

"Most of the band's income comes from tickets to our live shows, meet and greets, and merch. Also, I didn't buy my house with the band's earnings. I bought my house *because* of the band, remember? We needed a place to play, so I provided it."

"Then, I'm curious . . . How are you able to afford your house? And afford to travel internationally? And start a foundation?"

The only people I've ever told about my inheritance are Liz and Jess. Whenever people ask, I usually tell them I have a lot of investments and leave it there. While that's true, the money I invested with came from my inheritance. I don't like telling people exactly where my money comes from. It usually leads to them asking how my parents died. I hate having to retell the fake story, so the less I have to talk about it, the better.

Maybe because Arella understands what it's like to be parentless, I can tell her that I lost mine too—without all the meaningless *I'm sorry*s and pity looks. She probably knows how useless those are.

"My parents were wealthy," I say as a way to imply that they're gone without actually saying it. "They left me everything they had."

"What did they do for a living?" she asks without a hint of surprise.

Did she already know that they died? How? I haven't said anything to suggest that my parents are dead until now.

"They were researchers." Technically, that's true. My parents were researchers . . . for ZIRDA. They were the ones who spent years in a lab, working to uncover if it was possible to create a usable product from Healers' tears that kept its healing abilities.

Now that we know it's possible, who's to say we can't discover the source of an Ordinary's immunity, reproduce it, and create a pill, or a liquid, or anything that will give ZIRDA agents immunity over the Royals?

I swallow hard before asking, "How did you know my parents are gone?"

She looks away from me as she plays with the end of her long braid. "Um, I read about it when I Googled you. Your Wiki page mentions it briefly."

"I see," I say to the sidewalk. It's been years since I looked myself up. I didn't realize my Wikipedia page included that information.

A moment passes before Arella breaks the silence. "Do you wish I didn't know?"

"Nah, it's fine. I just don't like to talk about it."

"We can talk about something else," she says cheerfully, and I appreciate her attempt at bringing the mood back up. "What are *your* plans this weekend?"

I don't miss a beat. "Thinking up ways to win you over."

The mood officially changes the second Arella bursts into laughter. A hint of pink forms on her cheeks. "Is that so?"

"Yeah, and if you tell me how to do that, it'll make my job a lot easier."

It takes a few heartbeats before she says, "Maybe I'm not something you can win, Trey."

I narrow my eyes at her. "Are you saying that you're not an option at all? Or that I gotta work to *earn* you, not win you?"

She pauses to think. "Um, maybe I'm just not in the right place right now to start something new."

"Bullshit. Not buyin' that. I think that if a person, especially a woman, *really* wants something, she'll make it happen. So, that means you don't want me enough, and I'm gonna change that. You just gotta tell me how."

"Shouldn't that be something you figure out on your own?"

I theatrically slump my shoulders. "But I'm impatient. It'd

be much easier if you just tell me. If you don't, I'll have to resort to my own dumb ideas."

"Which are?"

"Doing lots of cheesy romantic things until you're swept off your feet and want me more than you want to bake. If that doesn't work, I'll try plan B."

"Which is?"

I grin. "Pulling my pants down."

Arella laughs again, covering her mouth with a palm in the most adorable way. "Does that usually work for you?"

"Hasn't failed me yet. Typically, that's plan A, but I figured you're not the type to fall for that."

She's still laughing, and I love the sound of it. Her laugh means I'm making progress. "Do you have a plan C?"

"Nah. I'm hoping I won't need one."

Her laughter fades as she rolls her eyes. "I still don't understand why you're trying so hard to date me. If you want something easy, you should look through that long line of women ready to throw themselves at you."

"You're different, Arella. I don't know why, but you've captured my attention." That's a lie. I do know why. Arella is the most unique person I've ever met. She's literally one of three people in the entire world that I know of who are immune to Zordi powers.

"Why do you always call me Arella?"

I press my brows together. "Because that's your name?"

"But everyone calls me Ari."

"Would you rather I call you that?" I call her Arella because for four weeks before I met her, I referred to her in my head as Arella. Calling her *Ari* now would sound weird. But if that's what she wants . . .

"I don't mind," she says. "I actually kind of like it."

I'm going to take her "kind of" as that she *really* likes it.

We talk easily until we arrive back in my driveway. One of my band's songs is playing from the backyard speakers. My time alone with Arella is almost up, and I haven't thought of a way to ask her out yet. I still get the feeling that she'll reject me.

When I asked her out before, she only agreed on the premise that we'd be going as friends. Victor made it clear that being friends isn't good enough and that getting intimate with her will encourage her to tell me secretive things about herself. How can I get her to date me if—

That's it! I can't present the date as a date. I've gotta make it sound casual. That's how I got her to come out to my show. That's how I got her out for dinner. And that's how I got her here tonight.

If I had texted her saying, "Hey, wanna come to a party as my date?" she absolutely would have turned me down. I informally invited her, nonchalantly asked her to bring Javina, and it got her to show up.

"What're you doin' tomorrow?" I ask with a newfound vigor.

"Work."

I don't hide my disappointment as I grunt. "Nanny or daycare?"

"Daycare. I only nanny over the weekends. Except this weekend because the family I nanny for is going on vacation. That's why I'm going to see my grandparents."

"Do you have a day off next week?"

She nods. "Monday."

Make it sound casual . . . "You wanna hang out?"

At the closed gate to my backyard, Arella stops and turns to me, tilting her head back a little to meet my eyes. "What do you have in mind?"

Thank fuck she didn't immediately say no. "I've got a video shoot in the morning. How 'bout something fun in the afternoon, and then we can get dinner afterward?"

She squints at me with a smile. "Is this your sly way of asking me out on a date?"

Abso-fucking-lutely. "Nah. We can just hang out as friends, if that's what you want."

Spending time with her as *friends* is the same as dating, just without the label. I don't need the label to work my mission, especially if it's the one thing holding her back.

Making our time together sound casual must be working, because Arella perks up. "Okay. Let's hang out on Monday."

14

TREY

Monday

It doesn't take me long to finish filming my solo scenes. While the rest of the band films their scenes outside the Soul House, I head inside, backstage. I've just started messing around on a loop station when Liz strolls in and stops at my side.

She has tense energy. "Hey, T-Bear."

I press my foot against the loop pedal to stop the beat. "What?"

She feigns innocence. "What, what?"

"You're all nervous and shit."

Liz knows how much I hate playing mind games, so she gets straight to the point. "She seems sweet."

"Who?" I ask, even though I know exactly who.

After Arella and I returned to my backyard party, I refused to leave her side. I felt Liz's glare on me the entire time. Every time I made Arella laugh, Liz didn't miss it. Anyone who noticed that probably thought Liz was jealous, but I know better.

She doesn't approve of me flirting with Ordi women, which I'll admit I tend to do sometimes just to get them into bed with me. She probably thinks that's all I'm trying to do with Arella, when that's not the case at all. Would Liz approve of me befriending Arella if I told her that this woman could be the key to saving innocent lives from the Royals' violence? I'm not sure.

Liz calls me out on my bullshit. "You know who I'm talking about. Ari. You seem really into her."

"Sure." I try to sound nonchalant. The last thing I need is for Liz to lecture me about women again.

"How into her are you?"

With a long sigh, I set my guitar down. "Are you about to reprimand me? 'Cause if so, we should go sit on the couch. It's comfier."

Liz heads there, and I follow her.

"You know what I'm about to say," she says, plopping onto the cushions.

I do the same. "What? That I shouldn't be fucking around with Ordi women?"

"Yes!" She gives me a *duh* face. "You're the only Zordi I know who actually finds Ordinaries attractive. They're meant to be our friends, not our partners. Plus, it's breaking the second most important Zordi law."

That second law was only established to enforce the first one. Since we aren't allowed to reveal anything from the Zordi world to an Ordinary, we're not allowed to engage in sexual or romantic relationships with them, either. Getting too close to them means there's a higher chance of exposure. Exposure means a scrub for the Ordi and z-prison for the Zordi. Depending on how bad the exposure is, sometimes it means death.

There aren't a lot of Zordis who like sex with Ordis. Most people think it's bizarre. Like as strange as it is to chew on glass or to purposely burn your own hair off. To me, sex with

Ordinaries feels just as good. Better, actually, because it's risk-free. Zordis can't catch Ordinary illnesses, and they can't catch ours either, meaning we can't transfer STDs. And since we can't reproduce with them, why not take advantage of the pregnancy-free sex?

"You're lucky you've never been caught doing it with an Ordi," Liz says as she leans back against the couch.

"The only way for me to get caught is for another Zordi to report me," I say. "Since you're the only one I see regularly, I think I'm fine."

"Either way, Ari's sweet and innocent, and that's dangerous for a guy like you."

My face screws together. "A guy like me?"

"You know I think you're a great man." She chuckles lightly and cocks her head to the side. "Complicated, but still great."

"Why do I feel another *but* coming?"

"But . . . as soon as a girl starts to have *real* feelings for you, you always drop them like they're lethal."

"Do not."

"Do too."

"Hey," I say with a finger up, "the last Zordi I dated used me to make her ex-fiancé jealous."

"What about the girl before that? The really busty Black one." Liz puts on her thinking face. "Kelly?"

"Keelah."

"Yeah. What happened to her?"

"She cheated on me, got pregnant, and tried to tell me I was the father."

Liz's jaw drops. "Were you?"

"Hell no. She's an Ordinary and a gold digger. She demanded money from me until I asked her to take a DNA test. I even offered to pay for it. Haven't heard from her since."

That woman ran straight back to the guy she cheated on

me with. I can only assume they're still together. At the time, I was pissed, but I wasn't too broken up about it. We'd only been sleeping together for a month.

"Rodrigo and I have been together for almost a year now," Liz says. "We met on Glimmer, that dating app for Zordis. Maybe you should try that. With your face, I'm sure you'll land a date in a snap. Even for our kind, you're one of the better-looking ones."

Zordis naturally have big eyes, clear skin, straight teeth, and healthy bodies. Because of that, we're seen as more desirable by Ordinaries. By Zordi standards, I think I'm average, but Liz always tells me otherwise.

"Thanks for the advice, Mom. I'll try that dating app sometime."

She backhands my chest, scolding me. "Look, I understand that you have a wall up against our kind because with your gift, it makes it hard for you to know if you truly like someone or if you're just mirroring their feelings. You stick to Ordis because it's easier. Legally and biologically, it won't work. There's no real commitment and no harm when you fuck it up. Because when you do fuck it up, which you will because you're a man, instead of taking responsibility for it, you can easily brush it off because, no matter what, that relationship wasn't bound to work anyway. However, that doesn't mean you should cut Zordi women off forever. Eventually, you'll get tired of this and want to find your soul mate."

What is this? Call-Trey-out-on-his-shit day? I've never thought about any of that as reasons why I steer clear of Zordi women, but when Liz puts it that way . . .

"Come on, Liz. You don't really believe in that soul mate bullshit, do you?"

"Of course I do!" She gapes at me like I'm insane for not believing it.

Besides our differences in bodily functions, another thing that makes Zordis unique from Ordis is that we have strong connections with our soul mates—or so people say. Apparently, there are ways to know when someone is your soul mate. Tons of books have been written about it. It's even taught in Zordi school, but it's all nonsense.

My belief is that when people claim to have found their soul mate, it's just a ploy to either steal someone else's girl or to justify adultery. Aunt Jodi used the soul mate excuse to rationalize leaving Victor out of the blue, turning him into the petulant asshole he is today. So yeah, soul mates are dumb.

"Please, Trey. Could you just leave Ari alone and give someone legal a chance?"

I toss my arms into the air, letting them fall back into my lap. "It's not like I haven't given Zordis a shot. All the ones I've been with have only wanted me for money."

"Well, you're not gonna find someone who wants you for *you* while fishing in the ocean of Ordinaries."

AFTER WORK, I HEAD STRAIGHT TO ARELLA'S APARTMENT TO pick her up for our date. We're only halfway into it when I decide we need to get out of the public. Two ladies recognized me while we were go-karting. A group of guys bombarded me at the bowling alley. Another girl recognized me when I was about to beat Arella at air hockey. I lost concentration, then the game. I'm supposed to be spending time with her and building a connection—not making her wait around for me to finish taking pictures with strangers.

"Do you mind if we cook dinner instead of going out?" I ask as we head back to my car.

"I thought you said you wanted to get Mexican?" Arella says.

"I did . . . until we kept getting interrupted."

"Do you normally get recognized everywhere you go?"

"Typically, but put me in a crowd with those over thirty-five, and I guarantee you I'm a nobody." After we climb into my car and buckle ourselves in, I say, "How 'bout we make tacos at your place? That way I won't have to drive you back."

"That sounds wonderful."

Perfect! I'll finally get to see the inside of her apartment.

At the grocery store, nobody recognizes me. We're able to get in and out within five minutes.

As I pull up to Arella's apartment complex, she gazes intently out the window.

"Whatcha lookin' for?" I ask, putting the car into park.

Her back snaps straight. "Nothing."

Bull. She does this every time she comes home, and I don't know why. I exit the car and skim my eyes across the parking lot. Nothing looks out of the norm, so I follow her inside.

Arella's little apartment smells like a bakery—sugar, bread, and frosting. There's stuff everywhere. Assorted trinkets litter the tops of her tables. Framed floral artwork covers the walls. All that can possibly be purple is purple. Violet curtains. Lavender pillows. Lilac throw blankets. Even her lampshades are purple.

She kicks her sandals off by the door, and I do the same with my shoes.

"Would you like something to drink?" she asks as she heads into her postage stamp of a kitchen.

I trail her. "How 'bout some coffee?"

"It's almost seven."

"And?" Caffeine doesn't affect Zordis the way it does Ordis. Our bodies absorb and filter the caffeine way too fast for it to give us any energy. It's the same reason why Zordis can't take Ordinary medicines and drugs. Our bodies need stronger remedies. I still like the taste of Ordinary coffee though.

"Sorry," Arella says. "I don't drink coffee, so I don't have any. I could make you some tea?"

"Tea sounds great."

From the cabinet, Arella pulls down a mug, fills it with water from the fridge, then sticks it into the microwave. Since I don't wanna be the one to tell her that's not how you make tea, I keep my mouth shut. Next, she grabs a large pan from under the stove and starts heating it up with some oil.

"What can I help with?" I ask as I slip out of my jacket and drape it over the back of a worn dining chair.

"You can just set the table while I do all the cooking." She points at a drawer. "Place mats are here. Silverware is right above it."

The tiny thing she calls a table looks like it belongs in an office with a printer on it—a *small* printer. Her apartment couldn't handle anything bigger anyway. I decorate the table with plum-colored place mats, then set down some napkins and silverware.

Since I can't be of more help, I casually saunter the two steps it takes to get to her living room. Off an end table, I pick up a framed photo of Arella standing next to an old couple. The man is tall and lean, with salt-and-pepper hair. The woman has wavy hair like Arella's, except it's shoulder-length with silver streaks.

"Are these your grandparents?"

Arella peeks her head out of the kitchen as I hold up the frame. "Yeah. That's them."

I set the frame down, then pick up another one. It features a kid version of Arella behind a cake with a 7 candle on top. Something drags the corners of my mouth down.

That was the last age I had a birthday cake. It's also the last age I celebrated a holiday, or had a family dinner of any kind—up until I met Liz.

She makes it a point to celebrate every holiday with me, which is good for her, too, considering her family has basically deserted her. For my birthday, she always gives me two gifts: one for that year and a second to make up for a past year. She does the same for Christmas. For Thanksgiving, she cooks me a huge meal with at least six sides, even though it's always just us. *What did I ever do to deserve Liz?*

The rest of the photos in Arella's living room all tell me the same thing: She lived a good childhood with two people who love her. There are pictures of her as a kid on rides at the fair, petting animals at the zoo, and getting piggyback rides from her grandpa at a playground. I've never gone to a fair or a zoo. Maybe my parents took me before they died, but I don't remember. *It woulda been nice to be able to do stuff like that . . .*

With a heavy heart, I plant myself onto the chair holding my jacket. The wood creaks under my weight. "How did your weekend go with your grandparents?"

Arella sets a steaming mug in front of me with a tea bag already in it. After I thank her, she goes back to the stove. "It was wonderful. Grammy and I baked some cookies, and we ate them while we played Scrabble."

"You any good at Scrabble?"

"I'm decent. Grammy is the best though. I swear she makes up words, but when I check them online, they're legal. Like, do you even know what a Q-A-T is?"

"Not a goddamn clue."

"Exactly. It's a legal word though."

While Arella cooks the taco meat, I focus on her emotions —or lack thereof. I concentrate as hard as I can, but nothing comes. I'm still sensing all the people from the surrounding apartments.

After a few deep breaths, I try again. This time, I close my eyes and imagine myself touching her heart. I do that for a few seconds before a sharp pain pinches my temples, then a headache eases into me. It's the same type of headache I get whenever I don't consciously dial back my Empath power all the time and I'm sensing too many people at once.

"You're quiet today," Arella says as she cuts up some lettuce.

"Just thinkin'." I take my first sip of the warm tea. *Mmm. Earl Grey.*

"About?"

The last thing I'm gonna tell her is the truth. *Oh, I was just thinkin' about how, for some mysterious reason, I can sense everyone's emotions but yours.* She would question the fact that I have the ability to sense emotions more than the fact that I can sense everyone but her.

"I was just wonderin' if you think your grandparents would like me or not."

Arella throws her head back, laughing so hard, she has to set the knife down on the counter.

"What's so funny?"

She continues to giggle. "Don't take this the wrong way, but they wouldn't like you. They wouldn't like anyone who shows interest in me. They're super-protective. When I told them I wanted to move to LA, they fought me on it for months."

"Why are they so protective?"

"I'm their only grandkid. It's expected." With a wooden spoon, Arella stirs around the taco meat. "Since my mom passed away so young, they treated me like their own child instead of a grandbaby."

Here's my chance! Make it sound unintentional. "What was your mom's name?"

"Bella."

"And your dad?"

"Aries."

I make a mental note to dig up everything I can on Bella and Aries Rance tonight. "What did they do for a living?"

"Dad was an accountant. Mom was his secretary."

"Sounds kinky." I wiggle my eyebrows, and it makes Arella chuckle.

"It's exactly what you think it is. Grammy said they hit it off during the job interview. Apparently, my dad only hired my mom because he wanted to date her."

"And you said they passed away in a car accident?"

"Yeah. They were driving home on a rainy night in September of '95. It was dark, and they went right over a cliff."

A rainy night? In September of '95? My heart stills, and my back straightens like a rod. No way in hell. It'd be too much of a coincidence.

But I have to ask . . . "What day was it in September?"

She pauses to think. "Um, I'm not sure."

I'm barely breathing as more words spew from my lips. "Where was the cliff?"

"Don't know." Arella shrugs nonchalantly as she goes back to stirring. I can't tell if she actually doesn't know or if she's trying to hide information. Seriously, what a time to not be able to sense someone! If I could sense her, maybe I could tell if she's lying or not. But what reason would she have to lie?

I try to keep my voice from shaking. "Do you remember where you lived when you were that age?"

She shakes her head. "I was three. I barely remember what I ate yesterday."

Since she doesn't seem to have the answers I'm looking for, I stop asking questions.

Eventually, dinner is ready. I'm quiet as we consume our meal, because my brain is too busy thinking up an excuse to leave.

When we finally finish the tacos, I say, "Hey, I just got a text from Liz. She needs me for somethin'. You mind if I head out?"

If she's disappointed about me leaving, she doesn't show it. I hate having to rely on someone's facial expressions to know how they feel.

"Don't worry about the dishes," she says as I'm about to pick up my plate. "I'll get it."

I'm halfway home when I realize I forgot to make plans with Arella to see her again. I'll have to text her tomorrow. Right now, my mind's a mess. The only thing I can think about is going home to research Arella's parents. I almost stop on the side of the road to do it. I don't though, because I know if whatever information I find jumbles my mind even more, I won't be able to get home safely.

I run into my house so fast that I trip over some shoes I apparently left lying in the middle of the entrance. In my bedroom, I wave a hand at my burner laptop. It flies toward me at full speed, and I catch it in midair. With it propped open on my mattress, I type, *Bella and Aries Rance.*

What comes up is a bunch of romance novels. Definitely not what I'm looking for.

I try searching for each of her parents' names on their own and find nothing useful. On a whim, I type, *Isabella Rance.* A lady from the 1200s shows up for that. Not Arella's mother.

Finally, I try *deaths in September 1995.*

It's too broad. What comes up is a bunch of dead famous people.

So I try again: *deaths in September 1995 California.*

I gasp when my parents' names pop up first. I don't know why I'm surprised. I already knew it was the same month. I click the first link and read it.

The article doesn't state anything I didn't already know about the tampered story. It highlights some details about a few propane tanks exploding, causing the immediate death of a thirty-three-year-old couple. There's only one line about me, the "seven-year-old son of the deceased," and I'm labeled as "the lucky survivor."

The article doesn't mention the body parts that were found that didn't belong to my parents. It says nothing about the intruders' car that was still parked in the driveway when the cops came, and nothing about how that car mysteriously disappeared after the cops left. The article is so fabricated that if someone read it to me with different names, I wouldn't even know it's my family's story.

The Royals have people everywhere. I wouldn't be surprised if all the cops that came that night were Royals. I wouldn't be surprised if this article's author was a Royal either. If not that, the Royals probably threatened the writer into telling these lies to cover up their crimes.

Back in the search bar, I try being even more specific: *deaths in September 1995 California down a cliff.*

The first article is about Arella's parents. At least, I *think* it's Arella's parents. The article states that a couple was driving when the rain and darkness made them lose control of their car and they went right over the cliff.

A few things are fishy about the article.

First, the couple's names are Stanley and Robyn Calder, not Aries and Bella Rance. Second, they weren't the only ones who died in the car that night. Apparently, their three-year-old daughter, Hannah, died with them. Third, this happened in Three Rivers, near the same mountain that Shadow Ridge is hidden under, and it happened on the *exact same night* my parents died.

Coincidence? I think not.

I came to the Internet for answers, and all I've got are more questions. Why would Arella lie about her parents' names? Or did someone lie to *her* about her parents' names? If that's the case, who and why? It's possible that the article printed false names to cover something up. If so, that begs the question: Who was trying to cover up what?

Next, why would the article state that the couple's daughter died with them? Arella—or should I say *Hannah?*—is very much alive. I'm certain this article is about her parents, because I spend the next hour scouring the Internet, and there isn't any other report of a couple driving off a cliff to their death in September of 1995.

It's too much of a coincidence that Arella's parents died on the same night that mine did in the same town. There's a connection here, and I'm determined to find it.

15

———

ARELLA

It's beginning to turn into something.

Three days have passed since Trey and I hung out, and every morning since, I have woken up to his text that says, *Good morning, beautiful.*

Whenever his name pops up on my phone, the corners of my lips get yanked upward. They stay that way while I read his message and giggle at all the funny things he says.

He has asked if we could hang out again this week, but our schedules didn't match up. While he's free during the day, I'm at work. While I'm free in the evenings, he's at work. I didn't realize how much goes into what he does. Everything from rehearsals to recording sessions to writing sessions to planning out their videos and filming them. Then there's all the meetings they have with their manager and potential collaborators. It all sounds complicated, but he seems to enjoy it.

When I'm not actively texting him, I'm on YouTube, watching as many of his band's videos as possible. I knew they were good after seeing them perform the one time, but I didn't know they were *this* good. The production value and creativity of their music videos are impressive. Their millions of subscribers and even more millions of views tells me I'm not the only one who's impressed.

On my lunch break today, the first thing I do is check my phone, hoping Trey has texted me. I can't hold back my smile when I see his name.

> Hey! You free tonight? My manager rescheduled my band's social media meeting to next week, so I'm open.

I'm flattered that his first thought after finding out he has some free time was to ask if I'm available.

> Sorry. 😕 I have a movie date with Javina.

I feel the same, but I won't ditch my best friend to hang out with him, no matter how badly I want to.

> Will I ever get to see you again?

> I'm free tomorrow night?

> I play a show every Friday and Saturday, then I've got meet and greets afterward. I won't be able to have alone time with you. How about Sunday?

My heart does backflips in my chest. He wants *alone time* with me. Why does that excite me so much?

> Sure! We can hang out after I'm done nannying at five.

> I'll take it!

Later that evening, it's late and dark on my drive home from the theater—so dark that I don't see the shattered glass outside my door until it crunches beneath my shoes. It's everywhere. My first thought is that someone broke my window, except I don't have a window by the door.

Crushed purple flowers are scattered all over my front stoop. Ripped into fourths is a little card. Careful not to touch any glass, I pick up the card pieces and hold them together like a puzzle. In all caps handwriting, it reads:

FILLING OUR TIME APART WITH PLAN A.
—T.G.

A wide, ridiculous smile spreads across my face. When Trey said he was going to do cheesy romantic things to win me over, he wasn't kidding. It's kind of working.

After shoving the ripped card into my purse, I scowl at the mess. *Who would do something like this?*

Suddenly, it clicks. There's only one person I know who's low enough to trash someone else's property—especially *my* property. It only takes me a second to wrench my keys out of my purse, but it's too late. The sound of his heavy footsteps rushing from around the corner sends a chill down my spine. Before I can do anything else, he slaps a palm over my shoulder and flips me to face him.

"Wish you coulda seen how big that vase was. Seems like that guy was tryna compensate for somethin'." Nathan's slurred words make the little hairs on my arm stick up.

My ex looks different from the last time I saw him. Now he's got a buzz cut, which is a huge upgrade from the long, greasy mop he used to have. Even with the upgrade, he still looks as cold and callous as ever.

"Who's T.G.?" Nathan towers over me, speaking so close to my face that his gin-and-cigarette breath poisons my air.

"None of your business." My voice comes out smaller

than I wanted it to. I can't stand how much this man affects me. Within seconds, he's already turned me into the scared little girl I was when I was with him. All that progress I've made over the past eight months, gone.

"Ari, Ari, Ari." Each time he says my name, a nasty bite nips at my skin. "Everything you do is my business."

I try to sound more firm this time. "Leave, or I'm calling the cops."

"Right." He chuckles low in his throat. "How many times has that helped you before?"

None . . . "I'm serious," I say, my voice growing stronger as I channel whatever confidence Javina always has. "If I keep calling about you, *someone* will figure it out eventually."

Nathan rips my purse from me. It falls to the ground behind him with a thud. Then he seizes me by my shoulders and yanks me toward him until his nose touches mine. I cringe, trying to push him back. It does nothing.

He's bigger. Taller. Stronger. And he's angry. "You won't be calling anyone about me."

I don't know what gives me the courage to do it, but I hack one back and spit it into his face. He releases me with a growl.

"You little bitch!" He swipes at the loogie dripping down his eye, then smacks me in the face. My head whips to the side as I yelp.

Ignoring the pain, I jab my keys into his stomach.

"Fuck!" He groans and keels over, grabbing his torso.

I take advantage of his temporary weak state by bashing my knee between his legs where it hurts. He cries out as I shove him to the ground.

After thrusting my key into the doorknob, I stumble inside. A hand clutches my ankle, and I fall face first against my living room carpet. My head bounces back as pain erupts up my jaw. I taste blood where my tongue got caught between my teeth.

"Let go!" I jerk my leg back and forth until he loses his grip. Then I kick him in the face, and I'm not even sorry.

Nathan's head snaps back as he roars, "FUCK!"

Finding my balance, I pick myself up and slam the door shut. Then I click the bolt lock in place and sink to the carpet with my back against the door. My chest heaves for air as my eyes water.

I knew it. It was only a matter of time before he showed up again. For a while there, I thought he had finally forgotten about me.

Not a chance.

He probably did that on purpose—gave me time so I'd think I was safe and lower my defenses before he came back to haunt me.

A fist bangs against my door three times. "You little bitch. My fuckin' nose is bleeding."

Good! I need to call the cops. This time, he didn't just verbally harass me. He *hit* me. The police have to do something about him. They just have to.

Now, where's my pho—I almost face-palm myself. My phone is in my purse. The one that Nathan chucked to the ground on the other side of this door.

With my heart still pounding and my tongue throbbing, I steal a look through the peephole. It's too dark to see anything, so I flip the light on. A dim yellow glow illuminates my front stoop.

Nathan's not there. Neither is my purse. *Did he take it?*

I don't dare twist the lock open to check. Not yet. Not until I know he's gone. Knowing him, he's probably hiding around the corner, waiting for me to come out.

"I asked you first!" Nathan barks.

Who's he yelling at? As if he can hear me, I tiptoe toward the living room window and peer out between a small opening in the blinds. Sure enough, there's that lame excuse for a human standing on the sidewalk with a phone pressed to his ear.

But not just any phone. *My* phone.

"Who are you? Why are you calling my girlfriend?"

Is he seriously still calling me that?

"She's not available right now. How 'bout you give me a message, and I'll relay it to her?"

Who's on the other line? No one ever calls me besides Javina and my grandparents, and Nathan's not brave enough to talk to any of them that way. My grandparents don't even know he's abusive. They think we broke up because he met someone else.

As he treads farther from my window, he says words I can't make out. All I can see is the side of his face when it twists from anger to something dark and dangerous.

With the bottom of his shirt, he wipes off the blood trickling down his nose. He's back to yelling again. "The fuck did you just say?" A short pause. "You listen here, douchebag. If you think you can come here and kick my ass—"

I don't stay to listen to the rest because it finally clicks who has called me. Within seconds, I'm out the door, because the last thing I want is for Trey to be involved in this.

"Nathan! Stop!" I run to him, reaching for my phone.

Big mistake.

He backhands my face with so much vigor that I plummet to the ground. Before I can even think about standing, he grabs me by my hair and jerks me up. I scream and punch at him, but it does nothing.

"Are you seein' this Trey guy?" Nathan holds my phone out to me. Trey's name appears on the screen, the call still in progress.

"Arella?"

"Let go of me!"

Nathan tightens his grip on my hair. "What did I say about seeing other men? I'll show you what happens when you disobey me."

16

TREY

I'M ON MY WAY HOME FROM DINNER WITH LIZ WHEN I CALL Arella. I'm excited to ask her if she likes the flowers I sent—until a man answers her phone.

At first, I play it cool and ask who he is. Once he gets angry at me for no goddamn reason and calls Arella his girlfriend, things aren't cool anymore.

"Could I speak to Arella, please?" I try to keep my tone patient but fail. One hand is on the wheel while my other presses the phone to my ear.

"She's not available right now. How 'bout you give me a message, and I'll relay it to her?" Whoever this guy is, he must be drunk, because he's slurring his words. My best guess is that this is the abusive ex. He's the reason why Arella jolts whenever I touch her. The reason why she looks over her shoulder all the time. The reason why she's so hesitant to move forward.

I despise him. Any man who makes a woman that fearful doesn't deserve to breathe.

I'm about twenty minutes from Arella's apartment. Fifteen if I don't get stopped by any lights. Ten if I drive like a maniac. So I stomp my foot against the gas.

"Where is she?" I'm still flooring it as I weave around some cars that honk at me.

"She's busy," the asshole says.

"Doing what?"

"Suckin' my dick." The man laughs as if he's just told the funniest joke in history.

I'm done being nice. "Tell her I'll be there soon to save her from your pencil dick. I'll bet yours resembles an overly sharpened pencil that's more eraser than anything."

His laughing stops. "The fuck did you just say?"

"I said give Arella her phone back, or I'll come do it for you." A truck angrily honks at me as I swerve around it. I don't blame him. I'm going at least double the speed limit.

"You listen here, douchebag. If you think you can come here and kick my ass, then come. I'll show you what I'm fuckin' capable of."

"Nathan! Stop!" Arella shouts in the background. I didn't realize she was in the room with him.

My heart drops when I hear a smack and a scream. *Arella's* scream.

Shit. Did he just hit her?

"Are you seein' this Trey guy?" Nathan yells.

"Arella?" I say, as if it'll help.

"Let go of me!" she shrieks.

Dammit. I pissed him off, and now he's gonna take it out on her.

Cars honk at me left and right. I ignore them, focusing on the only goal I have: protecting Arella.

"What did I say about seeing other men? I'll show you what happens when you disobey me."

More shouting comes from Arella and her drunk ex. I put my phone on speaker, drop it into my lap, then grip the wheel with both hands. Only a few miles to go.

Every car on the road drives at a snail's pace as Arella screams. Every yelp she makes tightens a knot in my chest.

"Shout all you want, Ari. I want him to hear you."

Next comes some grunting and struggling, then something heavy topples to the floor. Nathan groans, yelling out swear words.

"Get out of my apartment!"

"You bitch! How dare you hit me again!"

Yes! She's fighting back!

The line goes dead. *No!*

My wheels squeal as I whip around a turn. Going over sixty down a thirty is bound to get me arrested, but I don't care.

Eventually, Arella's apartment complex comes into sight. My tires squeal again as I jerk my car into park behind her car. I don't even bother shutting my door as I bolt out.

I'm about to fly into Arella's apartment when my body slams against her locked door. *Fuck exposure.* I wave a hand at the doorknob. The bolt lock clicks open, and I run inside.

A lanky guy with an ugly buzz cut straddles Arella on her living room floor. They're between the couch and her tipped-over coffee table. She struggles with him as he attempts to rip her pants off. Thank fuck I got here when I did. The man's rage storms through my head, mixing with my already boiling anger.

I don't think as I seize the guy's shoulder, twist him to face me, then hurl a fist into his already bloody nose. It's nice to know that Arella did some damage before I arrived. I'm so fucking proud of her.

A dull ache explodes into the middle of my face, exactly where I punched her ex. It makes my eyes water. Feeling other people's pain never stopped me from fighting before, and it sure as hell isn't gonna stop me now. I expand my mind power outward, because sensing more people will help me sense less of the piece of shit in front of me.

I draw my elbow back and punch him again. With a yelp, Nathan topples backward, trips over the coffee table, then tumbles to the floor. Like a spring, he jumps back up and charges at me. I leap around the table, getting as far away from Arella as possible.

Nathan swings at my head, and I almost laugh. Based on the way he stands and throws his fist, this guy doesn't know what he's doing. He's no match for my many years of training in hand-to-hand combat. It's too easy for me to duck and strike him in the gut. He collapses to his knees with a moan.

I think he's done for.

And I think wrong.

I'll give him some credit because he stands up again and moves so fast, he knocks the wind out of me with a kick to my stomach. I hunch over with a groan. Unfiltered agony shatters through my face when he slams his fist against my upper cheek. For a lanky guy, he sure does punch hard.

When I regain my composure, I pound my fist straight into his ribs, making him fall to his knees again. Then I grab his head and smash it against my knee. His head whips backward with a *crunch!* as his back slams against the carpet. I hope I broke something. I think I did, by the way my nose feels like it's twisted to the side.

Again, I'll give the guy credit, because somehow, he still has enough strength to roll onto his hands and knees. Blood pours from his nose onto Arella's beige carpet as he coughs. I feel worse about dirtying up her carpet than I do about beating up this man I don't know.

Kneeling, he wipes his nose off on the bottom of his shirt. Then he looks up at Arella, who's standing a ways behind me. I almost kick him for thinking he has the right to look at her.

Nathan smirks. Laughs even.

What the hell is so funny?

"You're lucky this bastard showed up," Nathan says. "I was about to fuck you like the dirty little whore you are."

That's it. No more holding back. I yank him up by his

shirt and punch him again. Agony tears through my jaw. I ignore it as I hit him again—harder.

Then again.

And again.

And—

"Stop!" Arella shouts from behind me.

My balled-up fist freezes barely a finger from the asshole's face. I don't dare take my eyes off him as I speak through gritted teeth. "You want me to stop?"

"Yes," Arella says firmly. "Let him go."

It takes everything in me to release Nathan's shirt. He thumps to the floor.

I still don't take my eyes off him, nor do I unclench my fist. "Arella, please tell me you have a good reason for stopping me from hurting the man who was hurting you."

Her voice goes soft. "He'll press charges if you keep going."

"And you're going to press charges against him for assaulting you!"

"I'd like to see you try," Nathan snickers as he stares up at the ceiling. His face is bright red, already swelling up in the areas I hit him the most.

I resist the urge to break his teeth in. "Babe, go call the cops."

In the corner of my eye, she snatches her phone off the floor. Nathan laughs as he finds enough strength to stand and hold the bottom of his shirt to his nose. Obviously, I haven't wounded him enough to keep him down. That can easily be changed though.

"Go ahead and call, Ari. When they get here, I'll explain that you and I were hooking up when your side toy walked in on us and attacked me."

"We're over!" Arella shouts, and it surprises me. I never pictured her as a shouter, especially not with such venom. "Why can't you get that through your head?"

Nathan continues as if she hasn't said a word. "I'll tell them that we have our moments here and there. I've been telling them that anyway, so they'll believe me. Everyone thinks you call me up weekly because you can't stay away. You know they'll listen to me with my dad there. Then I can press charges against this fuckwad."

The flames in my palms flicker. Heat forms between my fingertips. If I don't control myself, this entire apartment will go up in flames. If this guy knows what's good for him, he'll shut the fuck up.

I don't take my focus off his bloody face. "Call the cops, Arella."

In the corner of my eye, she sets her phone down. "No."

Finally, I look at her. "What?"

"He's right, Trey."

"Again—what?"

"I'm not going to risk him getting you in trouble."

"And I'm not going to let him get away with hurting you!"

Arella squares her shoulders. "You can, and you will. We're letting him go. We can talk once he leaves, then decide if we'll call the cops or not."

I shake my head. "Let's skip the talking part and call now."

"Trust me, Trey. Just let him go."

She's asking me to trust her—the one thing I've been trying to get her to do with me since we met. Victor's words echo in my head.

"To get, you need to give."

I'll trust that Arella has a good reason why she doesn't want to call the cops. But I still can't let Pencil Dick walk away freely.

With a grunt, I grab the shithead by his shirt and drag him down the hall.

"Let go!" He claws at my hand.

In Arella's bathroom, I shove him into the tub, where he

can bleed some more without getting it all over the carpet. He stumbles backward, landing on his ass.

I point a stern finger at him. "Stay here, asshole. You open this door, and I'll cave your face in so hard, a bat will make you its home. Got it?"

"Fuck you!"

I can't control myself. My balled fist strikes him in the gut. Twice. "Got it?"

The troll-faced jerk off curls into himself, gasping for air as he nods.

"Good." Shutting the door behind me, I make my way back into the living room. Arella is in the same place I left her. "All right, babe. Let's talk."

She hooks a thumb toward the front door, raising her eyebrows with a wordless question.

I nod, then follow her out.

A yellowy moon hangs above us in the black sky as we face each other on the front lawn of her apartment complex. Arella hugs herself as if she's freezing. She's not. It's June in California.

I think about holding her, but I don't know if that would comfort her or make her tense, so I decide against it. Quietly, I wait for her to explain. To tell me why we aren't calling the cops. Why we're standing outside instead of in there, making sure her ex knows he's never allowed to breathe around her again. Instead, she just stares at the grass.

"Arella?" My voice is calm, even though I'm fuming. "You know, I don't care about him pressing charges against me. I want him behind bars and away from you."

"Me too," she says softly.

"Then why aren't we calling the police?"

"Nathan's dad is the LAPD deputy chief. They'll twist this into something it's not. They'll make *you* look like the bad guy."

I'm not sure how else to say it to make her understand

how serious this situation is, so I tell it how it is. "Arella, he tried to *rape* you."

The way she doesn't flinch at the R-word tells me this isn't the first time he's forced himself on her. I'm gonna punch one of his teeth out for that.

"Do you have a record?" she asks.

Is that a trick question? I'm not sure what answer she wants, so I go with the truth. "Yeah . . ." When she doesn't respond, I feel the need to explain. "Two counts of disorderly conduct and another charge for attempting to run from the police. And maybe a parking ticket or two." *Or twelve . . .*

"I figured you had something."

"Look, I don't care about keeping my record clean. It's already dirty."

"It's not about that. It's that Nathan and his dad will dig up everything they have on you and turn it around to use to their advantage."

I only met Nathan a few minutes ago, and I've never met his dad, but they've both made it to the top of my shit list.

Arella continues, "With your record like that, they'll have no problem getting an attorney to make it sound like you attacked him first, which technically, you did. Think about your career, Trey. If this gets out, how will this affect your band?"

I didn't even think about how this would look for me. Social media would have a fit. So would Monique. And Liz. Honestly, Liz's opinion is the only one I care about.

"I'm willing to risk all that if it means you're safe." And I mean that with all my heart.

"I'm not."

With a heavy sigh, I accept that she's made up her mind. If this is what she wants, so be it. Just in case, though, I ask one more time. "Are you sure you don't wanna call the cops?"

A firm nod. "I'm sure."

"All righty, then. Stay here. I'ma go take care of Pencil

Dick lying in your bathtub." My Empath power tells me that he hasn't moved from where I left him and he's angrier than he was before. He's about to be even angrier when he sees my fist again.

An instant smile appears on Arella's face. It eases all the tension in my gut. "Pencil Dick?"

"You got a better name for him?"

"Nope. Pencil Dick is perfect."

"Great. Don't come in 'til I say so, 'kay?"

Once she nods, I head back inside and shrug my jacket off. With balled fists, I march toward the bathroom.

17

———

ARELLA

I SIT ON THE CURB AND PICK AT MY NAILS FOR A WHILE BEFORE my door finally opens.

Trey has Nathan in his grasp. My ex's face is swollen red. On his bare chest, written in big black letters, are the words I ASSAULT WOMEN.

That should be a tattoo.

"Hey, angel," Trey says tenderly. "Thanks for waiting. Come on in."

After I step inside, Trey shoves Nathan out the door. Dramatically, my ex collapses to the ground. Trey hadn't pushed him *that* hard. The same message on his chest is written on his back. That's not coming off easily.

When Nathan doesn't get back up, I ask Trey, "Is he alive?"

"He's just puttin' on a show." Trey scoffs. "I only hit him one more time, and only 'cause he wouldn't sit still."

"Not true," Nathan says from the ground. "You hit me twice."

"Okay, fine. When I finished my artwork, he swung at me, calling me every nasty name in the book. So I might have punched him once more."

I don't feel sorry for Nathan. None of the things Trey did to him tonight will ever compare to the many bruises I endured. This doesn't make up for all the days I missed work because I was too weak to move, or the times I cried all night because I was scared I wouldn't wake up in the morning.

Nathan pushes himself up and wipes the blood off his mouth with the back of his hand. "Where's my shirt?"

"Fuck off," Trey says.

"I'm not leavin' without my—"

With a cheesy smile and a wave goodbye, Trey slams the door and locks it. I wait a second and am pleasantly surprised when I don't hear any pounding.

A moment later, I catch a good view of Nathan stumbling past my living room window and around the corner. He must have parked his car on the street where I wouldn't see it. I shudder with the thought of what he planned to do if Trey hadn't shown up. Would I have been able to fight him off? *I was never able to before.*

"Sorry for taking so long," Trey says. "It took me a while to find a Sharpie around here. He won't ever bother you again."

"How are you so sure?"

"Because I threatened to slice off his micropenis if he does."

No words come to me. I'm still trying to process everything. It all happened so fast. My heart is still racing from when Nathan climbed on top of me and held my arms down.

A trickle of blood dripping down Trey's hand makes me gasp. "Oh no!"

He flexes his bloody knuckles, then shrugs. "I think that's mostly his."

"I'll go get the first aid kit." I rush away to rummage under the bathroom sink for my big red box.

When I return to the living room, Trey is in the kitchen, washing off. His right hand looks drastically less gory as he dries off on a paper towel. He's got some gashes, but they aren't too deep. Still, another man got hurt because of me. This is exactly what I was trying to avoid.

The first and only guy I've been on a date with since leaving Nathan got chased off by drunk Nathan with a knife. My date ran away and tripped on the curb, spraining his ankle. Then he hobbled to his car and drove away. I haven't heard from that guy since, no matter how many apology voicemails I've left.

Trey takes the first aid kit from my grasp. "I've got this, babe. Why don't you go sit down while I wrap up my hand?"

"I'd like to do it for you, if that's okay." I need to feel helpful.

He thinks for a second, then sticks his hand out to me. "Have at it."

After applying the ointment, I wrap some gauze around his knuckles. There's still blood oozing from the small gashes. Just looking at it makes me squirmy. There's a difference between seeing it on TV and seeing it in real life.

Trey doesn't seem to mind the blood. If anything, the expression on his face tells me he's proud of himself.

"I could get used to you being my doctor," he says, smiling at me all handsomely.

I don't respond. I feel terrible that I have to be doing this at all.

With his other hand, he tilts my chin up. "Don't look so sad, baby. It's not your fault."

I force a smile. He can tell me all night that it's not my fault, but I know it is. If I had gotten rid of Nathan years ago, when all the red flags started waving, I wouldn't still be dealing with him today. I allowed things to get too far. Now, I have to deal with the aftermath. I just wish the people around me didn't have to deal with it too.

"Now I understand why you freeze up whenever I touch you."

"It's not just you," I say faintly. "It's *all* men."

Trey's fingertips graze my jawline. I wince when he lightly brushes against the spot I fell on when Nathan grabbed my ankle.

Trey's mouth turns into a grimace. "He used to do this a lot, didn't he? Mark you up."

I nod, unable to respond any other way.

Leaning in to me, he gently says, "I will never hurt you the way he did. You have the power to stop me from touching you if you ever don't want it, okay? Just say *no* or *stop*, and I will."

I gape into his eyes, trying to make sense of his confusing words. What does he mean that I can just say *no* and he'll actually stop? *Is that even a thing?*

I finish wrapping his hand, then pack up the first aid kit.

"Thank you, Doctor Rance," Trey says, offering me a honeyed smile.

I smile back, and it's not forced this time. "You're welcome. I'll bill you next week."

"Can I pay you in the form of a dinner date?"

I don't miss a beat. "It's against the official doctor code for me to date my patients."

"Hmm. That leaves us two options, then. Either you quit your job or I will find a new doctor."

I'm not sure what comes over me. One second, I'm chuckling, and the next, I'm throwing myself into his chest. Trey doesn't hesitate to circle his muscular arms around me as I bury my face into his shirt. The longer he holds me, the more warmth washes through me.

"Thank you," I breathe as a tear drips down my cheek. It's more from relief than anything. "You have no idea how long I've been trying to cut him out of my life."

My throat closes up as I remember the threats Nathan used to hiss at me for saying I wanted out. He used to tell me he'd kill me before I could get away.

Trey draws back to look at me. "He's out of your life now, baby. And I'll be right here to make sure it stays that way."

Because I don't have the words to express my immense gratitude, I just smile at him. He smiles back, then pulls me closer against his hard body and holds me. Nothing else.

He doesn't talk.

He doesn't move.

He just holds me.

For the first time in years, I feel safe in a man's arms.

18

TREY

I'VE GOT TWO OPTIONS.

One: Don't show up.

Two: Play it off like it's no big deal.

I'd get more shit for ditching, so I text Liz and ask her to come to rehearsal early with her makeup bag. Then I suck it up and drive to the Soul House.

The second I enter the back door, Liz takes one look at me and plants a firm hand on her hip. "You know we have a show tonight, right? Like, in front of people?"

"Did you bring your makeup bag?"

She groans, glaring at me. "Sit your ass down so I can fix your face before the rest of the band comes, or more importantly, Monique."

On the sectional, Liz slips off her gloves, then unrolls a bag with a collection of items I have no idea what to do with.

Liz remains quiet while she applies skin-colored goop to my purple cheek.

When I can't take the silent treatment anymore, I say, "Please don't be mad."

"I'm not mad, T. I'm disappointed."

"Goddammit, Liz. I'd rather you be mad." Even though

she is three years younger than me, Liz is obviously the more mature one in this relationship.

"I'm disappointed because you were going so strong. It's been, what, two years since you got into a fight?"

"I had a justified reason this time." The reasons I fought before weren't justified in Liz's eyes. I, for damn sure, think they were justified.

She stops applying the makeup to lean back and scowl at me. "Were any drugs or alcohol involved with this one?"

"Nope. I was completely sober last night," I say proudly, like I should receive a gold medal for not shooting poison up my bloodstream anymore. "I was at dinner with you right beforehand."

"Did you try sleeping to speed up the healing process?"

"No." Zordi bodies naturally heal faster than Ordinary bodies, and even faster when we sleep. If I had slept last night, I probably would have woken up with a clear face. Unfortunately, my adrenaline was still pumping after I left Arella's apartment, so I couldn't sleep at all. It wasn't my night to, anyway.

Liz resumes covering up my bruise. "It doesn't look like you drank any Healing Water either."

"I didn't." I used my last bottle of Healing Water on Arella the night she was drugged—something I can't tell Liz. Using Zordi products on an Ordi is just another thing she'll scold me for.

"Don't you find it ironic that you're the son of the inventors of healing products but you had none when you needed it?"

"Sure." I wince when she presses a makeup sponge a little too hard against my cheek. I think she's doing it on purpose.

Liz yawns, covering her mouth with a hand. "So, what was this fight about?"

"Arella's ex-boyfriend attacked her."

With a gasp, Liz stops what she's doing. "Is she okay?"

"Yeah. She's a really strong person. Probably as strong as you."

My compliment works to ease Liz, because she's gentler with me as she pats some powdery stuff onto my face. "I've been thinking about you and Ari. Or Arella, as you call her."

I'm not sure why, but my heart rate kicks up a notch. "Okay?"

"I've been thinking about how perfect she is for you, except that she's an Ordi, of course."

Of all the things Liz could have said, I wouldn't have guessed it'd be that. "Perfect for me? How so?"

She leans back to look at me. "You really haven't figured it out?"

My tone goes dry. "Enlighten me, Liz. I'm an Empath, not a Mind Reader."

"Sometimes your gift makes it hard for you to know which of your emotions are real and which aren't. For some strange reason, Ari's invulnerable to our gifts. Whatever feelings you might have for her aren't muddled by what you'd be sensing from her if you could. Ari could be the first *real* relationship you ever have."

"I have a real relationship with you, don't I?"

Liz huffs. "You know what I mean. Like a real *romantic* relationship. Not what we have."

I swallow thickly. The idea of having a *real* relationship, the kind of *real* Liz is referring to, makes my stomach churn. Especially if it's with Arella. Not only is she an Ordinary; she's just a mission. Once I get the information from her that I need, we'll go our separate ways. I'll move on to helping ZIRDA figure out how we can replicate her immunity and use it against the Royals. She'll move on to having a real relationship with someone else. Someone who's capable of having real relationships. Someone who actually deserves her.

Liz finishes with my face, then tosses everything back into her makeup bag. "Don't you think that *my* feelings for you play a big part in what our relationship has become? Don't you think that because I care about you as much as I do that it makes you reciprocate it for me?"

I pause to think about that. I can't say it does, and I can't say it doesn't. I adore Liz—more than I adore anyone else in this world. Actually, she's the only person I adore at all. I would do anything for her. Do I only feel this way about her because she feels it for me? Would Liz and I be this close if I could separate my feelings from everyone else's? I'd like to think the answer is yes, only because that means I have control over my decisions. I hate thinking that I'm living my life based on how other people's feelings affect me.

Wait . . . What if that's all my life has ever been? The last time I slept with Jess was because she projected her desires onto me. Would I have done it otherwise? Maybe this is why I jumped on the idea of starting a band with Kevin. When we met, he got excited about the possibility, so I did too. Maybe this is how I got roped into becoming Elliott's mentor. Sharon brought up the idea of me mentoring a Deaf kid no one else wanted. She felt determined to include him, so I did too.

Have any of my life decisions been my own?

19

ARELLA

TREY'S BRUISES SURE HEALED QUICKLY. WHEN HE COMES TO pick me up, the shiner on his face is gone. The gashes on his knuckles have disappeared, too. His injuries were worse than mine, yet my face is *still* purple. It's only been three days. *How did he heal so fast?*

"Did you drink some magic potion or something?" I joke as he ushers me into his kitchen with a hand on the small of my back. I barely flinched when he placed his hand there, and I'm pretty proud of myself for it.

"Magic potion?" He drops his hand from my back, and I kind of wish he hadn't.

"Yeah, to heal your knuckles."

He flexes his fingers, staring at the places where the gashes used to be. "They weren't that bad."

Maybe, but his hand looks brand-new . . .

With a waggle of his eyebrows, he says, "So, am I allowed to classify tonight as a date?"

"Is that what you want?" I smile back and set my purse on his black countertop.

"I only want to call this a date if *you* want to call this a date."

I nod a little too eagerly. "I'd like that."

"Great!" He flashes me one of the biggest grins I've ever seen on a man. "For our date, do you wanna teach me how to bake?"

I perk up. "Really?"

We spend some time picking out a recipe online. After we decide on something easy, I teach him how to correctly measure out flour.

"When baking," I say as I dump the spooned white fluff into a mixing bowl, "you usually want to put the dry ingredients into the bowl first. Then you add the wet ingredients after you make a well."

"Make a what?" He's cute when he doesn't have any idea what he's doing.

"Here, I'll show you." After I measure out a few more dry ingredients into the bowl, I show him how to make a well.

He scoffs. "That's it? It's just a hole in the middle with a fancy name."

I laugh as I pour in the wet ingredients, and then I gesture for him to mix it all together. "You don't bake very often, do you?"

He takes the bowl. "I've never baked anything at all."

"Um . . ." I gesture at all the baking supplies scattered across his countertop. "You sure have a lot of baking tools for someone who never bakes."

"I just bought all this shit last night."

"Why?"

"Because I read on Google that baking can be a fun date activity. You love baking, so I figured you'd like this."

I laugh, slapping my palm against the counter. "Wait! You *Googled* date ideas?"

"Yeah . . ." He looks away sheepishly. "I've never done this before. I'm clueless, and Professor Google has never let me down."

"You've never done what before?"

"Date."

That can't be true. "How many girlfriends have you had?"

"Eh. Let's not talk about that." Trey passes me the bowl, then picks up his phone and pretends to read the snickerdoodle recipe.

"That many, huh?" The dough isn't completely incorporated yet, so I resume mixing it.

"No. I just didn't invite you over to talk about other women."

"Sorry, I was just curious."

Trey steps around to the other side of the island and takes a seat on one of the barstools. "How 'bout this? For every personal question you ask me, I get to ask you one."

"Deal. I'll start. How many girlfriends have you had?"

"Just one."

That's it? One seems low for a guy with a face like his. Although, to him, women he's slept with and women he's called his girlfriend are probably two different things.

"How long did that relationship last?"

"Nuh-uh." He wiggles a finger. "You're jumping ahead of the game here, Miss Rance. I believe it's my turn." He thinks while I line the baking sheet with some parchment paper. "Did you take your mom's last name or your dad's?"

"They got married before I was born, so technically, I have both their last names." Between my palms, I roll some dough into an inch-wide ball, dip it into the cinnamon sugar, then place it onto the parchment. "So how long did your relationship last?"

Trey digs his fingers into the dough and repeats my process. "Shit, I dunno. I think Jess and I made it, like, three months."

"Do you still talk to her?"

"Not really. And now, I get two questions. First: You mentioned that your parents worked together. Do you know which company they worked for?"

"No . . ." I don't understand why Trey is so interested in my family. I suppose since he doesn't have a family of his own, it's reasonable to be curious about mine, but he asks about my family a lot.

"Second question: Have you ever Googled your parents?"

"No . . ." I narrow my eyes. "Should I?"

"Nah." He rolls out another dough ball. "I was just wondering 'cause I Googled mine recently."

"Did you find anything interesting?"

"Not really, and now it's your turn."

"Okay." I've been thinking about this topic a lot, so the question comes easily. "Your bad-boy habits. All the fighting, drugs, and girls, and stuff . . . has it stopped?"

"That's a hard question. If you wanna know when I stopped doing drugs, it was about two years ago. The fighting stopped around then, I think. As for the girls, I'll still occasionally enjoy a good time here and there. I mean, if the opportunity presents itself."

It makes me happy to know he's been clean for two years. I'm not happy to know he still sleeps around, although I'm not surprised. "What changed you?"

We roll out a few more snickerdoodle balls before Trey finally looks at me. "Two things. First: music. The first time I picked up a guitar, I was hooked. Whenever I play, my mind feels less . . . chaotic. When I moved out of my hometown, I left my guitar behind, and it all went downhill from there.

"A few years later, I came to LA and met Kevin in a guitar store. We got to talking, and he told me about his dream to play in a band. I said I wanted to help him live his dream. So we started our band, picking up Marcus, Emmy, and Liz along the way. Once everything took off for us, I decided it was what I wanted to focus on, so I dropped the bad habits."

I finish rolling out the last doughball, then turn on the sink to wash my hands. Trey comes up beside me, running his palms under the faucet too.

"What was the second thing that changed you?"

"Liz." He doesn't offer any further explanation, and it makes the jealous green monster awaken inside me. Liz seems to be important to him. I know they're close. I just wish I knew exactly how close.

Are they the type of friends who come with benefits? Judging from the way the Internet talks about them, yes. Liz kept glaring at him for talking to me and not her at his house party, so I wouldn't be surprised if they have a past.

Trey dries his hands off on a towel, then leans his back against the counter. "Liz taught me that shit happens and you've got two choices. You can either let it bring you down or build you up. While the things she and I went through are completely different, they are equally as shitty, yet there I was, getting high and drunk and fucking faceless women, while Liz moved halfway across the country by herself to pursue her dreams in dance. If Liz can go through her battles and still make something of herself, why can't I?"

I stick the baking sheet into the preheated oven, then set the oven timer. "It sounds like she made a huge impact on you."

"Yeah, but don't tell her that. She'll get all mushy, and I hate it."

With a chuckle, I toss all the dirty baking supplies into the sink. "*Sure* you do. I bet on the inside, you secretly like it."

"I plead the fifth." His tiny smile confirms that I'm right. Then his smile dips into a light scowl as he gestures at his black countertops sprinkled in flour. "Damn, babe. You really know how to make a mess 'round here."

I run the dough-covered rubber spatula under the water. "It's baking. Messes are necessary."

"Maybe this is why I don't bake."

I don't even think about it. My hand simply digs itself into the bag of flour and plops it onto his countertop.

Trey's mouth pops open. "Oh, hell no!" In one swift

motion, his hand flies into the flour, and he throws a handful onto my chest.

I gasp, jumping back as white dust flutters to my feet. "Hey!"

I reach for the flour again, but he snatches it first. With a sly look, he dashes around the other side of the island.

I chase him, giggling. "Give that back!"

"Not a chance. If you wanna make a mess in my kitchen, then baby, we will make a mess."

He flings another handful of flour across the island at me. I put my hands up to block, but I'm too late. Flour lands all over my hair and dress. More of it flurries onto the floor.

I cross my arms over my chest with a pout. "I'm covered in it."

It only takes him a second to cave. Instantly, he's back at my side, setting the flour bag down. "I'm sorry, babe. I'll help you get it out." Gently, he shakes some of the white powder off my dress.

Too easy. My hand goes straight into the bag, and flour flies into his face. "Ha! Gotcha!"

A slow grin spreads across his lips as his tongue runs along the inside of his mouth. "Damn. I shoulda seen that comin'."

As he wipes the flour off his face, I laugh hysterically. "I can't believe you fell for that."

Trey goes motionless, staring at me. I see it in his eyes— the moment his willpower snaps. Before I can get a word out, he shoves the hair from my face, and then his lips devour mine.

20

TREY

She tenses at first.

I don't stop. I don't want to stop. If someone tried to pry me away from her, I'd blast them with a fireball.

My lips massage hers open until she melts into me. Her body relaxes in my arms as her hands circle the back of my neck. I draw her in by her waist, needing every part of her body to be touching mine. At the sound of her breathless moan, my cock hardens.

I kiss her as if I'm starving—because I am—for her.

I've been waiting to do this for what feels like months. I told myself I wouldn't kiss her until she told me she was ready. After seeing her so playful and laughing all adorably, I couldn't stop myself.

She tastes amazing—like honeyed watermelon on a warm summer day. My tongue explores her mouth as desire pumps inside my jeans. I desperately want to be inside her. Gently, I shove her back against the island, clawing at her dress. I want it gone. Anywhere but on her.

I grip the back of her thighs, lifting her onto the counter. We separate for barely a second before she pulls my face back to hers. I pant as I take her in. All of her. The feel of her tongue between my lips. The sweet way she smells. How she's making me lose my mind with each little moan she lets out. I draw back a little so I can take a breath, but a forceful tug of my shirt yanks me right back to her.

Fuuuck . . . Screw breathing. Who needs to do that, anyway? I consume her, taking all I can get. My hands travel everywhere on her, up and down her back and from her head to her thighs. Her fingers splay over my pecs, sending tingles down to my toes. When she pulls on my hair, my dick almost explodes.

I thought I was the one calling the shots.

Nope.

It's her. She's destroying me, and I want her to keep doing it.

I'm not sure how long it is before she finally releases me. With our foreheads pressed together, we pant—hard. My heart beats so fast, I'm pretty certain it's about to give out. My lips feel cold without her. I need to kiss her again.

So I do.

I ease her lips back open with mine, and she lets me. After pulling her hair to one side, I leave her lips to kiss her neck. She arches her head back, giving me full access. I savor her delicious skin, nipping at the tender spot behind her ear as I breathe in her inebriating scent. Sweet lavender, springtime and . . . Arella. Her scent is familiar to me now. If I could only smell her for the rest of my life, I wouldn't mind.

"Trey," she moans in a whisper, and damn if it doesn't make me weak in the knees. She could tell me to jump off a bridge, and I'd do it. No questions asked.

Finally, I lean back and breathe. If we continue this any longer, I might die from the lack of oxygen.

In a whisper, I say, "You wanna take a shower?"

"No," she answers sharply.

I laugh, realizing how that sounded. "I didn't mean together. We're covered in flour. I figured you'd want to wash off, but you don't have to if you don't want to."

Her cheeks turn rosy. "What will I wear?"

"My clothes. They'll be big on you, but you'll look great." I've never let anyone wear my clothes before. It feels too intimate. But the idea of Arella in my shirt makes me more eager to get her into the shower.

"We should finish the cookies first."

Right on cue, the timer beeps.

With some oven mitts on, I pull the baking sheet out and place it onto my new cooling rack. Then I offer Arella my hand. She takes it and allows me to help her hop off the counter. I like that she didn't hesitate. She took my hand as if we hold hands all the time, except this is the first time. *And it feels so . . . normal.*

I don't let go of her until we reach my bedroom. There, I point at my drawers. "Dig through these 'til you find something that fits. Bathroom is through there."

After returning to the kitchen, I wave my hands back and forth, making damp towels slide up and down the countertops. The towels erase the evidence of our flour fight. I've still got a semi under my belt, and it's super uncomfortable. *Saggy grandmas, foot fungus, math problems . . .*

"Trey?" Arella calls out.

Shit. My hands fall to my sides, and the towels freeze where they are. I glance up, but she's not there. I breathe out a sigh of relief. I never know where she is.

I peek my head around the corner. "Yeah?"

Her voice comes from inside my bedroom. "Could you show me how to turn your shower on? I can't figure it out."

After instructing her on how to work the nozzles, I go back to cleaning the kitchen. Once that's done, I grab some clean clothes, then run upstairs to my other shower.

By the time I'm out, Arella's still showering. It's no big deal, because I can start on dinner without her. This time, she's going to sit around while *I* do all the cooking.

At the fridge, I rummage around for some steaks and a do-it-yourself salad kit. When I close the fridge door, Arella's standing right there.

I jump back. This time, I don't drop anything. "Goddammit. You gotta quit doin' that."

"You didn't hear me coming?"

"No." I've always relied on my Empath powers to tell me when someone's near. Guess I'll have to start training my ears. It doesn't help that Arella's so fucking quiet.

I step back to get a better look at her. Long wet strands of hair drip water down my white T-shirt that dwarfs her. No makeup. Flushed cheeks. *And those lips!* I want to kiss her again.

Finally, my eyes make it down to her legs, and I laugh. "Are those my boxers?"

"Yeah. It was the only thing that would stay up on my waist. Do you mind?"

I'm about to say "of course not," then I stop. Instead, I grin like a mischievous little puppy. "Actually, I do mind. You should take my boxers off right now and just lounge in your underwear."

"I might have . . . if I was wearing any."

My dick turns rock solid again. "Say *whaaa*? You're not wearing any underwear?"

"Well, I was, but they got wet."

"How did they get wet?"

She bites her lip, smirking at me. Finally, I get it.

"Fuck." I throw the steaks and salad onto the counter, then stomp down the hall.

Arella giggles, and it only makes my cock twitch more. "Where are you going?"

"You're driving me crazy, babe," I say over my shoulder. "I can't stand to be in the same room with you right now."

Any longer and I'll lose what little control I have, put her over my shoulder, and strip her naked in my bedroom. She's not ready for that . . . yet.

"Okay," Arella calls after me. "I'll start seasoning the steaks."

HALF AN HOUR LATER

"Would you like some wine?" I ask, gesturing toward the three bottles on the shelf behind me. In addition to all the baking supplies, I also purchased these last night, just for her. I hope I got something she'll like.

"No, thank you," she says, and I have to keep from frowning. "Water's fine."

I'm curious to see how or if alcohol affects her immunity, but I can't do that if she doesn't accept the damn wine. If a little alcohol can break down her immunity walls and let me sense her, that might be the breakthrough I need to figure this out. *Maybe next time.*

I'm about to sit in front of my warm plate when I sense someone approaching my house. Their depressing energy weighs me down like bricks tied to my arms. Heavy emotions like that always come at me stronger. The more the energy seeps into me, the more I've got a hunch as to who it is. The curtains in the living room are drawn shut, so I can't peek outside to confirm, but nobody ever comes over unannounced with emotions like that—except one.

Jess is the last person I want to see right now, especially with Arella here. When the doorbell rings, I make no effort to stand.

"Aren't you going to get that?" Arella asks.

"Eh. It's probably just UPS."

The doorbell rings again.

Arella glances that way. "Maybe they need a signature."

Groaning, I get up. *At least she didn't barge in this time.*

When I open the door, my heart plummets. Liz has puffy eyes, red cheeks, and messy hair. My irritation from five seconds ago instantly melts into concern.

Liz runs her face into my chest, sniffling. I wrap a protective arm around her and slam the door shut. She quietly sobs as I hold her. Usually, crying makes me cringe, but this is Liz. She's the one who can turn any storm into sunshine. If she's crying, something is seriously wrong.

My tone comes out rough. "What happened?"

She lifts her head and wipes away some tears with her gloved fingertips. She's careful, as if not to ruin her makeup, but it's too late for that.

"I—" Liz catches a glimpse of Arella at the dinner table. "Oh, sorry. I didn't mean to impose on—"

"Stop." I grab her face with both hands, forcing her to look at me. "What happened?"

She breathes in heavily, not answering. Maybe this isn't a conversation we should have in front of an Ordinary. Taking her hand, I drag her toward my music room.

"I'll be right back, babe," I call over my shoulder. No reply comes.

Five guitars, a drum set, and various other instruments are scattered around the perimeter of my music room. Gently, I click the door shut. With a flick of my wrist, the curtains glide open to let some sun in. Liz loves the sunshine. Maybe it'll help lift her mood.

I sit on my long keyboard bench, then pat the empty space next to me. Liz plants herself at my side as she slips out of her satin gloves and drops them onto the carpet. Then she dabs her face off with the bottom of her shirt. Tenderly, I pull her against me, and her head falls onto my shoulder.

"Did I interrupt something?" Liz's voice comes out as broken as her energy feels.

"No." I could be in the middle of getting heart surgery, and Liz would have my full permission to interrupt. Sensing her pain makes me want to hit someone. Preferably the mouth-breathing toe-licker who upset her. "What happened?"

"Rodrigo broke up with me." Liz sniffles as her sadness rains over my head.

"Why?" I try to keep my voice steady. I need to control my emotions so she doesn't cry any more.

"He can't get over that I'm a Hydro and he's a Pyro. He's got issues with being with someone who's got a dominant power over his."

Having a best friend with the dominant element over mine has never bothered me. Liz has always been the stronger one in more ways than that anyway, and I admire that about her. Why can't Rodrigo see it that way?

I'm at a loss as to what to say because I suck at pep talks. Instead, I close my eyes and think of my happy place: my little cabin out in the Colorado mountains. I imagine the flowy trees and the scenic flowers. The peace and quiet. The calm of being alone in my own head since there isn't anyone else around for miles. Being there soothes me.

As soon as my emotions are controlled, I project them into Liz.

She immediately straightens up, breathing easier. "Whatever you're thinking about, it's working."

Growing up, I used to get beat for using my mind power to make Victor feel calmer and happier—two things he never felt after Aunt Jodi left. I thought I was being helpful. Turns out, Victor didn't want to be helped. Being able to use my gift on Liz, knowing that she *wants* me to, is freeing.

"You want me to kick his ass?" I'm mostly asking to get her to smile, but if she says yes, I'll leave right now.

"No." She doesn't smile.

"How 'bout I go over there and show him how dominant *my* Pyro power can be?"

"No." She still gazes somberly at the floor.

"How 'bout we sit outside his place and I'll wiggle my fingers around until all his furniture is upside down?" I motion toward a small table in the corner and theatrically circle my wrist. My songwriting notebook on top falls to the carpet as the table rotates and then drops back down with its legs sticking up.

Finally, Liz laughs and I get a sense of relief. "That'd be funny, but no."

I pull Liz up with me as I stand. Naturally, our hands intertwine. I'm the only person in the world she can hold hands with—bare.

After Liz saw my worst memory for the first time, any time our hands touched, she saw it again: my mother getting shocked with a lightning ball, my father's bloody face, the explosion, all of it. This went on until last November when I was at her place for Thanksgiving. As we both reached for the plates, our hands touched and she saw nothing. It's been that way ever since, and neither of us knows how.

Liz doesn't question it. She embraces it, holding my hand as often as possible. Like when we watch movies together or when we're just sitting around talking. I let her. Not just for her benefit, but for mine too.

I won't admit it out loud, but Liz makes me feel like I'm worth something. Like I'm more than just a body taking up space, breathing someone else's air, using up other people's precious resources. Sometimes, she even makes me feel like I have a purpose: to be the person who'll always be there for her because nobody else is.

I just wish that was enough for me. Enough for me to feel like I actually belong in this world. For me to feel like my life isn't pointless. To make me stop wishing I had died in that explosion too.

Liz tells me that surviving it wasn't luck. She says that I survived because I was *meant* to, but I can't have survived just to be her support person. There has to be something else, something more that I'm meant to do, and I think this mission is it. This is what the universe kept me around for.

"How 'bout we go out with the band after recording

tomorrow?" I say, pulling Liz in for a tight hug. "You'll forget all about what's-his-nuts by the end of the night."

"I'd love that." Liz squeezes me back so hard, the air leaves my lungs. "Thanks, T. I knew coming here would help me feel better."

She's starting to get sappy, so I need to counteract it. "My offer to kick his ass still stands."

Liz leans back, rolling her eyes at me. "Your fists can't solve every problem, T. In fact, they never solve *any* problems."

That's not true. My fists solved Arella's Pencil Dick problem in one night. "What kind of best friend would I be if I didn't at least offer?"

"Speaking of being best friends, as your best friend, I gotta talk to you about Ari again."

I don't miss a beat. "Uhh, my dinner's gettin' cold." I'm about to open the door when Liz pulls me back.

"Just hear me out, okay?"

With a slump of my shoulders, I remain where I am. "Fine. What?"

"Remember how I said that I think Ari's perfect for you?"

"Yeah?"

"Well, it doesn't change that she's an Ordinary. If you get caught doing things with her you shouldn't be, it'll affect more than just you. You're no A-lister, but people still recognize you on the street. I'm not gonna report you, but what if someone else does? If the Enforcers take you away, what happens to the band?"

A chill creeps up my spine at the mention of the Enforcers. Keepers are the ones who make Zordi laws. Enforcers are the ones who, well . . . enforce them. Together, they make up the Superiors, Supes for short, otherwise known as the zovernment, otherwise known as pieces of shit.

Enforcers are known to be tough and unrelenting. Zordi

parents like to use Enforcers as a threat to get their kids to behave. Now Liz is using them to try to get me to behave.

Nonchalantly, I wave a hand through the air. "Don't worry 'bout it."

"I can't not worry. I just read an article on the z-net yesterday about some guy who got arrested for kissing an Ordinary behind a mall. He's probably gonna get at least ten years, and that's just for *kissing* an Ordinary. Imagine how much time you'd get for having an ongoing sexual relationship with one. We can't hold our band rehearsals from inside a z-prison."

"And we won't," I say reassuringly. "I'm being careful."

"If you say so. Either way, I'm worried about Ari too."

"Why?"

"Because when you break things off with her, it'll break her heart. She's really sweet, T. I don't like the idea of you hurting her."

"We're just friends hangin' out," I say with a shrug. "It's not serious."

Liz arches an eyebrow. "You hate cooking, and you cooked dinner for her. When have you ever done that for a girl?"

"I've done that for you."

"I don't count."

I fake a gasp. "Liz! Is this how you tell me you've got a wiener?"

She backhands my chest so hard, it stings. "You're not taking this seriously!"

I rub the spot she hit. "Ow! You and Marcus should have an arm-wrestling match. I think you'd win."

"Trey Andrew Grant!" She scowls at me so hard, I'm afraid her face will stay like that.

I'm still rubbing my chest because, damn, that shit hurt. "All right. I get it. Be careful with the Ordinary. Can we be done now?"

"Fine," Liz says with a roll of her eyes.

Together, we head to the dining table to find Arella almost finished with her steak. I feel like a dick for leaving her to eat by herself.

"Sorry, babe," I say. "Thanks for waiting."

"That's okay." Arella shivers, and her teeth clack together.

"I'll be right back." I go down the hall to kick up the temp, then set it to stay in the mid-seventies from now on. It won't affect me, but it'll make Arella feel more comfortable whenever she's here.

I hear Liz talking to Arella, but I can't make out the words as I disappear into my bedroom.

When I return to the table, Liz is sitting in the chair next to Arella's. I interrupt Arella's explanation about why she's wearing my boxers to hand her my black hoodie.

"Thanks." She slips into it immediately, looking so adorable, I could kiss her. I'll wait until Liz leaves though.

"You hungry, Liz?" I ask.

She shakes her head. "Don't fuss about me. I'll grab something on the way home. I just wanted to say hi to Ari before I left, and tell her why I was upset earlier, and apologize for crashing your night."

"You don't have to stop anywhere. Here, you can have my steak. I'll reheat it for you." I pick up my plate and head toward the kitchen.

"What are *you* gonna eat?"

"We've got more food."

Liz's chair slides back as she stands. "No, really. I'll just—"

Turning on my heel, I glare at her. "Sit your ass down." I point at her, then at the empty chair. She just got dumped. There's no way in hell I'm letting her go home to eat by herself.

Liz raises her hands in surrender. "Okay. I'll stay."

A minute later, I return with a warm plate and clean silverware. I set it all in front of Liz with a fresh napkin, then leave to find myself something to eat.

In the freezer, there's some frozen mac and cheese and a frozen pizza. The mac and cheese won't take as long, so I choose that. Once it's heated, I join the girls with it.

"Damn you, T," Liz says, dropping her fork. "Now I feel bad. Are you sure you don't want this?"

"I'm sure. Now, you're gonna eat that piece of cow, and you're gonna like it." I take a bite of my highly processed pitiful excuse for nutrition, pretending to love it. "So, what were you ladies talking about?"

"Ari asked what I was doing this weekend. I told her that we're having an appreciation party on July Fourth for the crew and their families." Liz turns her attention to Arella. "As I was saying, Trey rents out the park, and the rest of the band brings all the food and drinks. This is our third year hosting an appreciation party, and we've decided to make it an annual thing."

I butt in. "We?"

Liz rolls her eyes. "Okay, *I* decided to make it an annual thing. Everyone loves it except you."

"And you know why," I mutter under my breath.

Liz shrugs nonchalantly as she shovels some mashed potatoes into her mouth. "Come up with a good excuse this year."

Arella's face crumples together. "Excuse for what?"

Liz and I glance at each other, then at Arella. I know Liz is gonna hate this, but I do it anyway because I just realized that my excuse this year is sitting right here.

"Hey, babe, you wanna come to the party with me?" If Arella's there, she can be my reason to leave early that people can't judge me for.

After Arella happily agrees to attend the party, we finish our meals, and then Liz heads home with a lighter spirit.

For the rest of the evening, Arella and I lounge on my couch and talk. Honestly, we kiss more than we talk, but I'm not complaining. I try asking more questions about her family until she asks me, "Why do you want to know so much about them?"

I give her a long-winded explanation about wanting to know everything about her because I really like her, then I go back to kissing her and stop with the questions.

Eventually, when my lips are numb, I lie back and motion for her to lie with me. Without hesitation, she does, nuzzling her head into the crook of my shoulder. She places a palm over my abs while I drape my arm around her back, resting it over her hip. Our bodies fit together as if they were made to.

It takes me a few minutes before I realize that I'm cuddling. *I*, of all people, am *cuddling*. And enjoying it! It feels so natural that it didn't occur to me that I was even doing it. Maybe this cuddling thing I've been avoiding isn't so bad after all.

Ultimately, our time together ends. Since her clothes haven't finished washing yet, I tell Arella she can wear my shirt and boxers home. It'll also be a good excuse to see her again.

When we arrive at her apartment, I walk her to the door like a fucking gentleman. Once our lips meet again, the gentleman in me is lost. Roughly, I shove her back against her door and pin her arms above her head. I kiss her until she's moaned my name at least three times.

"I can't get enough of you," I say. Based on the way she keeps tugging on my shirt to pull me closer, she hasn't gotten enough of me, either.

"I really should go now," Arella pants as I pepper kisses down her neck.

"Five more seconds," I beg. I count to five in my head about twenty times before I finally gather enough willpower to let her go. "When can I see you again?"

"I get off at four tomorrow?" She looks up at me all hopeful. It's cute.

"We've got a recording session from three to seven; then we're probably going out for dinner afterward."

"How about the next day?"

I sigh deeply. "We have a video shoot all day. I might be done by seven or eight. Would you wanna hang out for a bit after that?"

"Our schedules don't match up very well, do they?"

"Nope." I lean in to kiss her, and she opens her mouth for me willingly. "I'll text you, okay? We'll figure somethin' out."

With a dazed smile, she says, "Mm-kay."

I take a step backward toward my car. "Sleep well, angel." That name fits her perfectly. It embodies all of her innocence and beauty in one word.

"You too, Trey," she says with a wave. "Goodbye."

My body freezes in mid-step. I swallow hard as my words come out sharply. "Please don't say that."

Arella is just getting her door open when she turns to me. "Say what?"

"Goodbye. I'm not fond of that word." *An understatement.*

"Oh. Why's that?"

Because my mother said it to me the last time I ever saw her. I try to sound as nonchalant as possible, acting like all the chaos from that night isn't suddenly eating me alive. "There's just . . . a kind of finality to it, ya know? It makes me feel like I'll never see you again. I was taught that goodbye means forever. *Bye* is just for now."

Arella must see the distress on my face, because she comes to me, plants her hands on either side of my face, and brings me down to meet her lips. Our kiss is short but still satisfying. "Bye for now, then."

As she releases me, the pain instantly melts away.

21

––––––––––

TREY

I wake up to my phone buzzing on my nightstand. The name on the screen makes me groan.

When I tell Victor why I haven't seen Arella for five days, the truth isn't acceptable. Apparently, I need to drop everything in my life, including my "dead-end career," and dedicate myself to this mission until it's finished. He's delusional if he thinks I'm gonna do that. Finishing my parents' mission is important, but my band is important too. I can't just drop them.

"Tell me you have something of value." Victor growls into my ear. "Something that can give us a direction."

"Not yet," I lie.

"Wow, you really are useless." *Click.*

Victor can call me whatever he wants, but without a clear answer as to why or how Arella's parents died the same night mine did, I'm not telling him about it. The last thing I need is another reason for him to hound me, when besides that, all I know is what Victor told me when he assigned me this mission.

"Before your parents were killed," he said, "they were working on discovering how some rare Ordinaries could be immune to Zordi powers. They pretended to be part of the government and told the research subjects they were needed for a top-secret medical study.

"Every week, the subjects would come to Shadow Ridge to be analyzed, and ZIRDA paid them well for their time—until one day, the Royals found out about the Immunes project and tried to take it over.

"They stormed my house, demanding that I take them to ZIRDA California's hideout. And when I refused, they sliced my throat and left me for dead."

Since missions aren't to be spoken about between agents, Victor doesn't know anything else beyond that. At least, that's what he said. I wouldn't be surprised if he's keeping vital information from me.

Either way, I've come up with my own theory. My explanation for Arella and her parents being near Shadow Ridge that night is that three-year-old Arella—I mean *Hannah* —was one of my parents' research subjects. Maybe my parents were about to meet with them to take them to the base when Arella's parents got attacked by the Royals. I'd bet anything the Royals killed the Calders so they could take Hannah for themselves. Then somehow, my parents were able to save Hannah and get her somewhere safe.

I have a feeling that the same Royals who sliced Victor's throat are the ones who came crashing into my home, probably looking for Hannah. That would also explain how my mom's lip and my dad's face got slashed so badly—a sight I have yet to forget.

While this is a possible theory, I'm missing significant pieces to the puzzle. Like, how did the Royals find out about the Immunes project? Were there moles back then like the ones Victor discovered recently? Is that how they knew Victor was a ZIRDA agent and where he lived? Is that how they knew where my parents lived, too?

Also, how did my parents know where and when the

Royals were attacking Arella's parents? And if Arella was one of my parents' research subjects, does Victor know that the little girl back then is the same one he found and assigned me to? If so, why wouldn't he tell me that? Most importantly, why would my parents leave the house that night feeling anxious if they thought they were simply meeting with Arella's parents for another research session?

There's too much here that doesn't add up, and sadly, the person this entire thing revolves around seems to know the least. Based on the way she talks about it, Arella thinks her parents' car accident was exactly that—a car accident. She has no reason to think otherwise.

Do her grandparents know the truth? If my theory is correct, the ZIRDA agent who delivered Arella to her grandparents probably said nothing more than "Her parents were found in a car wreck at the bottom of a cliff, but this little girl survived." If that's the case, why is Hannah's name now Arella? And why would her grandparents move her around California annually if it wasn't to make her harder to find?

Her grandparents have to know something, which is why the next phase of my mission is to get Arella to introduce me to them. Maybe the more I know about them, the more answers I'll have.

It's just past noon when my phone buzzes again. I haven't eaten or done much beyond lie on my couch, trying to decipher my thoughts. My phone flashes with a picture of Jess. I almost let it go to voicemail but don't because I don't want her to take my silence as an invitation to show up.

"Happy Fourth!" Jess says. "You wanna get lunch?"

"Can't. Busy."

She snorts. "Doin' what?"

"Workin' on stuff." I'm playing with a little stress ball, throwing it into the air and catching it with my telekinesis before it lands on my face. The goal is to stop the ball as close to my nose as possible without the ball actually touching me. *Real important stuff.*

"Take a break."

"Can't. I've got a lot of work to do." I throw the ball up and stop it with my Kinetic power about a fingertip from my nose. *Eh. I can do better.*

"You really can't take off, like, a half hour? Not even for me?"

I know what that means, and I'm not interested. I'm not dating Arella for real, but having another woman over just to fuck still feels weird. Besides, I'm in the middle of trying to figure out a gift to get for Arella.

Earlier, Victor suggested that, to speed things up, I should shower Arella with gifts. The only problem is that I don't think she's easily impressed by material things. If I'm gonna get her something, which I fully intend to, it has to be something meaningful to her. I just don't know what that would be.

Jess isn't used to hearing *no* from me. After I keep denying her, she calls me nasty names and hangs up. I think about texting her that I'm sorry, but it'd be a lie. She's not my priority right now. Arella is.

The rest of the afternoon drags on. By the time I've thrown the stress ball into the air another hundred times, I still don't know what Arella's perfect gift is. I think about asking Liz for advice, then realize it's a dumb idea.

If Arella was a Zordi, Liz would probably have the perfect suggestion. Because Arella's an Ordinary, the only advice Liz'll give me is that I need to quit before Arella gets hurt. Little does Liz know, I don't plan on hurting this woman. When the time comes, I'll get *her* to break up with *me*. Problem solved.

I'm still thinking about a gift idea as I pull up to Arella's apartment. When she steps out of her home, I hop out of my car to greet her properly. Before she can say anything, I scoop her up, press her back against my car, and plant a heavy kiss over her lips. It's a full minute before I release her.

"Your kisses are getting addicting," I pant.

She's got a dazed expression as she responds with a breathy "Yours are too."

"You didn't stiffen up when I lifted you."

Her brows crumple together as she thinks. A second later, she leans back, and her eyes light up. "Wow. I didn't."

Gently, I pull her in for a hug. "You're so strong; you know that?"

Besides Liz, Arella is the strongest woman I know. For three years, a weak man stole that strength from her. It took a lot of courage for her to walk away, and not only did she do that, but she was brave enough to fight back.

On the night I kicked her ex's ass, she told me she used to always fight back until doing so only made him hit her harder. Eventually, she learned that taking it resulted in less bruises. I'm glad that she's finally done with his shit. Now she can live her life the way she wants. If only I could find the strength to fight my battles the way she has.

Beautiful waves of red and orange paint the sky as Arella and I arrive at the park. Vehicles of all colors and sizes are scattered around the lot. We find a parking spot toward the back; then I cut the engine.

"Babe . . ." I say, placing a hand over her knee. She doesn't flinch, and it makes my insides throw confetti into the air. "I'd like to leave before the fireworks start. Is that okay?"

"What? Aren't fireworks, like, the main part of a July Fourth party?"

I swallow hard and turn toward my window. "I guess."

"You don't like fireworks?"

It's not that I don't like them. I think they *look* cool. It's the bomb-like noises they make that I don't like.

"How 'bout I come back to pick you up after the

fireworks?” I say to the steering wheel. “That way, you can still see ’em.”

Arella’s tender hand cups my face. She trails light fingertips along my stubble before turning me to look at her. I go willingly. Her calming eyes and tender smile send a wave of comfort through me. It’s as if she has her own body power of easing my anxiety and it works by touching my face.

“I’ll be happy to leave with you, Trey.”

I place my hand over hers, pressing it harder against my cheek. I’m grateful that she didn’t ask for an explanation, because I’m not ready to give her one.

With Arella’s arm looped through mine, we join the party. Looming trees surround the park. A sand volleyball court already has a team on each side, with a ball in the air. Kids scream at the top of their lungs as they race around the playground. Most of the people are gathered at the pavilion where all the food is. More are down by the small pond, singing around a fire with Kevin on a guitar and Marcus on a box drum. The upbeat energy emitting from everyone lifts my spirits.

Arella and I head toward the pavilion where a couple of teenage boys are going through the buffet line. They pile food onto their plates as if they haven’t eaten in days.

I grab a beer from a cooler and hold it out to Arella. “Want one?”

“No, thanks.”

“How ’bout a hard lemonade?”

Between her fingers, she twists the ends of her hair. “I’ll just have a soda.”

I’m about to tell her that she should let loose and have fun when it hits me that I’ve never seen her drink alcohol. Not once during those four weeks I studied her. Not during these last few weeks since we’ve met, either.

I place the beer back into the cooler, then take her hand and give it a squeeze. “You don’t drink, do you?”

She doesn't pull her hand away. She doesn't squeeze my hand back either. "Not really."

"Sorry, babe. I didn't know." Which is stupid, because I'm supposed to know everything about this woman. How could I have missed this? What other details have I missed?

"That's okay. I never told you."

"Can I ask why you don't drink?" *Maybe this has something to do with her immunity . . .*

She keeps her eyes anywhere but on me as she, aggressively now, rubs more hair between her fingers. The distress on her face tells me all I need to know.

Instinctively, I pull her close and whisper into her ear, "I won't let him hurt you ever again."

She melts into me, circling her arms around my back. "He was always worse when he was drunk. Everything about it reminds me of him. Seeing it, tasting it, smelling it. Everything."

I know all about avoiding things that bring up bad memories. Alcohol to her is like fireworks to me.

After shutting the beer cooler, I open the one labeled NONALCOHOLIC, all while keeping Arella's fingers intertwined with mine. She plucks a Sprite off the top, and I grab one for myself too.

"Trey, you don't have to drink soda just because I am."

"Didn't you just say that the smell of alcohol makes you think of Pencil Dick?"

She nods slightly.

"Are you gonna make out with me later if I smell like beer?"

"Probably not, but—"

"Hey, if my choices are to taste you or some stupid beer, I'd rather have you."

I don't see it coming. She throws herself at me, kissing me like she's never kissed me before. Urgent, passionate, and needy. The Sprite slips from my hands. It falls, pops, and sprays everywhere, but I don't care. I need my hands free to take in as much of this woman as possible. Even with her breasts pressed up against my chest and my hands all over her back, she still isn't close enough.

Something hard hits my back, then thumps to the ground and rolls away. I don't let it stop me, because tonight is proof that I'm making progress. Arella initiated this kiss, and that's a huge step for her. I'm not planning to release her until she pulls back first.

My powers tell me that two people are approaching us from behind—probably the same people who just threw something at me. When the two stop at my heels, one of them clears their throat.

Only then does Arella draw back, and it takes a lot of willpower for me to let her. When I open my eyes, I find that hers have that dazed look again. Her flushed cheeks and plump lips are already begging for me to come back. *I will, baby. Later.*

Without looking, I already know who's behind me. No other two people would ever throw shit at me. I flip around to greet Liz and Emmy with a scowl.

"There are children here," Liz says, returning my scowl. Her dirty look has nothing to do with the kids. After her warning about getting caught with an Ordinary and how it could affect the band, it's probably not the smartest idea to kiss one in public. The Enforcers won't accept "This is all part of my top-secret ZIRDA mission" as a reason not to send me to z-prison. I'm fine though. Everyone in our crew is an Ordinary.

Emmy laughs, picking up a partly eaten apple off the ground. "Even my apple didn't stop him."

"Do you mind if we steal Ari from you, T?"

"Of course not." I need to show my face around the party before I dip out early, anyway. Having Arella at my side will force me to introduce her to everyone, and I'm pretty sure she would hate that. "Just make sure you feed her before you convert her to the dark side."

"We won't convert her into anything," Emmy says. "We're just gonna tell her all of your dirty little secrets."

I play along with her joke. With two fingers, I point at my eyes, then at my friends. "I'm watching you. If I catch my girl running outta here screaming, I'll—"

"Your girl?" Liz says, arching her eyebrows.

Arella gapes up at me with the same wide-eyed expression.

"What?" I feign innocence.

"Ari's *your girl* now?" Liz asks.

I nod confidently. "Yes, she is."

"I am?" Arella says, jerking her head back. Not the reaction I was hoping for.

Emmy chuckles, shoving me in the shoulder. "Most men *ask* the lady before they start telling people. Ya know, in case she declines."

I gaze into Arella's eyes. "What do you say, babe? You wanna be my girlfriend?"

Her cheeks fade to a light pink. "Um, I . . . I'll think about it."

My mouth drops. In my head, I shout some F-words to the sky. I thought for sure that if I asked her in front of Liz, she'd not only say yes but it'd help her feel better about Liz being my best friend. *Guess I was wrong.*

Arella's lips curve upward into a smile that she was holding back. "It's way too easy to mess with you."

I slap a hand over my chest, letting out a breath of relief. "Don't do that to me."

The women laugh, and it eases my tension.

"So, is that a yes?" I ask, because I need verbal confirmation.

Arella pretends to think for a second before grinning up at me. "Yeah. I'd love to be *your girl.*"

Disappointment slams into my gut from Liz's direction. In

the corner of my eye, she huffs out a frustrated breath and shakes her head slightly. Maybe one day, I'll be able to explain to her why I'm doing this. Why I'm risking going to z-prison. Why, one day, hopefully soon, I'll be able to stop the Royals from hurting more people like me.

22

TREY

I wanted to make things "official" with Arella because I thought it'd be a good reason for her to introduce me to her grandparents.

I was wrong.

It's been over a week, and every time I mention the possibility of us paying her family a visit, she says things like "It's too early for that" or "They're traveling right now."

I call bullshit. I think there's a family secret she's afraid I'll uncover, and it'll be the exact answers I'm looking for—answers that Victor won't stop hounding me about. He calls every other day to check in—or should I say to give me shit for being "worthless." He thinks I'm going too slow.

Sadly, he's right. I'm not utilizing my time well enough. If I keep going days between seeing Arella, it'll take me forever to finish this. That's why, for the last week and a half, I've made it a point to see her every single day, even if it's only for an hour. Either I drop by for breakfast in the morning before she heads to work or she meets up with me at the Soul House whenever she gets off.

So far, it's been working. I can feel her trust in me growing with each lingering hug, each prolonged kiss, and each time she lets me touch her somewhere new. I haven't seen her naked yet, and although I crave to, I don't push her. The last thing I want is to ruin all the progress I've made just because I wanna get my dick wet.

Yeah, this is the slowest I've ever gone with a woman. And yeah, the blue balls every night is torture. But in the end, when she trusts me enough to tell me everything about herself, it'll be worth it.

I've got two things with me when I arrive at Arella's apartment on Sunday evening: a backpack full of goodies and an extra helmet. I'm in the middle of admiring the beautiful sunset when she steps out, looking like a fucking snack. It takes everything in me not to drag her back inside and lick every inch of her delicious skin.

Instead, I take her in by the waist and spin her around before I plant my mouth over hers. Once I've had my fill of her lips, I hand her the extra helmet. *Her* helmet. The one I purchased today in her size, just for this. I help her strap it on, and she looks so adorable in it that I kiss her again.

When I let her go, I hand her the backpack.

She slides her arms through the straps. "It's heavy. What's in here?"

"Stuff."

"For what?"

I mount my bike, then gesture for her to hop on. "Stargazing."

"Oh!" A bright smile spreads across her face. "Where?"

"Uh, I haven't figured that part out yet. I thought we'd ride away from the city until we find a place that's secluded enough."

She perks up. "I know a place."

"You do?"

"Yeah, it's about an hour and a half away though."

"Perfect. Let's go."

The sun is almost gone by the time Arella tells me to park my bike on the side of a gravel road. When she said this place was secluded, she wasn't lying. I haven't seen another car in a while.

In my head, the low hum of other people's emotions is gone. A place like this is hard to find in California. I'm impressed.

I cut my Harley's engine, and the air goes still. Crickets chirp around us.

"I usually park my car right here," Arella says as she dismounts the motorcycle.

"Where is *here*, exactly?" I lift my helmet off, then a light breeze blows through my hair.

"You'll see."

We hang our helmets on the handlebars, then I steal the backpack from Arella so she doesn't have to carry it. From the side pocket, I pluck out a flashlight—another thing I bought today because I'd probably scare Arella off if I whipped out a fireball.

With my Ordinary torch in one hand and my girl in the other, I let her lead me down the ditch, then back up through some trees.

We hike through the woods for a while. It's a beautiful night. The air feels warm against my skin, and I can already see some stars above. I couldn't have asked for anything better.

Eventually, Arella leads me to a trail . . . sort of. It's more like a path of dirt, barely wide enough for one person. Our hands let go, and I offer her the flashlight, then follow her up the steep hill.

I duck under a tree branch. "This seems like a place where you'd take someone to kill 'em."

"Relax. I've only ever killed two people here. The third one got away."

A dry stick cracks beneath my feet as I stop to gape at her.

Giggling, she turns around and grabs my arm. "I'm kidding. Now, come on! We're almost there."

A few minutes later, we're out of the woods and the ground levels out into a grassy meadow. In the middle of it, slightly to the left, is a lone oak tree. The breeze is a little stronger up here, and it smells of ripe nature.

I follow Arella to the oak, then we stop under all of its long branches. Dark green leaves stretch out in all directions like an umbrella protecting us from whatever may fall from the darkening sky.

Arella opens her arms out wide and does a spin. "Welcome to my *thinking spot*."

"I like it." My backpack drops to the grass with a thump. "How did you find this place?"

"I found it by accident. Sometimes when Nathan—"

"Pencil Dick."

She laughs and rolls her eyes. "Yes, him. Sometimes when we got into a fight, I'd go for a drive. One night, I ended up here. I liked the atmosphere and the quiet. Later, I started coming back whenever our fights got really bad, because you know . . . he couldn't find me here."

With a hand splayed over the small of her back, I pull her toward me until her entire body is flush against mine. Tenderly, I place a little kiss on her forehead. I don't know why. I just feel the need to comfort her.

"He hasn't been coming around or contacting you at all, has he?"

She shakes her head.

"You'd tell me if he does, right?"

"You'd be the first to know."

"Good." I have a strong feeling that Nathan's out of her life now. That night, after Arella convinced me not to call the cops, I needed insurance that he'd stay away. Taking pictures of him with the words I ASSAULT WOMEN written across his body was my way of gaining that insurance. I made it clear that if he ever as much as looked at her again, I would post the pictures everywhere for the world to see.

From the backpack, I yank out a violet blanket. I spread it out under the tree, then bring out the meats, cheeses, crackers, and water bottles. Then I sit and pat the empty space next to me.

Arella smiles down at me. "You're adorable, you know that?"

"Hmm. Can't say I've ever been called that before."

"Well, it's true." She sits and helps me unwrap our snacks. "You come up with the most romantic things for us to do."

"I wish I could take the credit, but this was another idea I stole from Professor Google."

"What did you type in?"

"Um." I clear my throat as I tell her the truth. "Romantic things to do with a pretty girl."

"Really?" She laughs, and it sends a spark through my chest. I like hearing her laugh and seeing it too. Since I can't sense her happiness, seeing it is important.

"Yeah, really." I run my palm across the blanket. "This is for you, by the way. I bought it for you 'cause you're always cold at my house. You can leave it there to keep you warm."

Her bottom lip puckers out into a pout. "But I like wearing your hoodie."

"Oh! That reminds me." I dig toward the bottom of the backpack to find my black hoodie. The one Arella has been wearing every time she comes over. The one she looks irresistible in. "This is for you too."

Her eyes widen as she accepts it. "To keep?"

"Yep. I figured since you like it so much, you should just wear it all the time."

She lunges at me. Her kiss is quick—too quick. When she draws back, my hands instinctively reach for her. She comes willingly, and I get to kiss her for a little longer. I could probably kiss her all night.

Sometimes, it's hard for me to let her go. A few nights ago, when she came to my place and we were up talking past two in the morning, I almost asked her to stay the night. The only reason I didn't was because I had a feeling she wasn't ready for that step yet, and I didn't want to make her feel obligated to stay.

"Thank you, Trey," she says when I finally release her lips. "I love them both. Your hoodie more, but I love the blanket too."

It took me a while to decide on a good gift for her. I had already bought her this blanket when I realized that the perfect gift had been in my house the whole time. My goal was to give Arella something that would be meaningful to her. Based on her reaction, I'm gonna say I nailed it.

To Victor's knowledge, I bought Arella an expensive bracelet. He thinks I gave it to her last week and that she loved it so much, she cried. I'm glad I went with my hoodie instead, because I doubt a stupid bracelet would have elicited such a happy reaction from her.

We talk easily while we munch on our cheese and crackers. With passion, Arella tells me about her dream bakery. Everything from the paint color on the walls to what kinds of sugary treats she wants to have on display. It doesn't take long for me to get lost in the sound of her voice. It's so soft and sweet. She could be talking about a bloody massacre, and it would still sound like a lullaby to me.

Eventually, we finish snacking and find other things to do with our mouths. Mine starts at her lips before it maneuvers down her neck and behind her ear. She lets out breathy moans as I travel down her chest.

Panting against her cleavage, I ask, "Can I take your shirt off?"

I expect her to say *no* like she has every time I ask. Instead, she surprises me by nodding and lifting her arms up. My heart thrashes against my ribs as I drag her little shirt over her head and toss it behind me.

I barely have time to admire her lacy white bra before she climbs on top of me, straddling my lap. I feel like her prisoner. She's captured me, and I can't escape. I don't even want to.

My hands grip her plump ass as I jerk her body closer to me. With a grunt, I press my stiff cock against her inner thigh. She lets out a sexy moan that makes my arms go weak.

Our breaths are heavy as I pepper kisses along her collarbone. When she arches her head back, I take the hint. I nip, suck, and bite at every inch of her neck until I'm ready to go back to her lips.

When our mouths meet again, it feels like coming home. This is where my lips are supposed to be. Kissing her forehead is great, her neck is like heaven, and I love kissing her everywhere else, but *this* . . . This right here. This is where it's at.

With a finger, I pull the strap of her bra down her shoulder. When she doesn't stop me, I leave home to trail kisses down her chest. I suck a little bit of her cleavage into my mouth and wait for her to tell me *no*. Hope sparks inside me when she doesn't.

"Babe?" I say like a plea.

"Mm?" she moans.

"Stop me."

She shakes her head as she whispers, "I don't want to."

At that, my cock hardens so much, it's painful. Within a flash, I've got her breast out and her nipple in my mouth. She gasps as she arches her head back and grips my hair. While I suck on one nipple, I roll the other between my fingertips. It drives her insane. I know not because I sense it but because she writhes on top of me.

Before tonight, I thought the reason I always have great sex is because I can feel the woman's pleasure on top of my own. It never occurred to me that someday, I'd be going to second base with a woman I can't sense at all. If someone had asked me if I thought it'd be as good, I would have said *no*.

And I would have been wrong.

All I've done is touch and kiss Arella, and now I'm sucking on her breasts for the first time, and it already feels better than sex with any woman I've ever been with.

My fingertips graze against the button of her jeans for only a second before she grabs my wrist. I take that as a sign that I've reached her limit. Instead of tearing her pants off the way I want to, I fist her hair, yank her head back, and return to sucking on her neck.

It takes a lot of willpower, but eventually, I find Arella's shirt in the grass and help her put it back on. With a hand behind my head, I lie back on the blanket and motion for her to join me. Naturally, she rests her head over my shoulder, and I pull her close until there isn't a sliver of space between us.

For a long time, neither of us says anything. I appreciate the way we can be with each other and not have to fill the silence. Usually, quietness irks me because I hate being alone with my thoughts, but whenever I'm with Arella, my thoughts aren't that hard to handle. They aren't dark or depressing or what Liz calls self-degrading. When I'm with Arella, my thoughts are about her, which are light and cheerful.

I listen to the sounds of her easy breaths as I stare up at the black sky, where a few stars are shining. *Would my parents have liked Arella?* I bet they would have, only because there's nothing about her not to like. She's kind, beautiful, and she's got a great sense of humor. Her immunity is just the cherry on top of all that.

Suddenly, it hits me how special this moment is. For the first time ever, I'm alone in my head—and someone is right here! To be truly alone, I typically have to travel to my secluded cabin in Colorado. When Elliott died, I hid there for a month.

When I finally came back, I explained to a furious Liz that I had disappeared because I'd needed to clear my head. Getting everyone else out of it is the only way to do that. Yeah, it's lonely, but until now, I've never had another choice. Never did I imagine that it'd be possible to have a clear head minus the loneliness. Arella has made that possible. Here she is, cuddled in my arms, and the only emotions I feel are my own. It's amazing!

Now I'm more in awe of her than ever. She's so fucking special, and she doesn't even know it. Leaning down, I plant a hard kiss against her temple, but it's not nearly enough to fully express how much I enjoy being here with her. I wish I could tell her with words, but I don't know how. Not that I could explain it to her anyway. I'd have to tell her that I have an ability she doesn't know exists.

I kiss her temple again, harder this time, because I want to show her how grateful I am for her. I hope she can feel my gratitude through my lips.

"What're you thinking about?" she asks softly as she continues caressing little figure eights over my abs.

It takes me a second to gather myself with all the overwhelming fluttery thoughts I'm having. "You. I think my parents would have liked you."

"You think so?"

"Yeah. They probably would have loved to hang out here with us, too. When I was little, my parents took me hiking a lot. Our favorite spot was near this small town a few hours south of LA. We'd hike to this big rock, and they'd bring snacks like I brought for you tonight. The three of us would lay out on a blanket under the stars, just talking."

"That sounds wonderful. My grandparents never took me hiking. They like to do more indoor things."

"Like meet your new boyfriend? That's indoors."

She chuckles, and I'm not fond of how it comes out with a

hint of annoyance. With a deep sigh, she pushes herself up and sits with her legs in a pretzel.

"What?" I say and follow suit. My body feels a little cold where hers used to be.

"Nothing. I just feel like you're obsessed with meeting my grandparents. That's the third time you've brought it up this week."

"You're counting?"

She ignores my question. "What's up with you wanting to meet them so bad?"

"What's up with you *not* wanting me to meet them?"

"Like I said before, I think it's too early for that."

"Did Nathan get to meet them?"

She nods.

"How long did he have to wait?"

"About six months."

Six months? I don't have time for that.

"And," Arella continues, "I didn't introduce him to my grandparents until I felt like he and I had really connected, like on a level deeper than just two people dating. I don't think you and I are there yet."

"Okay . . . How can we get there?" *And fast . . .* I'm running low on time, and Victor's running out of patience—that is, if he had any at all.

She lets out a small laugh and shakes her head. "That's not how it works, Trey. A deep relationship takes time."

"How will I know when we've reached that point?"

"I think you'll just know."

Playfully, I narrow my eyes at her. "You're giving me too much credit, babe. I'm clueless about this stuff, remember? You're gonna have to give me more details. Like . . . what will it look like?"

"What does a deep relationship look like?" She shrugs and thinks. "I suppose the biggest factor is that we'll be in love."

"In love?" Just saying that word out loud makes my throat

dry. *Me? In love?* Is that possible? Probably, but not with an Ordinary. I could pretend though. "What does being in love look like?"

"You've never been in love?"

"Don't think so." I have an idea of what it looks like from hanging around Marcus and Emmy. They're always touchy-feely with each other, and they do everything together. Whenever one walks into the room, I sense the other's happiness spike upward. I assume that means they're in love.

"Love looks different between everyone, but I think the one thing that's constant is what my grammy always tells me. She says that when you love someone, you put their happiness before your own."

I think about that for a moment, racking my brain for anyone I've ever felt that way about. Sadly, I can't think of anyone. Even sadder, no one has ever felt that way for me. At least, not romantically.

I know my parents loved me—before they were murdered.

Victor *used to* love me. Maybe he still does . . . in his own sick, twisted way. If he ever verbalized it now, I'd be certain he's been replaced by a Shifter or a Mind Swapper.

I think I loved Elliott. Why else would I have taken his death so hard? I would have done anything to protect that child or to have saved him from the cancer.

Now that I think about it, I think I love Liz. I one hundred percent would put her happiness before mine, but I don't think the way I feel about her is the same kind of love Arella's talking about.

"How do you know the difference between regular love and romantic love? Like, I think I love Liz, but I don't wanna make out with her. At the same time, I'd do anything to make that woman happy."

Arella purses her lips together in thought. "My grandpa says that he knew he loved my grandma when, one day, he looked at her and couldn't picture the rest of his life without her."

"Hmm. If that's the case, then I might love Liz romantically. I can't imagine my life without her. Who will be there to yell at me for making dumb decisions?"

Arella bursts into a light chuckle. "Maybe if you stop making dumb decisions, she won't have to yell at you."

"That's impossible. I'm a man. It's what we do." I'm glad that Arella didn't take my loving Liz romantically comment seriously. I only said it to be funny.

"You don't have to be *romantically* in love with someone to want them around for the rest of your life. You can feel that way about Liz and still love her as a friend."

"Good, 'cause that's exactly how I feel about her."

Between a few fingers, Arella plucks a blade of grass and plays with it. Without looking up at me, she asks, "Do you ever think that Liz is secretly in love with you? Like, as more than a friend?"

Confidently, I shake my head. "Never."

"How are you so sure?"

"Trust me, baby. I, of all people, am sure." I can sense the way Liz feels about me, and it's never anything close to the way Marcus and Emmy feel about each other. Unfortunately, I can't tell Arella that.

"Then how can you say that you don't know what a deep relationship looks like, when it's exactly what you have with Liz?"

Good point. "I guess I didn't think about my relationship with Liz being that deep until now."

"How did you guys build such a strong connection?"

I know exactly how. Liz brings it up all the time. She even knows the exact date and calls it our friendiversary. It was the day our hands first touched. The day we shared about our pasts.

Would sharing about my past with Arella get her to share

everything about herself with me? Possibly, and I'm willing to do that . . . *I think.* Maybe I don't have to share every little detail, but I could tell her that my parents didn't actually die in a house fire.

An idea pops into my head, and suddenly, I'm ready to leave.

I toss our stuff back into my backpack. "Let's go, babe. I need to show you something."

23

TREY

It's well past midnight when we finally arrive at my place. On my bed, Arella's next to me wearing my hoodie—her hoodie now. Her new blanket is draped over her lap, keeping her legs warm. Between us, I have my most valuable possession: a shoebox-size wooden box.

"Please tell me there aren't any human body parts in there," Arella says.

I laugh a little. How does she know exactly what to say to ease the tension in my gut?

I've never shown this box to anyone before. My heart thrashes because I'm about to now. "Why would you think I'd keep body parts in a box?"

"I watch a lot of true crime shows with Javina. A big wooden box with a lock? Total grounds for a collection of eyeballs."

I make an *ick* face. "Gross, babe. No, I don't have any eyeballs in here."

"Wonderful. In that case, please proceed with showing me what's in this mysterious box."

I suck in a deep breath before sticking a little metal key

into the lock. With a twist, it opens, and I flip the lid. The first thing I pull out is a small framed picture.

Arella takes the scorched item as I hand it to her. "Are these your parents?"

"Yep, and that's me when I was four." I point at the little blonde boy with the shit-eating grin on his face. "This was the only picture I was able to recover from the fire. It was saved by this heavy-duty frame."

"You were adorable! I mean, you still are, just with darker hair. And you look exactly like your father."

"Everyone said that." The next thing I pull out is a small chain with a circle pendant hanging from it. On the pendant are three birthstones. "This was my mom's necklace."

"Do these colors represent you and your parents?"

"Yep." Next, I pick up a worn baseball. "I found this in the backyard the morning after they died. My dad and I went to baseball games pretty often. Whenever we played catch in the yard, he'd tell me that I'd play for the Dodgers someday."

"Do you think about them a lot?"

"Occasionally." *An understatement.* I think about my parents all the time.

Whenever I see people at the grocery store with their kids, I think about how my parents used to let me pick out what we got for dinner. The three of us would cook it all up, even if it didn't go together.

I usually think of my mom whenever I see flowers. She used to always have a vase of freshly cut ones sitting on the dining table.

Yesterday, I saw a kid with his dad in a big blue truck, jamming out to music while they played the air drums. My dad and I did that plenty. He's part of the reason why I love music so much.

My heart aches the more I think about my parents. This is usually when I distract myself with sex or music. Before Liz encouraged me to be sober, this was also when I'd get high. Thanks to her, now, I just live through the pain.

From the box, Arella grabs a small wad of cash paperclipped together. "What's up with this?"

I take it from her and slide the paperclip off. A ten, two fives, and four ones. "Twenty-four dollars. Back then, this used to be a lot to me."

"I thought you said your parents left you everything they had."

"They did, but my uncle didn't share that information with me until I turned eighteen. At first, I was ecstatic that my parents left me with money. Then, after reading through the paperwork, I learned that I could have been using it the whole time. My uncle purposely hid it from me."

Arella's face crumples. "Why?"

"Because he's a dick. When I first moved in with him, all I had were the things in this box and the clothes on my back. He provided me with two shirts, two pairs of pants, some underwear, and that was it.

"I went to school rotating through those same three outfits. Eventually, the other kids noticed, and that's when the fights started. I begged my uncle over and over to buy me more clothes, but he never did.

"Ultimately, I did what I could to make my own money. When I wasn't in school, I was with him at work. He ran a big business with lots of employees. I did small jobs for them around the office, like making coffee or cleaning their shoes. I'd earn a few quarters here and there. Depending on the job, sometimes they'd pay me a whole dollar. Eventually, I saved up enough cash to make a trip to a store.

"I was so excited to buy myself a new shirt, pants, and socks. I still remember how the cashier looked at me funny, and I don't blame her. I was an eight-year-old boy shopping by himself. I told her that my uncle was just down the road at a different store. Eventually, he noticed that I was wearing new clothes. When I told him I bought them myself, he didn't believe me. I was beaten that night for lying."

Arella's eyes water, and she uses the sleeve of her hoodie to wipe the tear away. I debate on ending the story there but feel the need to finish it.

"I didn't tell my uncle that his employees had been paying me to do stuff for them. I knew he wouldn't like it and would make me stop. Somehow, he found out and threatened to fire anyone who continued to pay me. Not only that, but he took what cash I had at the time and forced me to burn it."

The memory of that night flashes across my mind. Victor slapped my face and yelled at me until I did what he demanded. A fireball appeared in my palm, and I threw it at all my hard-earned cash. I cried as I watched it burn until every last flame had flickered out. I think it was only fifty-some dollars, but at the time, that could have been new shoes.

Arella places a hand over her chest as another tear rolls down her face. Usually, crying makes me uncomfortable. With Arella, all I want is to comfort her, so I take her hand in mine and kiss her knuckles.

She wipes at her damp face with her other hand, then squeezes mine in a way that offers me comfort back. "I'm so sorry that happened to you."

"Don't sweat it, babe. It turned out okay. In the end, I actually made more money. It'd been going on for so long that his employees were kinda dependent on me to do things for them. They got sneakier about paying me. Some of them even tipped me more because they heard about what my uncle did and felt bad."

"Weren't they afraid of getting fired?"

"Nah. If he was gonna fire one, he'd have to fire 'em all. I had a hand in almost every department. Everything from cleaning bathrooms to hauling boxes around to bringing people lunch."

She gives my hand another comforting squeeze. "I can't believe your uncle treated you that way."

"That's not even the half of it."

"Would you like to tell me more?"

Surprisingly, I do. Sharing deep stuff isn't easy for me usually, but with Arella, it's not only easy, it's soothing. I like how she listens without pity in her eyes. I hate when people look at me like that. I don't want pity. I want what Arella and Liz have given me—understanding. Except, Arella's version of it feels different. She doesn't look at me like I'm damaged the way Liz does.

"I would like to tell you one more thing." I've never said what I'm about to say out loud before. Liz only knows through seeing my memory. If it wasn't for that, she wouldn't know anything.

Do I really want to do this? I only think for a second before coming to the conclusion that yes, I do. I *need* to. If I share this piece of myself with Arella, maybe she'll want to share pieces of herself with me. *I can do this.*

"My parents didn't die in a house fire." The second those words leave my mouth, I almost wish for them to come back.

Arella cocks her head to the side. "What do you mean?"

"I just tell people that because it's easier than explaining the truth."

"Which is?"

"They were . . . murdered." That last word comes out cracked and broken. "And—I . . . I saw it happen."

"What?"

"I was home when . . . you know, the people came. They blew up my house with my parents still in it. I only survived because my dad threw me out the window just before the explosion."

Arella's warm hand cups my stubbly cheek. Like it has before, her gentle touch eases the pain. I press my hand over hers to make sure she doesn't pull away. I'm not ready for her to yet.

"Sometimes," I whisper, "I wonder how things would have turned out if I had done something to save them."

"You can't blame yourself, honey."

I don't . . . much. Mostly, I blame the Royals, which is why I'm working so hard on this mission.

Wait . . . Did she just call me *honey*? She's never called me a pet name before. I like the sound of it. It's the same name my mother used to call me.

With her fingertips, Arella caresses the spot behind my ear. No one's ever touched me like this before. So comforting and nontransactional. "Now I understand why you don't like fireworks."

"Yep. Hate 'em."

"Maybe this is a weird question, but why would someone want to harm your parents?"

"I dunno." It's not entirely a lie. I have theories, but nothing's confirmed. I've already accepted that I may never know.

"Can I see the rest of your box?" Arella asks.

With a nod, I draw out the last few items. Everything is either half-burned or got lucky in the explosion. My dad's green tie, a piece of my mom's floral dress, a chunk of her favorite vase, and my old teddy bear.

This is the luckiest stuffed animal in the world. It was on the couch when my dad threw me on it and tossed me out the window. Besides getting drenched in the rain, it never saw damage. "This is Andy."

Arella takes the bear from me and pets the top of its head. "He doesn't look like he was used much."

"He wasn't. I've barely touched him since I threw him into this box."

She squeezes the bear's paws. "Does it sing or anything?"

"Nah, it's just a regular ol'—"

Something mechanical clicks. A robotic voice comes out of nowhere. "Password?"

Arella perks up. "Oh, it talks!"

"What?" I snatch the bear from her and crush it against my ear. The bear goes silent. Frantically, I press the bear's stomach, willing it to speak again. "How did you do that?"

"Incorrect password," the bear says, making my heart pound.

Arella shrugs. "I just felt something hard inside and pressed it."

I shove the bear back into her hands. "Do it again."

After giving me a sideways glance, she presses on the bear all over. It takes her a moment to find the sweet spot again. When she does, something clicks, and that same robotic voice chimes. "Password?"

"Uh, Trey Grant," I say.

"Incorrect password."

Arella eyes me through a skeptical gaze. "You didn't know it did that?"

"No." Hastily, I toss everything back into the wooden box and lock it up. My chest is heavy, and my lungs feel tight. I can barely breathe as I say, "Let's get you home."

***

After dropping Arella off with a promise to see her in the morning, I'm back in my bedroom, staring at my old teddy bear. I've got a kitchen knife in my hands, hovering over the stuffed animal like I'm about to perform surgery.

"Sorry, Andy."

Carefully, I slice into the bear's back. White stuffing spills out of the hole. I dig most of it out before finding a black button-shaped object. I press it.

"Password?"

"Trey Andrew Grant," I say in a clear, crisp voice.

"Incorrect password."

I press the button again. "Andrew James Grant."

"Incorrect password."

"Suzie Marie Grant."

"Incorrect password."

Dammit.

It had to have been my parents who hid this device inside my bear. What password would they have chosen?

I try my birthdate in every combination I can think of. I try their wedding date. Our old home phone number. The name of my pet fish who died in the explosion. The name of my bear. Nothing works.

Defeated, I sink to the floor. *What could it be?*

An hour passes before Arella's words echo in my head. *"Does it sing or anything?"*

That's it! It seems obvious now that I think about it. My mom's song. The one she wrote just for me. The one I occasionally sing to myself whenever I'm sad. That's gotta be it.

I press the button again.

"Password?"

I sing each word clearly, "When you're lost without me, you'll always have Andy. When you feel you don't belong, hug this bear and sing this song. Look to the sky when you feel down. Know that things will turn around. Work twice as hard to the finish line. Now it's your time to shine."

I expect the device to reject me again. This time, my mother speaks.

"Hi, honey." I've forgotten what her voice sounds like. Hearing it makes me choke up.

I shoot off the floor and shove the device against my ear.

"If you're listening to this, it's probably because our plan didn't go as planned and something bad has happened. You're most likely with Aunt Debbie right now. We told her that if anything were to happen to us that she should tell you to hug your bear really tight and sing our song."

The next voice is my father's. "Son, your mama and I wanted to make sure that you'd be safe and taken care of. That's why everything we have is now yours, including a safe house by our secret rock. Aunt Debbie is the only person you should trust, and the only person you should take with you."

The only person I should trust? Why is the only person I should trust a woman who overdosed on z-drugs the morning my parents were killed?

I still remember the first thing I said when I arrived at Shadow Ridge and a grumpy Victor showed me to my new bedroom. "Why can't I go live with Aunt Debbie?"

He laughed, then said something people shouldn't say to seven-year-olds. "That bitch was found dead in her home yesterday with a syringe still in her hands."

That was how I found out that I hadn't lost only my parents the day before but also my only aunt. It clicked then why Aunt Debbie hadn't come to babysit me when she was supposed to. How could she, when she was dead? As I've grown older, I've come to realize that Aunt Debbie's death probably wasn't an overdose.

My mother continues talking on the recording. "When you get to the rock, take a hundred steps away from Cheesy. There, you'll find the safe house. You're the only one who can get into it. Remember that Trackers can't sense you once you're inside and underground."

"Take care, son," my father says.

"And don't ever forget that we love you."

The recording stops.

I stare at the small device with my mouth open. *That's it?* Who leaves a message for a child that basically says, "Hey, we're dead. Here's some money and a safe house. The only person you can trust is also dead, but have a good time at our rock!"

What bullshit! I've got half a mind to toss this stupid thing at the wall. I don't, only because I'm afraid I'll break it.

My whole life, I thought my parents just happened to cross the wrong Royals at the wrong time. Now it's obvious that they knew the Royals were after them. Why else would they have prepared a safe house for me?

If they knew something would happen to them, why not run and take me with them? Why stay in the danger zone? Could finishing their mission really have been that important? More important than me, their son? They knew they were risking their lives, risking leaving me to grow up alone, and they went on anyway. *They abandoned me on purpose!*

I wipe away the one tear rolling down my cheek. After regaining my composure, I drag my phone out of my pocket and open the GPS app.

I can't recall the exact town my parents used to take me to stargaze. It's been so long. All I remember is that it was a town named after a person with a name starting with a J. My parents used to make up stories about whoever it was named after, saying they were probably a janitor, or a journalist, or a jewelry maker.

Now that I think about it, maybe my parents made up stories on purpose to help my young mind remember the right town. If that's the case, that means they were putting things into place for over a year to keep me safe. Which would have been plenty of time for them to pack up and move away with me if they'd wanted to.

I scan the GPS for any J-named towns in California. Was it Jason? Jacob? Julie? Once I catch sight of the town Julian on the map, it clicks. Within a minute, I've got my helmet on and I'm mounting my bike.

Three hours later, my headlight illuminates a green sign that reads JULIAN 1 MILE.

It's been almost nineteen years since I've been around this

area. Everything looks the same. Quiet roads, quieter woods, mountain peaks in the distance.

Just before the main town is a single-lane road that leads me to the woods where my parents used to take me. I recognize the spot where we used to park the car. My mother would always say we had to park by the huge Y-shaped tree. Now I'm certain she made those comments on purpose. There's no way in hell a seven-year-old would have remembered where any of this was without her repetitive hints.

I cut my engine, then slide off my bike. After making sure no one's around, I wave a hand at my Harley. It floats through the air at my side as I step into the dark woods. Once the road is out of view, I leave my bike and helmet behind a cluster of trees.

With a little fireball hovering in front of me, I hike deeper through the woods. My ears catch sounds of small animals scurrying around, but they're gone before my eyes can spot them.

I step over a few fallen trees that I remember as bigger obstacles. My parents used to offer to lift me over them. Being the strong-willed kid I was, I insisted on climbing over them myself, without the help of a hover-log.

It feels like forever before I reach the big rock—or should I say biggish rock. *Do I have the right one?* I wave a hand to push my fireball closer to it. Like the fallen trees, it looks smaller than I remember.

My flame follows me as I head in the direction of Cheesy. It's a tree I named for all the holes in its bark. I find it about six trees away from the rock.

"When you get to the rock, take a hundred steps away from Cheesy. There you'll find the safe house."

At the rock, with the holey tree behind me, I begin counting.

One. Two. Three.

Ninety-eight . . . ninety-nine . . . one hundred. I glance around. There's nothing here. It's just more trees, bushes, and dirt. *Where's the safe house?*

The message said something about it being underground. I spend some time scouring the area but don't find anything that would take me underground.

Maybe I should try again. Back at the rock, I count another hundred steps. This time, I take kid-size steps. I end up about twenty paces back from where I was before. It's the same story though. Nothing's here.

With a fireball floating nearby the whole time, I spend the next several hours combing the area. My efforts are useless.

I can't find what I'm looking for, and it doesn't help that I don't even know what I'm looking for. A tunnel? A hidden passageway? A trapdoor? How about a sign that reads SAFE HOUSE HERE with a big fat arrow?

24

TREY

I'M PRETTY SURE MY PARENTS HID THIS SO-CALLED SAFE HOUSE on another planet. I've gone back to Julian several times over the last two weeks. With all the holes I've dug, earth I've moved, and for as many times as I've stomped on the ground looking for a trapdoor, I haven't found anything that remotely suggests there's a safe house nearby.

I'm in the middle of doing research on underground living spaces when my phone buzzes. It's a text from Arella that makes my face contort.

> I'm not sure if you should come over today.
> I'm sick. 😟

What? Her daily texts usually start with "Good morning, honey!" and "Did you have sweet dreams?" Even though Zordis can't dream, I always say that I dreamt of her. Where are those texts?

> I'm coming over anyway.

> Are you sure? I have the flu. It's highly
> contagious.

Positive. I'll see you soon.

The Ordinary flu isn't gonna stop me from seeing my girl, especially not on a Sunday. I don't get to see Arella for long on Fridays or Saturdays due to the nature of my work. Last night, she, Javina, and Javina's girlfriend came out to my band's show. I got to see them during the meet and greet for a bit, but I didn't get to have Arella alone. Sundays are precious to me.

I've got grocery bags dangling from my arms as I knock on Arella's door. She answers in pajama shorts and a baggy hoodie—*my* hoodie. Seeing her in it will never get old.

"Morning, angel," I say with a smile. "I brought you stuff to make you feel better."

"Yay!" She props the door open for me to enter.

For a while there, I thought maybe she was using the sick thing as an excuse not to see me. Now that I've seen her smile, it's clear she secretly wanted me to come over.

I rush in and place the bags on her kitchen counter. Then I hurry to greet my girl properly. Taking her by the waist, I lean in to kiss her.

She turns away, covering her mouth with a palm. "I have the flu!"

"Does it look like I give two shits?" I peck her forehead, then leave her to unpack the bags.

For the rest of the day, I make her soup, and we keep busy with card games and movies. During the second movie, I get her down to her panties as I massage her back, and well . . . we end up doing other things.

Even with her stuffy nose, the way she moans as I suck her nipples makes my cock hard. She clenches her hands in my hair as I kiss my way down her belly. Because my shirt is somewhere on the floor, I get the pleasure of feeling her skin on mine.

She's been good about stopping me whenever she feels like we're going outside of her comfort zone. I've been good about not pressuring her. The second she says *stop*, I stop. It's not only because I don't want to ruin this mission by breaking her trust, either. I have this deep need to show her that a man can be good to her. Arella deserves to be treated like a queen, and I'm enjoying being the one to do it.

With a finger hooked through her panties, I slowly tug them down, waiting for her to stop me. Instead of grabbing my wrist like she has been, she pulls her legs out of the fabric. I don't let the shock stop me as I marvel at the sight of her fully naked for the first time. It takes everything in me to not collapse my mouth against her clit and lap my tongue over it right now. I don't, because I'm afraid that if I go too fast, she'll shut down. If I take things slowly, she'll have the opportunity to stop me if she wants to. *Hopefully, she doesn't want to.*

Tenderly, I kiss her inner thighs. She squirms and runs her fingers through my hair. I get harder as her nails dig into my scalp and I take two perfect handfuls of her breasts. Between my thumbs and index fingers, I roll her nipples around. She tells me she likes this by arching her head back with a sexy moan. I need to hear her make more of those sounds.

On my way up her thighs, I pepper lingering kisses until I reach what I'm after. I hover there for a second to see if she'll stop me. When she doesn't, I go for it. She gasps sharply when my mouth presses against her clit. At first, I go slow, taking in how soft she feels against my tongue. I go in circles, then side to side. Once she gets used to me, her body melts beneath me.

I wish I could sense her. I wish I could feel everything she's feeling right now. I want to know how good it is for her without having to focus on her moans and watch her every move. Without my gift, I'm constantly second-guessing myself.

I keep asking for verbal confirmation. "How's that, baby? Do you like it better like this? Want it harder?"

Her answers come out in breathy yeses and a guttural "Just keep going."

I do. I lick and suck her clit until she cries out my name,

and I watch her fall apart with a scream. I don't even know she's coming until I see it on her face. I've never not known before. Every time I've made a woman orgasm, I could always sense it building inside her.

Not sensing Arella's climax but seeing it happen is surprisingly still as hot. Maybe a little hotter, because now, I know I can do that to a woman without the help of my gift. Plus, it's Arella. She's the hottest woman I know. My mind can't even comprehend it because she's an Ordi. I shouldn't be this attracted to her, yet here I am, craving to kiss every part of her body.

Lately, Arella's been consuming my thoughts. She's the first thing I think of when I wake up and the last thing on my mind when I fall asleep. During the long boring hours when I'm not with her, I wish I were, and it's not because I *should* be for the mission. I just miss her company. Her presence eases me in ways I can't explain.

When I feel anxious, her touch settles it. If a bad memory creeps through my mind, her smile erases it. I always feel lonely in my big empty house, but when she's around, my house feels full and lively.

When I'm with her, I don't feel like I have to put on a show like I do with other people. I don't have to act tough or pretend like I know everything, because Arella's not the type who likes that shit. Around her, I can simply be me.

I told her that I saw my parents get blown up, and not once did she give me a look of pity. I like how she treats me like I'm strong instead of someone who needs to be fixed. I know I need fixing. Liz has made that clear. The difference is that Arella seems to be fixing me without making me feel like I'm broken. She's doing it simply by the way she laughs at my lame jokes and the way she spends time with me without expecting anything in return.

Not sex.

Not money.

Not a performance.

Not a "better version of me" that she knows "exists under the fistfights."

Arella just wants me, and that seems to be enough for her. I've never had that before.

"Your turn," she says, still panting from her climax.

I chuckle, then hop off the bed in search of my shirt. I find it on the floor across her bedroom and slip it over my head.

Arella dips her eyebrows at me. "What?"

"What, what?"

"I said it's your turn."

I give her a firm shake of my head. "Don't think so, babe."

"Why not?"

"Are you ready for me to be inside you?"

The way she hesitates tells me all I need to know. "We don't have to do that. I can just do to you what you did to me."

"Nope. Can't. Thanks for the offer though." I can't remember the last time I turned down a blow job—don't think I ever have.

She side-eyes me, smirking. "Are you afraid that I'll see how small you are and break up with you?"

I let out a loud *ha!* and laugh deep from my chest. "Is that what you think?"

"Why else would a man who's had a plethora of one-night stands refuse to let me into his pants three weeks into the relationship?"

Three weeks? Is that it? It feels like I've been with her longer. She's probably counting it from the night we made things official, not the day we met six weeks ago.

"Trust me, baby. I want nothing more than for your lips to be around my cock, but I can't because it won't be enough. I'll want to fuck you properly, which means you'll be sore and screaming my name. You're not ready for that yet, so it's better if we play it safe. I can take care of myself when I get home, where I won't be tempted to cross any lines."

She gets this look on her face that I don't recognize. It's a mix of astonishment and something else. Before I know it, she's got me pinned to the bed and is attacking me with kisses. I'm a willing victim.

A feeling of warmth and light fills my chest. The only word I can think of to describe it is *happiness*. That's only half of it though. There's something else there that's making my stomach tighten into knots of bliss and panic all at the same time.

Arella pants as she draws back. "You're the best boyfriend ever, you know that?"

Her compliment warms and breaks me. I'm enjoying being her boyfriend. Unfortunately, this boyfriend-girlfriend thing is only temporary. In time, our relationship will come to an end. What then? Will she find a new boyfriend? Will she tell him that he's the best, too?

What happens to me? What will I do without her? What did I ever do before Arella? Lounge around? Drink excessively? Have meaningless sex? None of that sounds appealing anymore.

The idea of Arella with someone else sounds even more unappealing. I want her to be with *me*. I want her best to be *me*.

Internally, I slap myself. Things between Arella and me can't be like this forever. At the end of the day, she's still an Ordinary and it's illegal for me to be with her.

Besides, this relationship isn't real. Arella doesn't know that though, so of course, to her, this *is* real. To me, even though I know it's not, it *feels* real. Like when we hold hands and I get a sense of ease and joy. That feels real. The way she cups my face and makes the pain wash away. That feels real. How hard it is to let her go when we have our late evenings, making out against her apartment door. That feels real.

Does that mean what we have is . . . real? How is that possible? Maybe pretending to want her has tricked my mind into actually wanting her. Even so, that doesn't change that my body physically yearns for her whenever we're apart.

"Can I ask you something?" Arella asks as she slides off the bed to retrieve her clothes.

I would help, but all of a sudden, my mind feels foggy, and it's getting hard to breathe. My thoughts are consuming me.

"Trey?"

Shit. I haven't answered her yet. "Yeah, babe, what's up?"

"Maybe this is something we should have established three weeks ago, but I've been wondering . . . what do you want to get out of this relationship?"

"What do *you* want to get?"

Dressed now, she blows her runny nose into a tissue as she scowls at me. "I hate when you do that."

"Do what?"

"Answer a question with a question. You do it whenever you don't want to give someone a straight answer."

I won't deny that the second she asked that question, my throat closed up. My gut reaction was to ask her the same thing to avoid answering it.

I repeat her question in my head and actually think about it this time. What *do* I want to get out of this relationship?

A month ago, my answer would have been simple: I want information about her that will explain her immunity. Now, I think I want more, but I can't have that. We're from two separate worlds. Worlds that coexist but aren't meant to fully intertwine.

I stand to hug her because it'll ease the heaviness growing in my chest. Also, I can't take her looking into my eyes anymore.

I plant a soft kiss against her forehead. "What I want is more time with you."

It's the most honest answer I can give her because I'm so

torn. We're like different species of the same animal family. Like how lions and cheetahs are felines with different genetic makeups. They aren't meant to be together, and neither are Zordinaries and Ordinaries. It's unnatural. Except, the way Arella and I are together feels more natural than blinking. Everything from the way she fits against my body to the way she looks at me to the way she says my name.

The more I think about it, the more my feelings get jumbled up.

Feelings . . . something I know so much about, yet so little.

25

TREY

I DIDN'T INTEND TO STAY THE NIGHT. I'VE NEVER STAYED THE night at a woman's place before. I've never wanted to. With Arella, it was too hard to leave. We tried to say bye. I even got my shoes on at one point. When we kissed at her door, somehow, my shoes came off and we ended up back in her bed. Then I just . . . never left. How could I when she fell asleep in my arms, looking so peaceful? It would have taken a bomb threat to move me.

My beautiful angel wakes up with a sleepy smile plastered over her face. She gives me a look that says, *I'm happy you're still here.*

I am too, baby. I spent the whole night admiring how at peace she looks when she's asleep, and I'll happily do it again.

"How did you sleep?" Arella asks after we brush our teeth. I'm grateful that she had one of those free toothbrushes from her dentist for me to use.

"I slept well," I lie. "Dreamt of you," I lie again. It's not like I can tell her that I didn't sleep at all. I'd have to explain that I have a special body that doesn't need as much rest as hers does. That will lead to explaining that I have other special characteristics and abilities she's only seen in movies.

Then she'll run away screaming, and I'll go to z-prison for exposure.

Five minutes later, I'm slouched at Arella's kitchen table with a plate of waffles in front of me as she flips some eggs over in a pan.

"Are you okay?" she asks.

"Yep," I lie for the third time this morning, and I hate myself for it.

When can I stop lying to her? I'm not okay. Not even a little bit. My mind is racing with thoughts I can't reel in. I've been having breakfast with Arella almost every morning lately. But today, it feels . . . different. It's hard to put into words. The only way I can describe it is that I want to do this today, tomorrow, the next day, and every day after that. Knowing that I can't crushes me.

"You've been quiet this morning," she says.

I have to think about my response because I want whatever I say to her to be the truth. "I've just got a lot on my mind."

"Do you want to talk about it?"

"Not really. We don't have time, anyway. I have to be at a video shoot at nine. I also need to run home to grab some clothes first."

With the hot pan in hand, she scoops an over-easy egg onto my plate. Then she continues cooking her egg. I've never told her that I prefer my eggs runny. Throughout our many mornings together, she's figured it out. She's been making eggs for me like this ever since.

"What's the video for today?" she asks as the toaster pops.

"It's a cover of a Justin Timberlake song. This shoot was supposed to be a while ago. It's been rescheduled twice."

Arella slides a piece of toast onto each of our plates. Then she gives me three pieces of bacon and two for herself. Once she settles across the table from me, she says, "Should we leave right after breakfast?"

I pick up my fork but don't poke anything with it. "Actually, babe, I was thinkin' you should stay home."

"What? Why?"

"Because you were sick yesterday. Don't you wanna rest?" I hate myself. I can't stop lying. Her being sick has nothing to do with why I think she should stay home.

"I'm recovered now. Besides, I always go to your band stuff with you on my days off."

And I've been thoroughly enjoying it. During band rehearsal, she usually lounges on the sectional, working on her baking blog while I work. During video shoots, she helps out the crew any way she can. At our shows, she's in the crowd, singing along to the words. I like having her around, and people ask about her whenever she's not.

Besides me, the person who misses Arella the most when she's gone is Liz. Those two get along like fuzz on a peach. Once they're together, it's hard to separate them. They're constantly bonding over their mutual love of boy bands.

Last week, I caught them laughing hysterically about something. When I went over to ask what was so funny, neither of them would tell me. They were probably making fun of me, but I don't care. It made me happy to see my two favorite people laughing together.

I don't know what happened after I left Arella with Liz and Emmy at the July Fourth party, but ever since, Liz hasn't made a peep about my strange attachment to this Ordinary. If anything, she's been encouraging it by inviting Arella out to everything our band does. I wonder what changed Liz's mind. I'm sure she still thinks that having a relationship like this with an Ordinary is bizarre. Hell, *I* think it's bizarre.

Throughout history, Zordis have always been friends with Ordis, but never lovers. It's not that we see them as less than. It's that since we can't reproduce with them, we just biologically don't see Ordis that way. At least, we *shouldn't*. So, why do I? Is there something wrong with me?

I finally stick my fork into my perfectly cooked egg. "How 'bout I come over tonight after the shoot? If you want, I could stay the night again?" Hearing those words come out of my mouth sounds as unnatural as it feels to say them. Typically, I'm packing Arella's laptop for her because I can't get her to come to work with me fast enough.

My girl is too smart for her own good. She narrows her eyes at me. "What's the *real* reason you don't want me to come? Yesterday, you didn't care that I was contagious, and now that my symptoms are gone, you're insisting that I stay home?"

I sigh as I set my fork down. Neither of us has eaten a thing yet. "The treatment for this video was written way before we met. There's stuff I'm gonna be doing today that I think would be better if you didn't see."

"Oh . . . like, what kind of stuff?" The way she hesitantly asks that question tells me she already knows.

"Like, you know . . . stuff—with another girl."

She hides her discomfort behind biting into her toast. "Who?"

"She's an actress. Bailey. I've never met her."

Arella ponders that for a moment, then relaxes her shoulders as if to say, *This is no big deal.* Her eyes tell me otherwise. "Wouldn't I see the video later on YouTube anyway?"

"That's true." Selfishly, I want her to come. I don't like being away from her. I guess she could go into another room while we film the intimate scenes. So, if she's up for it . . .

I HIKE MY DUFFEL BAG FULL OF OUTFITS FOR THE DAY HIGHER up my shoulder as we climb the front steps of a little house in East LA. Whoever picked this spot as our filming location did a great job. The house looks beautiful. Colorful flowers line the walkway, and a cute floral welcome sign hangs on the front door.

Arella stops on the porch and fidgets with the ends of her hair. I grab her hand to make her stop, then kiss her knuckles. My duffel bag falls to my feet with a thud as I turn to face her.

"It's not too late to leave, babe. If you don't think you can handle what I told you is gonna happen today . . ."

"Technically, you haven't told me." She cups her sweaty forehead to shield her eyes from the sun. My Zordi eyes have already adjusted to the brightness. "All you said was that you'll be doing *stuff* with another girl. What, exactly, is *stuff?*"

I grip the back of her thighs and lift her onto the porch ledge. Naturally, she spreads her legs for me to slide between them. I hold her tight to make sure she doesn't fall.

"This video is about a girl who's been hurt so much that she's too afraid to get into another relationship. Throughout the song, I do things to show her that it's okay to fall in love again. We'll be cuddling. There are kissing parts. We'll be half naked. If you still want to stay, remember that it's just acting. It doesn't mean anything. At the end of the day, it's *you* I'll be going home with."

She doesn't hesitate to smile. "Okay. Just promise me you'll kiss me tons when you're done tonight."

"Deal. I'll even start now." My intent is to give her a short, soft kiss, but as soon as our mouths collide, I can't pull away. *She tastes so good . . .* My cock hardens as her fingers trail through my hair. I press my dick against her inner thigh, and she giggles adorably.

She's the first to lean back. "Should we go inside now?"

"In a sec. I need to calm down first." After a few cars pass, I readjust myself. " 'Kay. I'm good now."

The crew is scattered around the house, setting up lights and tripods, while others are standing around chatting. Everyone's emotions jump at me from all directions, so I rake my mind power into a three-foot circle. As soon as I do that, someone enters that circle. Their energy is upbeat.

"Ey! There he is!" It's Mateo, a Hispanic man in his late twenties wearing a Giants baseball cap over his thick curly hair. The top of his cap comes up to my nipples at best.

"Mateo!" I let go of Arella's hand to give him a man hug with a quick thump on the back.

As usual, he gets right to business. "We're gonna start with them performance shots first. We won't need the rest of the band after that, so they can leave early. As for you, you be stuck with me all day."

"I'm pretty sure it's *you* who's stuck with me."

Playfully, he punches my shoulder. "Ey, you ain't too bad to look at." He turns to Arella, whose hand I've returned to holding. "Who's this?"

"This is my girlfriend, Ari. Babe, this is Mateo, my favorite video director. He's got a knack for getting some unique shots."

"Ah, don't play me up too much. Good to meet you, pretty girl."

I don't miss the way Mateo's eyes skate up and down my girl's body. As he shakes her hand, I have to hold myself back from shoving him away. I know I shouldn't be this possessive of her, but knowing it doesn't stop me from feeling it.

"Nice to meet you too," Arella says with a smile that would send most men to their knees. No wonder Mateo's still staring at her.

"Where can I change?" I point at my duffel bag.

Mateo finally peels his eyes off what's not his and hooks a thumb behind him. "There's a bedroom back there."

I practically drag Arella with me as I head that way.

In the small bedroom, I dig through my duffel to find a purple dress shirt and black dress pants. Arella's planted on the end of the bed while I change my clothes and finish my outfit with a black tie. At the mirror, I'm rolling the sleeves up to my elbows when Arella's mouth parts behind me. The look in her eyes is all desire and something else I don't recognize.

I flip around with my arms out. "How do I look?"

"Yummy," she says breathlessly.

As if she's magnetizing me, I feel a pull to her. My feet move toward her before I even process that I'm doing it. I slip a knee between her legs, spreading them apart. I have every intention of giving her a light kiss until she yanks my tie and falls back onto the mattress, forcing me on top of her. I catch myself with a hand on either side of her head. I don't kiss her lightly after that. I kiss her hard, while clawing at her body to come closer to mine. I can't get enough of—

Knock-knock.

Arella freezes beneath me. I debate ignoring the intrusion until I sense that the person isn't moving from the door. Reluctantly, I stand.

"I'm not done with you yet," I whisper.

After adjusting my hard-on, I open the door to reveal a woman I've never seen before. She's pretty for an Ordinary. Nothing compared to Arella though.

"Hi." She hooks a finger behind an ear to pull back her long blonde hair. "I wanted to introduce myself. I'm Bailey."

"Trey." We shake hands. "This is my girl, Ari."

Arella still looks flushed from our kiss as she offers Bailey a small wave. "Hello."

I can't tell how she feels. Her face gives nothing away. *Is she uncomfortable? Jealous?* I want to tell her she has no reason to be. This would be a great time to be a Telepath instead of an Empath, except neither works on her anyway.

I grab Arella's hand and give it a squeeze. It's my silent way of telling her that I'm not attracted to Bailey at all. When I look at Bailey, I just see a person. That's it.

And that's what Zordis *should* see when they look at an Ordi. They shouldn't see anything sexual. They shouldn't see someone they want to devour all the time. Most of all, they shouldn't see someone who makes their heart race as much as Arella makes mine.

There's gotta be something wrong with me. In the past, I've read articles on the z-net about Zordis with mental conditions that cause them to have Ordi fetishes. They're put in rehab and therapy to correct it. *Do I have one of those conditions?* I don't know. Either way, it's not something I can think about right now. It's time for take one.

I make my way to the backyard, where the crew has set up a gazebo in the garden decorated with flowers. As we film, Arella lounges on a lawn chair, watching us. I'm glad she came to work with me today. I always perform better when she's around.

Fifteen takes later, Mateo calls out, "Cut! That's a wrap for the full band scenes!"

Without wasting a second, Arella hops out of her chair and begins helping the crew haul stuff back inside. I'm about to go to her when a hand on my forearm stops me.

"Ey, man. You nervous 'bout your scenes with Blondie?" Mateo nods his head toward Bailey, who's chatting in a triangle with Liz and Emmy.

"No. Why?"

"Of course you ain't. You're prolly used to kissin' strangers all the time. Bailey's not though, so I was hopin' you'd go break the ice with her."

"What do you mean?" I already know what Mateo means. He's not the first director to ask this of me. Typically, I'm down for it. Today, I'm not.

"You know, just make her feel comfortable with smacking lips with you before the cameras roll. It'll make the shots look more natural."

"She's an actress." I wave a nonchalant hand through the air. "She'll be fine."

"Even actresses get nervous, lover boy. Just go ease her nerves a bit, 'ight?"

With that, Mateo twists on his heel and heads inside. I have no intention of breaking the ice with Bailey. If she's nervous, she's just gonna have to get over it.

I glance to where Arella was earlier. She's gone now. I scan the rest of the backyard. No Arella. She's probably back inside.

I'm about to yank the back door open when someone calls my name.

I turn around with a fake smile on my face. "Oh, hey, Bailey."

"Mateo said you wanted to talk to me about somethin'?"

Damn you, Mateo. "Uh, yeah," I say, going along with it. *Might as well get this over with.* The faster we can get past her nerves, the faster we can film, the faster I can go home with my girl. "Let's talk over here."

Bailey follows me to the side of the house.

I stop under the shade of a tree and rub a hand behind my neck. "So, uh, I figured . . . um, that we'd kinda get used to kissing each other before the cameras roll."

Bailey's explosion of nerves fireworks through my head.

Great. Now she's making *me* nervous. "You cool with that?"

She nods eagerly. "Sure."

Taking her face into my hands, I press my lips against hers. She tastes like mint gum and not like Arella at all. Well, she's not Arella, so what did I expect?

Bailey's not a terrible kisser. She's just . . . different. I prefer the way Arella runs her fingers through my hair. And the way she lets out those soft breathy moans. And how her kisses always give me tingles that shoot down to my toes. The worst part is that Bailey doesn't smell like lavender and springtime. She smells of vanilla and coconuts. *Gross.*

Feelings of desire rush through me, but they aren't mine. I expand my powers to latch onto someone—*anyone*—else. Within seconds, it masks Bailey's emotions from my head. I don't want to want Bailey, and I especially don't want her emotions to control how I feel.

Disgusted, I pull back and drop my arms to my sides.

"Wow," Bailey says breathlessly.

At least one of us enjoyed it.

Without a word, I rush inside to go find my girl. Call me a dick for leaving Bailey like that, but I don't care. I need Arella.

She's not in the kitchen. She's not in the living room either. My chest gets heavier with each step I take throughout the house without seeing her. *Where is she?* I need to hold her to feel like the world is right again, and it needs to happen within the next five seconds.

Oh, fuck. What the hell am I gonna do once I complete my mission? Will my world ever feel right if she's not in it? Will I ever be able to kiss another woman without thinking of her? I know the answer, and it makes my lungs tight.

Maybe once I complete my mission, I can continue my relationship with her. I'll just have to hide her from the zovernment and make sure that she never finds out about my powers. I could stop using them, couldn't I? I'll do anything if it means I can keep her.

Then again, how will I explain to Arella that we can never get married? The Supes monitor all marriage licenses to ensure that our Zordi laws are followed. Maybe I can forge marriage papers to make her *think* they're official.

I'll also have to come up with an explanation as to why we can't have children. Telling her that I'm of a different human species with the inability to mate with her won't go over well. I could tell her that I'm infertile or we could adopt. How hard can it be to forge adoption papers?

Then again, what would happen to Arella and our fake family if I'm caught and taken away? How long will I go to z-prison for? Actually, having a secret Ordinary family with forged papers is totally grounds for a death sentence.

My chest aches as I continue my frantic search for her.

When I finally find her, it's in an upstairs bedroom with Liz and Emmy. She's stationed on an accent chair, about to say something, when I drop to my knees in front of her. Desperately, I clutch her face and press my lips against hers.

It takes her a second, but eventually, she eases into me and kisses me back. Our embrace is rough and intense. Still, it feels like coming home.

I slide my tongue into her mouth and bask in the familiar taste of her. The familiar scent of her. The familiar way she feels against me. The more we kiss, the more my anxiety flushes away.

Finally, after who knows how long, I pull back. We gasp for air as I press my forehead against hers and brace my arms on the chair.

When I open my eyes, her brown ones are looking back at me. That deep bliss and panic in my chest returns, rushing through me like a hurricane. It washes away the unease while also drenching me with pain.

I can't live the rest of my life without this girl.

I can't.

I won't.

26

TREY

THE NEXT DAY, MY MIND IS A CLUSTERFUCK. KISSING BAILEY made me realize that I never want to kiss anyone but Arella—ever. Now I just have to figure out how to make that happen.

On my way to pick up my girl for dinner, a wave of nausea hits me. My gut feels like someone's jabbing it with a wrench, so I drink the warm water from a half-empty plastic bottle that's been stewing in my car for a week. It does nothing to ease the tornado in my stomach.

This better go away soon, because I've got special plans to take Arella back to Long Beach, where we had our first date. I'm hoping that since she's more comfortable with me touching her now, she'll actually dance with me this time. I'm also hoping that being around her will help me figure out a plan as to how I'm going to keep her.

I'm about ten blocks away from Arella's apartment when my chest tightens like someone's got a tight grip on my heart and they're squeezing the life out of it. I white-knuckle the steering wheel as my lungs lose air. The dry-ass desert in my throat makes me cough, and I swear heavy sandbags have been dropped onto my chest and have made my lungs their home.

As my car pulls up to Arella's place, I tell myself the pain will pass. I'm still coughing as I knock on her door. A faint sound comes from inside. I press my ear against the door, wishing I was an Eavesdropper with enhanced hearing like Jess. I'm not, so all I hear is . . . screaming?

I try to turn the doorknob. Locked. With the wave of a hand, I fix that, and the door flies open.

My heart plummets. The sound I heard was definitely screaming. Arella's screams. And now, I know why.

Spiders.

Hundreds—no, *thousands* of little black spiders are crawling all over Arella's apartment. Some are so big, I can see the little hairs on their legs. The flames between my fingers flicker as I resist throwing fireballs at them and dash toward the screaming.

Arella's on her bed, screeching and flailing her arms. Spiders cover everything: the walls, the floor, the bed, *my girl*. I dart to her and wave a hand over her body, thinking it'll make the spiders fly off her. They don't.

In a panic, I've forgotten that my telekinesis doesn't work on living things. So with my bare hands, I swat the creatures away. Then I lift Arella into my arms and rush her out of the apartment.

She's still screaming when I set her bare feet down and flick away the last remaining spiders still crawling over her. They fall to the ground and scurry away.

"It's okay, baby," I say as calmly as I can, yet loud enough so she can hear me over her screams. It doesn't quiet her. With my thumb, I wipe away the tears running down her cheeks. "It's okay. It's okay."

I'm lying to her again. It's not okay. I'm freaking out too. It breaks me to see her like this. Roughly, I pull her against me and hold her like she's going to evaporate into thin air if I don't. I let her scream into my chest, and I clutch her until the screaming subsides. Eventually, all she does is tremble in my arms, hyperventilating.

I kiss the top of her hair. "It's all right, baby. I'm here."

I spot her phone on the ground. She must have been holding it, then dropped it on our way out. The urge to pick it up isn't as big as my need to comfort her. On the small of her back, I caress my fingertips in little circles, silently telling her that she's safe now.

"Don't worry, angel. I won't let anything hurt you."

I lean back to look at her. Her whole body is stiff. Her eyes are screwed shut, and she's still panting. I lift her and cradle her in my arms as I march to my car. She doesn't wrap her arms around my neck the way she usually does. She's just rigid and quivering, and it's scaring me.

Once I get her into the passenger seat, I lean in to examine her. Her eyes are still shut, and her hands are in tight, shaky fists.

"Babe?" I say tenderly.

She doesn't respond. I shrug my jacket off and drape it around her front. Then I click her seat belt in.

With a kiss on her forehead, I caress her cheek. "You're safe now."

She's still shuddering.

What do I do?

After closing her door, I fetch her phone off the ground. Then I round the front of my car and plop behind the wheel. I don't start the engine. I just stare at her.

"Angel?" I wait for her to say something.

She doesn't, and my throat closes up.

What's wrong? Why isn't she responding?

"Arella? Please say something." My voice breaks. I'm barely getting the words out.

She doesn't even stir. It's like she didn't hear me at all.

"Fuck." I punch the steering wheel. What the fuck is going on?

Breathe, I command myself, because I can't lose it right now. Arella needs me to be strong. I suck in a deep breath through my nose, then slowly blow it out through my lips.

I know what I have to do. I just don't want to do it. I hate hospitals. I avoid them at all costs. Sensing the emotions of dying patients, people in pain, and overworked nurses always makes me nauseous. Still, I start the car because I can't think of another option.

Arella barely moves as I pull up to the nearest hospital.

She's still unresponsive as I carry her out of the car and rush her into the building.

Her eyes still haven't opened by the time I burst through the doors of the Emergency Department.

All eyes fall on me. Sick women, irritated grandpas in wheelchairs, families in despair, and a guy holding a wad of red-soaked gauze against his eye. The cloud of depressing emotions forms a migraine in my temples. I just got here, and I already need to leave.

I rush to the front desk, ignoring the long line. "You need to see her right away."

A plump woman in her fifties glares at me from behind a pair of rectangular glasses. "Sir, you need to get to the back of the line."

"No. Someone needs to see her *now.*"

She glares at me—harder this time. "Is anything broken, bleeding profusely, dying, or on the pain scale of nine or higher?"

"What? No?"

She seizes a clipboard with paperwork already on it, thrusting it toward me. "Fill out this form. Someone will see you shortly."

I glance down at the sweet girl in my arms. Her face is pale. Her breathing is shallow. She's not shaking anymore, but that doesn't change how much I'm fucking losing it. I glance back up at the receptionist. "I need that someone *now.*"

"You need to fill out the forms, sir. And get to the back of the line."

"Fuck. The. Forms! Don't you see she's not responding?"

Dramatically, the lady yanks her glasses off and leans on her elbows. "You need to calm down, sir."

"I can't calm down. My *heart* is on the pain scale of nine or higher. Please! Help her!"

I feel like pulling out all my hair. I probably would if my arms weren't full of the one and only person who means everything to me. My lungs won't stop contracting, because I can still hear her screams. I can still feel her crying and trembling against my chest.

"Please," I beg. "Get someone to take her in."

The lady sighs, preparing to tell me some scripted rejection when a tan-skinned Indian woman wearing scrubs appears by the double doors. "I'll take her in."

Finally!

27

TREY

Doctor's orders. I'm doing everything she told me to. *Take her home. Help her relax. Comfort her. Don't leave her alone unless she asks to be.* No problem.

The whole car ride home, I never let go of Arella's hand once. Not until I parked in my garage and cut the engine.

Now, she's in my Jacuzzi. I thought a warm bath might help her relax. Sometimes it does the trick for me. I sit on the edge, gently rubbing a bar of soap up and down her back and around her shoulders.

I'm half expecting Arella to jump up and scream at any moment. The doctor said it's a common side effect of post-traumatic stress. The moment she explained Arella's shakiness and unresponsiveness with the word *trauma*, the blood drained from my body.

My chest has been feeling lighter ever since the color has been returning to Arella's face. Now, I just need to hear that sweet voice of hers tell me she's okay.

I don't know if she wants me to kiss her, nor do I ask. I just do it. Not for her. For me. It soothes me to kiss her shoulders, her forehead, and her cheeks. She hasn't told me not to, so I guess that's a good sign. I hope it's as comforting to her as it is to me.

After about twenty minutes, I drain the tub and assist her out of it. Then I dry her off with a towel and dress her in a pair of my boxers and a T-shirt. It takes me a few tries to get all her hair out of the messy ponytail I put it in earlier. Once I do, I kiss her forehead and pull her close.

The feel of her body against mine immediately alleviates the churning in my gut. I'm not sure why *I'm* the one who needs consolation. It's *her* who was attacked by hairy eight-legged monsters.

Where the fuck did they come from? And how were there so many? And so big? I'll have to do some research later. For now, I just want to focus on making Arella feel safe.

We stand in the middle of my bedroom, holding each other for a while, never saying anything. I don't know what I could say to make things better. All I know is that after a few minutes, her arms rise to hug me back, and my insides throw a mini party.

"Trey?" She tilts her head back to look at me. The sound of her voice makes me tear up.

"Yeah, baby?"

"Thank you for taking care of me."

I can't help myself. I seize her face and glue my mouth to hers. She doesn't hesitate to kiss me back. For me, it's more of a need than a want. It's full of anxiety, and relief, and pain, and desire all at once.

I only let go of her when my stomach rumbles. The whole hospital fiasco took several hours. I haven't eaten a single thing. Neither has Arella.

With her hand in mine, I lead her to the kitchen. She sits silently at the island while I whip up something for us to eat.

Ten minutes later, I place two plates onto the counter. They're full of pancakes, bacon, eggs, and some fresh-cut strawberries. I inhale my food like a starving animal.

I'm almost done when Arella speaks again.

"This was the first meal we ever had together. Breakfast. Right here."

That day feels like forever ago. So much has changed since the moment I met this puzzling brunette on the side of a highway. In only six and a half weeks, I've grown to adore this woman. I care more about her than I do my own limbs.

Like an annoying little alarm, my brain chimes in to remind me how ridiculous it is that I feel this way about her. It keeps reminding me that what we have is wrong. My heart though . . . It tells me that Arella is right. She's everything I want and need in ways I never imagined could exist. She understands me in ways even Liz doesn't. She doesn't make me feel like I have to fake happiness either. With her, I am genuinely happy.

I know this relationship isn't sustainable, but when it comes down to it, when my mission ends, can I really just walk away?

I already know the answer to that without having to think about it.

It's hitting me now that I haven't been actively trying to complete my mission for a while. The more time I spend with Arella, the less I've been asking to meet her grandparents. I haven't been pursuing answers about her parents, her genetics, or anything else either.

Maybe subconsciously, I haven't wanted my mission to end. This incomplete assignment is the only reason I have to stay with her. Until I find a better one, I'm gonna cling onto that for as long as possible.

DURING LUNCH THE NEXT DAY, I TELL YET ANOTHER LIE.

"The doctor said you can't go to work for a week." Yeah, I'm a piece of shit, but I'm not ready for Arella to leave my side yet. What if something happens? I can't protect her if I'm not near her.

"I can't miss work for that long," she says defiantly.

"Doctor's orders. You're in recovery."

For the next twenty minutes, Arella argues with me about being "fine" and how she "can't go that long without getting a paycheck." The more I offer to help her, the more she argues with me. I can't comprehend it. Jess and just about any other woman I know would love to hear that I'll pay for anything she wants for the rest of her life. When Arella says something about wanting to be able to buy things without having to ask me, I offer to transfer her ten thousand dollars. She still says no. *Seriously?*

"You can buy whatever you want, babe. No need to tell me what it's for, and no need to pay me back. Whenever you run out, just let me know, and I'll transfer you more."

She groans, throwing her head back. "You don't get it."

I raise my arms up and drop them to my sides. "You're right. I don't. It still doesn't change that the doctor said you can't go to work for a week."

Eventually, she stomps away to call her bosses.

When she comes back, I'm in the middle of loading the dishwasher.

"My nanny family is going to get a backup nanny lined up. As for the daycare, my director is not happy. We're already short-staffed, and she thinks I made up the whole spider thing."

I shrug as I insert a dirty plate into the dishwasher. "Fuck her."

Arella glowers at me, crossing her arms over her luscious breasts. She's braless, and I've been staring at her nipples peeking out of my T-shirt all morning.

I feign innocence. "What?"

"Have you ever had a job?"

"I once worked on a cruise ship as a musician."

She rolls her eyes. "Like a *normal* job."

"Um, the guy who owned the music store in my hometown used to pay me under the table to help around. Does that count?"

"No. My director said that I need a doctor's note if I'll be out for more than three days in a row. Company policy."

"No problem. I can write you one." I stick another plate into the dishwasher.

"No! I need a *real* doctor's note. Do you even care that I could lose my job?"

"You won't get fired, babe." Even if she did, I'd take care of her. She has nothing to worry about.

While Arella goes off to make a few more calls, I head upstairs to work out. I'm in the middle of my weight-lifting routine when Arella peeks her head through the door. I pause the rap music that's blasting over my speakers.

"My landlord said she'll get it taken care of immediately."

"Perfect." The weights clank as I set them back onto the rack.

Arella hugs herself, staring at the carpet. "Sooo . . . where do you think all those spiders came from?"

I did some research last night, while she was asleep. According to the Internet, it was either an infestation through a hole in the wall or a spider egg sac that hatched inside her apartment. What confuses me, though, is the number of spiders. The infestations I saw online were much smaller. More like ten to twenty at most. If a spider egg had hatched inside her place, it would have only been a few hundred little baby spiders. What I saw looked like thousands, and those fuckers weren't babies.

"Have you ever seen *Charlotte's Web*?" I ask. "There's a scene in the movie when Charlotte's egg sac hatches and all her little babies come crawling out."

"Those things were too big to be babies," Arella says. "Is it possible that this was Nathan's way of getting back at me for you beating him up?"

I pause to think about that. Is that hairy-balls-eating douchebag capable of pulling off a spider infestation that big? Maybe, but would he do it knowing I have those reputation-destroying photos of him? Perhaps he thinks we can't prove he did this. Arella has mentioned that his dad's got money. For the right price, you can hire someone to do anything.

I make a mental note to look into it later. Maybe I'll pay Pencil Dick a visit. With my mind power, I can usually tell if people are lying. In the meantime, I'll keep focusing on taking Arella's mind off the whole thing. Last night, she woke up from a nightmare about being attacked by furry arachnids the size of her face. It broke my heart to see her cry like that.

After I finish my workout, I rummage through my drawers to find the clothes Arella left here that night we threw flour on each other—the night we had our first kiss. I still think about that heated moment whenever I have a date with my right hand.

Once Arella's dressed, we climb into the car to go run some errands.

As I back out of my garage, Arella asks, "Do you think there's a chance all the spiders have left?"

"I think there's a higher chance that by tonight, you'll be shooting webs out of your wrists."

She chuckles, shaking her head at me. "If I were to have superpowers, Spidey webs would not be my first choice. Now where are we going?"

"Target."

"What for?"

I press a button to shut my garage as we pull out onto the street. "To get some things you said you need—clothes, shampoo, makeup . . . a flamethrower."

Her mouth pops open with a gasp. "Flamethrower? We're not setting my apartment on fire!"

With a wink, I say, "At least you wouldn't have to pay rent anymore."

2 8

———

ARELLA

I'VE GOT A FULL BELLY AS WE LEAVE THE RESTAURANT IN LONG Beach where Trey took me the first time we had dinner together. We slow-danced as a female duo sang perfectly harmonized love songs accompanied by their keyboard.

A dark sky stretches above us as we head to my thinking spot for another evening of stargazing. It was Trey's idea, and I didn't hesitate to say yes. I love being able to share the place that used to be my safe haven with my new safe haven.

"I liked waking up next to you this morning," I say with his hand in mine. It's rare for us to be in the car without holding hands.

A quick "same" is his response. He doesn't even look away from the road.

"I can see us having more mornings like that."

He answers with a slight nod and a somber "Me too."

He's been somber a lot today. Always staring off into space with a pained look in his eyes. Whenever I ask what he's thinking about, I get the feeling he only tells me a version of the truth.

My truth is that I can see Trey and me having more than just mornings where we wake up together. I can see us

252

spending more days together like we did today, barely leaving each other's side. I can see me going on tour with him and his band after they finish their album. I can see him helping me paint the walls of my future bakery and him being there when I sell my first cake. I can see us having it all together. Only problem is . . . I'm not confident if *he* sees all that.

Whenever I bring up the topic of our future together, he avoids it. Earlier today, I casually asked if he ever wants kids. His answer was a gloomy "Yes, but I'm not sure if that's in the cards for me."

"Why is that?" I asked.

Instead of answering, he changed the subject.

Besides owning a bakery, my other dream is to be a mom. I love children, and working with other people's kids every day isn't enough. Someday, I want my own. If Trey doesn't ever want kids, I'm not sure if this can work.

My quiet man parks his car on the side of the gravel road where I normally do. Together, we grab our things and head into the woods. At the top of the narrow trail is that same giant oak tree that's always provided me comfort whenever I needed it. A slight breeze blows my hair around as Trey lays out a blanket for us.

"You're gonna do great," he says as he unpacks his guitar from its hard case. He thought it'd be fun to teach me some simple chords. I don't even know the difference between a simple chord and a not-simple chord. Still, I'm willing to learn because it'll make him happy.

We're about an hour into my first guitar lesson when I'm finally getting the hang of it. So far, Trey has taught me four chords. Learning to play guitar isn't as easy as he makes it look. I can barely remember where to put my fingers, let alone switch between chords fast enough to play a song.

"That's perfect!" He flashes me one of his panty-wetting smiles. "Now play a D."

I glance at my numb fingers with the string indents in them. "But it hurts."

"That's normal. Once you play enough, you'll build up some calluses, then it won't hurt anymore. See?" He shows me his hard fingertips.

"How long will that take?"

"Depends on how often you play. Maybe a few weeks. Maybe months."

"Months?" I grip the neck of his guitar and hand it back to him. "Thanks for the lesson, Mr. Grant. Now, how about you serenade me instead?"

Through dazed eyes, he runs his tongue along his bottom lip. "Don't say my name like that. It does things to me."

I narrow my eyes and smirk. "Oh? What kinds of things?"

"The bad kind."

I like the sound of that. "Tell me, Mr. Grant. What are these bad things you speak of?"

His expression darkens. "I mean it."

"Mean what, Mr. Grant?"

His guitar gets thrown to the side with a loud *clank!* The next thing I know, he's launched himself at me, pinning my back to the blanket. Our lips meet roughly. His sweet scent drapes over me like warm air on a chilly day. He fixes my wrists above my head with one hand while his other hand cups my neck to hold me in place. He doesn't need to cement me down like this. I'm an enthusiastic captive.

Eventually, our kiss turns into a clothes-clawing, lip-biting, beautiful mess. As I slide his shirt up, I run my fingertips along every hard dip of his abs. Our mouths part for the split second it requires me to tear the fabric over his head, and then we're back to kissing in a frenzy.

"I can never get enough of you," he groans.

"Take more, then."

Every part of me craves to feel his hands on my bare skin. I rip my dress off to reveal the new matching bra and lacy panties I got today. Trey attacks me with his mouth. He goes for my neck first before sliding his lips down my chest. He scratches at my bra hooks and unhooks them within seconds. The lace gets thrown behind him. I arch my head back as his mouth latches onto one of my nipples.

"Trey," I moan toward the stars.

I grip his hair, heaving him closer as my other hand clutches the blanket beneath us. He hooks a finger through my panties and drags them down. They get tossed behind him too. They haven't even touched the grass before his tongue is lapping me up. I grab a handful of his hair as a tingling pleasure shoots up my body and down my legs.

With the perfect pressure, he circles his fingers over my clit. I squirm beneath him as he slides a finger inside me, then two. The entire time he moves them back and forth, he never stops licking me. My hands claw at his shoulders, begging for him to suck me harder. He must hear my silent plea, because he does, and I let out a whimpering moan.

His wet lips pepper kisses up my belly until he reaches my nipples again. He sucks on one while his fingers keep hammering inside me.

"You like that, baby?"

My response is an animalistic "Mmm."

That encourages him to keep going.

My fingertips graze his muscular chest and abs, all the way down to his zipper. I've barely gotten his jeans unbuttoned when he snatches my wrist and slams it above my head. Then he continues to lick my breast as if he didn't just deny me.

My other hand tugs at his messy hair to pull him back to look at me. "I want to touch you."

"If you touch me, I'll need to own your body."

"Then own me."

He groans, biting his lip. "Don't tease me, baby."

"I'm not. I want you."

He freezes. "Really?"

I take in the beautiful sight of him. His gorgeous face that I love to kiss. His defined arms that hold me tight. And his eyes. Those beautiful blue-gray eyes that always stare at me with desire and admiration. I nod firmly. "Yes. Own me."

His lips smash against mine again. He holds himself up with one hand while the other drags his zipper down. I shove the denim off his hips as he nips at my neck.

Soon, his jeans are thrown onto the grass too. Kneeling next to me, he hooks his thumbs behind the elastic of his boxers, then stops. I gape at him, urging him to shed the fabric, but he hesitates.

"You sure about this, babe?"

I nod eagerly. *Will you just get naked already?*

Finally, his boxers come down and his thick, hard erection springs up. It bounces a few times as I lose my breath and marvel at his size. Before I can touch him, he pins my arms down and kisses my neck. I moan and wrap my legs around him, desperate for him to enter me. He presses his erection against my inner thigh as he sucks my bottom lip into his mouth.

Panting, he releases my arms to grab his cock. With a dazed look in his eyes, he slides the tip up and down over my wet clit.

He's right outside my opening when I push him away. "Wait."

He stills above me. Then suddenly, he's off me, lying on his side, roughly dragging a hand through his hair.

"I'm sorry," he whispers, shaking his head at himself. "I shouldn't have pushed you this far. I knew you weren't ready."

What is he talking about? "I'm more than ready, Trey. Having you inside me is all I can think about right now. I just want you inside my mouth first."

All the worry dissipates from his eyes as his breath hitches. I climb on top of him and take his throbbing length into my hands. I wrap my fingers around his base, then stroke him up and down. His massive cock pulses and jumps between my palms. It's everything I imagined it would be. Firm, full, and satisfying.

Impatiently, I take him into my mouth, and he lets out a deep, guttural growl.

"Oh, baby." His hand grips the hair at the back of my head, guiding me into a rhythm as my head bobs up and down. "That feels so good."

That motivates me. I take him deeper and harder, changing pace from fast to slow, then fast again.

His breaths grow heavy and short. "Shit. Babe. Stop."

I don't.

"Please. I can't hold back any longer."

When I still don't stop, he forces me to. In a single motion, he flips me onto my back and straddles me.

"Do you want me?" he asks, his nose barely a hair from mine.

Each pound of my heart against my chest screams, *Yes, yes, yes!*

This man has done things to me. He's made me feel safe again when I wasn't sure I ever could. He's healed me. He's made me feel like I deserve to be with a man who touches me with affection, not abuse. He's made me feel like I'm me again. The me I was before I was made to feel weak and scared all the time.

Do I want him? Yes. More than anything.

"Own me, Trey."

That is all the permission he needs to press his cock against my opening and push inside.

I whimper, gasping as he fills me. Pain and pleasure ripple between my legs. He goes slow at first, allowing me to stretch and get used to his size. Each time he draws back and pushes in again, he goes deeper. I moan beneath him, arching my head back as I take his cock the way I'm meant to.

With a grunt, he plunges into me all the way.

An uncontrollable wail escapes me as my fingernails dig into his back.

He stills. "Am I hurting you?"

"No," I pant. Total lie, but I don't want him to stop.

He kisses my forehead as he moves inside me. Soon, the soft pain turns into pure pleasure as all the protective walls I've spent years building up come crashing down.

29

TREY

HER LIGHT CHESTNUT WAVES ARE SPRAWLED OUT ALL OVER THE grass. Her hands are clenched in the blanket beneath us. Her eyes are rolled back as her body trembles, taking every inch of me. This woman has never looked more irresistible.

She wraps around me perfectly—tight and dripping wet. Every time I thrust into her, she lets out the sexiest of moans. Arella could ask me to do anything for her right now, and I'd do it, no questions asked.

Every emotion running through me as I pump inside her is mine. The desire that shoots through my veins, the yearning in my heart, the need I feel to keep thrusting—all mine.

I'm close to the edge, but ending this too soon would be a tragedy. I've been waiting to have this moment with her for too long, and I'm not gonna ruin it by coming this fast. *She feels so good though . . .*

When my arms get tired of holding myself up, I lie on my side, facing her, and pull her leg over my shoulder. Easily, I find her damp opening again and slip back in. As every inch of me pushes its way through, my lungs lose air.

"Don't stop," she moans.

No worries, baby. I wasn't planning to.

She arches her head back. "Yes. Harder."

I obey, giving her what she wants. She screams as I thrust deeper into her, relentlessly rubbing her at the same time.

Harder.

Faster.

Harder.

Faster.

"Trey!"

I love hearing her scream my name as I watch myself disappear and reappear inside of her. Her breathless moans, her quivering hands, her curled toes. This is all I want to do—forever.

My will to hold back is dwindling. I need to release soon. I pull out to take a mini break, but Arella's not having it.

She grabs my cock and strokes me into submission. "Come back."

Breathlessly, I obey, climbing back on top of her, but I'm done being gentle. I drive into her so hard, she screams out. She keeps screaming as I pump, and pump, and pump.

"Come for me, baby," I beg.

"I'm so close," she half gasps, half moans.

That makes me almost erupt. I circle my fingers around her swollen clit over and over until, finally, her nails dig into my forearm and she shrieks. The sound of her orgasm is my sweet release. She pulsates around me as I pour into her.

Suddenly, it comes to me, clear as day. All her emotions rush through my mind. Arousal, gratification, relief. I sense her feelings for me, all desire, and need, and . . . something else. I drink in every second of it as I thrust one more time, groaning as I hammer every last drop inside her.

Then, as quickly as it came, it's gone.

I collapse over her with an arm on either side of her face, careful not to crush her. My ear presses against her thrashing heart. A thin layer of sweat coats her body, sticking to my dry skin. Together, we pant hard, and we stay like this until our breaths slow.

She lets out a little gasp as I pull out. Flopping next to her, I stare up at the stars with my mind in disarray. I *sensed* her. Only for a few seconds, but I sensed her! *How?*

I gape at her, searching for an explanation. I will my mind power to work on her again. It doesn't. She's blank, like always, except . . . *not* always. *How did that happen?*

However it happened, I can't try to figure it out now. My brain can't process anything—not after that. It was crazy. The best I've ever had. Uncontrollable passion. It unearthed a deep intensity in my soul that I don't know how to explain. All I know is that I was meant to be inside this woman.

"You didn't pull out," Arella says, interrupting my thoughts.

I pat my chest and gesture for her to scoot toward me. She does, nuzzling her head into the crook of my shoulder.

"You're on birth control, right?" I don't even pretend to sound concerned.

"Yeah."

"And you're consistent with it?"

"I have the implant."

I give her a look that says, *What the hell is that?* I know nothing about Ordinary birth control options, except that they have pills and backup pills.

"It's a little rod they stick into your arm, and it works for three years."

There's a Zordi version of that. I'm pretty sure Jess has it. "Is your three years up?"

"Not yet."

"And the success rate is . . . ?"

"Over ninety-nine percent."

"Sounds like we're good."

She makes a *pfft* sound. "That's not the point."

"Then what is?"

"The point is that you just came inside me, and you didn't even know if I was on birth control or not. You've never even asked. What if I wasn't?"

I've always been careful to use protection with Zordi women. Once, Jess tried to get me to fuck her without a condom. I'm a risk taker, but I'm not *that* much of a risk taker. One percent is still too high, and with my luck, I'd be part of that tiny statistic.

With Ordis, though, there's no risk. I couldn't have a baby with Arella even if the Zordinary fertility gods floated down from the fucking sky and sprinkled us with their golden baby dust.

I have no concerns, but if it'll make Arella feel better . . . "How 'bout we get you some Plan B pills tomorrow?"

She nods firmly. "That would be great. And next time, let's use a condom, just to be safe."

"Okay." I grin. "That means there's a next time."

THE NEXT MORNING, I WAKE WITH MY LIMBS TANGLED AROUND Arella's body. It's as if throughout my sleep, I wouldn't allow her to get more than a breath away from me.

I still feel high from last night. When we got home, we had sex two more times before we finally passed out from exhaustion. I'm rested now, and more than ready for my next dose of her.

"Morning, angel," I say when she stirs. Even when she's rubbing the crust out of her eyes, she's the most gorgeous woman I've ever seen.

"Morning, honey."

For a few minutes, we cuddle as we go over the things we need to do today. Our two priorities are getting the backup pills and dropping off a "doctor's note" for Arella's daycare director. When Arella asks why we aren't getting a *real* note, I make up some excuse about how the doctor had already written one but I misplaced it in the shuffle of getting her home from the ER.

"I suppose I wouldn't want to bother that doctor again," Arella says with her head over my shoulder.

"I'll write you something that's official-looking," I say, still holding her close. "Besides, it's not like your boss is gonna check up on it. If she does, there's a medical record of you being at the hospital."

Arella trails a finger down my abs, making my morning wood harder for her. "I suppose you have a point."

"I've got an afternoon photo shoot with the band at a park, then rehearsal after that. You're cool to come with me?"

"I'd love to."

"Good. Now, before we start our day, I need to have you again." My hands, which were caressing her shoulder, trail down to her luscious breasts.

"So have me."

Those three little words are all I need to break through the ropes that were tying back my inner beast—the part of me that wants to tear her clothes apart and eat her up. My mouth doesn't waste a second to suck in her nipple, and once again, we become a tangle of arms and legs.

Right before I'm about to enter her, she stops me and asks for one of those stupid condoms. I comply because I can't stand to be outside her for much longer. Once I roll the rubber on, I return to where I belong—on top of her.

When she orgasms, her emotions rush through me the same way they did our three times last night. I soak up every second of it until it disappears.

Out of breath, I collapse at her side, gaping at her. Whatever immunity walls she keeps up somehow come tumbling down when I make her come. Is it only possible when she orgasms, or can this happen another way? What about the orgasm makes it possible for me to sense her? Why did this only start *after* we had sex? I've made her come before, and her emotions didn't rush into my mind until last night. Is it only me this can happen with, or would it work with someone else?

I don't know the answers to any of those questions or the other ninety-some racing through my mind. The only thing I know is that when my mission ends, there is no way in hell I'm letting her go.

30

TREY

I can see why Arella and Javina are best friends. They complement each other well. When Javina talks, Arella listens. When Javina says something negative about herself, Arella corrects her by turning it into something positive. They laugh at the same things and know how to speak to each other without saying anything at all. It's fascinating to watch.

We're having lunch together at a restaurant near the park my band just finished our photo shoot at. Arella and Javina are deep in a conversation about work. Neither Javina's girlfriend nor I have said a word in almost ten minutes.

I turn to Rachel, who's across the high-top table from me. In a low voice, I say, "Do you think they'll notice if we just leave?"

Rachel giggles. "Doubt it. These two can go on forever. Speaking from experience."

After another minute, Arella hops off her seat. "I have to use the potty. I'll be quick."

Rachel follows her. "Me too."

As Arella saunters away, I only have one thought: *That ass is mine.* Mine to touch, to slap, to squeeze, and—

A hand smacks my arm. "Hello?"

"Huh?" My attention snaps up to Javina.

"I said, don't hurt her." She flashes me an icy glare. "That girl's been through a lot, and she deserves the best. So, I'm warning you, don't hurt her. If you do, I'll hunt you down and rip your balls off with my bare hands. Ari and I watch enough true crime shows for me to know how to hide the evidence and make it look like the fucking Easter Bunny did it."

The idea of hurting Arella scares me more than Javina's threat. Actually, it scares the fuck outta me. My original plan was to get Arella to break up with me. Now I'm not so sure she will. I also don't want her to. Besides, Javina is right. Arella does deserve the best. Unfortunately, this achy feeling in my chest tells me that I'm not it.

For the rest of the weekend, I push all thoughts of my unpredictable future with Arella aside. In the little free time we have between my band activities, I perform many satisfying, mind-boggling experiments with her in my bed.

By Sunday evening, I conclude that as long as I'm touching Arella as she orgasms, my mind power works on her. By touch, I mean any skin on skin works. My hands, my tongue, my dick, anything. When I wear a condom and I'm not touching her anywhere else, she's blank. If she comes while I'm licking her, the second I pull away and that physical contact is lost, so are her emotions. One hundred percent of the time, though, as long as we're touching, my mind power works. *How?*

I try to figure out if she's aware of what she's doing. After I ask some awkward questions like "What do you think about when you're coming?" it's obvious that she has no clue she's doing anything at all. It only further confirms that her immunity to Zordi powers is outside of her knowledge.

We're about to head to bed when my phone vibrates in my pocket. It's Victor. Since Arella's been staying with me, I've been ignoring his calls during the day and only answering them at night. Since this is the second time he's called today, I should probably answer it.

I head toward the backyard. "Why don't you climb into bed first, babe? I'll be right there."

Arella nods, then she shuffles down the hall. After I close the sliding glass door behind me, I answer the phone.

"Bring her to me," Victor says.

I stiffen in mid-step. "What?"

"This project is taking too long. It's been almost three months since I assigned you this mission, and you have nothing to show for it."

Actually, I have lots to show. I've found out that even though Arella's immune to Zordi powers, Healing Water works on her. I've discovered that her parents died on the same night mine did and that she wasn't born with the name she has now. I've found out that her grandparents have background checks that come up mostly blank. And then there's this whole thing where I can sense her emotions under certain circumstances. I haven't told Victor about any of this, and I don't think I want to.

My parents' secret message in my old teddy bear stated that the only person I should trust was Aunt Debbie. Why isn't Victor on that short list? He and my dad were very close before Aunt Jodi left. They did everything together, from things like playing in bowling leagues to drinking beers on the deck over the weekends. Lots of people even got them mixed up because they looked and talked so much alike.

Lately, I've been getting the feeling that Victor knows more than he's letting on. How is it that he knows so little about my parents' mission? Yes, there's that secrecy rule between agents, but he's the head of ZIRDA California now. Doesn't he have access to those files? Doesn't he have the power to order someone to tell him what happened the night his little brother died?

I've considered questioning him about this, but I already

know the outcome of that. Victor will turn it around on me, like "How about you stop being concerned about past missions you weren't a part of and start focusing on the one you've got?"

Besides, if Victor is up to something and I start snooping around, he'll get suspicious. He might take me off this assignment and give it to someone else. I won't be forced to sit on the sidelines while Arella falls for the next guy Victor sends to her. For now, I need to act as if everything is okay.

I drag a hand through my hair as I pace my backyard. "What makes you think this is something we can crack within the span of a few months? What if we're close and we just need to give it more time?"

"We don't have time, kid. Who knows what the Royals are doing while we aren't?"

That's true. While I'm over here fucking around with Arella, the Royals are probably out there murdering innocent children. All I've ever wanted is to make the Royals pay for what they did to my parents and to stop them from ever doing something like that again. Now, I'm acting as if it doesn't matter.

"I'm making some progress. I just need more time to see it through."

"Did something happen to her at birth?" Victor snaps.

"Not that I know of."

"Did she fall into some chemicals? Get attacked by a mutant animal? Was she dropped off here by aliens? Goddammit, kid. Find out."

"I will. Just give me more time." I'm almost begging.

"No. I want her here within the week."

"What am I supposed to tell her?" My palms shake. Somehow, my voice remains steady.

"Tell her you wanna go on a road trip, get her in the car, and drive over. I'll take care of the rest."

I don't like the sound of that. "What are you gonna do once she's there?"

"We'll run tests on her like we did with the other two Immunes."

I still don't like the sound of that. "Did the tests on the other Immunes come up with anything?"

"No, and we couldn't find any matches in their DNA either. That's why we need her here to perform more tests."

"What kinds of tests?"

"Nothin' too fancy. Physical, mental, intellectual."

I *really* don't like the sound of that. "You can't just send those tests to me, and I can do them with her myself?"

Victor clears his throat impatiently. "We have an entire team of people here to perform the tests and to monitor her health during the process because we need to be extremely careful with this one. We can't lose her too."

I stop pacing. "What?"

"The other two couldn't handle the pressure of the physical tests. Sadly, we lost them."

What? I was already having trouble breathing during this conversation. Now I'm suffocating. The other two Immunes are *dead?* And it's ZIRDA's fault? Since when do we ever put Ordinaries in danger? **ZIRDA** has a history of taking measures to the extreme for a greater cause, but killing innocent Ordinaries?

"It didn't happen on purpose," Victor says defensively. "How are we supposed to know how much they can handle until they can't handle any more? Besides, losing two Ordinaries to save the other billions of people will be worth it. Once we've got the upper hand over the Royals . . ."

The man keeps going, but I stop listening. I don't care what he's got to say, because nothing—I repeat, *nothing*—justifies killing innocent people. The anti-Royals department was created to help *save* Ordinaries, not hurt them. I thought that's why Victor came up with this grand plan for our agents to date the Immunes to learn about them without causing any harm. Now he's performing deadly tests on them? *Is he fucking serious?*

Victor refuses to let me off the phone until I agree to have Arella at Shadow Ridge within a week. I agree without any intention of ever doing so. If there's a chance that Victor's brutal tests will harm my sweet girl, fuck that. I don't care if the results from those tests are the key to taking down the Royals. I cannot and will not allow anyone to hurt my girl.

That's when it hits me.

It's over.

My mission is over.

If finding out what makes Arella immune puts her life at risk, I'd rather never know at all. Keeping Arella safe is more important to me than defeating the Royals. Yes, I still want to see them gone, but that's somebody else's job now. As for me, I'm shifting my focus from understanding Arella's immunity to protecting it.

31

TREY

THE NEXT MORNING, ARELLA AND I ARRIVE BACKSTAGE AT THE
Soul House fifteen minutes late. It took her a while to orgasm,
and I refused to let her leave my bed until she did.

The entire band and our manager are all crowded around
the sectional. I sense the heartwarming energy before I hear
the synchronized *aws*. Once my eyes land on the
photographer from our photo shoot at the park, I get a good
feeling that I know what everyone's looking at.

"This one's my favorite!" Emmy says, handing a 4x6 print
to Arella.

I glance over my girl's shoulder at the breathtaking photo.
There I am, holding the most precious woman in the world,
kissing her cheek. I get lost in Arella's sweet smile as I recall all
the fuzzy feelings I got during that shoot.

Emmy had convinced Arella and me to take couples
photos after she and Marcus did theirs. I'm amazed by how
good the pictures turned out. *Do Arella and I always look that
happy together?*

"I like this one the most," Liz says, handing Arella another
4x6 print.

I agree. It was one of our last shots, where Arella and I

had our faces in each other's hands, looking deep into the other's eyes. The photo looks like it belongs on the cover of a sappy romance novel. With anyone else, I might have gagged and made jokes. Because it's Arella, I can't stop staring. The knot in my chest tightens. Any day now, I could lose all this.

When did things get so fucking complicated? This mission was supposed to be simple: Find out what makes this Ordinary immune, duplicate it, and move on. I knew I was gonna fuck this up. I just didn't think it'd be because I fell for my assignment.

"Could I get a copy of this picture?" I ask the photographer, pointing to the photo in Arella's hands.

"Sure," she says. "You can take that one, or I have a wallet size here."

I accept the wallet size. "Thank you."

"Could I get a wallet size too?" Arella asks.

"I only have one wallet of that photo, but I have many others you can choose from."

Beaming, Arella searches through the options and picks one out.

"Oh!" Emmy perks up. "You guys should do what Liz and I do with our pictures."

"Which is . . . ?" I ask with a feeling that it's something super girly.

"We write a cute note on the back for each other."

Yep. Super girly.

"Let's do it," Arella says, handing me her picture.

I trade photos with her and roll my eyes, even though I kinda like the idea. "I'll come up with a cute note to write later."

"Me too."

After we're done going through the photos, the band and I sit down with our manager to go over social-media shit for a couple of hours. Monique spends at least half the time urging me to get "more connected" with our fans through my personal accounts. As always, I refuse. I don't care that it'll help "sell more tickets" or "gain viewers." I play music because I love to, not for the money or the fame.

Once the torture is over, I grip Arella by her hand and we leave for lunch.

"I've got a surprise for you," I say a while later as I push my empty bowl aside. We've just finished eating at a nice ramen place in Chinatown.

Arella wipes her lips with a napkin, then straightens up. "What is it?"

"If I told you, then it wouldn't be a surprise."

Forty-some minutes later, we pull up to an extravagant spa with fancy lights running along the frame of the gold-painted door. Arella's jaw drops, but it's not the place she's astonished by. It's her best friend waiting for us on the golden chairs outside.

I've barely shifted the car into park when Arella runs out to greet Javina with a giant hug. "What are you doing here?"

Javina shrugs. "Dunno. I got a text from pretty boy this morning to meet y'all here at two, so I'm here."

"I'm treating you both to a spa day," I say.

Javina's excitement blasts through my head. "No way! For real?"

"Yep. You're both booked to get your nails done, have an hour-long facial, and a hot-rock massage."

Javina shrieks, then turns to Arella, patting my shoulder. "This one has my official stamp of approval."

My girl laughs. "Thanks."

I peck Arella on her cheek and give her a quick hug. "I'll come pick you up around six."

Now that Arella's preoccupied with getting pampered, I'm free to prepare the rest of my "preserve Arella's immunity" plan.

My first stop is at a jewelry store. I walk in without any idea of what I'm looking for. All I've got is one request: same-day engraving. It takes me a while to decide on a piece to purchase. When I finally do, the woman behind the counter rings me up, and I'm off to my next destination.

At a floral shop, I ask for enough rose petals to fill a swimming pool. The lady tells me she can do three dozen at most, and I accept that.

With a velvet jewelry box, a bag of rose petals, and an arrangement of flowers in hand, I head home. There, I set up the bedroom the way I want it and shut the door.

In the living room, I plant myself on the couch with a pen and Arella's photo. I write up at least fifteen drafts in a notebook before finally deciding on the right words. In my best handwriting possible, I transfer my draft to the back of our picture.

Once I'm done, I read it over a few times. It's the realest thing I've ever written. No song I've ever penned can compare. I hope Arella likes it.

A little after six, I'm waiting in my car outside the spa when Arella and Javina come out, practically glowing. I step out to greet them.

"How was it, ladies?" I hold my arms out for Arella to embrace me.

She does, giving me a hard kiss on the lips too. "Amazing! Look at my nails!"

I once-over her outstretched fingers. They're cleaned up nicely, finished with a lavender-colored polish. "Looks great, babe."

"That massage was exactly what I needed," Javina says. "Thanks, handsome. Out of Ari's two boyfriends so far, you're definitely my fave."

I chuckle lightly. "Not hard to be the favorite when the bar was set so low."

Back at home, while I make dinner, Arella interrogates me on why she's not allowed in the bedroom.

"You're not hiding any dead bodies in there, are you?" she asks playfully.

I shake my head with a chuckle. It's always dead people with her. Maybe she should lay off the true crime shows for a while.

"It's a surprise," I say for the tenth time.

"You can't give me a hint?" She puckers her bottom lip out.

"Nope, and you can pout all you want, but I'm not giving in. You'll find out as soon as we finish eating."

Arella is quick to inhale her pork chop and vegetables. If I could sense her excitement, I'm sure it'd be on the same level as Javina's was earlier outside the spa. Apparently, my girl has no patience, and neither do I, because I finish my meal within minutes of her.

My gut churns as I lead her down the hall and stop outside my bedroom. "Wait here while I put on the final touches."

She nods, then I slip inside, shutting the door behind me.

First, I turn the nozzles to fill the Jacuzzi with warm water. Then I press play on my speakers, and the bathroom fills with soothing piano music. After that, I float a little fireball around to light the wicks of the many candles I've already placed around the tub and bed. The last thing I do is position the velvet box behind some strategically stacked candles on the edge of the Jacuzzi. Finally, I open the door.

Arella clasps a palm against her face as her jaw drops. "Wow . . ."

Rose petals cover everything from the bed to the floor. The candlelight sways to the soft music, inviting her in.

I intertwine my fingers with hers and lead her to the bathroom, where more rose petals are sprinkled everywhere. "You like it?"

She attacks me with a kiss. "I love it!"

Internally, I do a happy dance. There's no way she'll say no.

A minute later, we're naked in the tub. Arella sits between my legs with her back against my front and her head leaned against my shoulder. I wouldn't have it any other way. As I caress her arm, I tenderly kiss up and down her neck.

"My apartment will be ready for me this weekend," Arella says, bursting my bubble of peace.

I scowl, even though she can't see it. I don't want her apartment to be ready. That means she won't sleep here anymore. Well, if she says yes, neither of us will be sleeping here anymore.

It's time . . .

"I have another surprise for you." From behind me, I grab the jewelry box and hold it out in front of her.

"Another? How many do you have tonight?"

Oh, just you wait . . . "Open it."

She dries her wet hands on a towel, then accepts the box from me. It's so big, it's almost double the size of her palms. Slowly, she flips the lid.

"Aw, it's our picture." She takes the photo out of the box, then gasps. "Wow! Honey! It's . . . wow!"

The flickers of candlelight reflect over a gold pendant necklace hanging from a dainty gold chain. The pendant's angel wings are spread, with a two-carat diamond heart in the middle.

"Read the back of the picture."

She does aloud. "Arella, you are my angel. You're the purpose in life I've been searching for. I want to spend eternity with you by my side. We belong together. —Trey."

The next moments of silence tear at me. The expression on her face is unreadable. Does she think it's cheesy? Does she not feel the same way? *Fuck.* I should have written something better.

She tilts her head back and grabs my face, then we embrace in a long kiss. It relaxes the nerves simmering in my gut . . . kinda.

"This is so sweet, honey," she says after she pulls away. "I love it. All of it. The surprise spa date with Javina. The delicious dinner. This candlelit Jacuzzi bath with rose petals. This beautiful necklace. Your wonderful note. Thank you so much."

"Anything for you, baby. Now, turn the necklace over."

"Let me put this down first." She leaves the tub to set the picture on the bathroom counter, where it will stay dry. When she returns, she sits in the spot next to me and flips the necklace over to read the engraving.

"Paris? T.G." Her face crinkles. "Paris? What about it?"

"I wanna take you there."

Her face goes blank. "Seriously?"

"Seriously."

She's quiet. This would be a great time to be able to project some excitement into her or, at the very least, know how she's feeling.

"Trey! That's amazing!" Her giant smile relieves me. That was the easy part. Next is the hard part. As if on cue, she asks, "When do you want to go?"

"As soon as possible," I say, then lower my voice. "Preferably . . . tomorrow."

"Tomorrow? I have to go back to work in three days."

"You don't have to work anymore. I'll take care of you."

She makes a *that's ridiculous* face. "I can't do that."

I take the jewelry box from her and set it aside. Then I squeeze her hands in mine and look straight into her eyes.

"Arella, you are the greatest thing that's ever happened to me. You make me feel happy and full and . . . well, a bunch of other things I can't put into words right now. You deserve way more than what I can give you, but I want to try, and it starts with taking you to Paris. You mentioned that you've always wanted to go there."

"I do. Not tomorrow though. Maybe in a few weeks, after

I can make sure I've got the time off. How long do you want to go for?"

I swallow thickly. My answer is going to freak her out. I say it anyway because I want to be as honest with her as I can. "Forever."

"Forever? What do you mean, *forever?*"

I run my wet fingers through my hair, staring at the rose petals floating in the water. "Like, as in, we won't be coming back."

As expected, her face screws together. "What?"

"You said you've always wanted to go to Paris, right?" My tone is nonchalant, as if it's normal to ask your girlfriend to run away to another country with you.

"Yes, to visit. Not to live. You haven't even asked me to move in with you, and now you're asking me to move to Paris? Haven't you ever heard of baby steps?"

I'm not fond of how quickly she's turning me down. "Can't you at least *entertain* the idea?"

"Okay, sure. Where will we live?"

"I'll buy us a nice place there. Any place you want." I've already got options saved on my phone for her to look at. Everything from cute little apartments to fancy mansions.

"What about my grandparents?"

"We can take them with."

She shakes her head with a face that says, *You can't be serious.* "They're not going to want to move to Europe."

"Didn't you say they love traveling?"

The way she rolls her eyes at me drives me crazy. "That's different. Besides, what about your band?"

"They'll be fine without me."

"So, you're just going to abandon them?" I don't like the accusative tone in her voice or that she used the word *abandon.*

"No band stays together forever."

"But you're working on a second album together and planning to go on tour after that."

I stare at the water again because the bewildered look in her eyes tells me I'm not winning this. "We can tour in Europe."

"Okay, sure. Where will I work?"

"You won't need to."

In the corner of my eye, the face she gives me makes me feel like I'm an ignorant child. "How will I pay for things?"

"I'll pay for everything."

"Right, so you're going to quit your current source of income here and get a job in Europe?"

"I could, but I have more than enough money for us to live on for the rest of our lives." Even if I didn't, I'd make sure she was taken care of. Whether that means I'd be waiting tables or going back to school, I'd do it for her.

"You do not." The way her eyes narrow irks me. I haven't told her how much money I have, but for her to be so skeptical . . . ?

"Don't underestimate what I have in the bank."

"This is insane." She rolls her eyes again. I wish she'd stop doing that.

I lean back and drape an arm over the edge of the Jacuzzi. "It is, but I want this more than anything."

"*You're* insane."

"Only a little." This idea sounds crazier out loud than it did in my head. There, it sounded reasonable, like I'm offering her an all-expenses paid vacation . . . for life. Who wouldn't want that? To never have to worry about paying bills, and her only concern would be whether she wants to visit the Louvre or the Gardens of Versailles for the tenth time.

"Why do you want to move to a whole different country?" she asks. "No, sorry, a whole different *continent*?"

"Don't you think it'd be a fun experience?"

"Yeah, for a few days, or even a couple of weeks, but for life?" The tops of her tits keep peeking up above the water, distracting me from our serious conversation.

I lean back with my best *I promise I'm not losing my mind* face. "If you don't like Paris, we could go to any other place in Europe."

"Why Europe?"

"If you don't like Europe, we can move to Australia, China, or Africa. Whatever you'd like."

Trackers sense other Zordis by the use of their elemental and body powers, but it doesn't work underground or overseas. Since I'd rather not live in a hole, Arella and I have to move.

To be safe, I plan to live out the rest of my life without ever using my powers, in case Victor decides to send someone overseas to locate us. Hopefully, he doesn't have connections with any of the **ZIRDA** bases abroad. The idea that he could have a bunch of people there on the lookout for me is terrifying.

"Trey, I don't want to move at all."

"Can't you at least think about it?" I don't give a shit that I sound desperate. At this point, I'm willing to get on my hands and knees and beg if it means she'll say yes.

Frowning, she crosses her arms over her chest. "What's the *real* reason you want to move? For a 'fun experience' is not going to cut it."

Coming clean about everything was on the list of options I came up with to get us outta this mess. It didn't take me long to decide against it. If I tell Arella the truth, she's gonna run, and I'll lose her. Then she'll definitely be in danger. I've got a feeling that if I'm not the one who takes Arella to Victor within the week, he'll send someone to replace me, and I doubt that person would hesitate like I am.

Arella lowers her tone and cups my cheek. It only settles half the anxiety swirling inside me. "Honey, are you in some kind of trouble?"

"I can explain everything once we get to Paris."

She drops her hand from my face. "Why not now?"

"Because . . . then you might not come with me." I hang my head low. "Actually, you might never want to see me again."

A loud *pfft* echoes throughout the bathroom. "Well, that just makes me want to pack up and head out right now, doesn't it?"

Once it's safe to, I have full intention of telling Arella everything. How the way we met wasn't an accident, how the Royals faked her death when she was three, and everything about the Zordi world. Is it a huge risk? Of course, but I want to be done lying to her. My gut tells me she'll be mad at first but, in the end, she will understand. *She has to . . .*

With her damp hands, she rubs her face and lets out a little groan. "So, let me get this straight. You're saying that whatever secret you're hiding from me might make me leave you, but you want me to move across the world with you before you tell me?"

I guess when she puts it that way, it sounds bad. I'd tell her now if I had a guarantee that she wouldn't freak out and run away. I can't keep her safe if she leaves me. If we're in another country, at least she'll be safe while she processes all the stuff I have to tell her.

I nod firmly. "Yes."

She throws her hands up. "That makes zero sense!"

"I know, babe, but that's just the way it is." I reach for her, but she shoves me away, stinging me deeply. Then she stands and exits the Jacuzzi, grabbing a towel to wrap around herself as she storms out.

I'm left feeling like my entire world is crumbling.

32

TREY

Throughout the night, I think it over. Maybe asking her to move to Europe with me was a little rash. I should have come up with something better. Sadly, with my limited time, it was the best solution I could think of. I just need to get Arella somewhere safe, and Paris seemed like my highest chance of getting her to say yes. My other idea was to ask her to bunker down with me in my parents' invisible safe house, but since I still can't find it, I tossed that idea right out the window.

In the morning, the air between us feels stale. The rose petals sprawled out all over the carpet are a reminder of a night gone wrong. Neither of us mentions Paris during breakfast. I doubt bringing it up again this soon will benefit me anyway. As for Arella, she acts as if last night never happened.

As I place our dirty dishes into the dishwasher, Arella mentions going back to her apartment for the weekend. The thought makes me grind my teeth.

"Babe, I still want you to stay the night with me—every night."

With a smile, she cocks her head to the side. "Are you asking me to move in with you?"

I nod, trying not to look too eager in case she declines my request.

"I don't know. You're kind of hard to live with."

I jerk back a step, my hands still wet. "How so?"

"You're messy. You leave your dirty dishes in the bedroom. You toss your smelly socks all over the house. You make too much noise, and there's just not enough space for me here."

What? "I don't do any of the bullshit you just listed. If anything, I'm tidier than you!"

The corners of her mouth curve upward.

I roll my head back, half grunting, half relieved. "I never know when you're fucking with me."

She laughs adorably. "It's too easy."

When I finish with the dishes, I pull Arella into the bedroom with me. Then I make a big show of emptying a drawer, tossing all my stuff to the floor. "See? There's tons of space for you here." I head into the walk-in closet and move all my clothes to one side, then gesture toward the empty space. "See? This whole side can be yours."

She grins as she runs a hand along the bare hanger rod. "You really want me to move in that bad?"

"Yes, baby. I do." What I actually want is for her to move to Paris with me, but this is a good start.

"Okay, then I will."

My eyes widen. "Seriously?"

"Yeah, seriously."

In the middle of the closet, I pick her up and spin her around. I plant a heavy kiss on her lips as she giggles.

"You know," she says when I release her, "it wouldn't kill you to put some color into your wardrobe."

"You don't like what I wear?"

"All you've got are jeans and plain T-shirts. Don't you ever get sick of wearing the same thing over and over?"

Suddenly, I'm flashed back to elementary school, where

the kids made fun of me for wearing that same striped shirt every three days. "It's what I'm used to . . ."

Arella slumps her shoulders. "Oh, honey. I'm sorry. I didn't mean it like that."

I know she didn't. "It's okay, babe."

With a seductive look in her eyes, she drops to her knees. "Here, I'll make it up to you."

There's no need to make up anything, but I allow her to anyway. Within seconds, she's got my zipper down, then my jeans. I'm rock hard before she's even wrapped her hand around my dick.

When I get my fill of her mouth on me, I pump into her against the closet wall until the pleasure ripples through me, and I jerk myself empty into a clean shirt I tear off a hanger.

"Did you come?" I ask, even though I know the answer. Her emotions didn't course through my head.

"No, but that's okay."

"The hell it is." I take her hand and lead her to the bed. "Lie down, baby. Let me take care of you."

It takes her a while to get there. Eventually, she does, and her release sends a wave of her emotions through my head.

I could get used to this.

"Do you mind if I get a workout in before lunch?" I ask as Arella gets washed up.

"Sure. I have to get some work done on my blog anyway."

An hour later, I saunter downstairs from my workout room to find Arella on the couch, typing away on her laptop.

She looks up from her screen, then frowns. "Did you work out?"

"Yeah, why?"

"You didn't even break a sweat."

"I only weight lifted," I lie because any Ordinary would be sweating through their clothes after the fifteen-mile run I just completed on the treadmill.

Arella knows I'm fibbing, because she gives me a fishy look.

I turn my back to her and head to the bedroom. "I'ma get cleaned up, then I'll make us lunch."

When I come back out, Arella is in the same spot, still working. In my palm is her diamond necklace. Sadly, I found it still in its box, where it doesn't belong.

Standing behind her, I hook the diamond around her neck, then gently pull her long waves out of the loop.

"Trey . . ." she says uneasily.

I knew she'd protest. "I want you to wear it, babe."

"But I didn't agree to the Paris thing."

"Doesn't matter. I got this for you, and it's yours whether you agree to the Paris thing or not."

"I'm never going to agree though."

Those words tear at me. They hold so much conviction. Gracefully, I flip my legs over the back of the couch and plop at her side. I take her laptop and set it onto the coffee table. Then I squeeze her hands in mine. "Could you at least think about it? Please?"

I hate how quickly she shakes her head. "There's nothing to think about. I'm not moving to Paris."

I swallow the dry lump in my throat. "Baby, I swear, with anyone else, I wouldn't give a damn. But it's you. I *really* need you to come with me."

"If you can help me understand why, I'll consider it."

I want to tell her everything. I really do, but I need to get her somewhere safe before I tell her that there are people out there who possess powers she doesn't know exist, and that I'm one of them. And that for some strange reason I still don't know, she's immune to those powers. And that my uncle wants me to bring her to him so he can perform deadly tests on her because I'm doing a shit job at solving the mystery myself. In Paris, she can get mad at me for as long as she wants, but at least she'll be away from Victor.

I sigh heavily. "I promise you, baby. I'll explain everything in Paris."

She yanks her hands out of mine, only to toss them into the air. "This is ridiculous. No, I can't wait until we're on another continent to hear why you've shipped me away from home. I want to know why now."

Don't get me wrong. I love seeing the side of her that's strong, defiant, and stands up for herself, but does she really have to choose *now* for it to come out?

With a huff, she folds her arms together. "You know, Liz told me that you like to run when the going gets tough. Whatever happened, Trey, you can't just run from it and drag me with you."

"Why the hell is Liz telling you shit like that?"

"It's not shit if it's true." That's the first time Arella's ever sworn in front of me. It sounds odd coming from her. "Liz told me what happened after Elliott passed away. About how you ran off to some cabin in Colorado for a month. Did something happen, Trey? Did you get into legal trouble or something? What's making you want to run again?"

"This isn't the same as what happened with Elliott." I choke up a little. It still hurts to say his name. "This is about you and me."

"Then why are *you* the only one who's clued in on the details?"

"I told you. I'll tell you once we get to Paris. Once we're safe."

"Safe from what?"

My eyes fall to my hands. "I can't say."

She groans and gets to her feet. "This conversation is getting us nowhere. If you want to move to Paris so bad, then why don't you just go yourself?"

The words leave my mouth before I can stop them. "Because I wouldn't be able to breathe without you."

33

———

TREY

A yellow Sunrise Daycare T-shirt and the angel-wings necklace—that's what Arella wore when she left for work earlier. It's her first day back to work since the spider incident. No matter what I said to encourage her to stay, she wasn't having it.

When she said she needed to work so she could make rent, I offered her triple the money. She still wasn't having it. Leave it to me to find the most difficult woman in the world to fall for. Any other person would have accepted that offer in a heartbeat. Not Arella. I guess I got my wish when I told Liz that I wanted someone to want me for something other than my money.

The only reason I didn't keep pushing Arella to stay was because she told me that Nathan used to use money to control her. He'd make her dependent on him and his daddy's money as a way to hold power over her. That's nowhere near why I'm offering her money, but I can understand why she feels the need to make her own. So, that's why I'm heading to work today—alone.

"You 'ight, bro?" Marcus slaps a palm over my shoulder in

the middle of our writing session. "You been quiet, and now you be hella red in the face."

The rest of our band turns their attention to me, and their concern soars through my mind. I must look sick. I definitely feel it. A minute ago, my chest started burning out of nowhere. Now I'm getting nauseous and my arms feel numb.

"I'm fine," I lie.

I push through another two minutes before the dizziness takes over. As the room spins, my guitar slides off my lap and clanks to the floor. Emmy shrieks, and it makes the migraine in my head blister.

"You wanna lay down, man?" Kevin asks, picking up the guitar for me.

Nausea rises up my throat. *Am I about to . . . Yep, I am.* I rush behind the mini bar and find a trash can just in time to heave into it. I cough as the vomit leaves my throat. Then I heave again. I feel everyone's eyes on me as I throw up my lunch.

When I think it's done, I tie a knot into the trash bag and replace it with a new one. Then I rinse my mouth out under the sink faucet. I was right. My bandmates are gaping at me.

"Are you guys cool with finishing this song without me?" I ask. "I'ma head home."

"Of course, T," Liz says.

"Yeah, go get some rest," Emmy adds.

As I mount my motorcycle, I check the time. Arella got off work twenty minutes ago, and she planned to meet me here. She's probably already on her way, so I call her. The phone rings to her voicemail. I end the call and shoot her a text.

> Hey, babe. I'm not feeling well, so I'm leaving work early. Can you meet me at home instead?

I ride for about fifteen minutes with a splitting headache before I pull over to call her again. I end up at her voicemail . . . again. This time, I leave a message.

"Hey, angel. I'm heading home because I don't feel well. Just letting you know so you don't go to the Soul House and expect me there. I'll see you at home, 'kay?"

I wish there was a way to know if someone's listened to your voicemail. I check my messages again to see if Arella has read my text. It still says *delivered*, not *read*.

In my missed-calls log is a call from Victor from five minutes ago. Whatever he's got to say can wait, because right now, I'm too focused on figuring out where Arella is. I know we didn't leave things on the best note this morning, but she wouldn't ghost me, would she?

I ride for another ten minutes before I get impatient and pull off to the shoulder again. After I yank my helmet off, I Google the number for Sunrise Daycare. Someone picks up on the third ring.

"Sunrise. Javina speaking."

"Javina, it's Trey. Is Arella there?" I don't know what I'm hoping for. Maybe for her to tell me that Arella got held up and she's just finishing up work. Maybe that one of the kids is pulling a bad prank on her by hiding her phone, and she's running around looking for it as we speak. I would have accepted anything except the answer I actually get.

"Sorry, pretty boy. Ari left when her shift ended."

"Thanks." I hang up.

I call Liz, and she picks up right away. "Hey, T-Bear. You okay?"

Not really . . . My nausea has gotten worse, and it's not like Arella to not answer her phone. "Is Arella there?"

"Nope, why?"

"Dammit." I slap a hand against my handlebars as I hang up. *Where is she?*

A thought stops my heart. What if this is her way of leaving me? She's had enough of me hiding shit from her, and she's probably at my house, packing her stuff up right now.

When I get home, her drawer will be empty, her side of the closet will be too, and I'll never see her again.

Please don't let that be it . . .

With my helmet back on, I race home. Her car isn't in my driveway. As I dismount my bike, my heart pounds against my lungs like fists against a sandbag. *Thump, thump, thump.* I rush inside, shouting for her.

"Babe? You here?"

Silence.

I wrench her drawer open so hard, it comes out of the nightstand. My nausea settles a tiny bit when I find her things still here. I don't even bother putting the drawer back in. I've got more important things to do—like find my girl.

Maybe she's at her apartment. Maybe she's surprising me by packing up her things to bring here. Even as I think that, I know it's unlikely. Still, I climb back onto my bike and head to her place.

It feels like forever getting through traffic. When I finally arrive at Arella's apartment complex, her car is missing from the parking lot.

I knock on her door and wait all of two seconds before I point a finger at the lock and let myself in. The place smells of ripe chemicals and cleaning supplies. At least it's spider-less. Unfortunately, it's also Arella-less.

"Babe?" I yell, just in case.

Nobody answers.

I head into her bedroom and find zero signs that she's been around. *Where could she be?*

I jump when my phone buzzes in my pocket. It's a number I don't recognize. Usually, I don't answer unknown numbers, but . . . "Hello?"

"Hi, is this Trey Grant?" asks a calm female voice I've never heard before.

"Who's this?"

"I'm Sara Benson, a nurse at the LA Community

Hospital. I'm calling on behalf of Miss Arella Rance. She wanted me to tell you where she is."

My lungs tighten. "Why couldn't she call me herself?"

"I'm afraid she's in no condition to—"

"What happened?"

"I . . . I, um, can't tell you exactly."

"Why not?" I shout, and I don't care that it's rude.

Sara is unfazed. She replies in the same calm tone. "Because I don't know all the details. I wasn't here when she was admitted up from the ER. I was just told to call you."

"The ER?" I shout again. "What?"

"Look, all I know is that she was brought in by ambulance."

"Ambulance?" I can't breathe.

"She's on floor two. You're welcome to come here and speak to the doctor in charge of—"

"I'll be there in fifteen minutes."

34

TREY

To my ears, the hospital is quiet. To my head, it's a madhouse of insanity. Sadness, fear, anxiety, dread—it's all here, clawing at me to feel what everyone else feels. I can't shut it off. I can't even tone it down. I'm too tense to control my mind power.

"Where is she?" I ask the woman stationed behind the first desk I can find on floor two.

She looks up at me from behind a pair of sparkly pink eyeglasses. The name badge clipped to her chest reads: Sara Benson, RN.

"You must be Trey Grant."

"Yes. Where is she?" I sound rude and impatient, but I can't help it. I won't be okay until I see Arella again.

The woman doesn't seem to care that I'm on a one-track train going three hundred miles an hour toward one goal and one goal only. "Wow. You got here quick. Do you live nearby?"

Not at all. I probably broke at least sixteen laws with my motorcycle coming here as I weaved between cars and ran stop lights. "Where. Is. She?" That's the third time I've asked, and I'm not asking again.

"Look, I understand you're probably scared right now, but don't worry. She's fine." Sara smiles as if to soothe me. "Just calm down, and take a deep breath."

I hate when people tell me to calm down. It only irritates me more. Still, I obey her and suck in a deep breath. It does nothing to settle me.

"Great. I'll go grab Dr. Jordan. He'll meet you in the family waiting room." She points toward an open room down the hall with a kiddie table and chairs. "In the meantime, could you check in?" She hands me a clipboard.

I sign the damn paper, then slap a sticker with my name on it against my upper chest. Then I force my body into the family waiting room. It's small and smells of musty carpet and old shoes. In the corner, a little TV plays an animated movie at a low volume. A large round table sits in the opposite corner with an unfinished puzzle scattered on top.

My phone buzzes in my pocket. It's Victor again. I don't want to be in the middle of a conversation with him when the doctor comes, so I let it go to voicemail.

All my nails are chewed down when I finally hear, "Mr. Grant?"

A tall man with rich bronze skin and graying hair appears in the doorway. My zense activates as he offers me the knowing smile that Zordis do whenever we first meet another of our kind. "I'm Doctor Jordan. Thanks for coming so quickly."

I don't return his smile. "What happened?"

The doctor places a pen into the chest pocket of his scrubs, sighing. "Miss Rance was in a car accident."

My knees almost give out. *A car accident?*

The doctor throws his palms up. "She's fine. Just whiplash, a few stitches, and some bruises."

Whiplash? Stitches? Bruises? My brain can't comprehend what any of those words mean when it comes to Arella. How can this man talk about all of that as if it's normal?

"Can I see her?" My voice comes out broken like the way my chest feels.

"I'm sorry. You'll need to wait until she's done testing."

"I can't just *see* her?"

"Not while she's going through an MRI."

The little patience I have left snaps as I growl, "How long is that gonna take?"

"Maybe an hour. Two at most."

Two hours? My heart can't take another minute of this. "What caused the accident?"

"A car T-boned her at an intersection and fled the scene."

I plop into the closest chair. The doctor continues, but my mind doesn't process it. All I hear is *blah, blah, blah.*

When Dr. Jordan leaves, the tingling in my chest leaves with him. I barely get a moment to myself before that same nurse knocks on the doorframe.

"Could I get you anything? Coffee? Tea? A snack?" Sara's got that pointless smile glued to her face again.

"No, thank you," I reply blankly as I stare aimlessly at the TV.

"If you wanna pass some time, there's a gift shop downstairs."

"Thanks."

Twenty minutes later, I pace the hospital with a large gift bag in hand, trying to pull myself together. They said she's fine. I shouldn't be so worried. But if she's fine, why does she need MRI scans? And stitches? What if she's not fine, and they lied to me to prevent me from freaking the fuck out and tearing this place apart until I find her? If I don't see my girl soon, I might do just that.

A person in the room at the end of the hall has five miserable people surrounding them. All their feelings of despair are drowning out the emotions of everyone else in the hospital. I do my best to channel my mind power toward Sara, who seems to be the only one around who's spirit isn't dying inside. The most that does is lower everyone else's murky energy to a constant whisper—a loud whisper.

Eventually, I hide in the stairwell to call Liz. She'll have something good to say. She always does.

Liz answers on the first ring. "What's wrong?"

"What? Are you a Seer now too?"

"You never call me, and this is the second time you've called me today after you abruptly left our writing session looking like you caught a zirus. So, what's wrong?"

I pound my forehead against the wall. It echoes in the stairwell. "It's Arella. She . . ." I can't even say it without choking up. "She was in a car accident."

Liz gasps. "How bad is the damage? To her, obviously, not the car."

"The doctor said she's okay. I haven't confirmed it yet since I haven't seen her. She's going through some bullshit MRI thing that takes forever." I still don't understand what the point of an MRI is when she's "fine."

"Oh, T. I'm so sorry. What can I do for you?"

I sigh deeply, trying my best not to lose it. "Just talk to me. I hate hospitals."

"Yeah, that's not the best place for you, is it?"

"I'm getting a headache." Actually, my head pounds as if little elves are chopping wood in my brain while listening to heavy metal. The only good thing is that the nausea has simmered down and my arms don't feel numb anymore. *Which reminds me . . .* "Liz, I need to tell you something, and it's gonna sound crazy."

"Okay?"

"I—I felt it."

There's a long pause, and I picture Liz's eyebrows creasing together. "Felt what?"

"That sensation Zordis talk about. I knew that something was wrong with Arella. My *body* knew. My stomach wouldn't stop whipping around, and there's this constant burning in my chest."

"That's not possible, T. We only feel the glimmer with our soul mates."

I know that. That's why this doesn't make any sense. "Well . . . maybe, I dunno. Maybe Arella—"

"Stop. I know what you're about to say, and there's no chance. She's an Ordi."

"I know, but here's the thing. Today is not the first time I felt it. It happened last week too. I thought it was just a coincidence, so I brushed it off. I've always thought the glimmer was just some stupid thing Zordis made up to put claim on each other—until I felt it *again* today. I mean, I dunno. Maybe it was a coincidence, but it doesn't feel like it."

"Hmm . . ." is all Liz says. The call goes silent for a moment before she continues, "Ya know, if you think Ari could be your soul mate, that means you're in love with her."

I don't respond. I don't know how to.

Liz presses on. "Are you?"

In the depths of my soul, I know the answer. I inhale a few breaths of courage before I'm able to admit it out loud. "Yes, I am."

Liz perks up, and I hear her grinning through the phone. "Ah! I've been waiting for you to fall in love for years. I never thought it'd be with an Ordi though. I mean, do you know how outrageous that sounds?"

I slump onto the bottom step of the stairs and shove my face into my hand. "I know it's bizarre, but it doesn't feel that way."

"I agree."

I don't hide my shock. "You do?"

"Yeah. I've said it before, T. That girl is perfect for you, except for the one thing. If you haven't noticed, I've stopped giving you shit for being with her, 'cause you light up whenever she's around. Lately, the lyrics you've been writing aren't as dark, and your smiles look genuine. I've never seen you so happy. I wasn't about to keep nagging at you for being happy, no matter how strange and illegal it is."

As always, Liz is right. Arella does make me the happiest I've ever been. For my best friend to have recognized that and encouraged it, even when she believes it's wrong, means a ton. I already thought Liz deserves the world. Now I think she deserves the entire universe.

"What should I do?" I ask, unsure what exactly I'm referring to. I need advice on a lot of things right now.

"Have you told her?"

"Told her what?"

Liz scoffs with a *duh* tone. "That you're in love with her."

"Considering how I only admitted it to myself for the first time just now, no."

"Do you know if she feels the same?"

"I can't sense her, so I dunno." I'm still trying to process the idea that I'm in love with someone. The concept that someone might feel the same for me is even harder to swallow.

"Seriously, T? You rely on your Empath power way too much. You need to tell her."

"How?"

"I dunno. Just tell her."

Admitting that I'm in love with Arella is one thing. Now I have to tell her, too? *Since when was that a rule?* "What will that accomplish?"

"I dunno. I just think it's important for you to verbalize this to her."

"Okay, then what?"

"Then, well . . . that's where it gets difficult, doesn't it? It's not like the Superiors are gonna allow you to have this relationship just 'cause you're in love. They'll still lock you up if they find out. In court, they'll ask you about intent to determine if they should put you behind bars or in an asylum.

"In your case, I'ma guess the asylum. The second you tell

'em you felt the glimmer with an Ordinary, it'll be case closed. *Bam!* Next thing you know, you're sitting in a room with a bunch of weirdos who eat their own toenails and—"

"Liz."

"Oh, sorry. I'm not helping, am I?"

Not a fucking bit. "Not really . . ."

"Okay, how 'bout I stop over at the hospital? Would that help?"

"Yes, actually. If they discharge Arella tonight, could you drive her to my place? I rode the bike here."

"Sure. Text me the address. I'll come now."

Almost an hour later, Liz strolls through the sliding glass doors with a brown paper bag.

"What's that?" I ask as my chest tingles.

"Tacos!" She beams. "Grabbed some on the way over. I figured you probably hadn't eaten yet."

My belly rumbles from the delicious scent of food wafting from the bag. I don't know what to say. This woman never stops wowing me. I heave her in by the shoulder and snake my arms around her. Then I squeeze her as hard as I can. Her warmth washes away a bit of the stress I've been carrying.

Liz coughs. "Stop, T. I'm gonna drop these tacos if you keep suffocating me."

I release her. "Sorry. I'm just so fucking grateful for you."

"As you should be. No one else would ever put up with your shit." She leans into me and lowers her voice. "I mean, seriously, any other Zordi would be calling to get you into rehab right now. Your obsession with Ari is still a little wacky to me, but I trust that you, of all people, know that your feelings for her are real."

"They are," I say with full conviction. "Speaking of other Zordis, her doctor is one."

Liz clasps a gloved hand to her mouth. "Oh no. Does he know you're dating Ari?"

I shrug.

"Do you think he's gonna call the Supes?"

Another shrug. "I hope not. I've been too worried about Arella to even think about that."

"I'll back you up. I'll say you two are just friends."

I let out a light scoff. "Like they're gonna listen to you."

She puts a fist up. "I'll make 'em!"

Liz checks in and gets a name sticker from Sara, and then we head into the waiting room. There's a different kid's movie playing on the TV now. On the table, I push the unfinished puzzle aside to give us space to eat our tacos.

Between bites, Liz asks, "Do you think it's possible that she's one of us?"

With my mouth full, I say, "No, why?"

"Because I don't think you have a mental condition. Crazy people don't think they're crazy, and you've admitted that this thing you have for Ari is bizarre. Yeah, you like to sleep around with Ordis, but I think that has more to do with your past and your gifts than having an actual attraction to them. But to fall in love with one? And to experience the glimmer? I doubt that's stemming from your trauma. There's gotta be another explanation, and the only one I can think of is that Ari's one of us. What if immunity is her power? What if her immunity is what blocks us from feeling the zense around her?"

Wow. That's a lot to take in. "First off, my past? My trauma? How does that have anything to do with why I'm willing to sleep with Ordinaries?"

Liz eyes me, lifting an eyebrow. "Do you really wanna unpack that right now?"

I'm about to say yes because I want to hear her explanation, but now, I'm not so sure. I've got a feeling she's gonna say things I won't like.

"I'll give you a hint. It has to do with your low self-worth, what you think you deserve, and how your past affects that."

Yeah, I don't wanna hear any more. I clear my throat. "Moving on . . ."

After I chew down the rest of my first taco, I lean back in my chair. "The idea that Arella is a Zordi has crossed my mind. I did some research on it over the z-net a while ago, and the closest ability I could find to her immunity is force fields. Even then, Blockers can only block *external* powers, and Arella's immunity seems to only block the *internal* ones.

"Also, those Zordis can't block the zense. According to the z-net, nothing can. If Arella was a Zordi and didn't know it, she'd feel the tingle around us, and I don't think she does. Plus, she doesn't have any other powers."

Liz finishes the taco she's working on as she thinks. "Maybe she's defective, and that's what causes her body to not feel the zense or have any other powers?" Liz is doing what I did before: looking for any possible cause that could explain the anomaly that is Arella. I've stopped trying to explain the unexplainable. It didn't amount to anything.

I pick up another taco and bite into it. "The correct term is *restricted*, not defective. Zordis with complications in their gifts get offended when people call them defective."

"I know, but my family calls me defective all the time, and it's true, so why correct them?"

This isn't the first time Liz has called herself defective, and I hate it. In the Zordi world where everyone's born with three powerful gifts and natural beauty, having anything wrong with you results in immediate disownment. Liz's family is no exception, and it's part of the reason why I will forever stick by this woman's side.

I scowl at her. "You're not defective. Your body power works—just not in a way you'd like it to."

"You know, you're the only one who ever gets mad at me for calling myself defective. Everyone else just agrees."

I shake my head, sighing. The Zordi community needs to

do better. "Anyway, if Arella is one of us, then explain how she gets cold all the time? Or how she sweats when she's hot?"

Liz bites into her second taco. "Hmm. Good point. With our bodies' natural equilibrium, it's not possible for us to sweat."

"Exactly. Also, Arella sleeps every night. She even has dreams and nightmares. She doesn't heal as fast as we can. She can't see as far as we can, either. The other day, while in the car, I asked her if she could read a sign way down the road. While I could read it perfectly, she could barely see it."

After wiping her mouth off with a napkin, Liz says, "Ya know, I've always wondered what it'd be like to have dreams or Ordinary vision. Once, I Googled what Ordinaries see when they take off their glasses. Did you know that some of their eyes are so bad, they can barely make out shapes or colors?"

"Yeah, I knew that."

A knock on the doorframe causes Liz to jolt.

"Sorry!" Sara giggles. "Just wanted to let you know she's done. You're welcome to see her now."

I shoot out of my chair before the nurse even finishes her sentence. Liz and I follow her down the hall and around a corner before stopping at a closed door. I don't sense anyone on the other side, so it must be Arella.

Sara turns to us. "Maybe just one at a time?"

Liz steps back and gestures for me to go first. With my giant gift bag in hand, I enter the small hospital room. Sara quietly shuts the door behind me.

The square room is dimly lit and smells of disinfectant. My girl is propped up on the bed in a light-blue gown, wearing a neck brace that looks like it's suffocating her. Cords are tangled around her body in every direction, hooked up to machines that do who knows what.

I'd do anything to take her place. I'd go through a

thousand car accidents if it means she'd never have to go through another one again.

"Trey." Her voice cracks, sounding weak and fragile. I want so badly to hold her until the pain is gone.

After setting the gift bag down, I slide a chair closer to her bedside and sit. Then I take her hand and squeeze it between both of mine. Once again, I draw strength from her touch. A tiny beam of light shines into me, erasing some of the darkness in my chest.

"Hey, beautiful."

She lets out a little *pfft*. "I doubt I look that beautiful right now."

"You'll always look beautiful to me." I mean that with all my heart.

This catastrophe only confirms how much of a wreck I'd be if something ever happened to her. Silently, I vow to myself to never let anything else happen.

With a smile, Arella turns her head to fully face me. The stitches on her lip flash me back to when my mother's lip was cut. She had blood dripping down every curve of her face. Her screams echo in my mind as that big man drags her away from me to pound his fist into her head. I should have protected her, like I should have protected Arella.

A pang of nausea hits me hard, except this time, it's not from the glimmer. I swallow thickly, trying to keep it down.

"What's in the bag?" Arella asks.

"Something for you." The bag crinkles as I pull out a big purple teddy bear.

Her eyes light up as she accepts it from me. "Awe. It's adorable! Thank you."

My phone vibrates in my jeans. It's Victor—again. What the fuck does he need so badly? This is the worst time to be calling. I don't want to leave Arella, but in all my twenty-six years, Victor has never been this insistent about reaching me.

"I'll be back, angel," I say as I step away. I gesture for Liz to enter the room as I head down the hall to answer my phone. "Hello?"

As always, Victor sounds snippy. "Are you with the girl?"

"Yeah, why?"

"Any updates?"

"No." I could tell him that the very person we need alive for any of this to work almost died today, but she didn't, so that information isn't relevant.

"Seriously? Have you been able to sense *any* emotions from her?"

"Nope," I lie again.

"Not a single one?"

"Nope."

"Hmm. We'll have to try something else."

I enter the stairwell as my heart clenches. "What do you mean?"

"These tests aren't working."

Something inside me flips into panic mode. Careful to keep my tone steady, I ask, "What tests?"

"You know . . . the flu, the spiders, the truck."

I stop breathing as everything clicks together. I try to sound less angry and more surprised. "Wait, all of those things happened to her . . . because of you?"

"Weakening her immune system. Invoking trauma, then a near-death experience. Since you're taking so long to get results, I thought we'd do some testing in the meantime. Our team thought lowering her natural defenses or raising an extreme emotion in her would do the trick. If we can get you to sense her when she's most vulnerable or when her emotions are at their highest, maybe we can find out the source of her im—"

"Why wasn't I informed of this?" I can barely contain myself through gritted teeth. "You could have killed her."

"Are you questioning my methods? Everything was highly controlled. The flu was a minor one, those spiders weren't poisonous, and the accident was thoroughly organized. I wouldn't risk her life without having our best agents on it. Also, I made sure she was sent to a hospital where one of our ZIRDA doctors is stationed. He's already sent me the reports from her MRI scan, and we'll cross-reference it with the others. She's completely safe."

Safe? Is he fucking kidding? I just saw her in a neck brace. It takes everything in me not to curse at him. I need to get off this call before I say something I shouldn't.

"Do you have any other tests planned?" I ask, trying my hardest to keep my tone stable.

"Yes, actually, and they involve you, but they need to be performed here. When can you bring her in?"

Never! He's insane if he thinks I'm going to allow him to breathe around Arella after he killed the last two Immunes. *Over my dead body.* "I can't convince her into a road trip now that she's in a neck brace."

"Why not?"

"Trust me. I know this woman. She's gonna wanna rest up. If I push her into it, she'll be more hesitant to do it. How about we wait until she's fully healed first?"

In the background, a spoon clinks against a mug. Victor takes a sip of the liquid. "When will she be out of the neck brace? A week?"

"At least two." I have no idea how long it'll be. I just need to buy some time. "Also, it'll be important for me to meet her grandparents first. They could give me some insight into something that may have happened to her when she was young that she doesn't remember."

"Fine. Meet them within the week and report back." *Click.*

Pulling at my hair, I collapse to the dusty floor.

This can't be happening.

35

ARELLA

THE DOCTOR SAID MY LIP WOULD HEAL WITHIN A WEEK. AFTER two days, my lip was fully healed without even a scar to show for it.

The doctor said my body would be sore for two weeks. It's been a week now, and my body feels like it's functioning at one hundred percent again.

I'm not wearing the neck brace anymore, despite what Trey wants. He thinks I should follow the doctor's orders and wear it for the full fourteen days, but why wear something that's awkward and itchy when I don't need to?

Ever since the accident, Trey's been intense. Even when we're home, not really doing anything, he insists on being next to me at all times. If I leave the room, he comes with. I understand that I was injured, and that's been hard on him, but nothing is going to happen to me in the safety of his house. The more I remind him of that, the more protective he gets.

Lately, his eyes have been swimming with anxiety. I wish he'd open up to me and explain what's bothering him. Despite what he says, it's not only the car accident that's eating at him.

However, the more I ask about it, the more he shuts down, so I let it go.

Something he *won't* let go is the Paris thing. He brings it up every day—sometimes multiple times a day. He's shown me housing options and talked my ear off about the wonderful sights. He even looked up storefronts where I can start my dream bakery. It's enticing, but at the end of the day, I'm not willing to move to Paris on the promise that he'll tell me why once we get there. No way. Whenever I urge him to tell me the reason, he refuses.

I'm climbing into bed when I ask, "Are you trying to get away from the feds?"

It's the only thing I can think of as to why he wants to flee the country. While I'm flattered that he's so into me that he won't move without me, I'm not trying to live a life on the run. He mentioned that he's got lots of investments. Maybe some are illegal and it's finally catching up to him.

"No, baby," he says somberly, sliding under the covers with me. "I'm not running from the feds."

The sincere look on his face makes me believe him, so I throw out other guesses. "Did you mess with the wrong mob boss? Is someone after your money? Did you find out you have a child somewhere, and you don't want me to find out about it?"

He pulls my back against his front. "No, baby. It's none of those."

I'm out of guesses. "And this is something that might make me break up with you?"

"Maybe, but I hope not. I'm one hundred percent sure you'll be freaked out at first, but I also have faith that you'll understand and forgive me."

I am a forgiving person—sometimes too forgiving. "Can you give me a hint?"

"No, but what I can tell you is that I care about you more than anything in this world and I hope that's enough to earn your forgiveness. It doesn't even have to be right away, just eventually. And I'll do everything in my power to make sure you'll never regret it."

He didn't have to tell me that he cares about me for me to know it. I *feel* it through the little things he does. Like the way he always brings me a fresh glass of water before bed and the way he holds me *so* tight until I fall asleep.

I'm torn. I'm nowhere closer to knowing what he's hiding from me, yet I trust that whatever it is won't change my feelings about him. This last week of watching him cook for me, clean for me, and treat me like a queen has made me realize that I'm in love with this man. While he hasn't said it, I think he's in love with me too. I can see it in his eyes every time he stares at me.

"Good night, baby." Trey wraps his arms around me tighter, then kisses my neck the gentle way he has been since the accident. While it does send a spark down my body, I miss the way he kissed me before—long, hard, and passionate.

He's the same when we make love too. He thrusts inside me like he's afraid he'll break me. I prefer the rough, animalistic way he pounded into me before. Yesterday, when I told him that, he said, "I don't wanna hurt you." No matter what I said, I couldn't convince him that my body can take it.

The other thing I couldn't convince him of is going to meet my grandparents. For weeks, he practically begged to meet them. Now he suddenly doesn't want to anymore? What changed? I'm off work, with a *real* doctor's note this time, so this is a great opportunity for us to go. Trey's excuse is that he's not ready for me to be in a car yet, but that's not true. He's been dragging me with him to work every day.

Either way, arguing with him is pointless—like the argument we've been having about my car. Since my Civic is totaled, I've been online shopping for a new vehicle. It's been hard to find something that I like and can afford. Trey keeps telling me to pick out whatever I want with any price tag because he'll get it for me, but I refuse to allow that.

Nathan used to buy things for me so he could use them against me later. Whenever we fought, he'd say things like "You wouldn't even have that if it wasn't for me." I recognize now that it was just another one of his many ways to guilt me into doing whatever he wanted. While I don't think that's Trey's intent, I still don't want to feel like I owe him.

Two weeks after the accident, I'm finally able to convince Trey to leave my side for the first time. His band has an all-day video shoot, and I want to stay home to bake. Lately, my blog hasn't seen much new content, which has been affecting my traffic, which affects my paycheck.

"I'm staying home," I say firmly. "Being out of work for the past two weeks means I need the extra money now more than usual. I promise you, honey, I'll be fine by myself."

"You're so goddamn difficult," Trey says with a huff, before getting into his car and driving away. It'll do him some good to have a few hours away from me. He needs to relearn that in life, things will happen, and he can't take me everywhere with him just to ensure I'm okay.

I'm in the middle of grabbing flour out of his cabinet when the doorbell rings. I expect it to be the mailman or someone trying to convert me into their religion, so I'm pleasantly surprised when it's neither.

"If you don't marry him, I will," Javina says when I open the door.

"What are you doing here?"

"That man of yours called me—at work, mind you, because I wasn't answering my cell, because ya know, I was *working*—just to ask me to hang out with you today. When I told him I couldn't, he offered me another spa day to get me to fake a family emergency."

My jaw drops. "Did you?"

Dramatically, Javina slaps a hand over her chest. "Please

pray for my mother, who broke her ankle from falling down a ladder. She's in desperate need of my care right now."

With an eye roll coupled with a light chuckle, I gesture for Javina to step inside. "Aren't we short-staffed?"

Javina kicks her shoes off. "Yeah, but luckily, we're down five kids today, and I was able to call in Carrie last minute. So, it's all good. Besides, I wasn't gonna turn down another spa day. Also, he Venmoed me five hundred dollars after I agreed to his terms. The note said, "for missing a day of work.' " She scoffs. "As if I get paid that much to watch over children."

"Wait . . ." I lead Javina into Trey's kitchen. "What were his *terms*?"

"He just asked that I don't let you out of my sight. For five hundred dollars a day, tell that boy I'll babysit you whenever he wants!"

I roll my eyes again. "He's been overprotective lately."

"Girl, I am too. First a spider invasion, now a car accident? What's next? A building falling over you? A stampede of hyenas? If I could, I'd shrink you and put you into a padded box. Then I'd carry you around in my pocket to make sure nothing can harm you."

On the spectrum of overprotectiveness, it goes Javina, then Trey, then my grandparents. Growing up, Gramps and Grammy rarely let me out of their sight. Even when we were doing simple things like hanging out at a playground, my grandparents were always one step behind me.

I'm used to people being overprotective of me. It's part of the reason why I didn't pick up on Nathan's red flags for so long. I've since learned that there's a difference between being overprotective and being controlling. Javina, Trey, and my grandparents keep me close because they genuinely care about me. Nathan kept me close because he needed to exert power over me.

Thankfully, Trey hasn't done or said anything that's felt controlling. Yes, he's a little possessive sometimes—like the other day, when his security manager made me laugh and touched my arm, Trey stormed over within seconds to pull me away. Still, he has yet to tell me what I can and cannot wear. Not once has he tried to read my text messages over my shoulder, or suggest that I'm not allowed to see or call Javina. The second he does, I'm out. I don't care how much joy this man brings into my life. I'm not going through another three years of abuse, gaslighting, and feeling unwanted. If anything, Trey has been making me feel overly wanted.

WHEN MY MAN RETURNS HOME FROM HIS VIDEO SHOOT, HE shows up in a car I've never seen before. Javina and I step outside to greet him in the driveway, where a brand-new white crossover is sitting.

Javina whistles through her teeth. "Damn, pretty boy. Lexus ain't doin' it for ya no more?"

Trey flaunts a megawatt smile from the driver's seat with the door open. "I'm good with my car. This one's for Arella."

In sync, Javina and I gasp. For the first time ever, my talkative friend is out of words.

I'm not. "Honey, you didn't . . ."

"I did." He beams and even has the nerve to do it proudly.

I'm not sure if I should be mad, glad, frustrated, or thrilled. I'm a little of all. It's the anger that comes out though. "Why would you do this? After all the reasons I told you not to?"

Javina flashes me a *What the hell?* look. "Ari! Ungrateful much?"

Trey hops out of the car with his arms up in surrender. "I bought the car under your name. It's all yours. Fully paid for. No strings attached."

I pretzel my arms together. "I'm not accepting it."

Trey sighs heavily. "How 'bout you get in and drive it around before you make that decision?"

I'm about to protest again when Javina shoots her arm up. "Shotgun!"

Later that evening, Javina's gone, and Trey and I are still arguing about the car thing.

I'm heated. "You know I have a meeting with a guy tomorrow to talk about buying his used car."

"Exactly. I overheard you on the phone with him, and his car sounds as shitty as your ex. He said it's missing a side mirror. What's wrong with me buying you a nice car with *all* the mirrors and extra safety features?"

"Because you got me a car I can't afford!" I'm shouting, and I don't want to be. I'm not a shouter, but Trey's turning me into one.

He replies calmly, and it only pisses me off more. "Did you miss when I said that it's *fully* paid for?"

"I'm gonna have to pay you back."

"No, you will not." It's the firmest and loudest thing he's ever said to me.

I return the conviction. "Yes, I will."

Things between us feel tense as we get ready for bed. We've stopped talking about the car, only because neither of us will back down. He's told me that I'm "so goddamn difficult" at least four times now. Eventually, I get tired of arguing with him, and I fall asleep.

The need to pee stirs me awake. Blackness engulfs the room. I flip the lamp on to discover that Trey is missing. *Of course.*

Typically when I wake up in the middle of the night, he's gone, doing who knows what around the house. Typically, it doesn't bother me. And typically, I just go back to sleep and wake up in the morning with him here. Tonight, though, I'm not feeling typical, and I want to know what's so important at three in the morning.

I shuffle down the quiet hall toward the living room. My feet stop when Trey's voice comes from around the corner. His tone is low and laced with frustration.

"Not yet. She's still recovering." A pause. "It's a three-hour drive and—" It goes silent as he listens to whoever is on the phone. "Maybe it wouldn't take this long if she wasn't hospitalized."

This isn't the first time I've heard Trey on the phone at this odd hour. However, this is the first time I've caught this much of the conversation. Where is a three-hour drive, and who is he talking to?

"All right. Just give me more time," he says, then there's a clatter. It sounds like he chucked his phone onto the coffee table. As he lets out a long, aggravated groan, I tiptoe back to bed.

A few minutes later, my bladder is empty and I'm cuddled up in bed with my teddy bear from the hospital. Trey is quiet as he slowly slips back under the covers.

"Who was that?" I ask with my back facing him.

"Shit." He bounces backward. "I thought you were sleeping."

I turn to face him, and it goes quiet as I wait for him to answer my question.

"Sorry, babe. I didn't mean to wake you."

"Who were you on the phone with?"

"Nobody important." He said that the last three times I asked him this question.

Trey gestures for me to scoot closer, then pats his shoulder for me to lay my head on. Usually, I would. This time, I don't budge.

"What's wrong, angel?" Whenever he calls me that, I think about the necklace I haven't taken off since he hooked it around my neck. It's the most beautiful piece of jewelry anyone's ever given me.

I sit up, hugging the bear to my chest, then click the lamp

on. Trey does the same on his side. For a moment, I only stare at him, admiring his adorably messy hair, sexy stubble, and those blue-gray eyes. Something in them is deeply sad. I wish I knew why, and if it has anything to do with what he's hiding or what's strange about him. Maybe it's both.

I draw in a breath and slowly let it out as I think of how to ask the question that's been burning in my mind since our first night together in Long Beach. "Is there something I don't know about you? Like, besides whatever mysterious reason you want to flee the country?"

In the time it takes for him to answer, I could have walked to Paris. His face says he's impassive, but his eyes tell me he's torn. "What makes you think there is?"

There he goes . . . answering a question with a question. "You're just different sometimes."

"Different how?"

I was hoping you'd tell me. "There are little things I've noticed about you. Things that don't make sense."

"Like?"

"Well, first, let's talk about your late-night phone calls, and how you never want to tell me who it is."

"It's not your business," he says, a little clipped.

"It is if you're talking about me."

His eyes go wide. "What did you hear?"

"Who were you talking to?"

With a heavy sigh, he gives in. "It was my uncle. He wants to meet you. I told him you need to recover first."

Reasonable, I suppose. His uncle lives in Three Rivers, which is three hours away. If that's the case, why all the secrecy? And why did he sound so exasperated? "Why is your uncle calling you at three in the morning?"

"He's not much of a sleeper."

"What about you? Do *you* ever sleep?"

"Of course."

I arch my eyebrows. "*Every* night?"

"I sleep with you every night, don't I?"

"Not really. Some nights, I feel like you're just laying there."

His eyes fall to his hands, speechless. I'll assume that means I'm right.

"Are you afraid of anything?"

"Everyone has fears, babe."

"Not you. You walked into an apartment crawling with spiders and carried me out like it was nothing."

He shrugs a shoulder. "Spiders don't scare me."

"Why do you tint your windows?"

Silence.

"Why don't you ever sweat during your workouts?"

No answer.

"How does your body heal so fast? You had a bruise on your face and gashes in your knuckles that were gone within days."

Still no answer.

"What was up with your old teddy bear asking for a password?"

Nothing.

"How did you know Lucas was in trouble?"

Finally, he looks at me. "Who's Lucas?"

"That teenager getting beat up in Long Beach."

"Oh."

"You knew something was wrong from all the way at the restaurant. How?"

Trey drags a hand through his hair, letting out a huffy breath. "I can't explain how. I want to. I just can't. And for the record, I tried to ignore it. It wasn't until I realized it was three against one that I assumed it was a girl getting raped or something. I couldn't live with myself if I allowed that to happen. I didn't want it to turn into something like this for us. That's why I asked you to stay at the damn restaurant."

"If I had, I wouldn't have known there's something unusual about you, and I think it's time you tell me what."

"I can't."

I hug my teddy bear tighter to my chest. "Are you an alien?"

His face screws together. "What? No."

"Are you a superhero?"

"No."

"Are you from the future?"

"No."

Well, that's the last of my theories. "Does anyone know your secret?"

"No."

That's a total lie. Somebody knows, and I'd put money on that somebody being Liz. "Are you dangerous?"

"No," he answers easily. "Not to you."

"Who are you dangerous to?"

"Anyone who tries to hurt you."

That makes my heart swoon until a thought hits me: Is there more to why he's been so overprotective lately? "Is there someone out there trying to hurt me?"

He swallows thickly. "Kinda."

"Were you, like, sent from another world to protect me?"

"Something like that." His gaze softens as he takes my hands into his. Instant warmth washes over me. "You asked if I have any fears, and I do have one. I'm afraid of losing you."

That's heartwarming and scary at the same time, because if he's lost me, that means I've lost him too.

36

TREY

Last month, I made a special trip into Chinatown to purchase more healing products, and I'm so glad I did. I'm surprised by how well Healing Water and Healing Goo work on Arella. It works like it does on any other person. It only took two days of light application for that cut on her lip to disappear. As for the rest of her body, it took a week of me sneaking doses of Healing Water into her system.

I offered her "Sprite" with all of her meals, because lemon-lime flavored Healing Water tastes just like Sprite. Whenever she said *no*, I filled her glass with regular Healing Water instead. Since it looks, tastes, and smells the same as filtered water, she didn't notice a difference.

I've stopped giving her Healing Water now that it's been over two weeks since the car accident. Thankfully, Victor hasn't pulled any more stunts since then. Not for a lack of begging.

Lately, our phone calls have been conversations where I'll spit out any excuse in the book to keep Arella away from him. Something's been bugging me about Victor, and it's not just that he purposely crashed a truck into Arella's car.

It's that he said he wanted to see if causing her to feel an "extreme emotion" would get me to sense her. If that's the case, why did he cause a car accident when I was nowhere near Arella at the time? Wouldn't it have made more sense to do it while I was *in* the car with her? I'd like to think he didn't want to risk my life, but let's be real—he doesn't give a shit about me. So why did he lie? What's he up to?

I don't know the answers. What I do know is that it's my job to keep Arella away from him. That's why as she leaves for work in her new car for the first time after the accident, I call her so we can talk on her drive. This way, I'll know immediately if Victor pulls another car crash. On her way home, I call her again, and we talk until she pulls into the driveway.

I do this every day for a week.

All is well until the next Monday. On Arella's way home from work, I call her three times. Each time, it goes straight to voicemail. I'm at home, staring at my phone, waiting for either the glimmer to hit me or another call from the hospital with bad news. I swear, if that happens again, I'll rush to Shadow Ridge myself just so I can punch Victor in the face.

I keep staring at my phone, willing for Arella to call me back.

She must hear my silent plea, because finally, her name and picture pop up on my screen.

"Where are you?" I ask.

"I just got to my apartment." She sounds hesitant, and I don't like it.

"Okay?" Woulda been nice if she had told me she was going there, but whatever. "When are you gonna be home?"

"Actually, I was thinking about having a night to myself."

I shoot up from the couch. "What?"

"I haven't spent a night in my own place for a while. I'm still paying rent on this, ya know?"

"Then stop paying rent and move in completely."

"I can't. My lease isn't up."

I pace toward my kitchen. My hands are jittery, antsy to hold her. "I'll pay whatever fee your landlord wants."

"Honey," she says slowly, "I just want a night to myself, okay?"

"What for?"

"I . . . I need some time to think."

"About?"

I wait for what feels like a whole minute before she finally says, "I don't know. Everything."

"Cool. We can think together. I'll be there soon." I'm done with this shit, and I need to see her. Now.

"Nooo, Tr—"

I'm already out the door by the time I hang up. *What the hell does she need to think about?*

I'VE ONLY BEEN IN HER APARTMENT FOR FIVE MINUTES, AND our conversation has already turned into a heated argument. I want to know why she's pushing me away, and she keeps giving me vague answers. She's hiding something from me. I can feel it.

I'm the first to raise my voice. "What the fuck does that mean?"

"It means that I wanted to be alone tonight. Is that too much to ask?" She's planted on the edge of her mattress as I pace her bedroom floor. My hair is all messy from how many times I've run my hands through it.

"Did I do something wrong?"

She groans, exasperated. "For the third time, no."

My knees thump onto the carpet as I kneel in front of her. In my sweetest voice possible, I say, "Tell me what's on your mind, baby."

She rubs her long hair between her fingers, looking anywhere but at me.

I grab her hand to stop her from fidgeting. "Babe, please. What's wrong?"

"I . . . I've been having doubts . . . about us."

I shoot up onto my feet. "What?" I've never been so sure of anything in my life, and here she is questioning it? "Why?"

"I dunno. I feel like lately, we've been having too much sex. I feel like it's all you want me for. You want it all the time. When we wake up. After lunch. After dinner. Before bed. It's just a lot."

"First off," I say, scoffing because my ego is slightly bruised, "sex is not the only thing I want you for. And second, I didn't realize you weren't enjoying it. I can tone it down."

"I *do* enjoy it, Trey."

"Then what's the problem?" This isn't the real issue. There's something else. Is it because of all those things she listed off that's weird about me? Last week, I made it a point to stay in bed with her throughout the night, and I haven't been working out lately, to avoid her questions about how I don't sweat.

"I . . ." Her tone softens. "I don't want to end up as a part of your list."

"My list?"

"Yeah. You know. The list of girls you've fucked and forget about later."

List of girls I've fucked? What? Obviously, she doesn't understand how special she is to me, probably because I haven't told her that I love her. I want to say those words, but I don't know how. And now isn't the right time.

I kneel in front of her again, taking her hands into mine. "Arella, you are *not* a part of any list. Don't ever think that. You mean so much more to me than that. You have no fucking clue how broken I'd be without you. Honestly, I don't think I'd be able to function." Those are the realest words I've ever said to anyone, and I mean all of it.

Her voice gets small, and she places a hand over her heart. "I didn't know you felt that way about me."

"I've been asking you to move to Paris with me. How else would I feel about you?"

She rolls her head back, yanking her hands away. "Ugh! Paris!"

"What?" I hate the way she says *Paris* like it's a poisonous word.

"You keep bringing it up."

"And?"

"Trey, I'm not moving to Paris!" Now, it's her who's shouting.

"Why not?"

"Oh my god." She clasps her hands against her face. "I cannot keep having this same conversation with you over and over."

I throw my arms up in surrender. "Just hear me out, okay? Picture this. You. Me. In a villa. Every day, we wake up to a beautiful sunrise. Every night, we fall asleep together with our little puppy. We could even travel for a while before settling into a place. Eventually, you could own your own bakery down the road. I could help you run it. It'll be perfect."

"What about my grandparents?"

"I'll buy them a villa too. Just as long as it's not right next to ours. At least down the road or something. Don't want 'em to hear you screaming my name all the time." I smirk, waggling my eyebrows up and down. She doesn't take the bait. She remains serious.

"What if they don't want to move?"

"Then they're just a plane ride away."

"Where will we get the money to fly back and forth all the time? Plane tickets around the world aren't cheap, ya know."

"Arella . . ." I say with a groan. "I have plenty of money."

"You keep saying that. How much money do you actually have?"

I shrug. "Enough."

"Care to put a number on that?"

"Millions."

She slumps her head to the side. "Yeah, right."

Why does she have to say it like that? Like it's too impossible to believe. Like I'm embellishing it. She doesn't even stop to consider that I could be telling the truth.

"I could prove it to you. Just need to log into my online bank accounts."

She presses her eyebrows together. "You don't *act* like you have millions of dollars. I mean, sure, you have nice things, but millions? What did your parents research that you inherited that much?"

Exasperated, I stand, crossing my arms over my chest. I'm not here to try to convince her that I could buy her a private island if she wanted it. I'm here because for some odd reason, she's pulling away, and I'm not going to allow it. "Look, the way I see it, you've got two choices. You can either come to Paris willingly, or tied up and duct-taped."

"Would you *really* do that?"

"Pretty close to it." I'm dead serious. We're running out of time.

Arella glares at me. "Kidnapping is a federal crime, Trey Grant."

I roll my eyes. I'm not *actually* gonna kidnap her—unless it's absolutely necessary for her safety.

She pushes off the bed to open a drawer. A shirt and a pair of boxers fly at my head.

I catch them against my face. "What the—"

"It's the clothes you let me wear home that day we threw flour at each other. I keep forgetting to give them back to you."

My heart drops. "Why are you doing so now?"

"Trey." She sighs. "I just need some time to myself, okay?

Please, just take your things and leave. We can talk more tomorrow."

My mouth pops open, but no words come out. It takes me a moment to gather myself. "Why does it feel like you're breaking up with me?"

"I'm not," she says, and it only makes me feel a sliver better. "But I still need you to go. And take your belongings."

In a single motion, I scoop her into my arms and storm out of her bedroom.

She squirms, smacking my chest. "Put me down!"

"No," I say firmly. "You said to go and to take my belongings, so I am."

She goes limp, slapping a hand over her forehead, but with a hint of a smile. "And you say *I'm* the difficult one."

In the living room, I set her back onto her feet before firmly taking her face into my palms. I stare straight into her eyes, silently pleading for her to hear my next words with her whole heart.

"You belong with me, Arella, and I belong with you. I'm not leaving here without you, and if you're not leaving, then I'm staying."

She blinks up at me with her long black lashes. Before I can take another breath, she crashes her lips against mine, stealing all the air from my lungs.

37

ARELLA

"Arella, get up." Trey shakes me awake.

I jerk out of my slumber. "Huh? Where's the fire?"

"No fire. I just need to talk to you." The panic in his tone lurches me upright.

He flips the bedroom lights on, making my eyes burn. I sit up, rub my eyes, then squint to see him. He's got an expression on his face like he just witnessed someone jump off a skyscraper.

"Is everything okay?"

"Not really." His voice sounds deep and husky.

I'm still naked from our before-bed activities. Trey has finally stopped treating me like I'm made of porcelain, and he's gone back to being rough. Earlier, I was so exhausted from how good it was, I couldn't even get up to get dressed. Instead, he wiped me off with a wet towel and I passed out.

"What time is it?" I ask.

"Two thirty-ish."

In the morning?

Trey climbs into bed and sits an arm's length away. He doesn't usually sit that far from me. "I have a question to ask you, and I can't wait until the morning for an answer."

"Okay?" What could possibly be this urgent?

"Is there anything you're hiding from me?"

I freeze with the blanket held to my chest. There's only one thing I've been hiding from him, but how could he know? I haven't told anyone, not even Javina. Did his weird intuitive sixth sense tell him?

I play dumb. "What're you talking about?"

"Just answer the question."

"I . . . um, I dunno what you're talking about."

"This! I'm talking about this!" From his back pocket, he yanks out some folded papers and tosses them onto the sheets between us. I recognize them immediately.

My eyes go wide. "Where did you get those?"

"From your purse."

"What were you doing in my purse?"

"I was cleaning the kitchen. Your purse fell onto the floor, and all your shit spilled out—including these." He points a hard finger at the pregnancy brochures I got when I stopped into the doctor's office to take a test. "Just tell me it's nothing and that I'm freaking out for no reason."

I lower my head because this reaction is exactly what I was afraid of. Three nights ago, when I told him that I think we have too much sex, I didn't mean it. We have the perfect amount of sex. That night, I wanted to be alone because I was panicking for other reasons—reasons I've been keeping from him because there hasn't been a good time to tell him.

At least, that's the lie I've been telling myself. Really, I'm just scared. What will he say? How will he react? Will he take it better than I did? It's been three days, and I'm still trying to process it. How long will it take him?

When that test came back positive, my first fear was that he's not ready to be a father and that he doesn't want to be yet. Right now, he's validating that fear.

My voice comes out soft and breathy. "I'm sorry. I didn't know how to tell you."

"No!" He shoots off the bed and paces the floor. "No! No! No!"

Suddenly, I feel more naked than I already am. I clutch the blanket closer to my body, wishing a shirt was within reach.

Trey rakes both hands through his hair. "How long have you known?"

I strain to keep my voice steady. "Three days."

"*Three days*? You've known for three fucking days, and you didn't think to mention it to me? Were you ever planning to let me in on your little secret?"

I shoot dagger eyes at him. "You should not be the one to lecture about secrets. I don't think I have enough fingers to count how many you're keeping from me."

His face turns pale as his chest moves up and down in short breaths. "Who is he?"

"Huh?"

"Who's the father?"

I tilt my head to the side. "What do you mean?"

"I mean, who did you sleep with?"

"You . . ." *Why would he even ask that?*

He chuckles low in his throat, shaking his head. "Unbelievable."

"Trey, I didn't sleep with anyone else."

For a split second, his expression falters. He heard the conviction in my tone. Then he glares at me. "Don't lie."

"I'm not."

"You're not pregnant with my baby," he says with just as much conviction.

"How are you so sure?"

He crosses his arms together. "Because I'm infertile."

"What?"

"You heard me. I can't have children."

I gasp, and my head lurches back. Is this what he meant when he said he wanted kids but that it wasn't "in the cards" for him? Is this why he wasn't the least bit concerned about whether I was on birth control or not? "When were you planning on telling me that?"

"I—I didn't think it was important." Here's another secret to add to his long list.

"Obviously, you're not infertile, because I'm pregnant."

"With who?"

"With you!"

He clenches his fists together. "Goddammit, Arella. Quit lying to me."

"I'm not!" I shout.

"Bullshit!" he shouts back.

That's it. I've had enough. I'm not going to sit here and be accused of lying and cheating when I haven't.

I slide off the bed and shove my limbs into the closest shirt and pair of pants I can find. I feel Trey's eyes on me the whole time. The lump in my throat grows with each wordless second that passes between us. Tears well into the corners of my eyes. I snatch my phone off the charger and storm down the hall.

Trey follows me. "What are you doing?"

I don't answer him. Speaking feels like it'll break me, and it's taking all my strength to keep myself from crying right now. On the kitchen floor is my purse with all my things still scattered everywhere. Frantically, I thrust everything back where it belongs, then I dig my keys out as I rush to the front door.

Trey grabs me by my waist the second I touch the doorknob. He spins me around. "Where are you going?"

I knock his arms away. "Home."

"You *are* home," he says so firmly, it almost makes the hurt evaporate. *Almost.* His house feels more like home than my own apartment—only because he's here. It doesn't feel like home right now though. Not when he's looking at me like I've betrayed him. If he really thinks I'd do such a thing, he doesn't know me at all.

"I'm leaving, Trey. Call me when you—"

He snatches the keys from me and shoves them into his pocket. "No."

Oh, god. It's like I'm watching a rerun of my episodes with Nathan. When I wasn't marked up, he'd let me leave, knowing I'd come back eventually. When I was bruised, he'd take my car keys and lock me in the bedroom like a prisoner.

On the outside, this may look like the same situation, but on the inside, it doesn't feel the same. Nathan forced me to stay because he was afraid someone would see the fresh wounds. Trey wants me to stay because . . . well, I don't know. The anguish in his eyes tells me he's hurt, but I did nothing to hurt him.

Okay, maybe I should have told him the moment I found out, but that was my only mistake. I don't even understand how this happened. Trey only came inside me once, I'm on birth control, I took a Plan B pill the next morning, and we've been safe ever since. The odds of getting pregnant were like .001%. I don't even get a regular period. With my birth control, I get a period, like, three times a year. How was my uterus able to produce life? It doesn't make any sense.

Angry at this entire situation, I swing the door open and stomp out, slamming it behind me. It's not until my bare feet hit Trey's driveway that I realize I've left without shoes on. How far am I going to get without a vehicle or shoes?

I wipe the wetness from my cheeks as I hurry down the sidewalk. Apparently, I've decided that trudging around barefoot without a destination is better than being in there with my heated boyfriend who thinks I cheated on him.

I'm already past his neighbor's house when the front door reopens.

"Arella!" Footsteps come running after me. It's not long before he's caught up. His breaths are heavy.

I expect him to yell at me. To smack me for disobeying him, or to call me names because I "wasn't listening." Instead, he takes one look at the tears rolling down my cheeks, then crushes me against his firm chest.

I attempt to push him off, but it only makes him squeeze me tighter. I'm too weak to shove him away, because I want this too. Nathan never chased after me. Some nights, I'd walk around for hours before finally coming back to find him *still* drinking, *still* angry, and *still* aggressive. All I ever wanted was for him to be sorry and for me to matter to him. I never did.

I matter to Trey though. I can tell by the way he's holding me as if I'm the only thing that's *ever* mattered to him. I sob into his shirt as he buries his face in my hair.

"Arella," he says, all choked up. "Please don't leave me. We can figure this out, okay? Just don't leave me."

38

———

TREY

If I wasn't perplexed by this woman before, I am now. She's a good liar. If I didn't know any better, I'd believe her. But I do know better, and at the end of the day, it's her word against biology. Believing her is like believing she can get pregnant from watching porn. It's just impossible.

After I convince her not to leave, I carry her back into the house. The second I return her feet to the carpet, she runs and locks herself in the bedroom—*our* bedroom—the one we've been making love in almost every night for weeks. Something I thought we were doing with only each other.

To give her some time alone, I pace the kitchen where my panic first started. My mind hasn't stopped feeling chaotic since I saw those brochures fall out of her purse. I can't wrap my head around the idea that she let another man put his grubby little raccoon hands all over her. The knots in my chest tighten just thinking about it.

When did she even find the time? When she's not with me, she's either at work or with Javina. I guess, now that I think about it, I don't have any proof that she's at work or with Javina when she says she is. She could have been sneaking off to see another guy this whole time.

Maybe this is why she refuses to move to Paris with me—why she didn't even consider it. She didn't want to leave *him* behind. What's he got that's so special? What am I missing that made her turn to someone else to fill that void? Maybe I should have—

No. I can't do this. I can't spiral down a hole of self-pitying thoughts right now. Not while I've got a woman in my bedroom who's crying her eyes out. No matter what she did, I still care deeply about her, and I'll do whatever it takes to make this right.

Lightly, I knock on our bedroom door. Again, *our.*

Nothing happens.

I knock again.

"It's unlocked," says a sniffling voice.

I enter to find red eyes, pink cheeks, and a bunch of crumpled-up tissues on the nightstand. I want to scoop her into my arms and tell her that everything's gonna be okay. I don't, because nothing's okay. Not while there's another man's baby growing inside her.

Silently, I bunch up all the tissues and toss them into the trash. She clutches her violet blanket against her front as if she needs a barrier between us. As if she's using it to protect herself from me.

I sigh deeply. I didn't mean to upset her. I'm just hurt. I want to know why I wasn't enough for her. I'd do anything for her, including drop my band and move to Europe to protect her. I'd spend every last dime I have on making her dream bakery become a reality. I'd even trade my life to save hers if it came down to it. *How is that not enough?*

I point to the empty side of our bed. "Can I sit?"

She nods, and I settle in.

"I'm sorry for yelling at you," I say gently.

"I'm sorry for yelling too."

"I've been thinking it over, and if you say you didn't sleep with someone—"

"I didn't." She says it so resolutely, I almost believe her. I *want* to believe her. I just can't when there's evidence inside her that points otherwise.

"Then there's only one explanation. You're not pregnant."

"I've had really sore breasts for a week now, and three days ago, I woke up slightly nauseous. That's why I went to take a test at the doctors. It came back positive, as did the home tests I took."

"Maybe the tests are wrong. Let's take another." How accurate can those tests really be? There's gotta be a chance they're wrong, right?

"Okay." She agrees so quickly, it makes me think the odds are not in my favor.

I jump to my feet. "Great. Let's go."

"Now? It's past three in the morning." She gives me a look like I'm insane. Maybe I am. Actually, I know I am. I'm in love with an Ordinary. It doesn't get any crazier than that.

What if, by some miracle, she *is* carrying my child? What if she really is a Zordi and just pretends to be an Ordinary for a reason I can't comprehend? It's possible to pretend to not see far. It's possible to fake shivering. It's possible to force your body to fall asleep every night.

But then, if she was a Zordi, why wouldn't she have said something by now? If she was a Zordi and didn't know it, why wouldn't she mention that she feels a tingle in her chest whenever she's around me?

Also, how does she fake the sweat that beads over her forehead whenever we're under the hot sun? How did she fake passing out from getting roofied by Ordinary drugs? If she was a Zordi, Dex would have had to drug her with z-drugs. If she was a Zordi, she'd have powers, and she'd heal faster than she does.

The more I think about it, the more my anxiety grows. There's no way in hell that baby is mine, and I don't care that it's three in the morning—I need to know the truth, and I need to know it now.

I head toward the door. "I can't wait any longer, babe. Let's go."

Arella shakes her head and gestures at her red face and messy hair. "Trey, look at me. I'm not in a state to leave the house. How about we do this first thing in the morning?"

I don't give two fucks what she looks like right now. On her side of the bed, I collapse to my knees with my arms in her lap. "Arella, please. For once, can you just do what I ask? This is not like when I asked you to stay at the restaurant. Or like when I asked you to take me to meet your grandparents. Or to move to Paris with me. Or to accept the new car. You've been fighting me on practically everything since the day we met. Can you, please, just give me this *one* thing?"

I slap a hand over my chest. "Try to see this from my side, okay? I'm an infertile man whose girlfriend just told him she's pregnant. I want to believe that you didn't sleep with another man, but can't you understand that this whole situation is tearing me apart?"

Forty-five minutes later, we step inside a twenty-four-hour superstore that smells of stale chips and sour milk. With Arella in hand, I head straight to the aisle with condoms and pregnancy tests.

"Why are we getting four?" Arella asks when I pull multiple brands of tests off the shelf.

"We need to be sure."

She scowls at the boxes tucked under my arms. The look on her face tells me I shouldn't grab another.

I guess four's enough. "Don't worry, babe. I'm paying."

"That's okay. I can get it." She reaches for the boxes.

I lean back. "I got it."

She shifts her scowl from the boxes onto me. "You *never* let me pay. Not when we go out to eat, not on our dates, and you just bought me a brand-new car. Let *me* buy something for once."

"No."

She doesn't give up because lately, she's been making it a point to be as difficult as possible. "Why do *you* always get to pay for everything?"

"Because I'm the man." The moment I say that, I want to face-palm myself.

She scoffs and jerks her head back. "Are you saying I can't pay because I'm a *woman*?"

"No." I let out an exasperated breath. "I'm paying because these things are a smaller percentage of my bank account than yours. You work hard for your money, and all I did was lose my parents to a fucking explosion. Thousands of dollars I don't deserve appear under my name every month, so I'm paying. Besides, this was *my* idea. I was the one who dragged you out here in the middle of the night."

For a moment, her glare falters into sympathy. It looks like she's about to give in, until she crosses her arms over her chest. "Nathan always had more money than I did, and he never let me pay for anything. At first, I thought it was because he wanted to be nice. Eventually, I realized he just wanted to control me."

Ouch. I can't believe she's comparing me to that ugly scumbag right now. I cup her face with my free hand and lean in to her. "That's not what I'm doing, and you know it."

"Then when I say I want to pay for something, don't stop me."

This woman is one of the most easygoing people I know. She's also the most difficult. I've learned by now that once her mind is made up, there's no changing it. So reluctantly, I hand her the boxes.

She clutches all four against her chest. "Thank you for understanding that I need to do this."

I do understand. Things are falling out of control, and she

wants to feel in control of *something*. Not only that, she doesn't want to repeat her situation with Nathan. I applaud her for standing firm the way she just did. *My strong, independent woman.*

I lower my voice. "If you want to pay, that's fine, but please, don't compare me to your ex ever again. I don't buy you things to control you. I buy you things because I want to take care of you. Because I—" *Because I love you.* The words almost leave my lips. They don't, because 4 a.m. in the middle of the family-planning aisle of a grocery store is not the right time or place. "Because you're special to me."

"I'm sorry. I didn't mean to compare you to him. I was just trying to explain why I wanted to pay."

With a palm on the small of her back, I pull her in. She steps into me and allows me to kiss her forehead, but it's not enough, so I cup the back of her neck and collapse my mouth over hers. We embrace in a hard kiss that soothes the ache in me.

The second we part, the ache floats right back in like a cold black fog. Our moment of truth is coming, and my heart knows it.

"The car is this way," Arella says after we check out.

"But the bathroom is this way." I point toward the big RESTROOMS sign hanging from the ceiling.

"What? We're doing this *now*?"

"What part of 'I can't wait any longer' wasn't clear?"

"Can't we do this at your house?"

Ouch. It stings that she didn't call it *our* house. "Arella, please . . ." I hold out the shopping bag.

With a huff, she snatches the bag. I'm about to follow her into the family bathroom when her palm against my sternum stops me.

"What do you think you're doing?"

I give her a *duh* look. "Trying to see if you're pregnant?"

"Nuh-uh. You need to wait out here. I don't want you to stand around and watch me pee on a stick."

"What's the big deal? It's not like I've never seen you naked."

"It's weird."

Things will move along faster if I stop arguing with her, so I step back with my hands up. "Fine. Just take all four, and let me in as soon as you're done."

The bag crinkles in her grasp as she vanishes behind a locked door.

After an eternity, Arella peeks her head out and motions for me to enter.

Breathe, I remind myself. I've been forgetting to do that.

"So?" I say as an electric current of nerves shoots up my core. "What's the verdict?"

"I just took them."

"Okay?" I wave my hand in a *keep going* motion.

"Do you not know how these things work?"

"Not really. Don't you just pee on it?"

"You have to wait two minutes for the results."

"Oh."

It's the longest two minutes of my life. My heavy footsteps echo as I pace the tile back and forth. Arella remains at the sink, watching the four sticks intently. I can barely contain myself.

"Are they done now?" I ask like an impatient child.

"Yeah."

I rush to the sink. *What the hell?* It's just a bunch of lines. "What do they say?"

"They're all positive."

"What's that mean? You're positively pregnant or you're positively *not* pregnant?"

She chuckles, making me feel stupid. "Positively pregnant."

39

TREY

I'm pathetic.

We've confirmed that she's pregnant, and the first thing I do when we arrive home is climb into bed and ask her to cuddle with me. She does and falls back asleep within minutes. I don't blame her. She has to work in the morning, and because of me, she'll be running on barely five hours of sleep.

I've got her back crushed to my front, and I'm pathetically gripping onto her like I never want to let her go. Because I don't. Because I'm so fucking pathetic!

I shouldn't want her. I should be telling her this is over. But I don't. I'm too weak. I still need her like I need air to breathe. All I can think about is how I can convince her to leave the other guy and be with me—only me. And to love me—only me.

I'll give her anything she wants. *Anything.* Does she want me to change? Name it. I'll do it. Does she want me to give her more attention? Less? I'll do it. Does she want me to find her a fluffy unicorn that shits glitter? What color, baby? I'll fucking do it.

The longer I hold her, the more I fall apart inside. My thoughts keep diving deeper and deeper into a black hole of *I deserve this pain* and *I'm not worth anyone's love*. That second thought is the one that keeps repeating in my head like an annoying beeping sound I can't get rid of. Why did I think for even a second that Arella could love me back? What's there to love about me anyway? I can't do anything without fucking it up.

My chest won't stop burning like I've swallowed hot coals. My throat's dry like the goddamn Sahara. It's hard to breathe because my lungs feel constricted. Every breath I suck in is laced with her scent. Someone else got this close to her. Close enough to smell her and touch her. Close enough to put his load inside her.

Someone else.

Someone else.

Someone else.

In the morning, we barely speak to each other. As Arella leaves for work in a rush, she tells me that she'll come right back when she's done so we can talk. That gives me a small sense of hope. Maybe that means she's willing to work things out.

That hope quickly drains out of me as I watch her taillights disappear, and I'm left alone. It's not long before my mind spirals again. How could this happen? What did I do wrong? What can I do moving forward to be a better man for her? To be the man she wants to spend the rest of her life with.

If she could just be honest with me, I'd forgive her. I'll even raise her child like it's mine if it means she'll stay with me.

Are there some logistics I'd have to figure out to make that happen? *Of course.*

Am I risking going to z-prison for life? *Yep.*

Am I willing to do it anyway? *Abso-fucking-lutely.*

I'm twenty minutes into murdering a punching bag when the doorbell chimes. I almost miss it with how loud my music is. *Who the hell is here?* No one ever shows up unannounced.

Except for one.

"I thought you were dead." Jess makes my zense prickle. Behind her, droplets of water sprinkle from the gray clouds above at a steady pace. I didn't realize it was raining.

"Nice of you to use the doorbell this time." I don't invite her in, and apparently, she doesn't need the invitation. She struts right past me and dumps herself onto my couch, throwing her legs up onto the cushions.

Reluctantly, I shut the door. It mutes the sound of water falling that seems to get heavier every time I blink.

Jess looks me up and down, and it's only then that I realize I'm still shirtless from my workout. I hate the way she stares at me like I'm property that belongs to her. I don't.

"Did something happen to your phone?" Jess is wearing the world's tightest pink shirt and a pair of denim shorts that cover more of her hips than her ass.

"No." I don't move from the door.

"Then why haven't you been answering my calls or texts?"

Because I don't want to or care to. "I've been busy."

"With what?"

"Stuff."

She blows out a breath, making her lips smack together. "All right, Mister-Fucking-Details. I see how it is."

"What do you want?"

"Well, damn. Aren't you a ray of fucking sunshine? Excuse me for checking up on a friend I haven't heard from. I texted you at least four times last week and, like, three times the week before that. I honestly thought you were dead."

"I'm not."

"Good." She kicks off her heels, then gets to her feet. "Got anything good to eat?"

Sighing, I follow her to the kitchen. "Take whatever you want, then leave. I've got shit to do."

"Do it later." She steals an apple from my fridge and takes a bite, leaning her elbows on the counter. "Come on, Grant. Don't you miss me? You haven't seen me in months, and now you're kicking me—" She gasps and shoots up. "You're seeing someone!"

Seeing Arella isn't the right term for it. *Madly in love with her* is more like it.

A pang of jealousy slaps me in the face as Jess takes another bite of my apple. "Tell me about her."

"Look, now isn't a good time."

"Sure it is! I'm here. You're here. We both got nowhere to be." Smirking, she heads to my bedroom. I follow and watch through unamused eyes as she jumps onto my sheets and shoves her face into the pillows. "Ya know, I'm not a Sniffer, but I can smell her. She sleeps here, doesn't she?"

I don't answer. Jess bounces off my mattress.

"She has clothes here!" she shouts from inside my closet. "Wow. You must really like this one."

"It's complicated." I lean against the doorframe, debating on whether or not it's appropriate to throw her over my shoulder and dump her back out in the rain.

Jess returns from the closet and settles on the edge of my bed. "How so?"

"It just is."

"Is it 'cause she's an Ordinary?" Jess takes my silence as a yes. "Trust me. Relationships with them Ordis never work. Been there, done that plenty. They're only good for one thing: sex without the consequence of children. I'm actually seeing this new guy. He's an Eavesdropper, like me. Things are working out so far. Maybe you should try dating Zordis again."

The idea of that is like hearing tires screeching into my ear. I don't want to date other Zordis. I only want one person. I just wish I was the only one she wanted too.

Jess stands from my bed to meet me in the doorway. She

slides her hands up my bare chest. "Do you need me to remind you what being with your own kind is like?"

She intensifies her erotic emotions, knowing it'll make me want her. It's always worked before, but it's not going to work now. I'm done with this woman. I'm done with her using me. And I'm especially done with her making me feel like the only time I'm worthy of her presence is when she needs a fuck and some cash.

Arella's never made me feel like an ATM. If anything, she makes me feel like I'm worth more *without* the money. Plus, she's never tried to use my mind power to manipulate me into giving her what she wants.

So I grab Jess by her wrists as I expand my Empath power out. I need to sense anyone but her, because if I don't control my emotions, she will end up controlling me.

Her jaw drops as her confused shock rushes through my head. I wish I could say that I give a shit, but I don't.

I'm more concerned about my situation with Arella. Thinking about it again makes me want to crawl into a dark hole and never come out.

The last time I felt this terrible was when I lost Elliott. The time before that? When I lost my parents. Maybe this is my fate—to lose anybody who means anything to me. I've lost Arella to another man. Next, I'll lose Liz and—

"Seriously?"

I whip my head toward the voice coming from down the hall. Arella's standing there with her jaw dropped and tears forming in her eyes. Before I can say anything, she runs away.

40

TREY

Barefoot, I dash out in the rain after Arella and catch her by her arm, just as she yanks her car door open.

Water pelts my bare back. "That wasn't what it looked like, I swear."

She's got wet hair, flushed cheeks, and tears streaming down her face. At least, I think those are tears. They could be raindrops. "You're shirtless, and she had her hands all over you. What am I supposed to think?"

Without waiting for me to answer, she shoves me away and climbs into her car.

I grab the door and hold it open. "Please, don't go." I sound desperate—because I am. "Just let me explain."

She wipes the wetness off her cheeks with the back of her hand as she chokes on a breath. "There's no need. I know what I saw."

"Look, I know what it looks like, but I swear to you—"

"Who is she?" Arella wipes more tears from her face.

I hang my head low. "Her name is Jess."

"Your ex-girlfriend?"

I nod, and her face contorts.

"So we get into one big fight, and the first thing you do is booty-call your ex-girlfriend?"

"No. She just showed up today." It's the truth, but it sounds like a goddamn lie coming from my lips.

"What did she want? Sex?"

"Yeah."

"And you agreed?"

"No. I was about to tell her to—hold on." I put a hand up, palm forward. "Don't sit there and pretend like you're not guilty of doing worse. There's proof living inside you." At least I stopped Jess before it got that far. I can't say the same for Arella.

"This is *your* baby!" she yells so loudly, all of California probably heard her.

"I'm infertile!" I shout back, just as loud.

She throws her hands up in surrender. "Nope. That's it. If you really think I have it in me to be unfaithful to you, then I'm done. This isn't worth it."

And there it is. The truth. I'm not worth it to her. Like how I wasn't worth it to my parents to quit their mission. Like how I'm not worth anything to my uncle. Like how I'm not worth Jess's time outside of a bedroom. It's nice to know that I'm not worth it to Arella *after* I've already fallen in love with her.

Hiccuping through a sob, Arella shoves me back a step.

I manage to catch her door before she can shut it. Then I grab her arm. "Stop trying to leave! We're not done!"

She jumps. She actually jumps. Worse, her hands shoot up to protect her face. "Don't hit me."

I step back. *Hit her?* No! I would never. Why would she think—*Dammit.* I shouldn't have grabbed her like that.

My shoulders drop. "Baby, no. I'm so sorry. I would *never* hurt you like that. Ever."

Her dagger eyes slice at me. "What you've done is worse. Bruises heal, Trey. The pain I feel from seeing you with another woman will stick with me forever."

My gaze sinks to the raindrops pooling in my driveway. I wish for something to come erase this. *Anything.*

I wait.

Nothing happens.

Water continues to attack me.

"I'll prove that I didn't cheat on you," she says through a sniffle. "As soon as this baby is born, I'll get a DNA test."

"Fine, and when that test comes back with the truth, don't bother telling me, because I already know." I'm being an ass, and I don't give a fuck. I'm hurt, and I want to drown myself in this rain. Why can't she just be honest with me? I'll forgive her in a heartbeat. I'll be a father to her baby. I just want her honesty.

She shoots me a foul glare. "And when that test comes back confirming that you're the father, be prepared to pay child support."

"Child support?" *What?*

That's what this is about, isn't it? That's why she's trying so hard to convince me she's carrying my baby. She's trying to milk me like I'm a cash cow. *Wow* . . . She played me good. Not once did I think this was her game. *Well, too bad.* Someone else has already tried pulling this stunt on me. It didn't work then, and it won't work now.

I let out a scoff. "You'd be stupid to think you're getting a dime from me."

She gapes at me with a pain in her eyes that makes me want to hold her and make everything right again. But how can I? Nothing's right. Nothing makes sense.

Arella turns and reaches into her purse. When she twists back around, she's got something in her hand.

"The only stupid thing I did was fall in love with you." She slams a piece of paper against my wet chest.

I peel it off to find our happy faces in a small photograph. This. This is all I've ever wanted. To be happy. To share my life with someone who understands me and makes me feel whole. I thought that person was Arella. I thought—*Wait. What did she just say?*

Two words leave her mouth that will scar me forever. "Goodbye, Trey."

CAPTURED IMMUNE

SECRETS TRILOGY: BOOK 2

A ZORDI WORLD NOVEL
SECRETS
TRILOGY
2
CAPTURED
IMMUNE
HE'S DETERMINED TO SAVE HER,
BUT HE'S THE ONE WHO NEEDS SAVING.
MELISSA LAM

1

TREY

"*Goodbye, Trey.*"

She knew that word would crush me. She knew, and she used it anyway. *Goodbye* is the word my mother taught me to use only when I'd never see someone again.

"*Goodbye* means forever. *Bye* is just for now," my mother said to me countless times when I was a kid.

Exactly nineteen years ago, on a rainy night in September, she said goodbye to me. I never saw her again.

Arella purposely used that word to hurt me, and it worked. I'm so wrecked by it, I haven't found the strength to move yet. My bare feet are standing where her car stood in my driveway a minute ago. Where we both stood a minute ago, shouting at each other, saying things we didn't mean. *At least,* I *didn't mean them.*

Rain pelts my bare back like little bullets shooting from the sky. The hems of my workout shorts drip water down my legs. I'm not even wearing shoes, because I didn't have time to put any on before chasing after Arella.

I tried getting her to stay. I wanted to explain and make things right, but she refused to listen.

So now I'm here . . .

Alone . . .

With a wallet-size photo of Arella and me gazing deeply into each other's eyes.

It's slowly curling in my hand. She shoved it at me right before taking off. I want the happiness we had when we took this photo. The happiness I have whenever I'm with her. Whenever we're cuddling until the very last second we have to get out of bed. Whenever we're exchanging looks from across the room that say *I admire everything about you* without actually saying it.

I've got half a mind to mount my Harley and chase after her right now—after the only person who's ever made me feel whole. I'll come clean. I'll tell her everything. I'll confess that the flat tire that brought us together wasn't an accident and tell her what Zordinaries are. I'll show her my powers and explain how I know for a fact that the baby growing inside her isn't mine.

Am I risking going to z-prison? *Yes.*

Do I care? If it'll get me my girl back, *no.*

Even knowing she's pregnant by another man, I still want to be with her. I love her too much to not forgive her. I'll raise that baby like it's mine, if that's what it takes for her to forgive me too. *Will she?*

She was pretty upset after finding me shirtless with another woman. But she was off sleeping with another guy for who knows how long, so what's the difference? I guess the difference is that she *saw* me. I suppose if I saw her half-naked with someone else, she'd be harder to forgive. But I'd forgive her—after bashing the other guy's face in.

No one touches my girl.

No one.

Except, she's not my girl anymore. *Was she ever?*

"What happened?" Jess asks when I step back into my house. She's draped over my couch with a slight grin on her face.

I wasn't in the mood for her when she showed up unannounced, and I'm definitely not in the mood for her now, so my tone comes out rough. "Cut the shit. I know you heard everything." *Or did she?*

With her enhanced hearing, Jess can hear something as small as dust fall. Arella's immunity probably blocks Jess's power like it blocks mine.

"Okay, fine." She perks up. "Was that the Ordinary you've been fucking around with?"

I hate the way she says that, as if my relationship with Arella was only "fucking around." Arella means a hell of a lot more to me than that.

"How well could you hear our conversation?" My soaked workout shorts cool against my skin as I drag my feet behind the couch. I'm dripping water all over my clean carpet, and I don't care.

Jess twists to face me. "As well as any other person can hear. I didn't need my gift to catch what you guys were saying. You were screaming at each other so loud, I'm sure the moon people heard y'all."

Dammit. I didn't mean to shout at Arella. I just couldn't control myself when she kept lying to my face, demanding that I pay child support for another man's child.

Okay, technically, she wasn't demanding anything. What she actually said was that she'll be taking a DNA test to prove that I am the father and that I should be *prepared* to pay child support. Because I'm an asshole and was pissed off to shit, I told her she'd be stupid to think she's getting a dime from me, when in reality, I'd give that woman anything she wants.

Money? *Done.*

My house? *Take it.*

My car? *Here ya go.*

Just be with me.

With a sigh, I scold myself. I shouldn't have let her go. I

especially shouldn't have grabbed her the forceful way I had. Add those to my long list of mistakes.

Jess continues with a sparkling grin. "Sooo, she's pregnant?"

"Yep." Admitting it out loud to another person makes it more real.

"Who's the father?"

Isn't that the million-dollar question? I wish I knew. At the same time, I don't think I want to know. I'll obsess over it, and I'll want to know everything about him so I can figure out why she chose him over me. "I dunno, but she tried to tell me it's mine."

Low laughter bellows from Jess's gut. "Wow! I'm so glad I was here to witness this. An Ordi trying to convince a Zordi she's carrying his child? Holy shit! This is better than TV."

Seriously? I glare at her. "Get out."

"What?"

With the fingers not holding my precious photo, I point at the front door. It swings wide open, coming to a firm stop just before hitting the wall. "Get the fuck out."

"Hell no! I need to know all the deets! Like, what's her motive? Is she trying to get your money?"

"Out! Now!" I give her two seconds. When she still doesn't move, I lose it. With a flick of my wrist, the couch shoots toward the door with her still on it.

"Whoa! All right, all right. I'm leaving. No need to be such an ass."

She's right. I am an ass, and she's a bitch, so I don't give a flying fuck what she thinks of me. I just lost the most important person in my life, and she's laughing about it like I'm on some stupid reality TV show. I'm done being her entertainment, and I'm done being her last-minute rebound. *Just get out!*

Once she stands, I point at the couch and fly it back to where it belongs. The second Jess has crossed the threshold, I wave a hand at the door. It slams shut behind her, and the bolt lock clicks. I hope I never have to see her face again. Ever.

I push the sopping strands of dark hair away from my face as I storm into my music room.

Minutes later, my pen flies messily across notebook paper as lyrics tumble from my mind. It's not long before I've got two new verses and a chorus written. I grab my guitar to play some chords along to the melody.

When I was eight, I learned that playing and writing music helped settle the tornado of misery swirling in my head all the time. That, and lighting stuff on fire. And throat-punching people.

As a teenager, I found out that getting drunk helps too.

As an adult, I discovered that z-drugs work the best. The higher I get, the less agony I feel. I wish I had some right now, because writing this song isn't helping.

"Fuck!" I smash my guitar against the floor. The wood breaks with a loud *crack!* as the instrument snaps in half.

For the first time since I got the call about Elliott passing away, I burst into tears. Thinking about losing my Deaf mentee kid only makes me sob harder. He meant so much to me, and I only had him for a short amount of time. Sadly, I had Arella for less.

My shoulders are shaking, and I'm wheezing. I don't even understand why I'm crying. Maybe it's because of the way things ended with her. Maybe it's because it happened on the anniversary of the worst day of my life. Either way, my relationship with her was doomed from the start. Whether it was now, like this, or later when the Superiors hauled me off to z-prison for having close relations with an Ordinary, eventually, our relationship would have ended, and I knew that.

So why the hell do I feel this broken? Why, for weeks, did I try to convince myself that we could make it work? Zordinaries and Ordinaries aren't meant to be together. We *can't* be together. Knowing that didn't stop me from falling in love with her, especially when everything with her feels more natural than blinking.

MY BODY LURCHES UPRIGHT AS I WAKE. THE SKY OUTSIDE MY window is black. I don't remember falling asleep, especially not on the floor. My eyes are sore, and my neck aches from the way I was lying. Next to me is my shattered guitar in a helpless heap of broken pieces. At least my shorts are dry now . . . mostly.

I flop onto my back and stare at the motionless ceiling fan. I'm not sure how long I stay like that. Maybe it's five minutes. Maybe it's five hours. It doesn't matter.

Eventually, my stomach rumbles. The sky is still black, so it's not time for breakfast. It's been a while since I ate, so I should probably eat *something*.

Inside the fridge, I find salad for two, chicken for two, and pie for two. Disgusted, I slam the fridge shut. Suddenly, I'm not hungry anymore.

The bedroom is worse. My sheets smell like her: sweet lavender and springtime. Groaning, I rip the linens off the bed and hurl them at the wall. The gentle way they slump to the floor pisses me off, so I rip my lamp from the outlet and chuck it across the room. It hits the wall, and the lightbulb shatters to pieces.

What else can I throw?

A book? *Sure.* It lands with the pages open.

Bluetooth speaker? *Definitely.* It leaves a dent in the wall.

Cologne bottle? *Hell yeah.* I thought for sure it would crack, but it merely falls to the carpet, unharmed. *Lame.*

This throwing stuff thing isn't working. *What can I light on fire?*

I glance around for something to burn and find Arella's

dress on the floor. I pick it up and crush it against my nose. As I inhale, every memory I have of holding her in my arms comes rushing back to destroy me.

After I suck up my sorrows, I grab all the sheets and take them, with Arella's dress, to the laundry room. Just before tossing all the linens into the washing machine, I smash her dress against my face again. *Mmm.* It smells so good. Like a mix of happiness and the only sense of peace I've ever had.

I can't do this.

Huffing, I stomp out of the laundry room, leaving her dress on the floor.

With an achy chest, I crawl onto my bare mattress and lie facedown with my arms out wide. I could put another set of sheets on, but why? That sounds like a lot of effort right now.

My bed feels bigger without her on it. Emptier too. I can still picture her here with her back flush against my front. I'd trace my fingertips up and down her arm while kissing her neck. We'd talk about nothing and everything at the same time. I never cared what we talked about as long as I could hear her voice.

"The only stupid thing I did was fall in love with you." Those were some of her last words to me. They keep repeating in my head.

Love. What does that word mean, anyway? Liz once told me that love is a beautiful and fulfilling experience. So far, my experience with love has only been full of pain and regret.

I should have listened to Liz when she told me to stop messing around with Ordinaries. Liz was afraid I'd hurt Arella. Little did we know Arella would be the one to hurt me.

Whatever happened to that "Ari's perfect for you" thing? Those were Liz's words. She said that since I can't sense Arella's emotions, anything I feel for Arella is real and not a reflection of her feelings for me. If Arella is perfect for me, then why do I feel like I've just lost a war?

I want nothing more than to see my girl right now. More

so, I want to see her happy. The image of her that keeps replaying in my mind is the way I last saw her: weepy and angry. I don't want that to be what I picture whenever I think of her. *Hold on. Where's our picture?*

I fly off the mattress and scour my bedroom. It's not here.

I sprint to the living room. I search between the couch cushions, then the kitchen. Nothing.

Where did I—Oh! My music room! I rush in there and find the photo waiting for me next to my notebook, where I wrote that sad guitar ballad about her. It's a song that will never see the studio. The lyrics are too raw. I'd never be able to sing it without choking up.

Thankfully, the rain didn't ruin the photo. It's a little curled at the corners, but it still showcases a happy couple gazing lovingly at each other.

The more I stare at the picture, the more I want to rip it up. I can't bring myself to do it though. I'm weak. Too weak to leave her when I should have. Too weak to throw her dress into the wash. Too weak to destroy the only picture I have of us.

Ripping up this picture will be like admitting it's over.

It's not over.

It *can't* be over.

Back in my bedroom, I search for my wallet. I find it lying open on the carpet. All my cash is gone—all two thousand dollars. *Of course.* Why wouldn't Jess use the time I was outside with Arella to dig through what's not hers? Unfortunately, missing cash is the least of my problems right now.

I'm carefully tucking my precious photo between the fabric of my bifold when I catch a glimpse of some writing on the back. I flip the picture over. The loopy handwriting makes my breath hitch.

I love you, Trey. You are right.
We do belong together.
—Arella

I read it again.

And again.

And again.

The sunrise appears out of nowhere. I haven't slept, I haven't eaten, and I don't feel like doing either. I also haven't let go of this picture since I saw Arella's note.

The absence of her is driving me insane. I need to do the one thing that will completely block her from my mind. Unfortunately, I promised myself—more importantly, Liz—that I would never drink that much or get that high again. Although, back then, I didn't know I'd feel so devastated.

Maybe I can black out for one day. I just won't tell Liz.

No, no, no. I scold myself for even considering it. Nothing good can come from that. Except I could feel better, even if it's just for one night. *That'll be worth it, right?* Probably not. The second I wake up sober, this chest ache will come right back. It always does.

What I truly want is a permanent healing solution, and she's probably in the arms of that other guy right now. The mere thought of it scratches at my throat, leaving it coarse and dry. Instead, I imagine her alone in her bed, sulking like I am. I let out a groan toward the ceiling. Neither image makes me feel good.

Should I call her? Has she tried to call me? Where's my phone? After rubbing my sore eyes, I force myself to go phone hunting.

I don't find it in my bedroom. Or the living room. Or the kitchen. When I still can't find it, I search my music room twice. Nothing.

Huffing, I trudge upstairs to my workout room. Finally, I

find the damn thing sitting next to my Bluetooth speaker. Now that I think about it, this was the last place I used my phone before Jess showed up during my workout yesterday.

Damn. Was that only yesterday?

My phone has five percent battery left. I've got two missed calls. Neither is from Arella. Three texts. None of those are from Arella either. They're all from Liz, dated yesterday.

> You coming to perform tonight or what?

> T?

> Shit. I'm sorry. I didn't realize it's September 5th. Don't worry about coming if you don't feel up for it.

The anniversary of seeing my parents get blown up is not the reason why I skipped out on my band's show last night, but I'll take it.

My phone vibrates in my hand. Liz's name and picture appear on the screen. I let the call go to voicemail, because I'm not in the mood to talk to Liz right now—or anybody. Well, except for one. If Arella called, I wouldn't hesitate to pick up.

A second later, my phone buzzes. It's a text from Liz.

> Are you planning to come tonight?

If I'm not in the mood to talk to people, I'm definitely not in the mood to perform. Especially not on a Saturday, when the Soul House is always packed. But if I skip again, my band manager will have my head. Monique lives for any chance to yell at me. I don't have the energy to deal with her wrath, so I suck it up, grab my leather jacket, strap on my helmet, and head toward downtown Los Angeles.

Riding my motorcycle is lonely without Arella. I can still feel her behind me and her fingers drawing figure eights over my abs. It's not until I've arrived at my destination that I realize I should have stayed home.

Arella usually comes to work with me. Whenever she doesn't, everyone asks about her. Typically, I can tell people she'll be coming when she gets off work. This time, I can't. What will I say instead? I sure as hell am not explaining what actually happened.

I find a parking spot in the back lot, then force myself to dismount my bike. I'd much rather go home, but I drag my feet to the backstage door anyway. On the keypad, I type in the access code.

Beep! The little light turns green, and I step inside.

Marcus is behind his drum set, spinning a drumstick around his fingers when he glances up at me. "Hey, man! Where you—" His face drops. "Damn. Who died?"

I must look like a train wreck. Definitely feel like one. I rub my stubbly cheeks. Maybe if I had trimmed my beard, I wouldn't look so defeated.

"Is Ari comin'?" Kevin, our bass guitarist, asks through a mouthful of chips.

"Marcus! Kev!" Emmy, our pianist, rushes out of the women's bathroom with Liz right behind her.

Liz flashes Marcus and Kevin a stern look, then pretends to zip her lips shut. The room goes silent.

The girls know. I don't know how they know, but they know. I can tell by their distraught emotions whipping me in the face like a chilly gust of wind. Plus, they're staring at me with a sorrowful look in their eyes.

I hate that look. It's the pity look. It's the same look people used to give me when I was known as the little boy whose parents died in a "house fire." *I shouldn't have come.*

Liz whispers something to Emmy, who nods, turns to the boys, and gestures toward the door. Without a word, the guys obey, and they rush outside with Emmy.

When the door clicks shut, Liz approaches me with gentle

steps. The closer she gets, the deeper her sadness bleeds into my head. It mixes with the pain that's been throbbing inside me since yesterday. *I really shouldn't have come.*

"T," she says, all tender and shit.

I hate it. I hate this. I don't want to be treated like I'm wounded. I mean, I am, but I don't want to be treated like it.

"How do you know?" I ask dryly.

"Well, you weren't answering your phone, so I called Ari. She said you broke up with her."

Is that the story she's telling people? Hearing the words *broke up* doesn't help me accept it. I won't accept it. I'm still holding out for the moment someone pops out and tells me this was all just a cruel joke. *The cruelest fucking joke ever.*

I drag a rough hand through my already messy hair. "What else did she say?"

"Not much."

I swallow the hard lump in my throat. "How is she?"

Liz studies me with furrowed brows. "Uh, I'm not sure."

Is she as miserable as I am?

"How are *you*?"

I shrug halfheartedly. "Fine."

"You don't look fine. You look heartbroken."

Is that what I'm feeling? Heartbroken? I guess I wouldn't know. It's never happened to me before. No wonder people say it sucks.

Liz keeps talking to me like I'm a lost puppy. "I thought you were in love with her?"

"I am."

"Then I'm confused as to why you dumped her, but let's talk about this later, okay? We've gotta get ready for our show."

The idea of performing sounds as bad as explaining to Liz what happened. "I don't wanna talk about it."

"I didn't ask if you wanted to. We're gonna talk tonight whether you like it or not."

"Liz . . ." I sigh through her name.

She lifts a gloved hand to my face. "No. Don't argue with me. You won't win."

She's right. With her, I never win.

I guess if there's one person in this world I can talk to about Arella, it's Liz. Liz befriended me even when I was a drunk z-drug addict headed nowhere in life. Liz, of all people, will understand.

I WAS WRONG. LIZ DOESN'T UNDERSTAND, AND I DON'T THINK she cares to.

"What do you mean, you didn't break up with her?" Liz has left her satin gloves lying on the backstage coffee table and has forced me to sit on the couch with her.

The rest of the band and crew left a while ago. I delayed this conversation by taking a long bathroom break. I'd still be in there if Liz hadn't waltzed into the men's room to call me out on my bullshit. Leave it to her to know that I was simply hiding in a stall to avoid this.

"I didn't break up with her. Technically, *she* left me." I can still hear Arella's tires squealing from driving away so fast.

"Why would Ari do such a thing?"

"Because," I groan, "it wasn't working."

"Do you want it to?"

I rub my hands over my face and groan again—louder this time. "Why are you doing this?"

"Because I care about you."

It's ridiculous that Liz cares about me at all. I'm a fuckup. She should start investing her precious energy into someone who actually matters.

I slouch back against the couch. "You've never had to have a therapy session with me about any other girl before. Why do you have to start now?"

"Because Ari's different, and you know it. With her, you're more vibrant and happy. You two have something special most people can't find in a lifetime. It doesn't even make sense, because she's an Ordinary and it's totally illegal and against all biology for you to love her, but I've never seen two people more meant for each other than you and her. I know you believe that too. So why are you acting like you're just gonna let her go?"

Liz is right. Arella *is* meant for me. She's my soul mate—something I didn't even believe in until I felt the *glimmer*. I used to think getting a sickening sense whenever your soul mate was in danger was just some stupid thing Zordinaries made up to put claim on each other—until last month. I was on my way to Arella's apartment when a sudden wave of nausea hit me like bricks to the stomach. My throat went dry and I couldn't stop coughing. Then I found Arella being attacked by spiders.

The week after, when her car was hit by a truck, my body knew something was wrong. I was nowhere near her when it happened, yet sudden nausea hit me again. I got so dizzy, I threw up. Given that Arella's an Ordinary, my sicknesses at those exact times could have been a coincidence, but that's one hell of a coincidence.

"Tell me what you want, T," Liz says. "What would make you happy?"

"I dunno." Happiness seems like a foreign idea right now.

"Do you want her back?"

"I dunno."

"Yes, you do. You either want her or you don't. Which is it?" Liz isn't stupid. We both know the answer. She's just trying to get me to say it out loud.

"Of course I want her back," I grumble.

"Then go get her. Whatever you guys fought about, talk through it."

"It's not that easy."

Liz scoffs. "You're a smart man. Figure it out."

"I can't."

"Why not?"

"I just can't," I snap.

Like always, Liz isn't having my attitude. She snaps right back at me. "Why not?"

I give in. "Because she slept with another man."

"No, she didn't."

I scowl at the conviction in her tone. "How are you so sure?"

"Because Ari would never do that."

That's what I thought too—until she showed me those two lines on a pee stick. "Well, she did."

"How do you know? Did she tell you?"

"No. I know because—" I choke up. "She's . . . She's pregnant."

Liz gasps, covering her mouth with her hand. "No. Maybe the test was wrong." She's going through the denial phase. That was me for the first fifteen minutes after I saw those goddamn pregnancy brochures.

I was cleaning up my house when I accidentally dropped Arella's purse and all her stuff spilled out. As I bent to pick it up, the words *Having a Healthy Pregnancy* caught my attention. I almost fell over.

"She took four store-bought tests and a test at the doctor's office. They all came out positive." I lift a finger. "Which, by the way, does not mean she's positively *not pregnant*."

Liz screws her face up. "Hold on. You thought *positive* on a pregnancy test meant positively *not* pregnant?"

"Well, I fuckin' hoped."

"You know, for a smart man, you're kind of an idiot."

I toss my hands into the air, letting them fall to my thighs. "Thanks for the pep talk, Liz. Really made me feel *loads* better. Same time tomorrow?"

Her hands go up in surrender. "Okay, okay, I'm sorry. I'm

just . . . trying to process all this. If Ari is pregnant, that means she really did sleep with someone else."

"That's what I've been trying to fucking tell you."

Liz slumps back, huffing out a breath. "Damn. That changes everything."

SUNDAY NIGHT USED TO BE *OUR* NIGHT. IT'S THE EVENING I usually have off, and I'd spend those hours just being with Arella. Most of the time, we'd just talk until she fell asleep. Sometimes we'd watch movies or play card games or take walks around my neighborhood.

Sundays are special to me. We had our first date on a Sunday. I took her to my favorite pasta place in Long Beach, where I made her laugh so hard, she wheezed and slapped her knee over and over.

A couple of Sundays later, she taught me how to bake snickerdoodle cookies in my kitchen. That night ended with us throwing flour at each other and sharing our first kiss.

Then there was that one Sunday when we went stargazing at her *thinking spot*, a secluded oak tree at the top of a woodsy hill. There, she explained to me what love is.

"When you love someone, you put their happiness before your own."

Later that night, I told her what really happened to my parents, and she comforted me with a simple touch of her hand to my face.

On a Sunday after that, we made love for the first time, right under that tree. It was the most magical and sensual experience I've ever had.

As I flop onto my still-bare mattress, I mope over the idea that this could be the first of many Sundays I spend alone.

On Monday, everything reminds me of her. Little things like waking up to her side of the bed empty, or walking into the kitchen, where she's not in my T-shirt, pouring herself a glass of apple juice. Or stepping into my shower without a naked beauty smiling back at me.

My shower water ran cold five minutes ago. My body's natural equilibrium is working hard to warm me because I don't care to get out. There's nothing waiting for me beyond these tile walls—the ones that I'm pounding my head against because I'm trying to get her out of my mind.

When I finally gather enough willpower to step out, the mirror is foggy. In the middle of the glass, I swipe a towel in a circle to reveal my face. *Ew.* Bloodshot pupils. Dark eyebags. Facial hair that hasn't been trimmed in who knows how long. I look like a homeless bum.

With a towel around my waist, I drag my feet into my walk-in closet. All her clothes are still hanging up on her side. I debate shoving it all into a box and driving it back to her. It'd be an excuse to see her, but returning her things means she won't be coming back. I'm not ready to admit that yet.

On Tuesday, I don't do anything productive all day. Unless lugging my feet around my empty house and finding things to throw fireballs at counts as productive.

Around noon on Wednesday, Liz FaceTimes me. I almost don't answer, but if I don't, she'll show up here, and that would be worse.

"Hey," I mumble when her face appears on my screen. I take a seat at my kitchen counter.

"Don't even think about skipping tonight. If you don't show up to rehearsal by four, I'll drive over there and throw water balls at you until you beg me to stop."

"Can't I get one pass?" I prop my phone up against my salt shaker. It's too much effort to hold my phone up.

"Hell no. I've given you passes for two days." That's true. I skipped our recording session yesterday and our writing session the day before that. "It's not good for you to be alone, T. I know how you get."

"What's that supposed to mean?"

"Have you been staying sober?"

"Unfortunately," I say with a scoff.

"Good. Now get yourself together and show up tonight."

Let's see . . . Get pounded with water by Liz or leave my house and be forced to talk to other humans? I think I'll take the water balls.

"Come on, T. Please?"

I sigh heavily. "Fine."

"Fabulous. I'll see you later then. And for the love of all things holy, please, trim your beard."

I rub my palm against my long chin hairs. "Is it that bad?"

"You look like the Wish version of Henry Cavill."

On Thursday, only because hunger is clawing a hole through my stomach, I force myself to make some lunch. For the first time in months, I'm cooking for one—that is, if sticking a frozen pizza into the oven counts as cooking.

On Friday, I arrive home from the Soul House mentally exhausted. The fans got a halfhearted performance from me tonight. During the meet and greet, I fake-smiled for all the photos until it was finally over. All of it felt trivial. What's the point when I don't have her?

I can't take it anymore. I need the pain to stop, and I need it to stop now.

I don't register that my feet have moved until I'm already in the kitchen with the cabinet open. From it, I drag down a half bottle of bourbon, some tequila, and a tiny bit of vodka. I don't think about it as I unscrew the vodka cap and chug it all in one breath. It burns on its way down my throat.

The tequila is next. It takes three breaths to finish.

The bourbon takes four.

This isn't enough to get me buzzed, and I need to black out. Years of being a drunk have built up my alcohol tolerance. Couple that with my body filtering it out way faster than the average Ordinary can, and I'm gonna need at least three more bottles—full ones.

My nights used to be filled with popping questionable pills and trying any z-drug I could get my hands on. Hollow sex with women in skimpy outfits. Meaningless fights with big guys in bars. Talking shit to bouncers at clubs, just to get them to drive a hard one into my face. I used to do anything so I could feel something other than the emptiness in my chest.

Two years ago, I cleaned up. Liz made me realize that a pathetic trainwreck isn't what I want to be. Tonight, I don't give a shit what I am.

Through heavy rainfall, I drive to the nearest liquor store, getting there ten minutes before closing. Something makes me go apeshit in the aisles. I toss practically every hard liquor in sight into my basket.

When I arrive back home, I don't waste a second. In my silent living room, on the vacant couch, I rip the seal off a bottle and chug.

The last time I drank with the intent of passing out was after I got the call telling me the cancer had finally taken Elliott. I would have given anything to cure that precious little boy. Right now, I'd give anything to have Arella back.

She would hate me if she saw me drinking like this. The smell of alcohol triggers bad memories of her ex in her head. Because of that, I never drank around her. *And now, she's gone.*

Only once two bottles lie empty beside me do I start to feel something. The blackout is coming, but it's not coming fast enough, so I reach for another bottle. *Bottoms up.*

ACKNOWLEDGMENTS

*To my **husband, Joe**:*
You are my best friend, my biggest supporter, my board game buddy, and my soul mate. I love doing life with you. I'm so grateful to be your bear, your bunnies, and your passenger princess. I couldn't have done this without you, so sit down, lean back, watch me sexily tie my hair up, and prepare to be properly thanked. ;)

*To my earliest **beta readers**:*
Sorry you had to read *absolute trash*. We all gotta start somewhere, right?

*To my **beta readers** who read this entire trilogy:*
Thank you for helping me craft this series to what it is today! Kaycee Racer, Priscillah Bancy, Kelsey Davis, Whitney Tanner, Mads Arlow, and Annie.

*To my **readers**:*
This novel took over ten years of late nights punching a keyboard and more rewrites than I can count. Thank you for taking the time to come on this wild journey with me. I'm thrilled for you to continue on, because things are about to get crazy.

To **Enchanted Ink Publishing**:
Natalia, Stephanie, Christian, Lisa, and Greg.
You are all so great at your craft, and I'm grateful to have
found you.

To my **Secret Keepers**:
Being an author can get lonely, but my street team members
have made this journey more exciting. They're the ultimate
hype girls, and I enjoy all of our NSFW conversations.

To **Krista Street**:
You are a strong example of a hardworking author. You
inspired me to strive for your level of greatness, and you
moved me to believe that I can do it too!

To my pup, **Truffle***:*
Thanks for making sure I always have a bathroom break
buddy, ya know . . . just in case.

ABOUT THE AUTHOR

Melissa Lam loves reading and writing romance books that take the reader on an emotional roller coaster full of mystery, suspense, and heartache.

As an extroverted introvert who doesn't like to leave the house (because it requires wearing pants), Melissa enjoys playing strategic board games and taking long showers. When she does find the will to put pants on, she can be found traveling, enjoying bubble tea, or experiencing the world through food.

TL;DR I like to eat and write about heartbreaking shit.

Website: authormelissalam.com
Instagram: instagram.com/authormelissalam
Facebook: facebook.com/authormelissalam
Newsletter: authormelissalam.com/newsletter

SUPPORT INDIE AUTHORS

The best way to support indie authors is to leave reviews, because it helps other readers discover us! If you enjoyed this book, please consider leaving your feedback on Amazon, Goodreads, and anywhere else readers hang out.

Grab the next book in this series at
www.authormelissalam.com